EDITED BY **JAMES LUCAS JONES**

DESIGN BY **ANANTH HIRSH**

LUCKY PENNY

ANANTH HIRSH   YUKO OTA

Published by Oni Press, Inc.

Joe Nozemack publisher
James Lucas Jones editor in chief
Cheyenne Allott director of sales
Fred Reckling director of publicity
Troy Look production manager
Hilary Thompson graphic designer
Jared Jones production assistant
Charlie Chu senior editor
Robin Herrera editor
Ari Yarwood associate editor
Brad Rooks inventory coordinator
Jung Lee office assistant

ONI PRESS

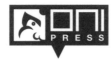

1305 SE Martin Luther King Jr. Blvd.
Suite A
Portland, OR 97214
U.S.A.

onipress.com
facebook.com/onipress
twitter.com/onipress
onipress.tumblr.com
instagram.com/onipress

johnnywander.com
@ananthhirsh
@aidosaur

First Edition: March 2016

ISBN 978-1-62010-287-9
eISBN 978-1-62010-288-6

Printed in China.

Library of Congress Control Number: 2015948229

2 3 4 5 6 7 8 9 10

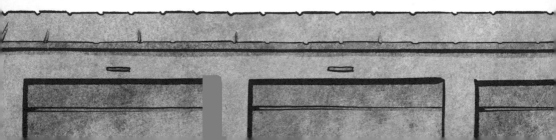

For our parents.

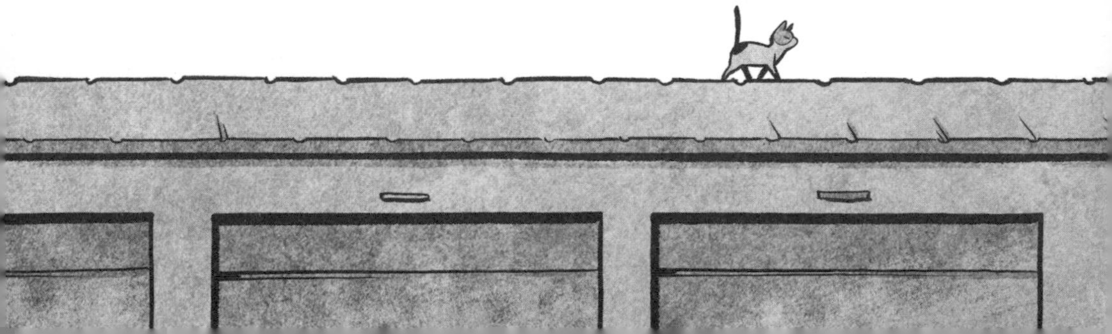

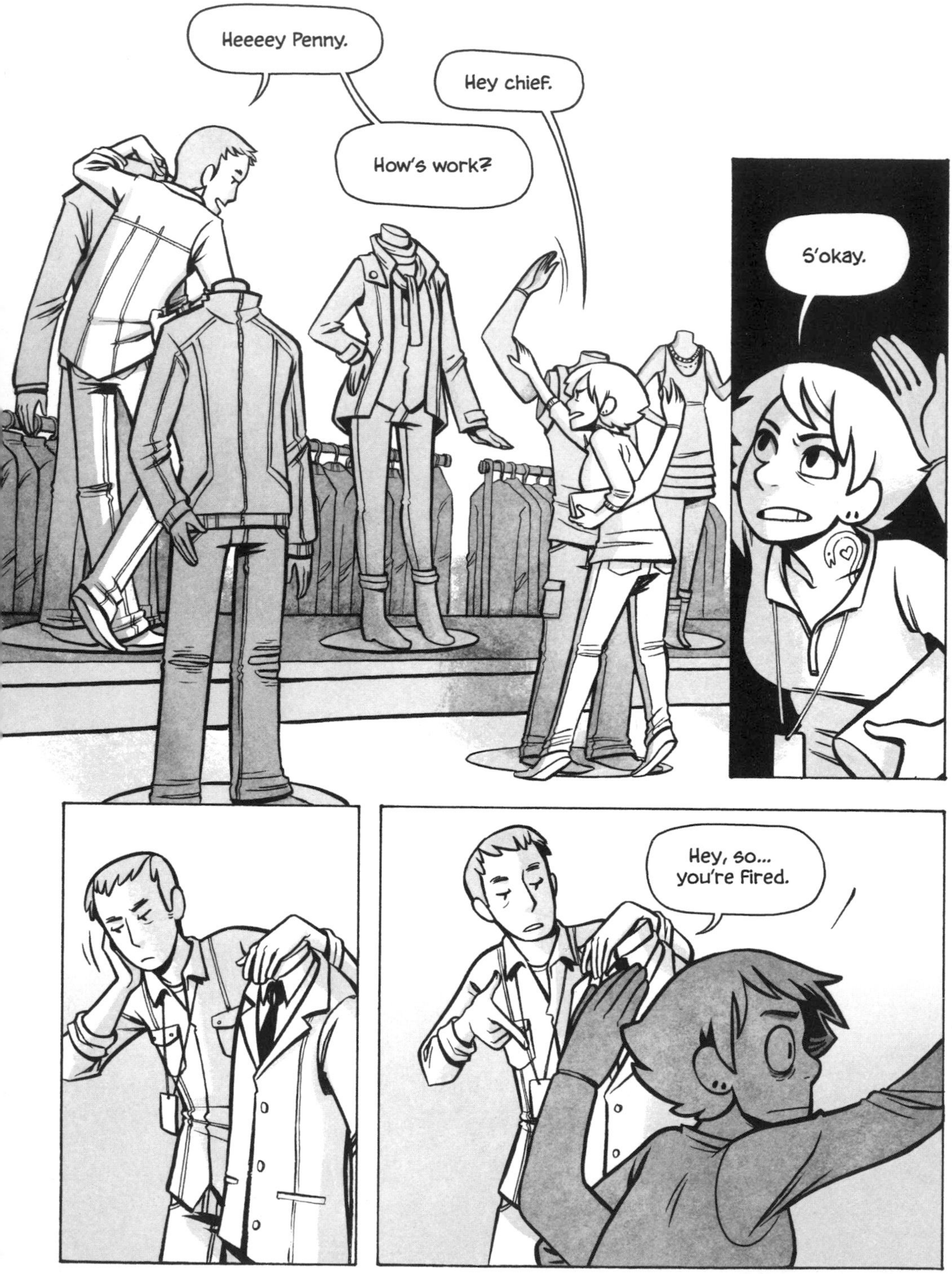
Heeeey Penny.
How's work?
Hey chief.
S'okay.
Hey, so... you're fired.

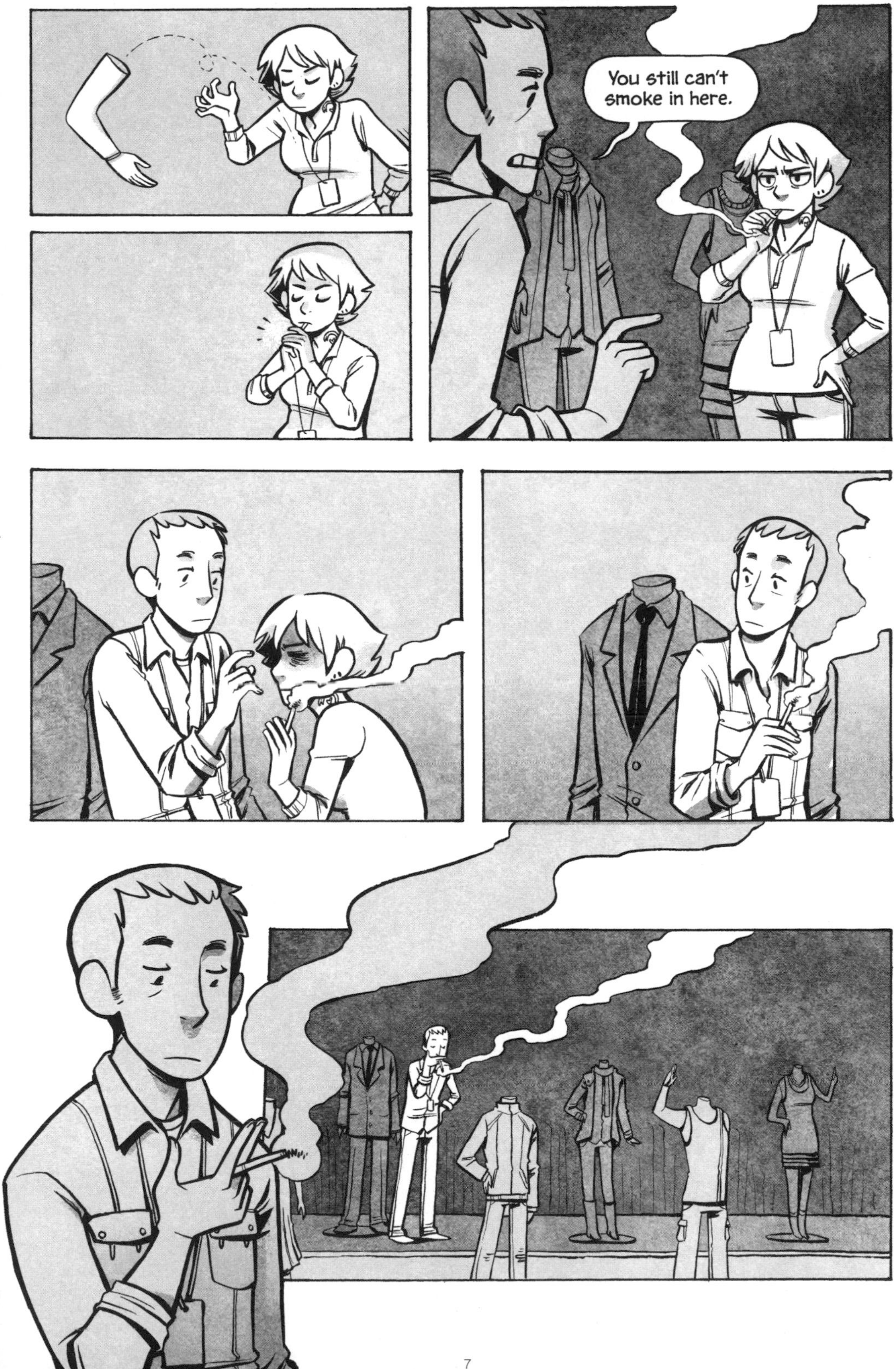
You still can't smoke in here.

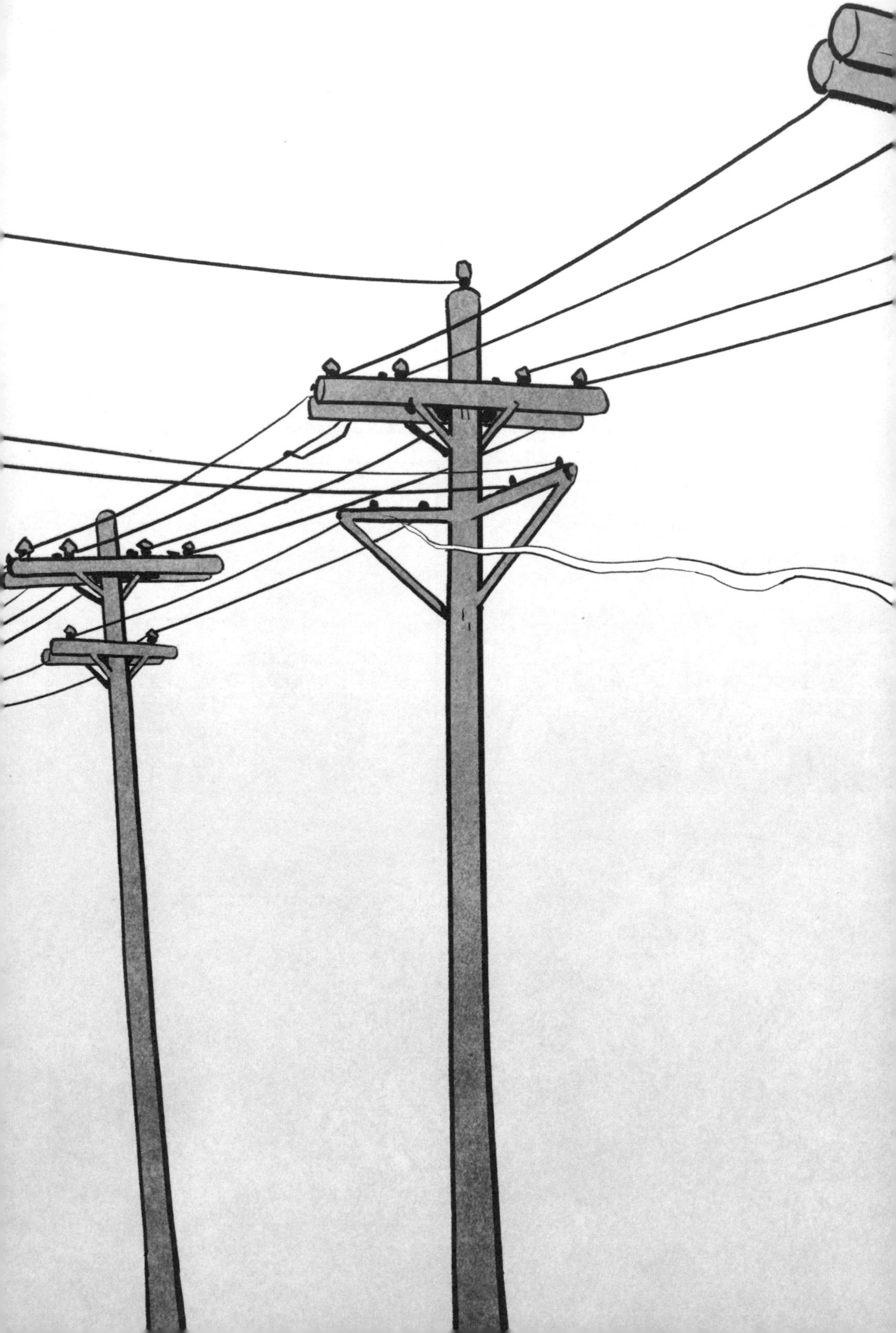

LUCKY PENNY

ANANTH HIRSH   YUKO OTA

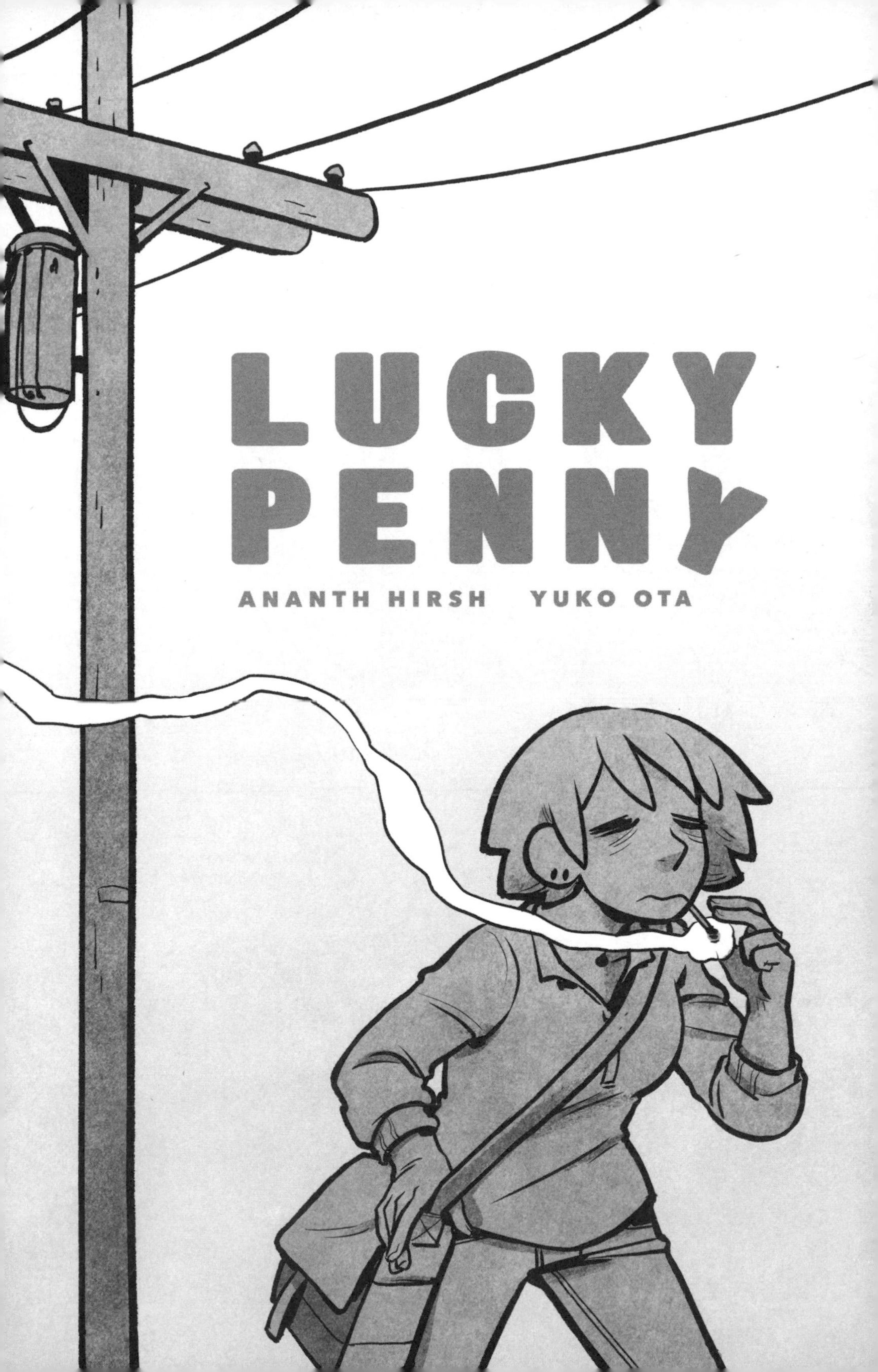

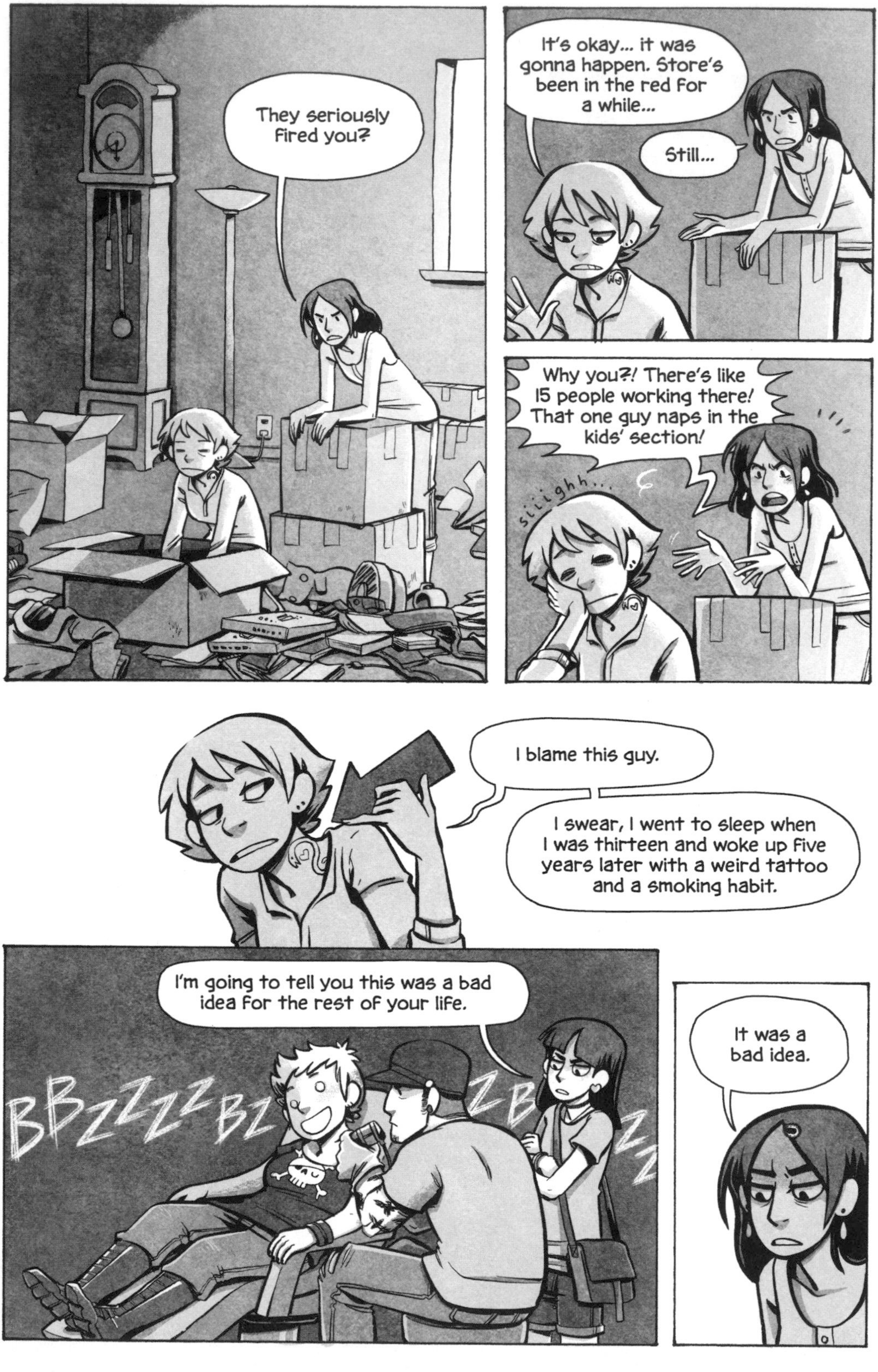
They seriously fired you?
It's okay... it was gonna happen. Store's been in the red for a while...
Still...
Why you?! There's like 15 people working there! That one guy naps in the kids' section!
siiighh...
I blame this guy.
I swear, I went to sleep when I was thirteen and woke up five years later with a weird tattoo and a smoking habit.
I'm going to tell you this was a bad idea for the rest of your life.
BBZZZZZBZ
ZB
ZZ
It was a bad idea.

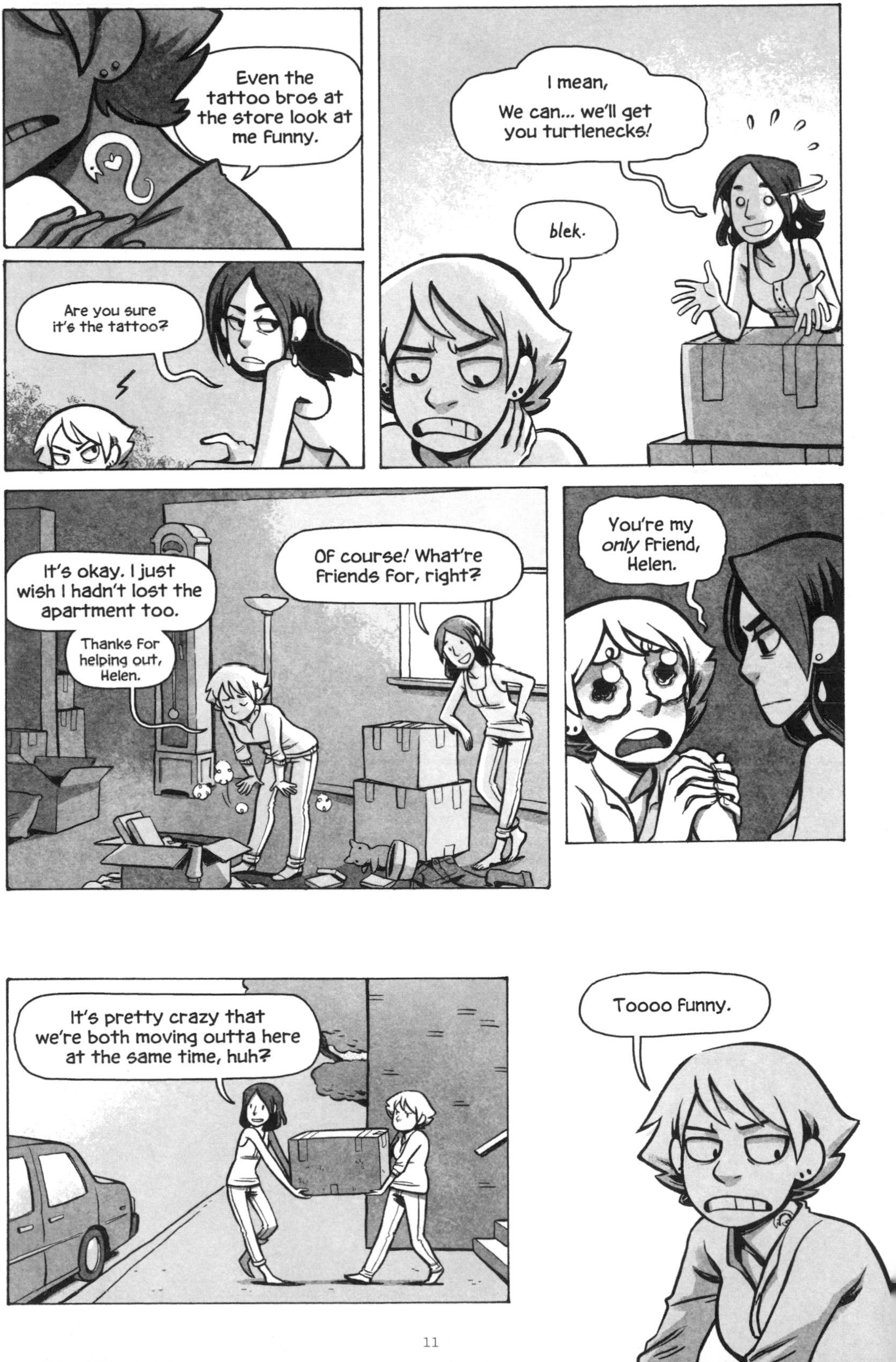
Even the tattoo bros at the store look at me funny.
Are you sure it's the tattoo?
I mean,
We can... we'll get you turtlenecks!
blek.
It's okay. I just wish I hadn't lost the apartment too.
Thanks for helping out, Helen.
Of course! What're friends for, right?
You're my *only* friend, Helen.
It's pretty crazy that we're both moving outta here at the same time, huh?
Toooo funny.

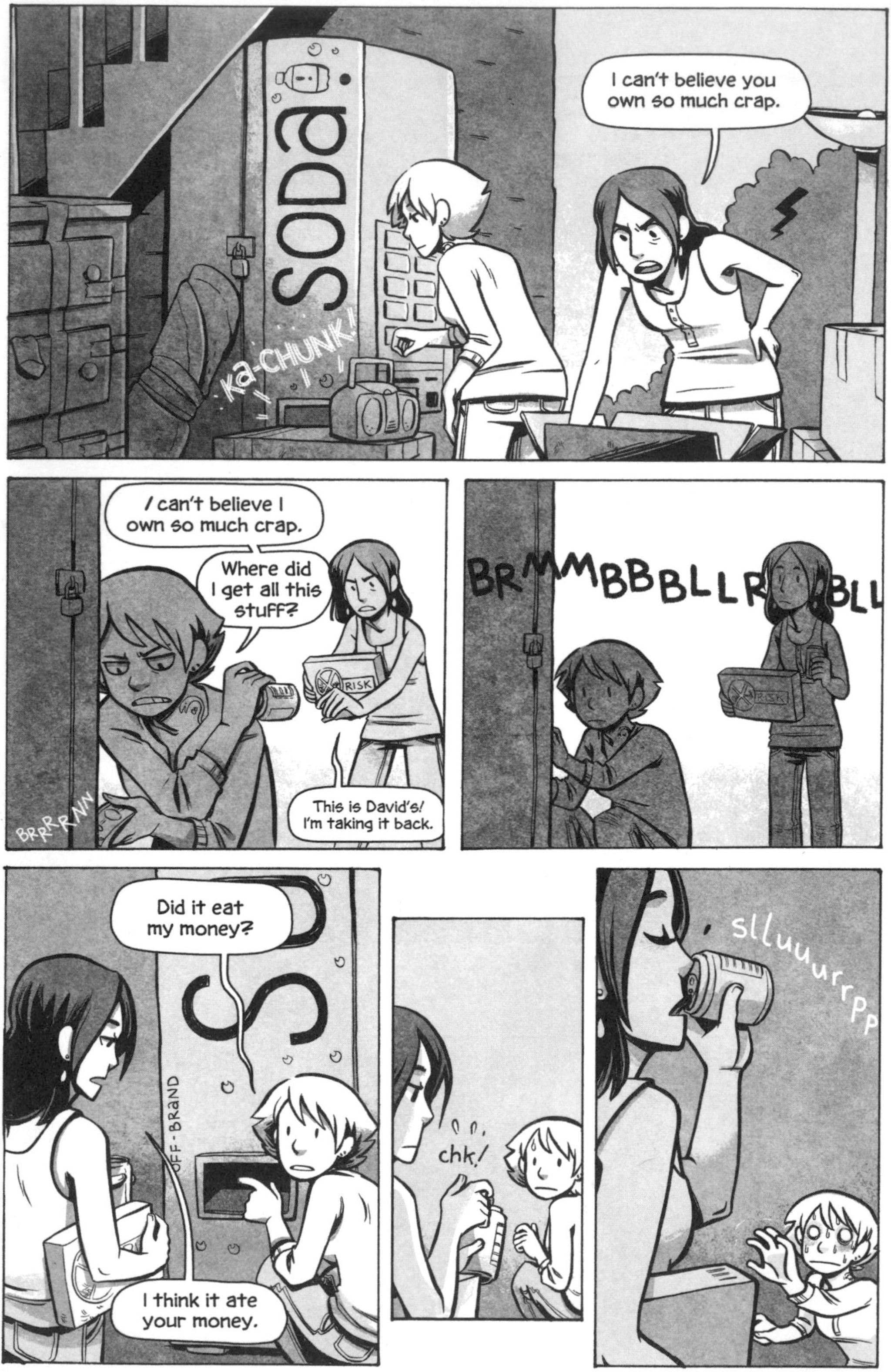
SODA
KA-CHUNK!
I can't believe you own so much crap.
I can't believe I own so much crap.
Where did I get all this stuff?
RISK
BRRRRNN
This is David's! I'm taking it back.
BRMMBBBLLR BLL
Did it eat my money?
OFF-BRAND
I think it ate your money.
chk!
sllluuurrpp

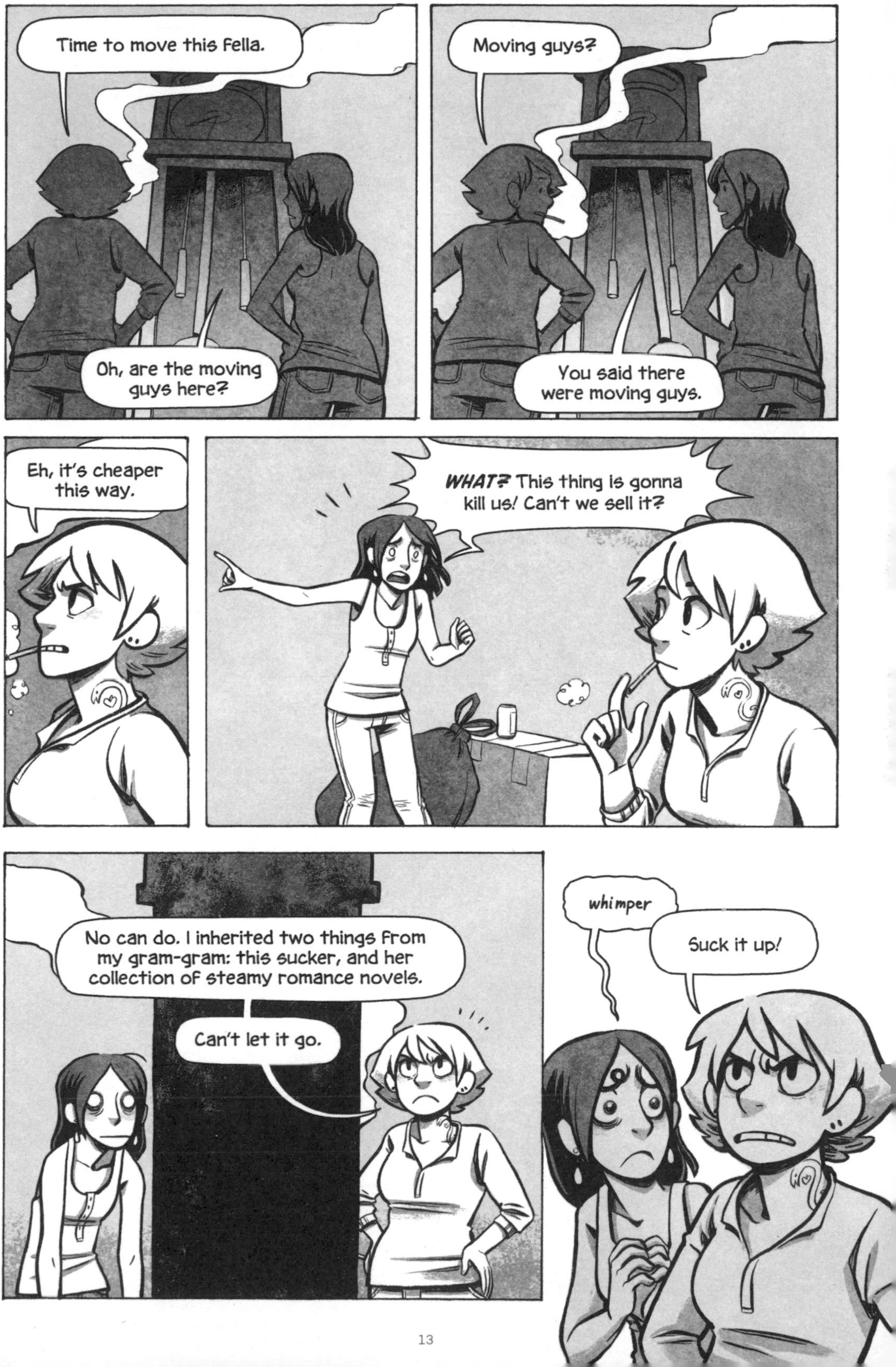
Time to move this fella.
Oh, are the moving guys here?
Moving guys?
You said there were moving guys.
Eh, it's cheaper this way.
WHAT? This thing is gonna kill us! Can't we sell it?
No can do. I inherited two things from my gram-gram: this sucker, and her collection of steamy romance novels.
Can't let it go.
whimper
Suck it up!

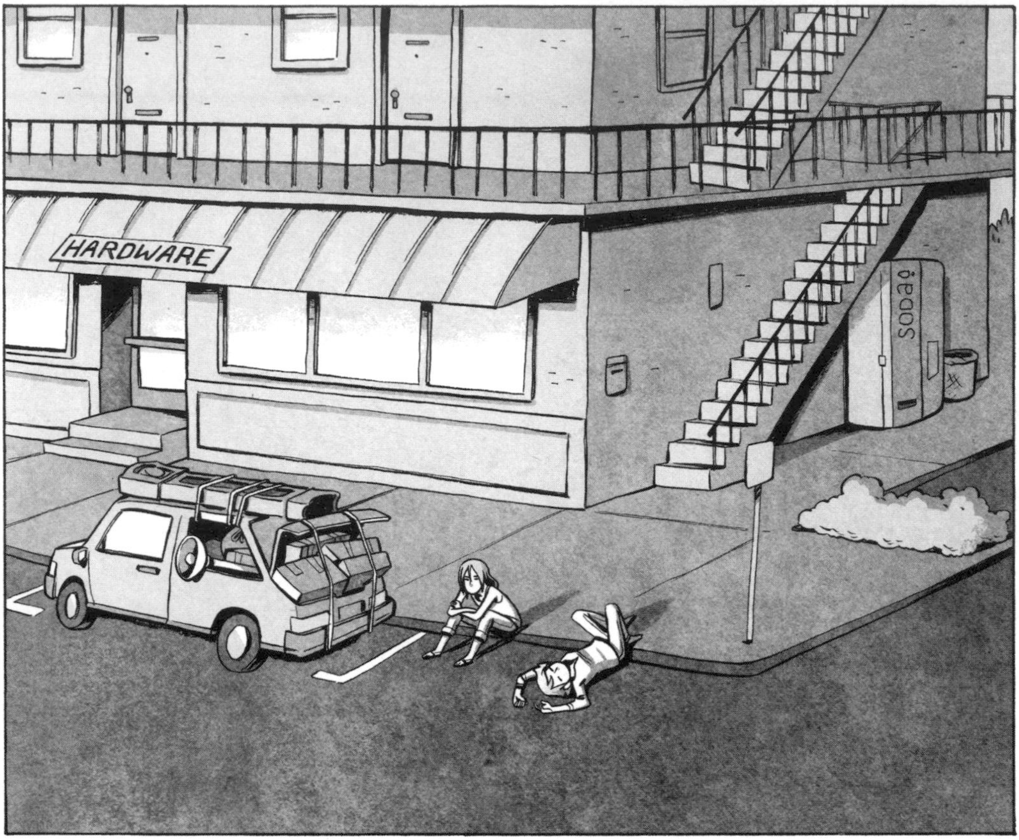
HARDWARE
SODA?

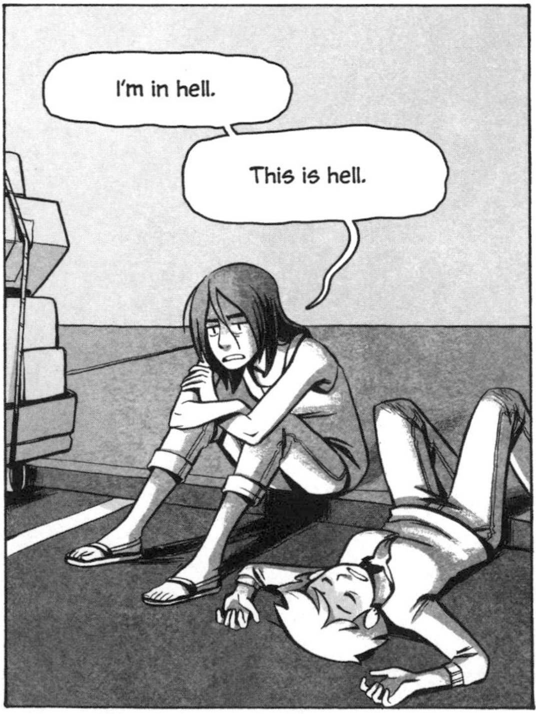
I'm in hell.
This is hell.

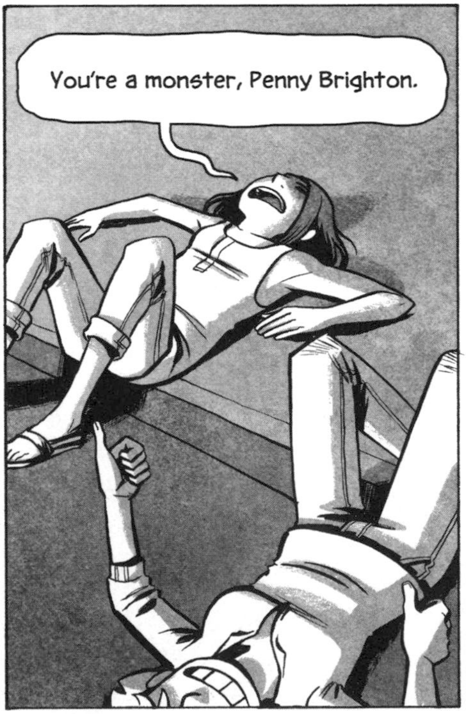
You're a monster, Penny Brighton.

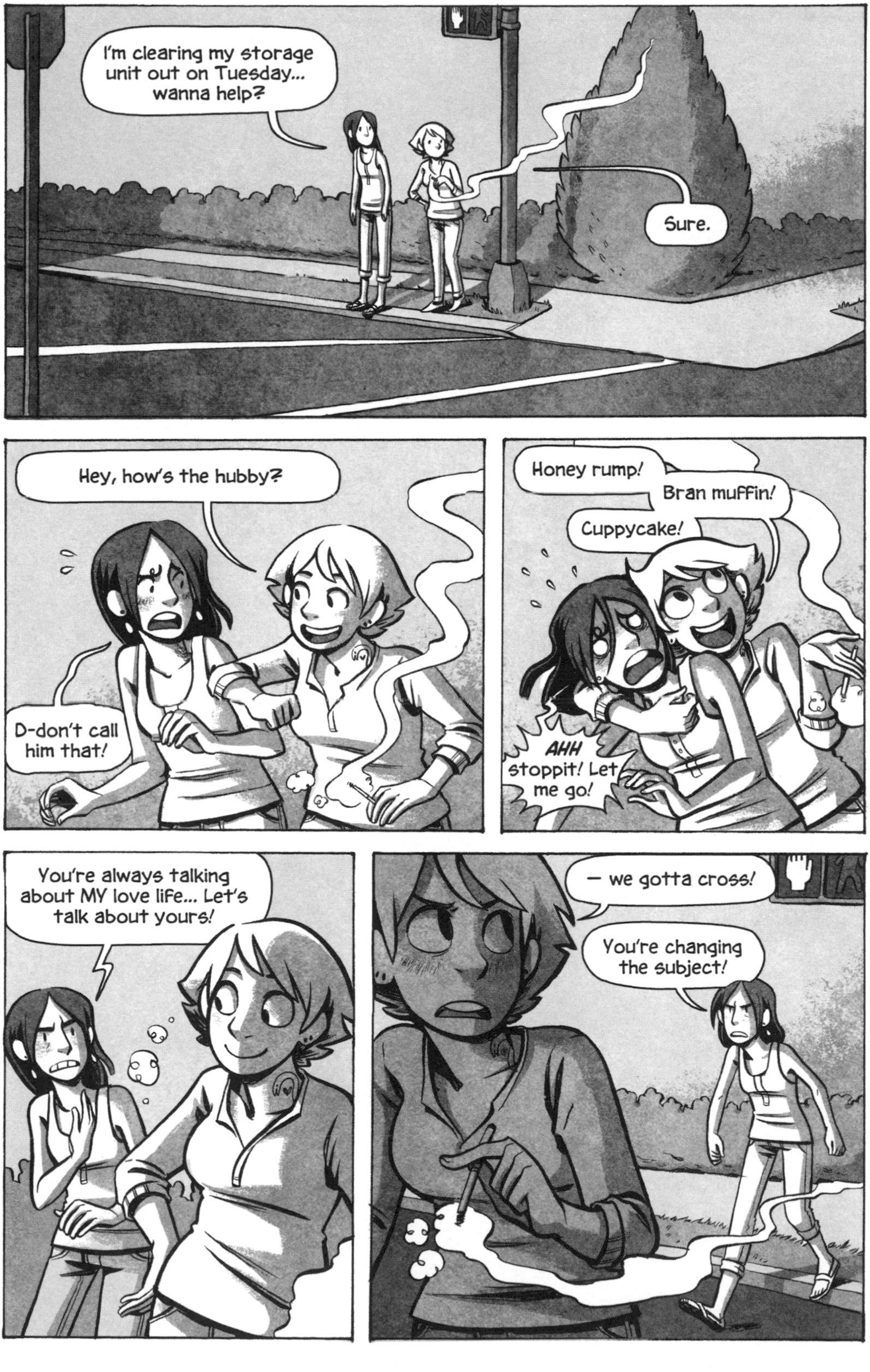
I'm clearing my storage unit out on Tuesday... wanna help?
Sure.
Hey, how's the hubby?
D-don't call him that!
Honey rump!
Bran muffin!
Cuppycake!
AHH stoppit! Let me go!
You're always talking about MY love life... Let's talk about yours!
— we gotta cross!
You're changing the subject!

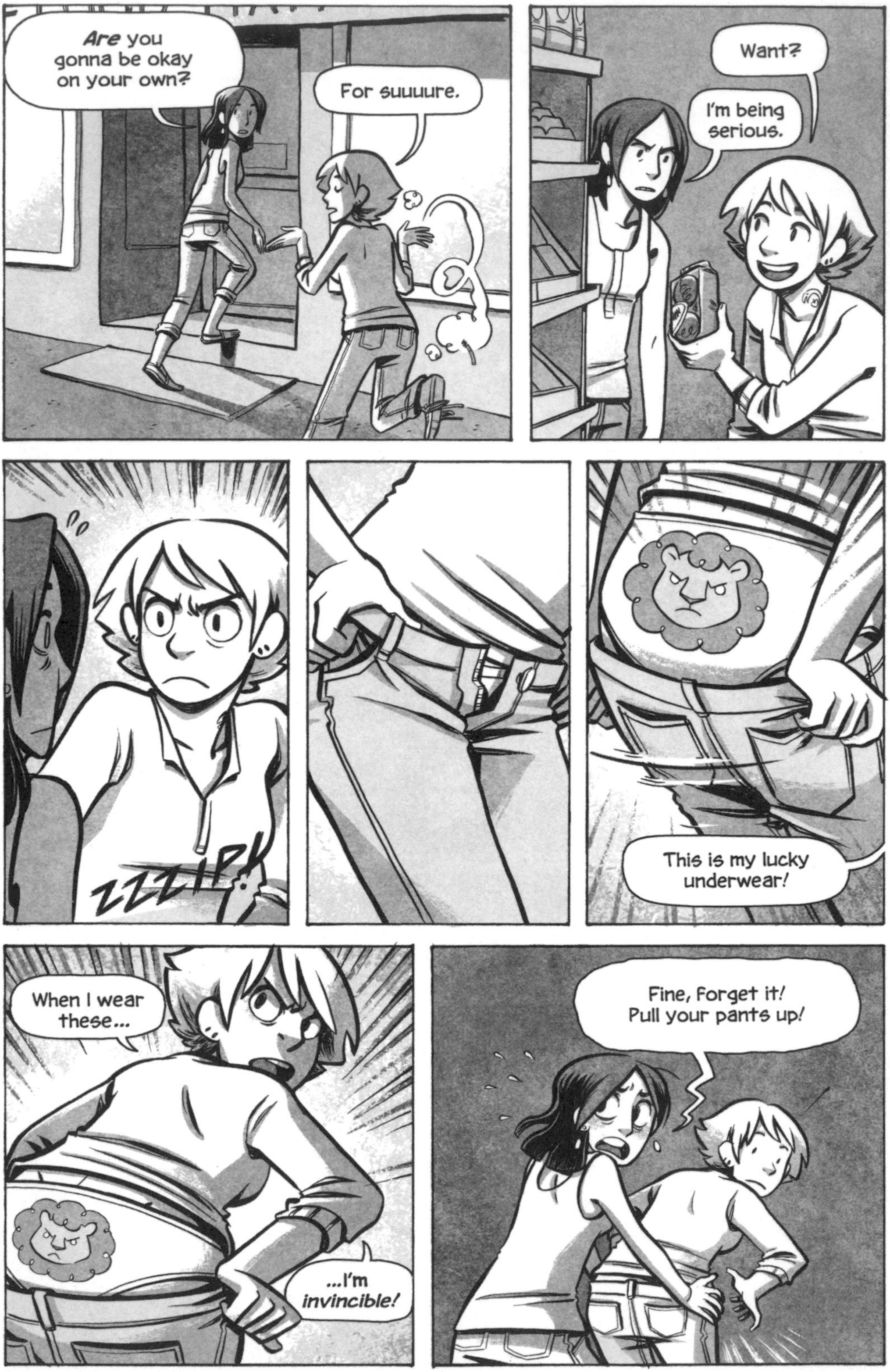
Are you gonna be okay on your own?
For suuuure.
Want?
I'm being serious.
ZZZIP!
This is my lucky underwear!
When I wear these...
...I'm invincible!
Fine, forget it! Pull your pants up!

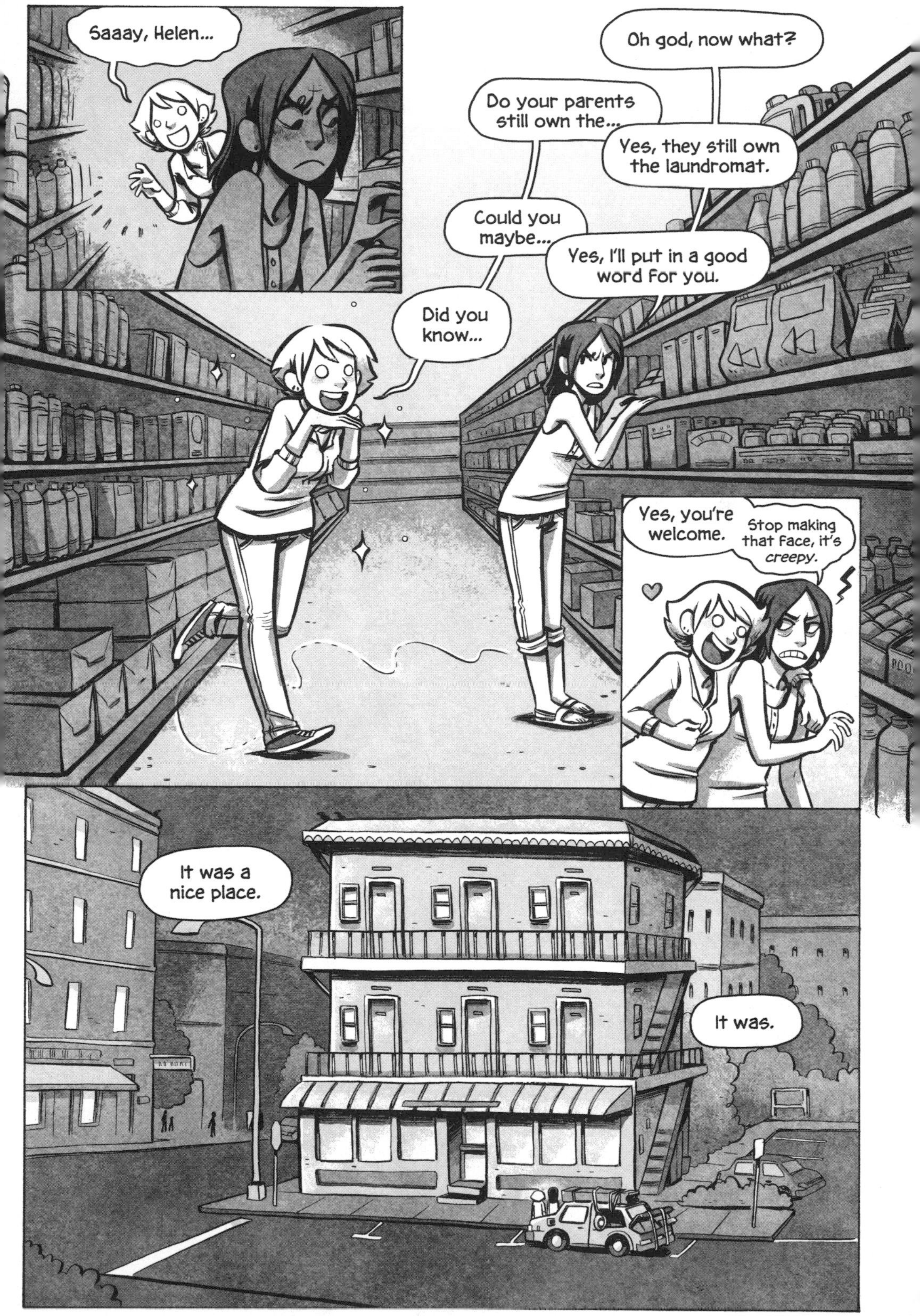
Saaay, Helen...
Oh god, now what?
Do your parents still own the...
Yes, they still own the laundromat.
Could you maybe...
Yes, I'll put in a good word for you.
Did you know...
Yes, you're welcome.
Stop making that face, it's *creepy*.
It was a nice place.
It was.

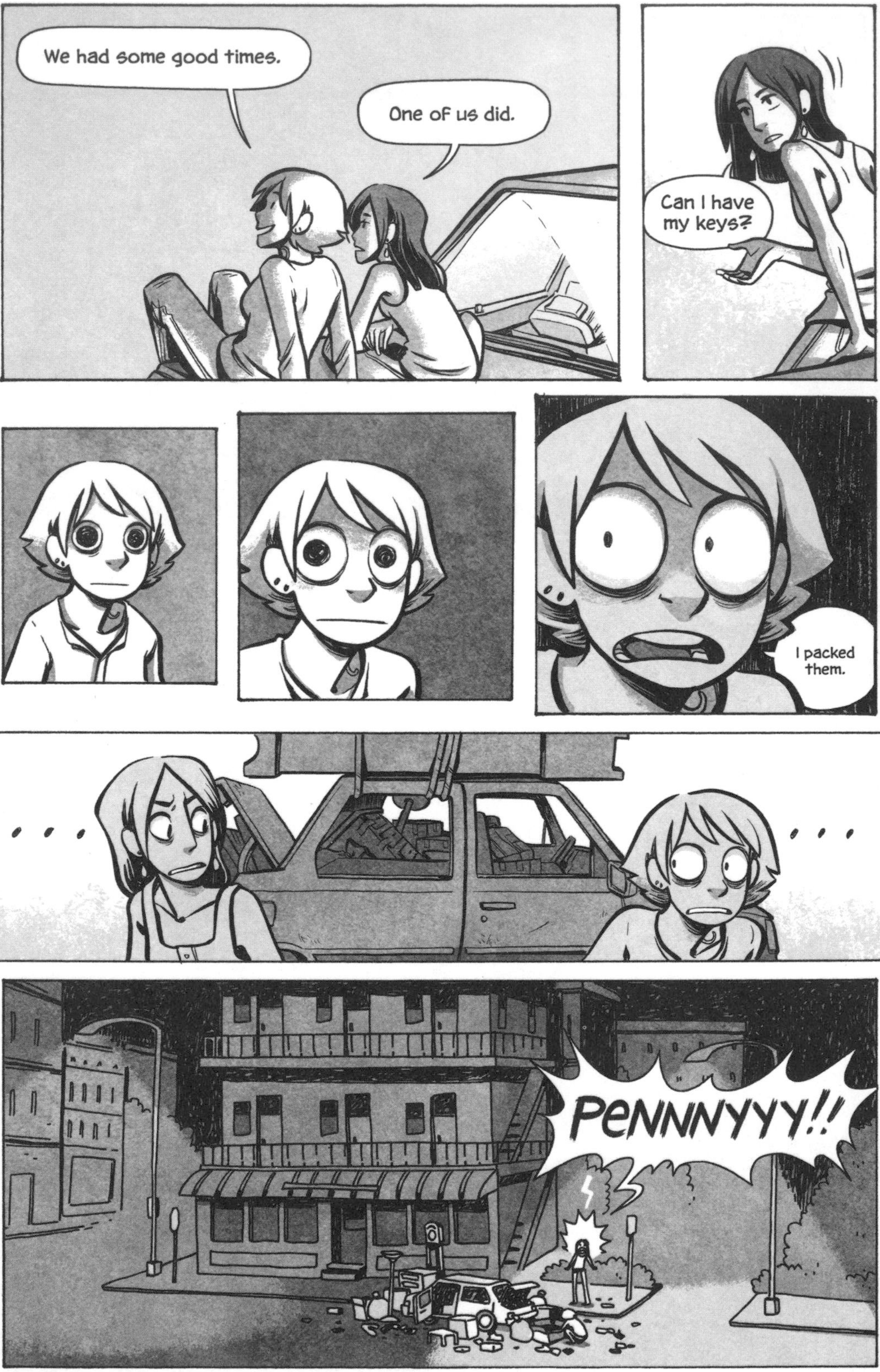
We had some good times.
One of us did.
Can I have my keys?
I packed them.
...
...
PENNNYYY!!

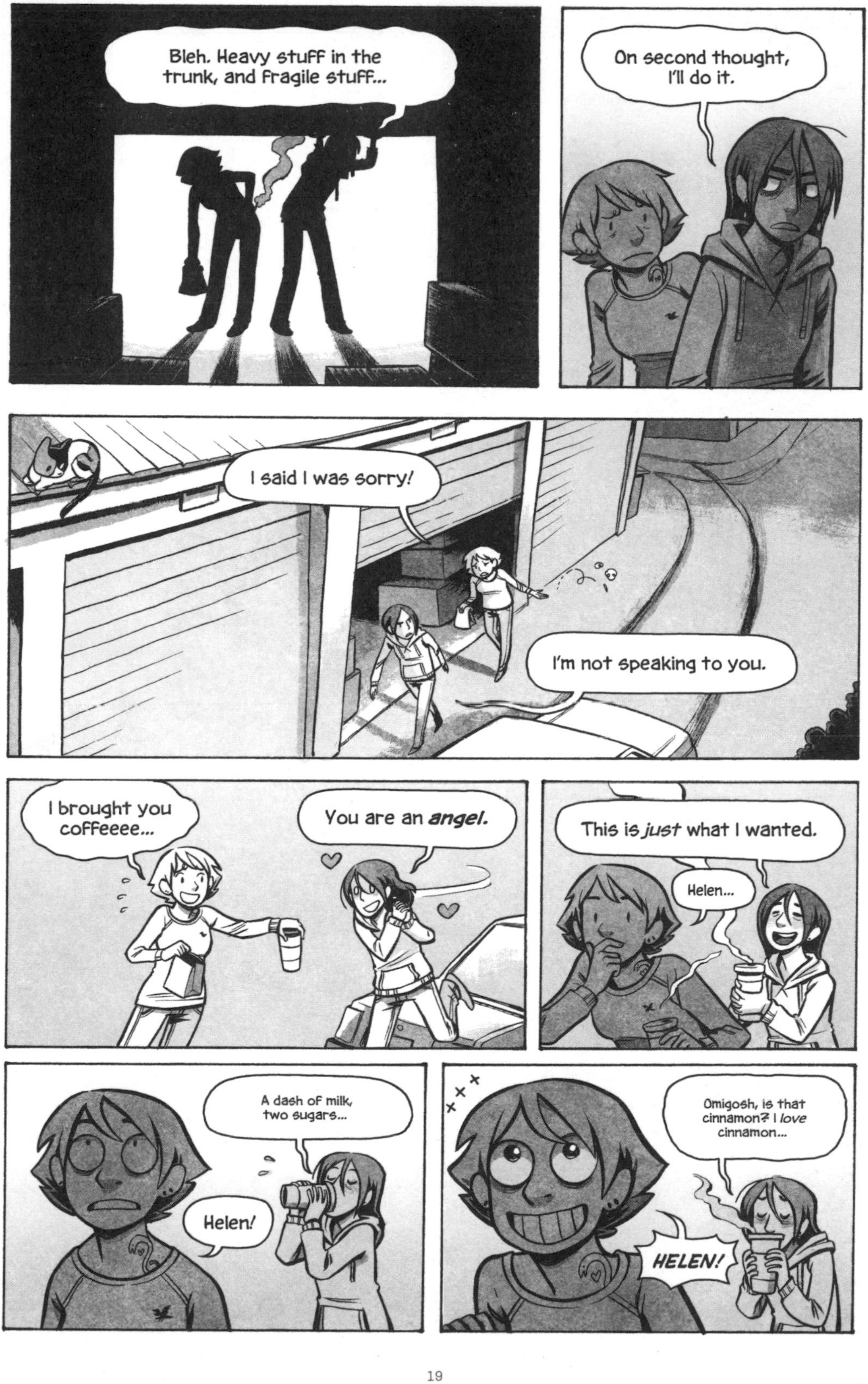
Bleh. Heavy stuff in the trunk, and fragile stuff...
On second thought, I'll do it.
I said I was sorry!
I'm not speaking to you.
I brought you coffeeee...
You are an *angel.*
This is *just* what I wanted.
Helen...
A dash of milk, two sugars...
Helen!
Omigosh, is that cinnamon? I *love* cinnamon...
HELEN!

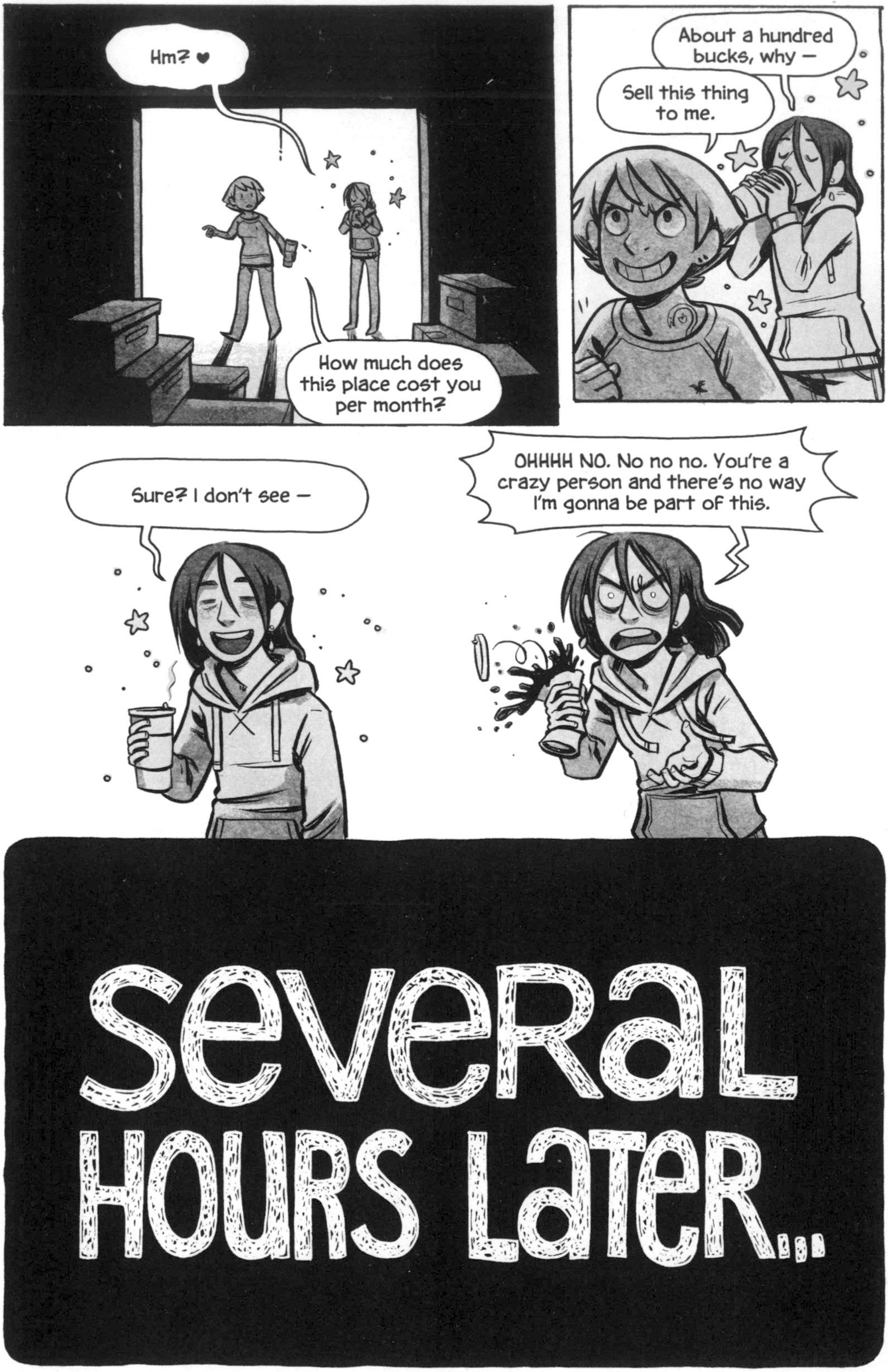
Hm? ♥
How much does this place cost you per month?
About a hundred bucks, why —
Sell this thing to me.
Sure? I don't see —
OHHHH NO. No no no. You're a crazy person and there's no way I'm gonna be part of this.
SEVERAL HOURS LATER...

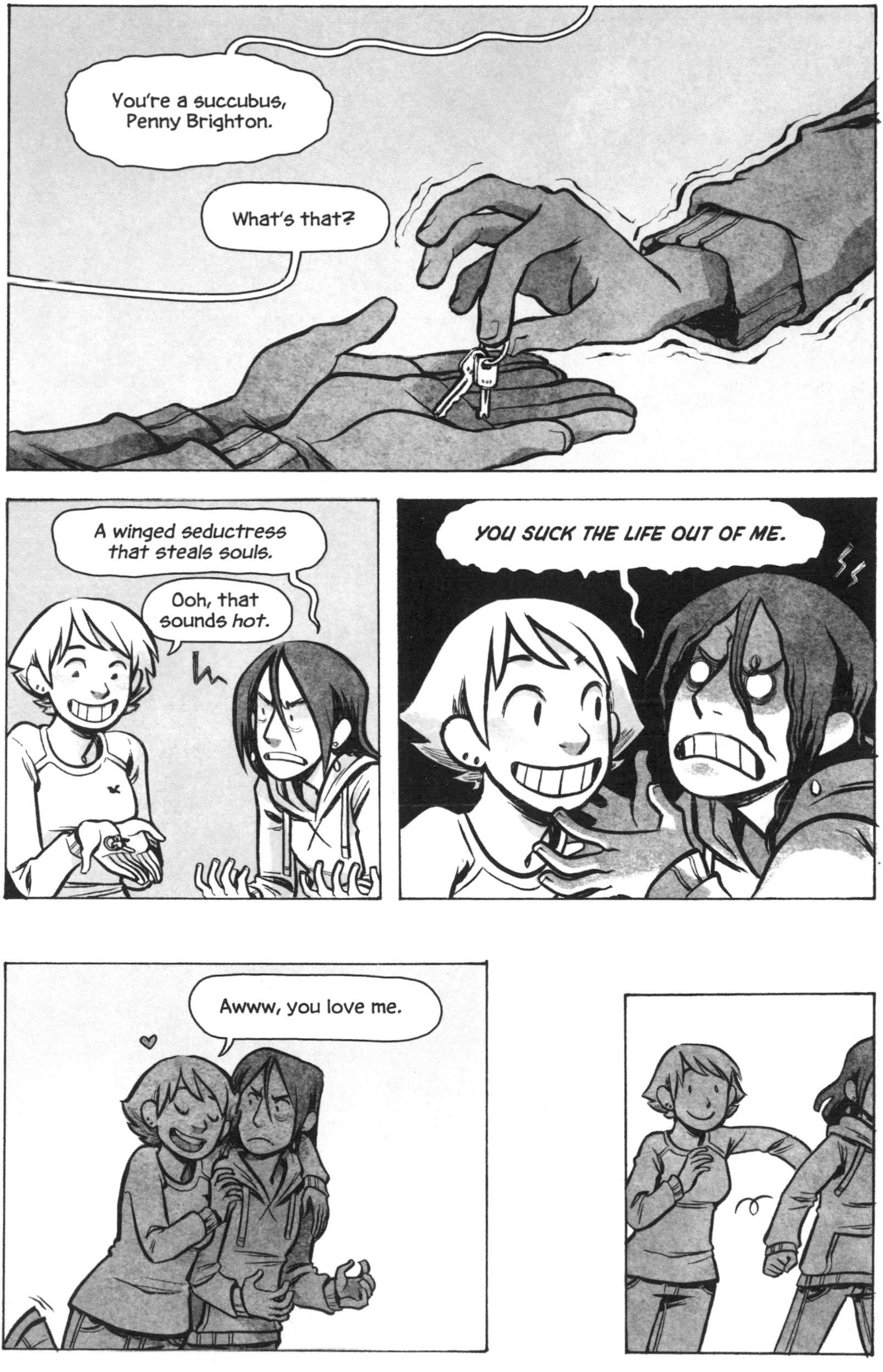
You're a succubus, Penny Brighton.
What's that?
A winged seductress that steals souls.
Ooh, that sounds *hot*.
YOU SUCK THE LIFE OUT OF ME.
Awww, you love me.

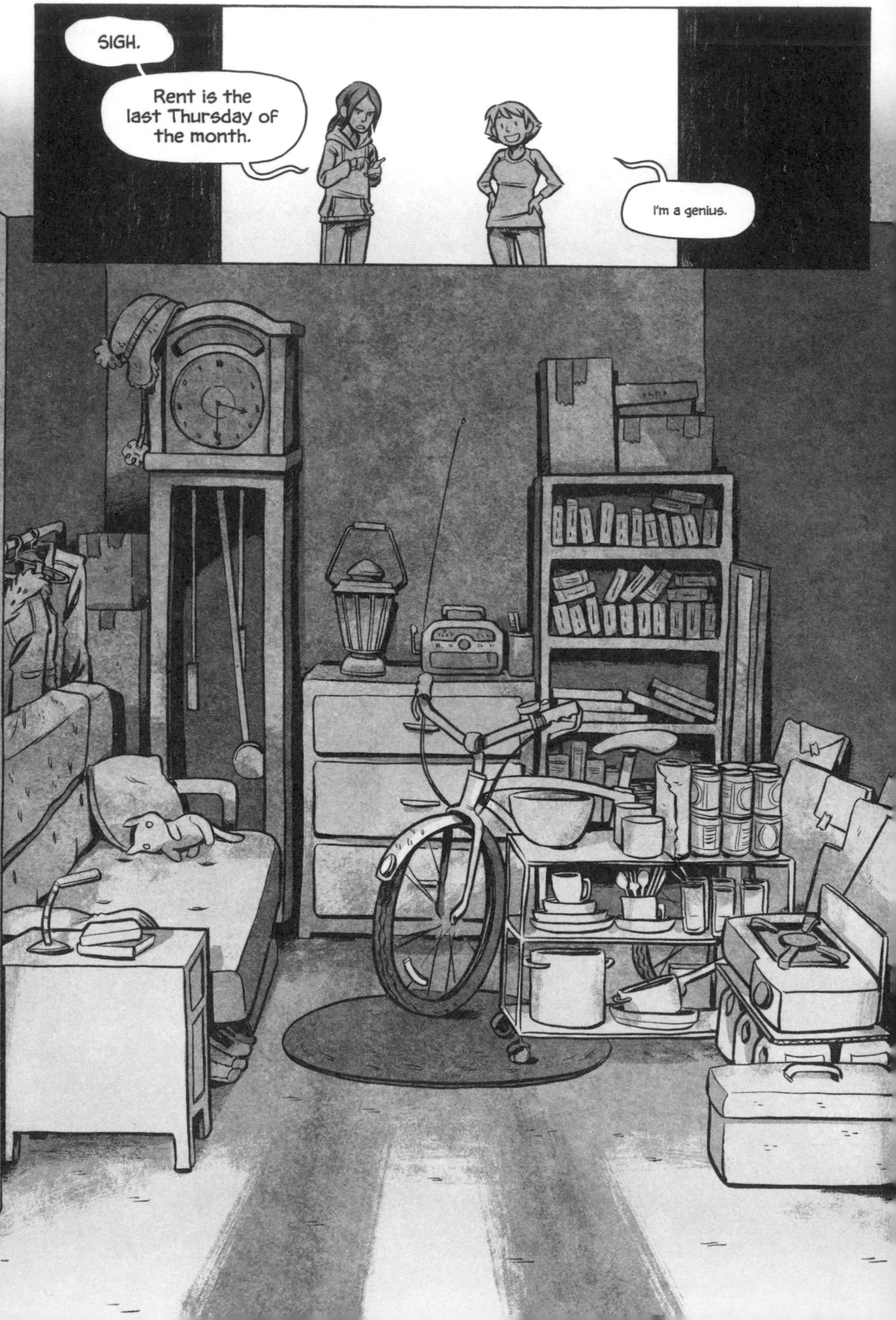
SIGH.
Rent is the last Thursday of the month.
I'm a genius.

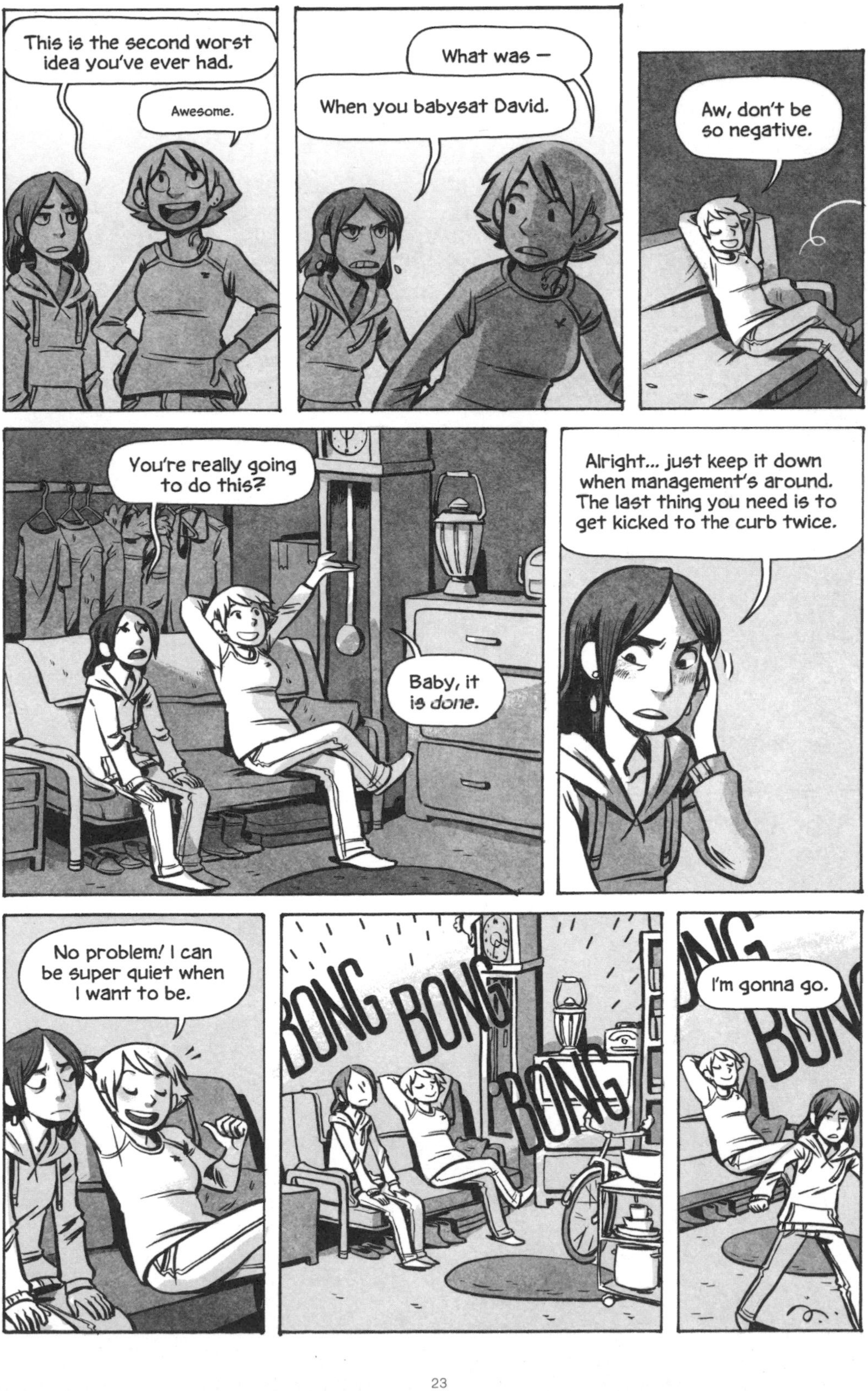
This is the second worst idea you've ever had.
Awesome.
What was —
When you babysat David.
Aw, don't be so negative.
You're really going to do this?
Baby, it is *done*.
Alright... just keep it down when management's around. The last thing you need is to get kicked to the curb twice.
No problem! I can be super quiet when I want to be.
BONG BONG BONG
I'm gonna go.

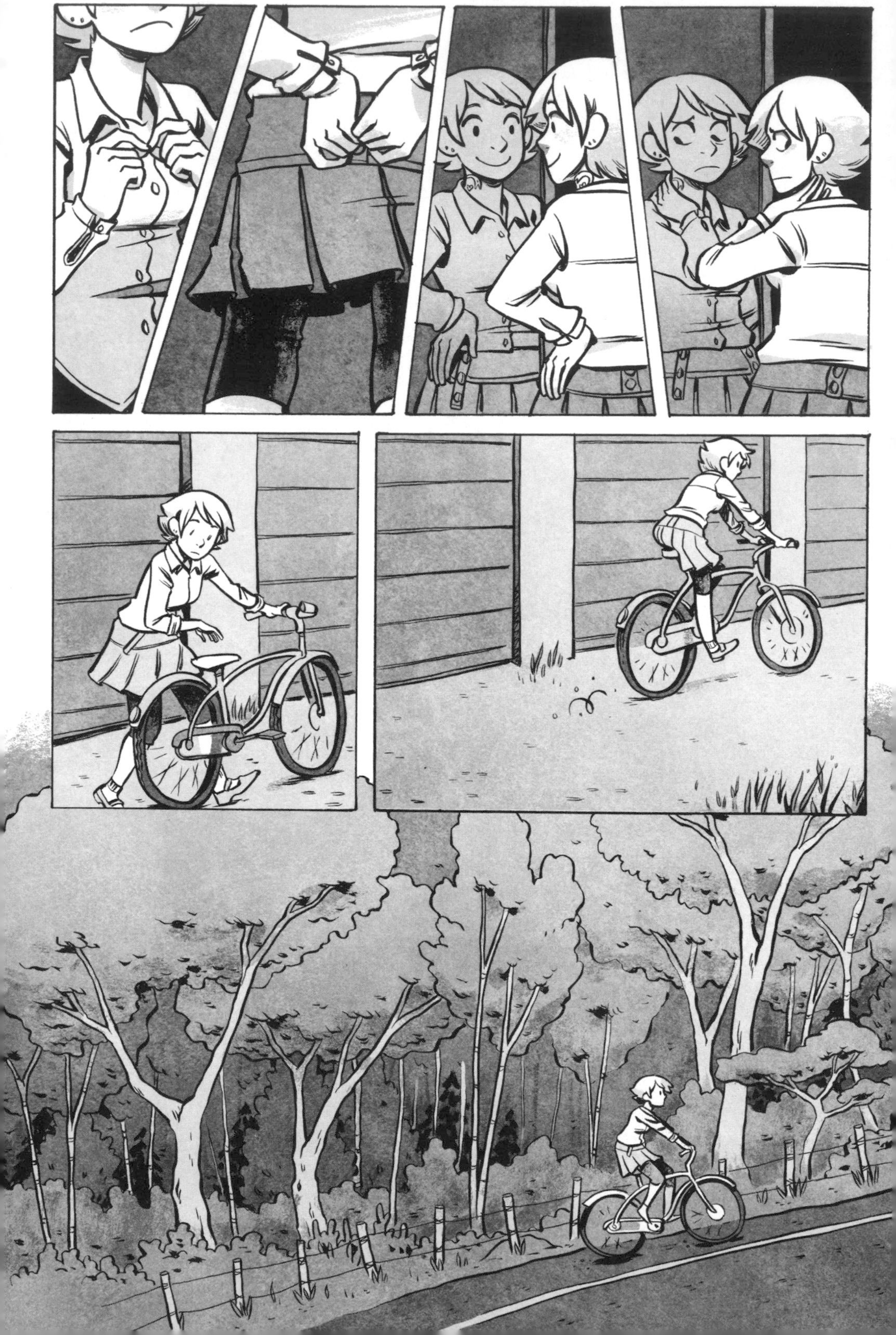

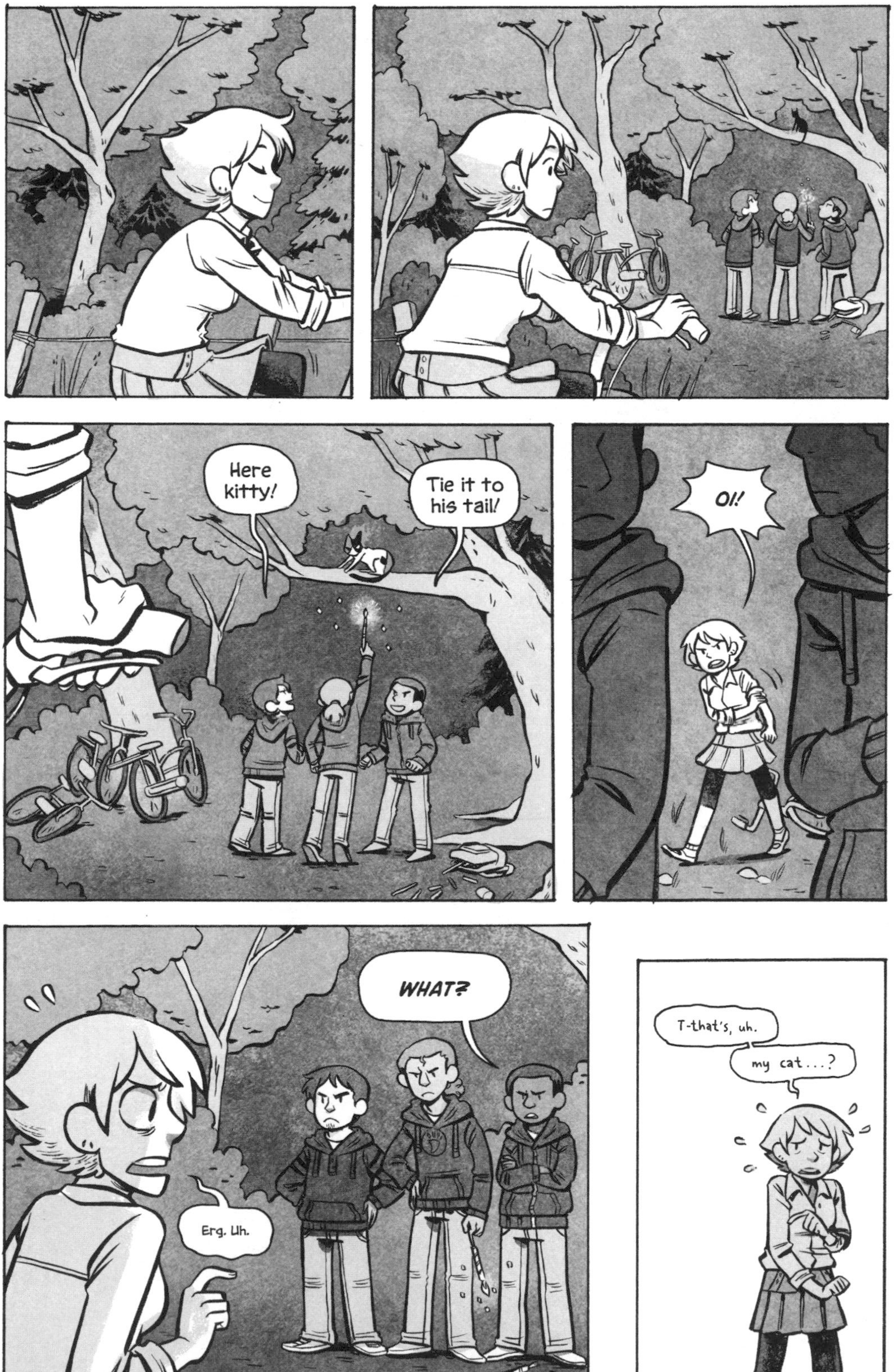
Here kitty!
Tie it to his tail!
OI!
WHAT?
Erg. Uh.
T-that's, uh.
my cat...?

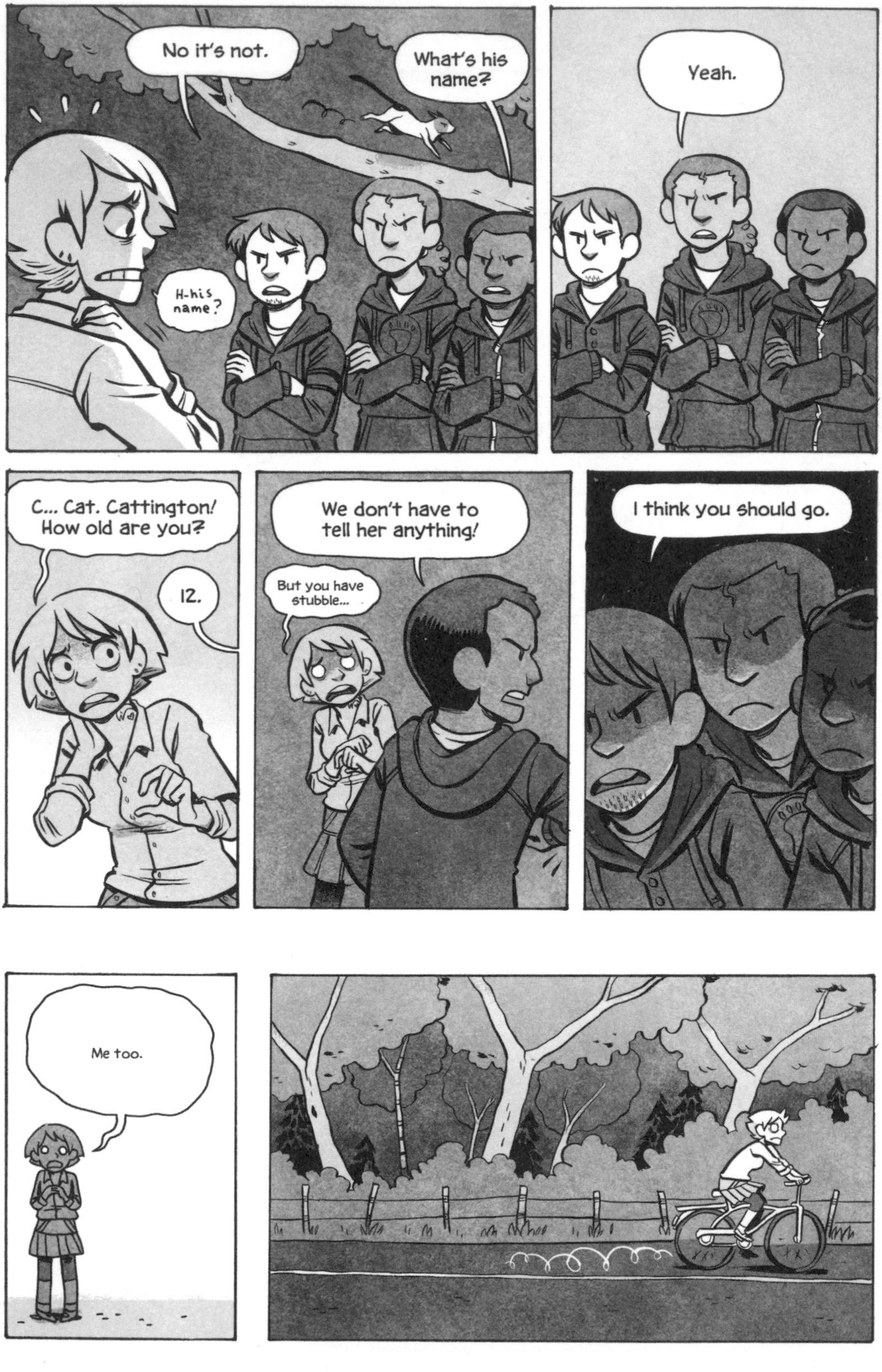
No it's not.
What's his name?
H-his name?
Yeah.
C... Cat. Cattington! How old are you?
12.
We don't have to tell her anything!
But you have stubble...
I think you should go.
Me too.

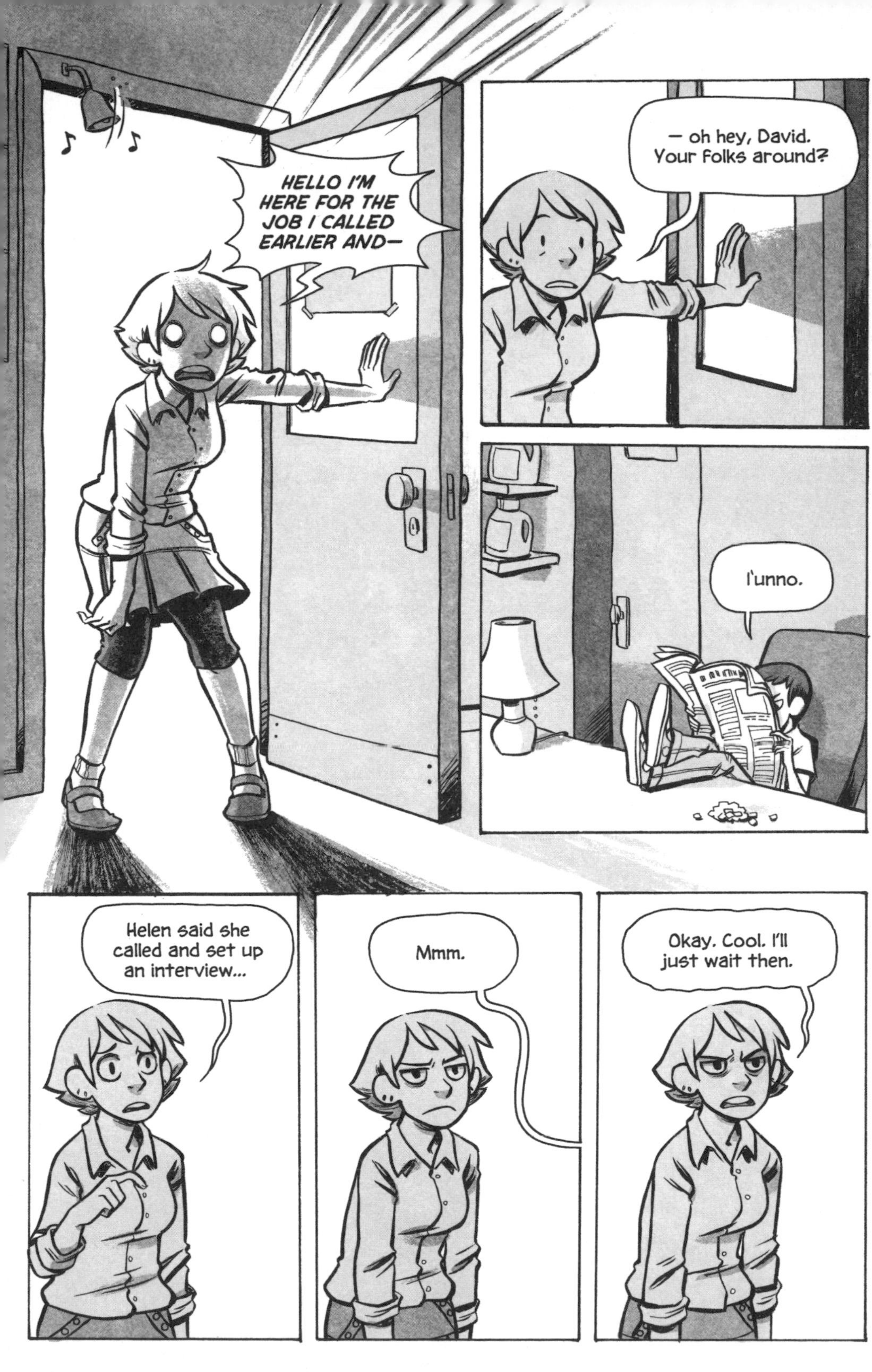
HELLO I'M HERE FOR THE JOB I CALLED EARLIER AND—
— oh hey, David. Your folks around?
I'unno.
Helen said she called and set up an interview...
Mmm.
Okay. Cool. I'll just wait then.

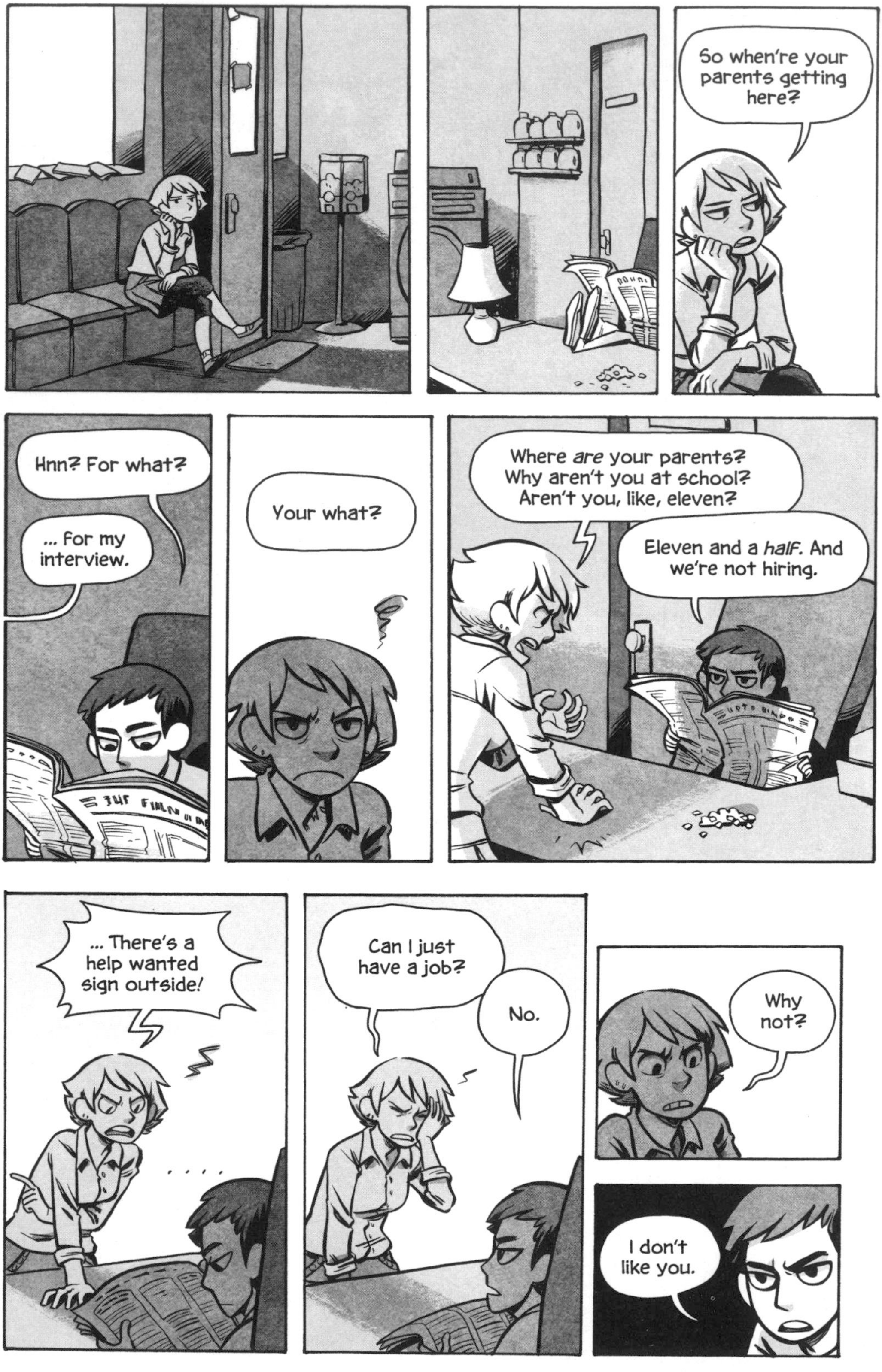
So when're your parents getting here?
Hnn? For what?
... For my interview.
Your what?
Where *are* your parents? Why aren't you at school? Aren't you, like, eleven?
Eleven and a *half*. And we're not hiring.
... There's a help wanted sign outside!
....
Can I just have a job?
No.
Why not?
I don't like you.

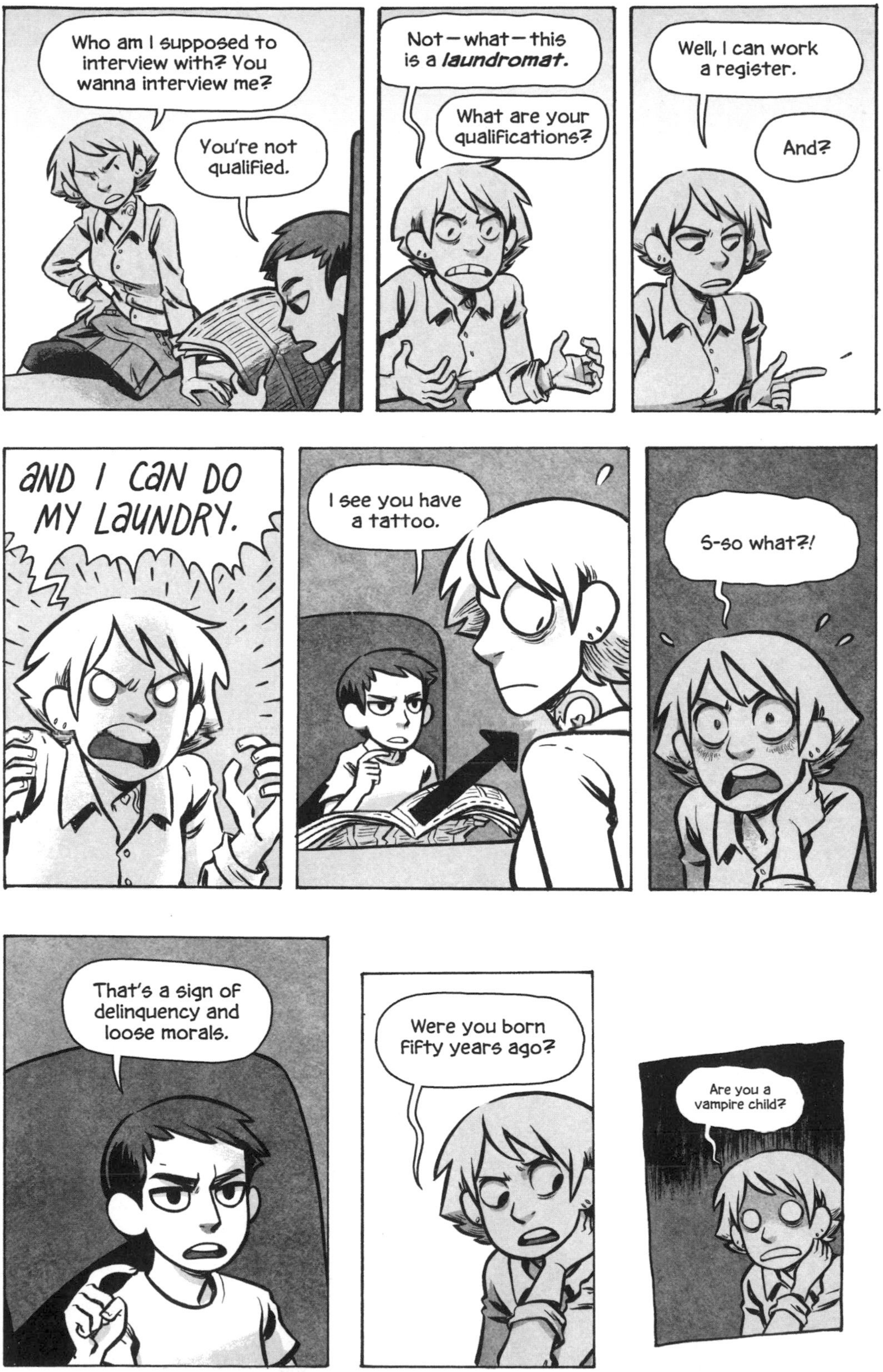
Who am I supposed to interview with? You wanna interview me?
You're not qualified.
Not—what—this is a *laundromat*.
What are your qualifications?
Well, I can work a register.
And?
AND I CAN DO MY LAUNDRY.
I see you have a tattoo.
S-so what?!
That's a sign of delinquency and loose morals.
Were you born fifty years ago?
Are you a vampire child?

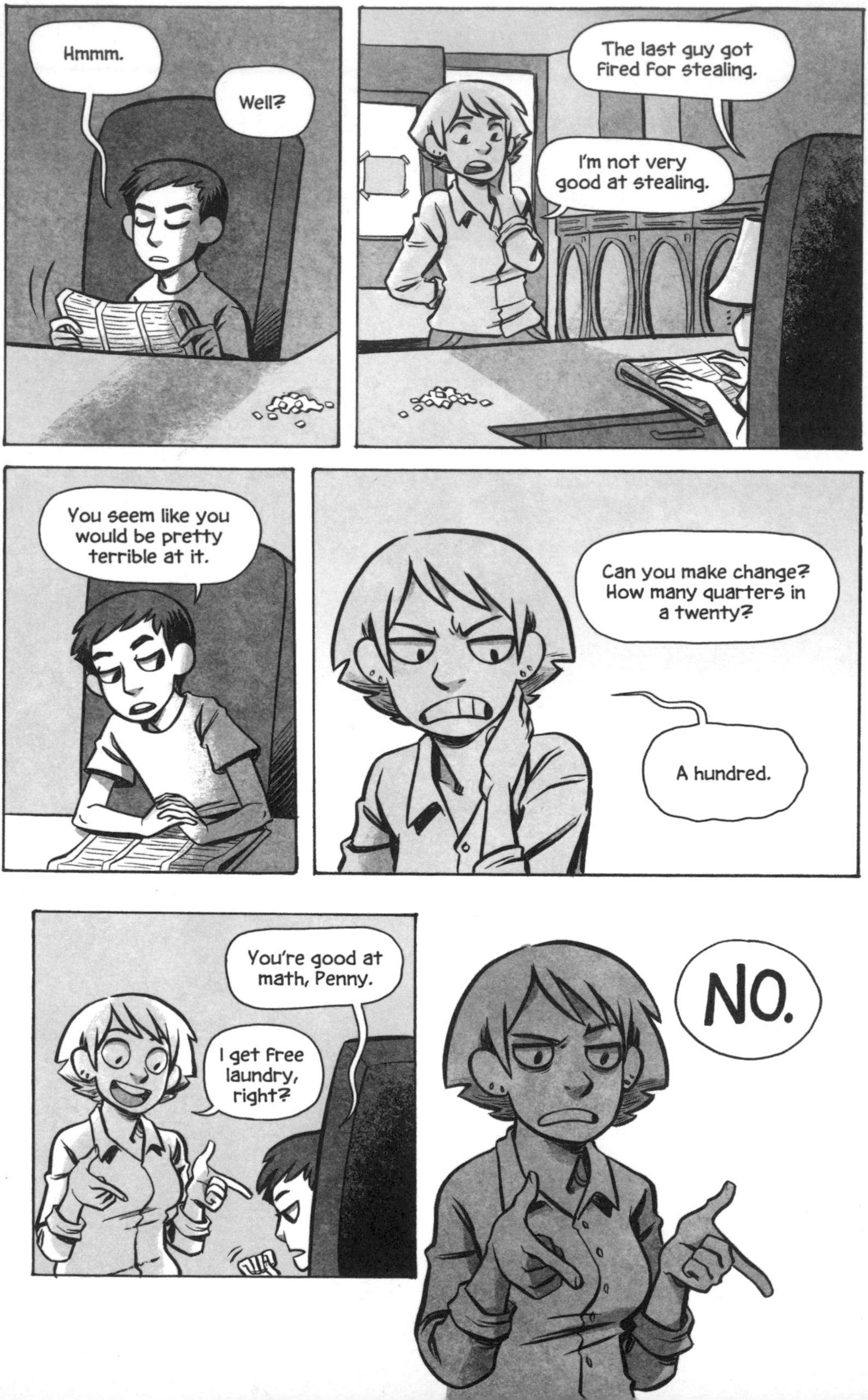
Hmmm.
Well?
The last guy got fired for stealing.
I'm not very good at stealing.
You seem like you would be pretty terrible at it.
Can you make change? How many quarters in a twenty?
A hundred.
You're good at math, Penny.
I get free laundry, right?
NO.

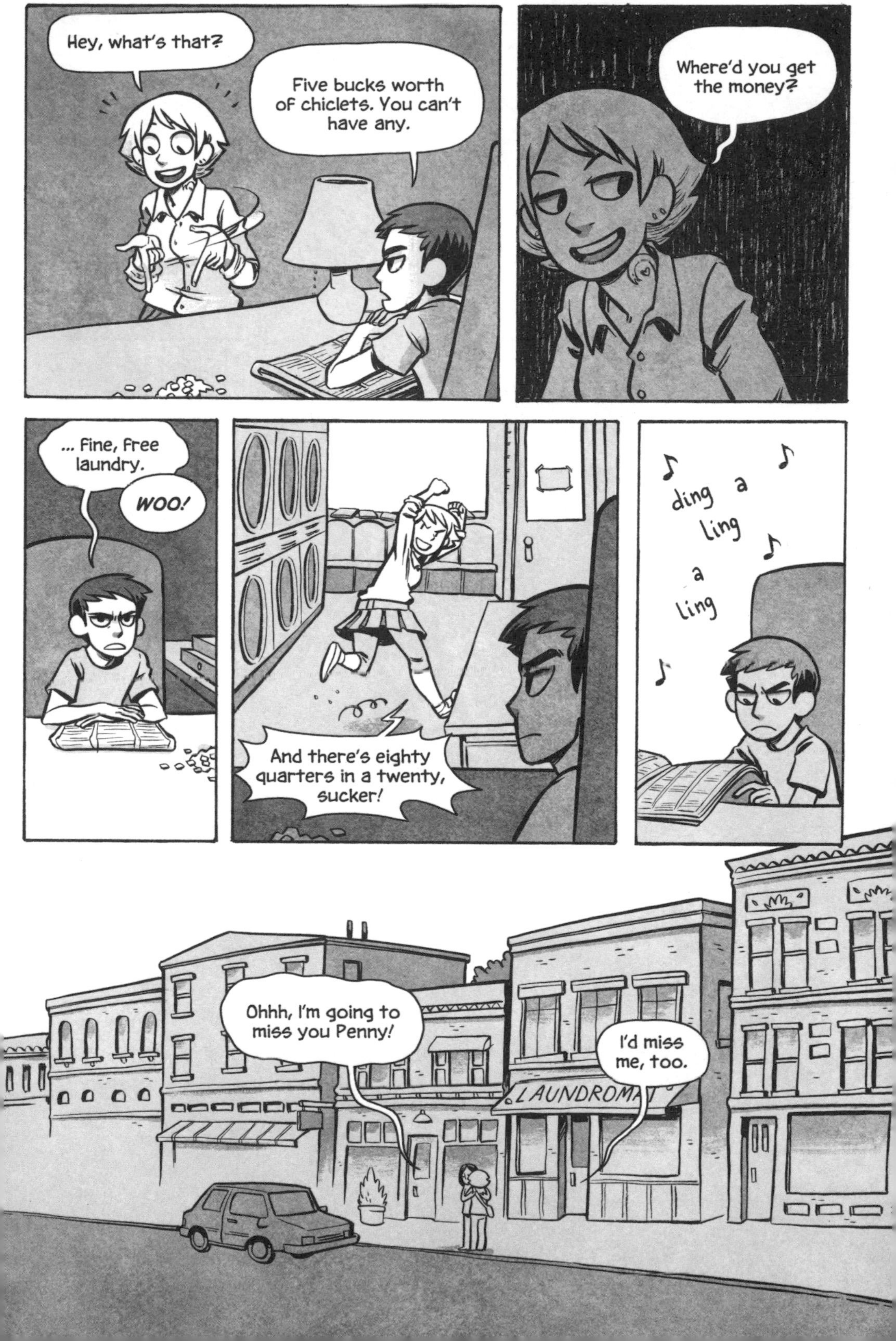
Hey, what's that?
Five bucks worth of chiclets. You can't have any.
Where'd you get the money?
... fine, free laundry.
WOO!
And there's eighty quarters in a twenty, sucker!
ding a ling a ling
Ohhh, I'm going to miss you Penny!
I'd miss me, too.
LAUNDROMA

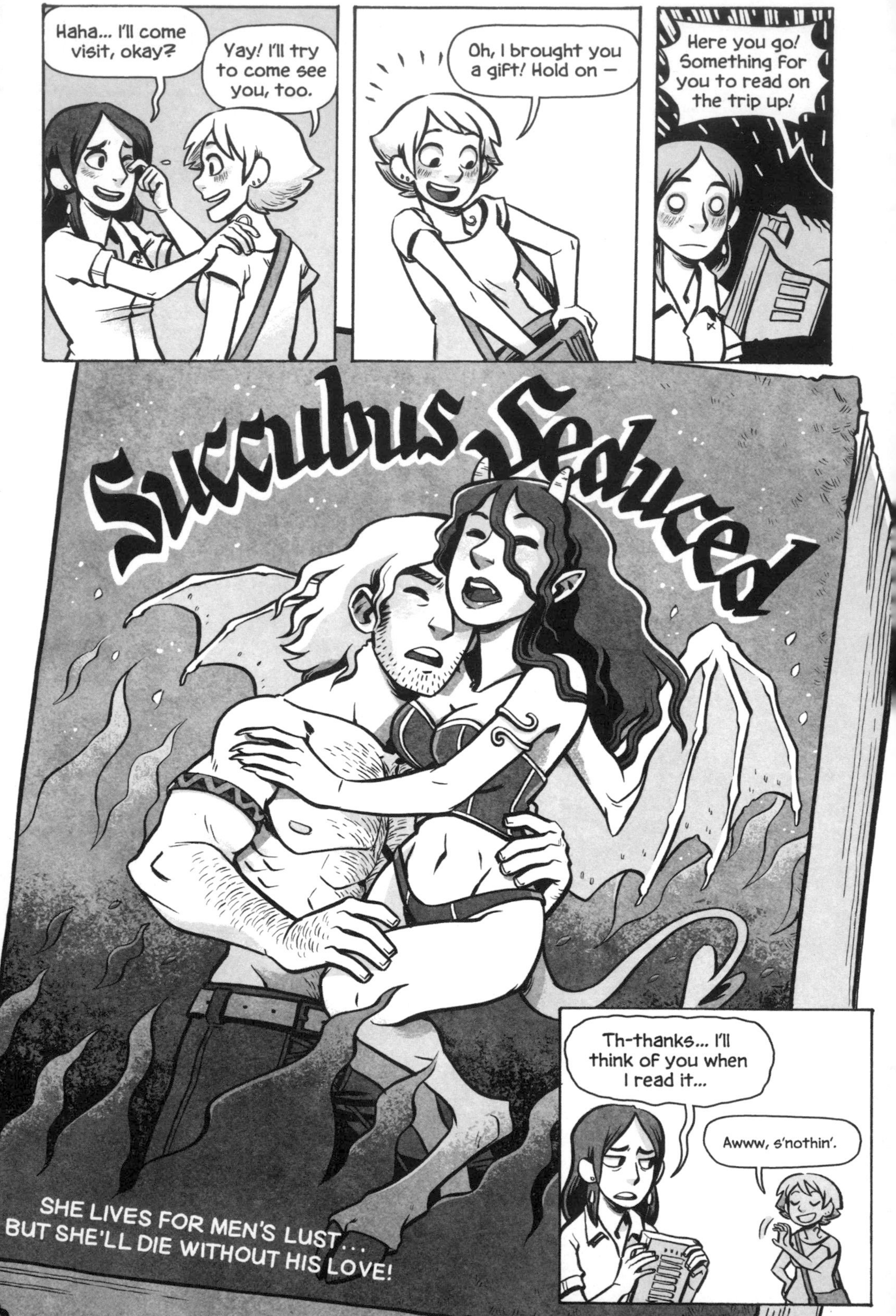
Haha... I'll come visit, okay?
Yay! I'll try to come see you, too.
Oh, I brought you a gift! Hold on —
Here you go! Something for you to read on the trip up!
Succubus Seduced
SHE LIVES FOR MEN'S LUST... BUT SHE'LL DIE WITHOUT HIS LOVE!
Th-thanks... I'll think of you when I read it...
Awww, s'nothin'.

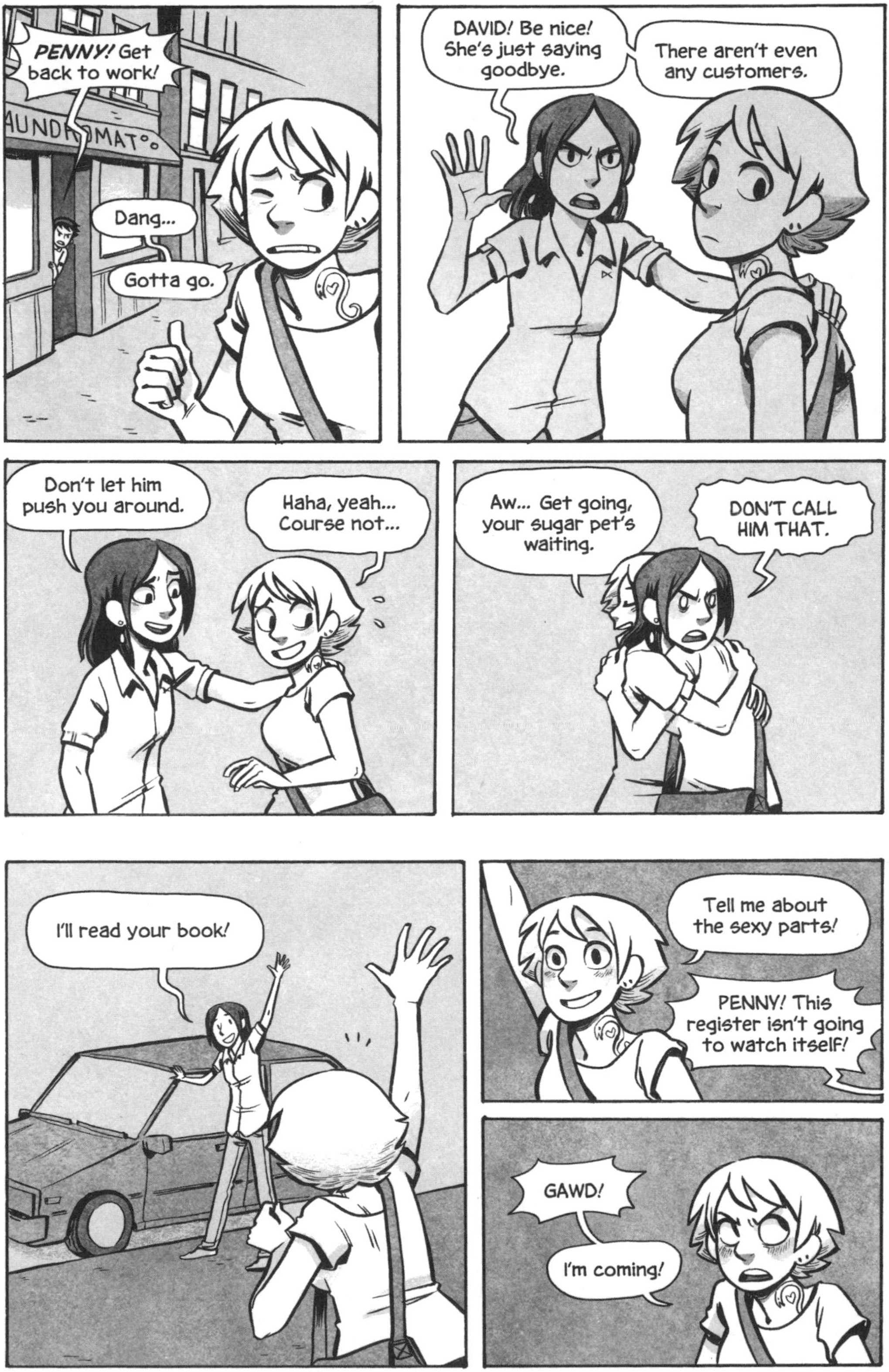

PENNY! Get back to work!
AUNDROMAT
Dang...
Gotta go.
DAVID! Be nice! She's just saying goodbye.
There aren't even any customers.
Don't let him push you around.
Haha, yeah... Course not...
Aw... Get going, your sugar pet's waiting.
DON'T CALL HIM THAT.
I'll read your book!
Tell me about the sexy parts!
PENNY! This register isn't going to watch itself!
GAWD!
I'm coming!

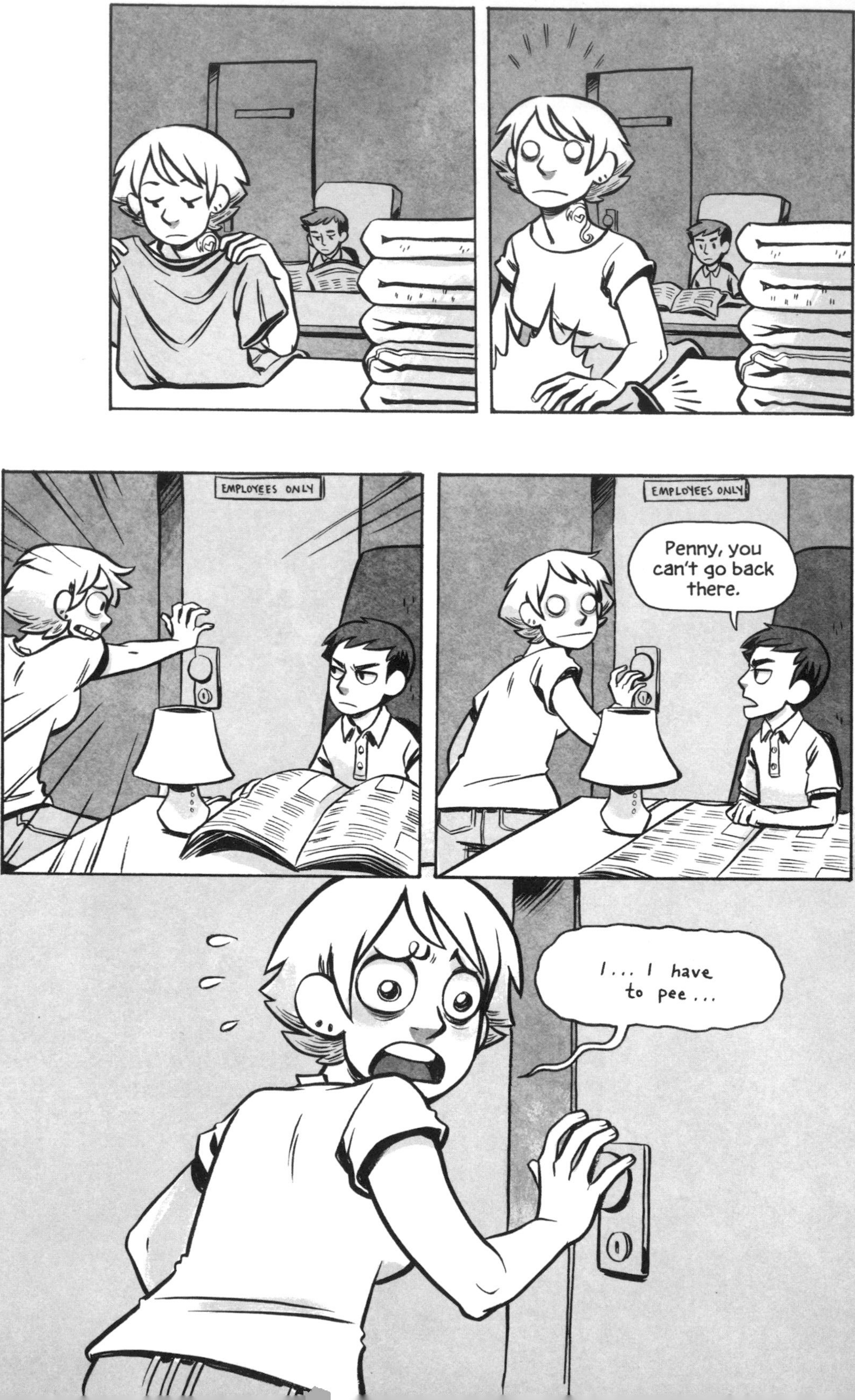
EMPLOYEES ONLY
EMPLOYEES ONLY
Penny, you can't go back there.
I... I have to pee...

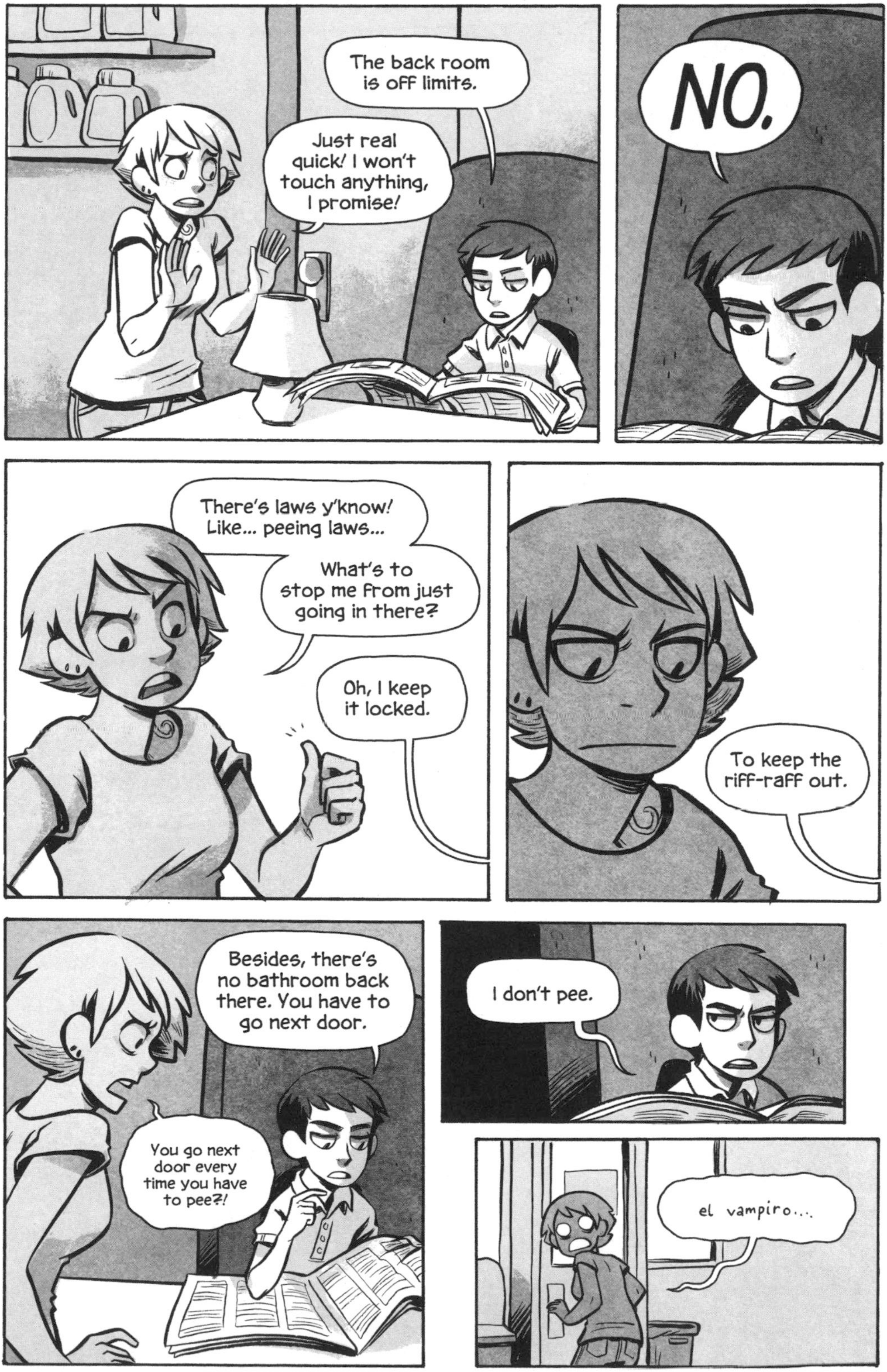

The back room is off limits.
Just real quick! I won't touch anything, I promise!
NO.
There's laws y'know! Like... peeing laws...
What's to stop me from just going in there?
Oh, I keep it locked.
To keep the riff-raff out.
Besides, there's no bathroom back there. You have to go next door.
You go next door every time you have to pee?!
I don't pee.
el vampiro....

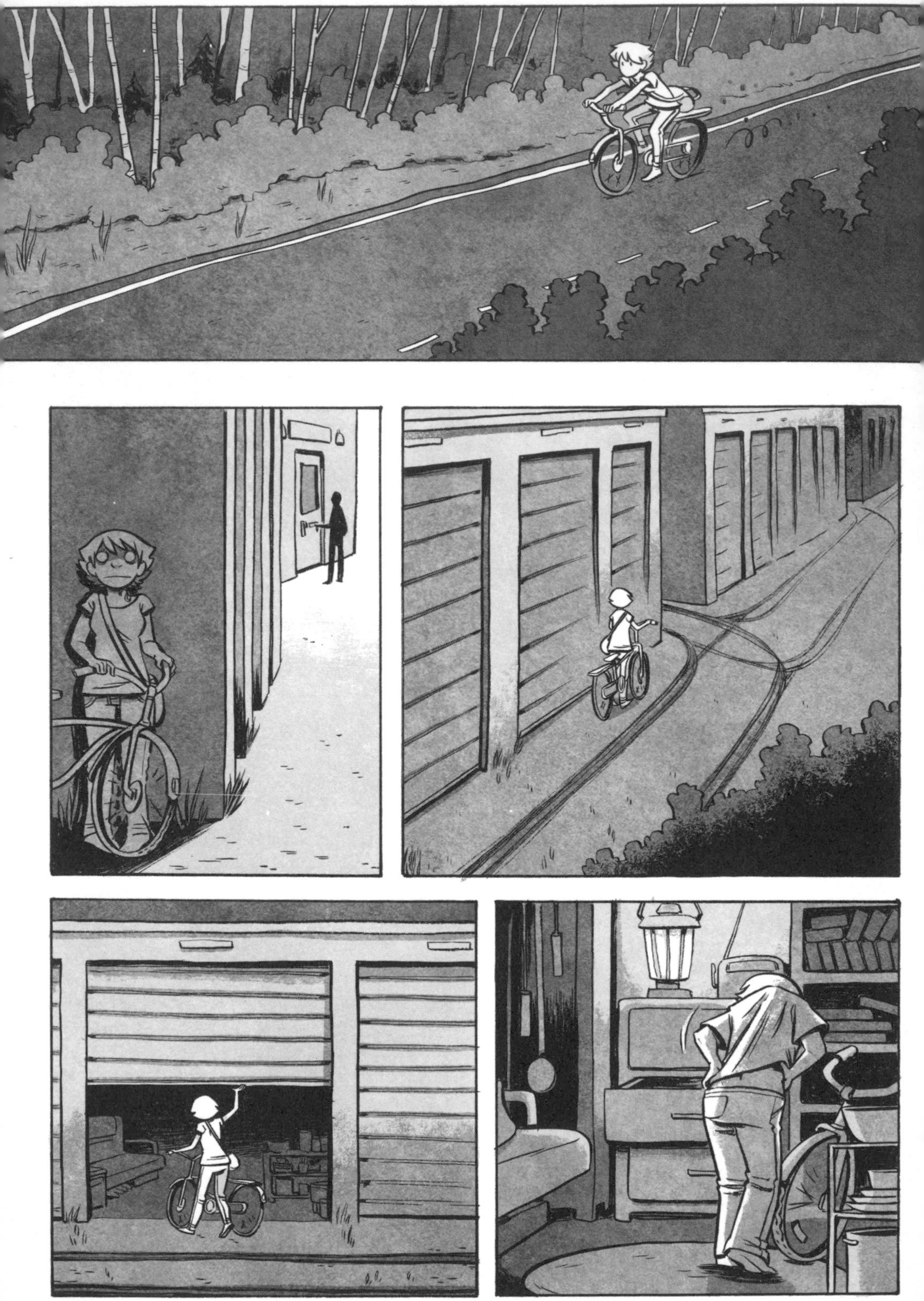

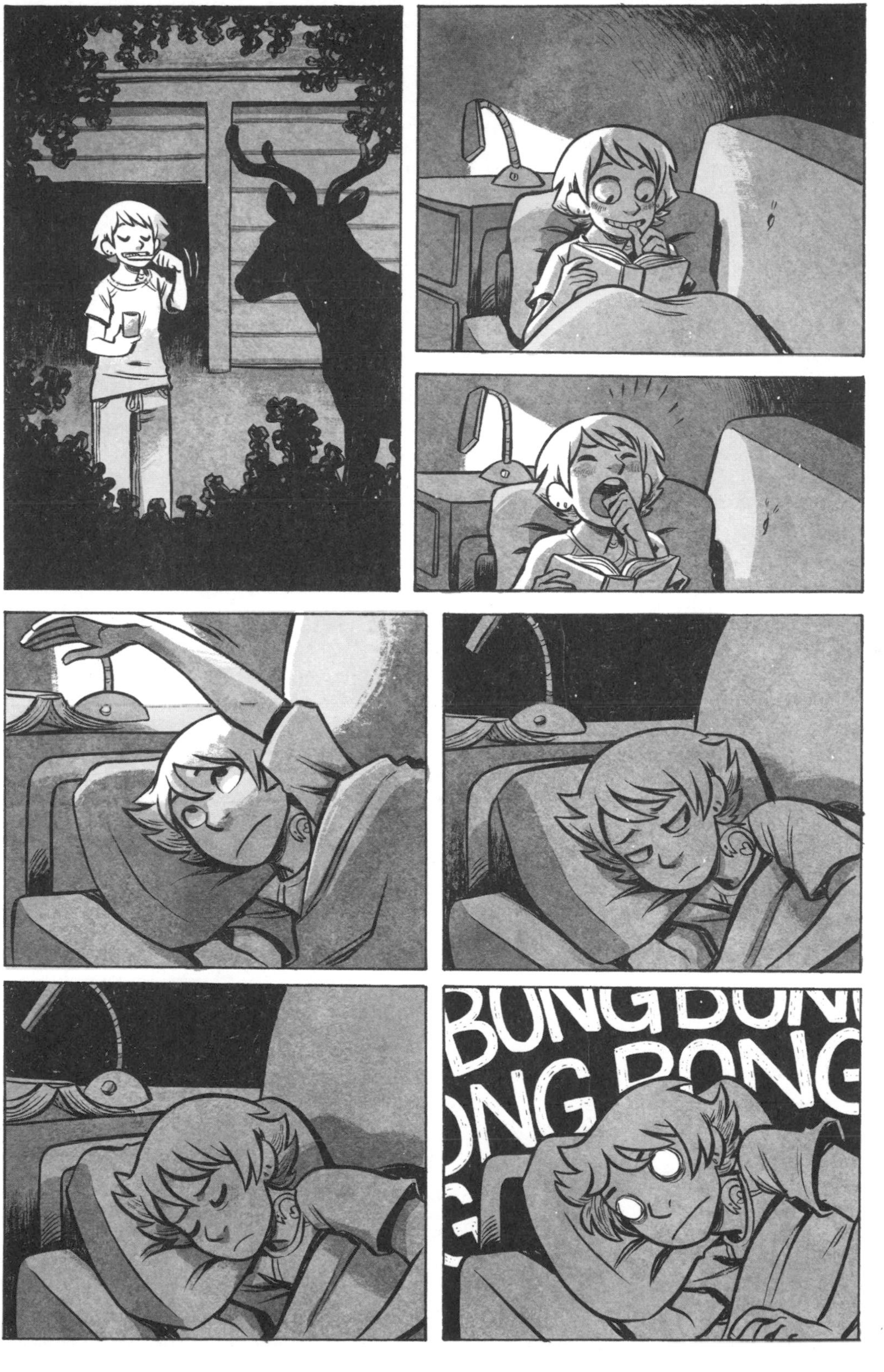
BUNG BUNG
BONG BONG

LION'S PRIDE

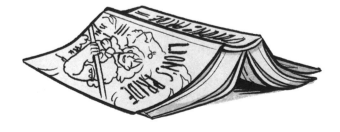

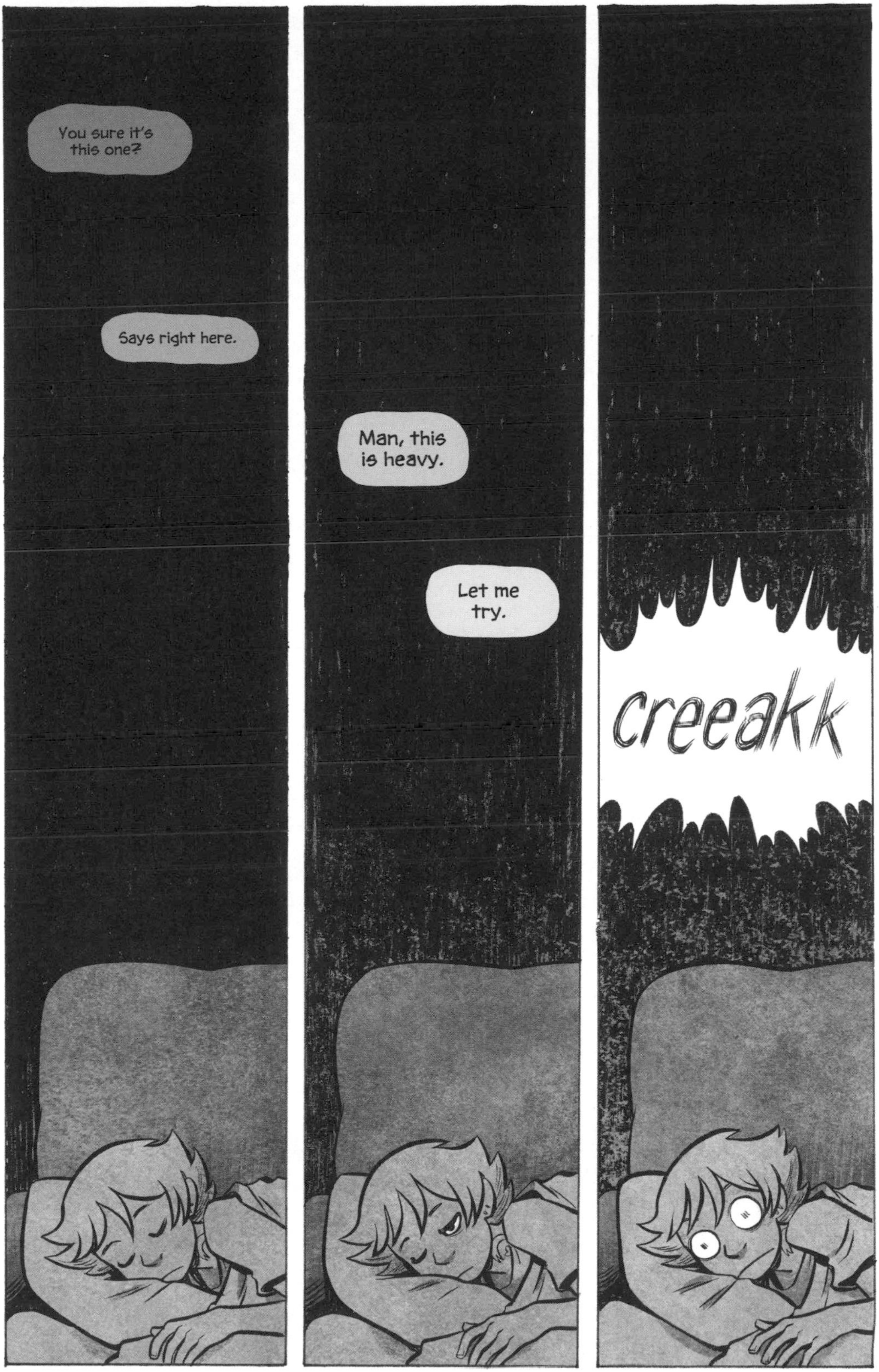
You sure it's this one?
Says right here.
Man, this is heavy.
Let me try.
creeakk

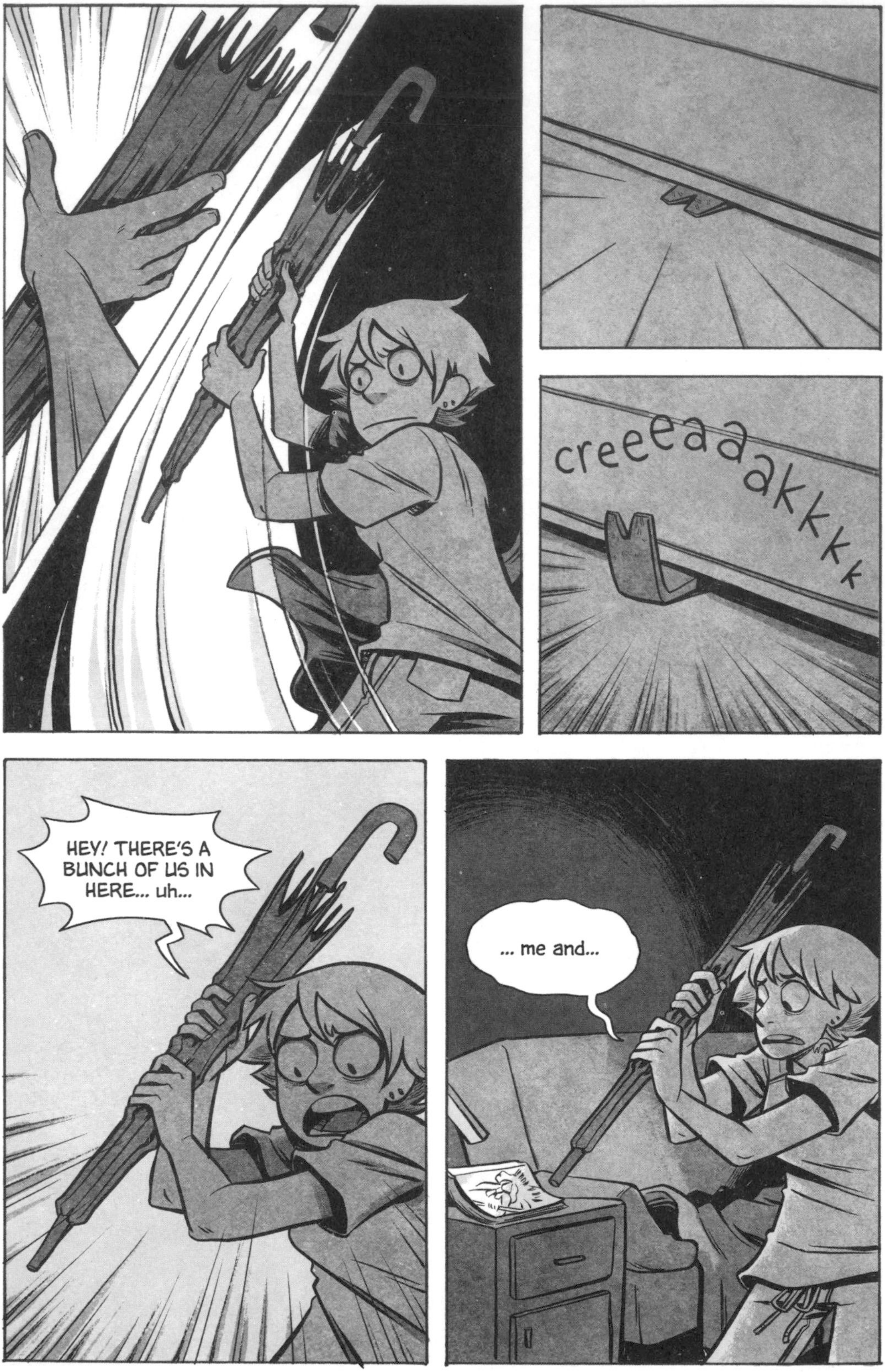
creeeaaakkkkk
HEY! THERE'S A BUNCH OF US IN HERE... uh...
... me and...

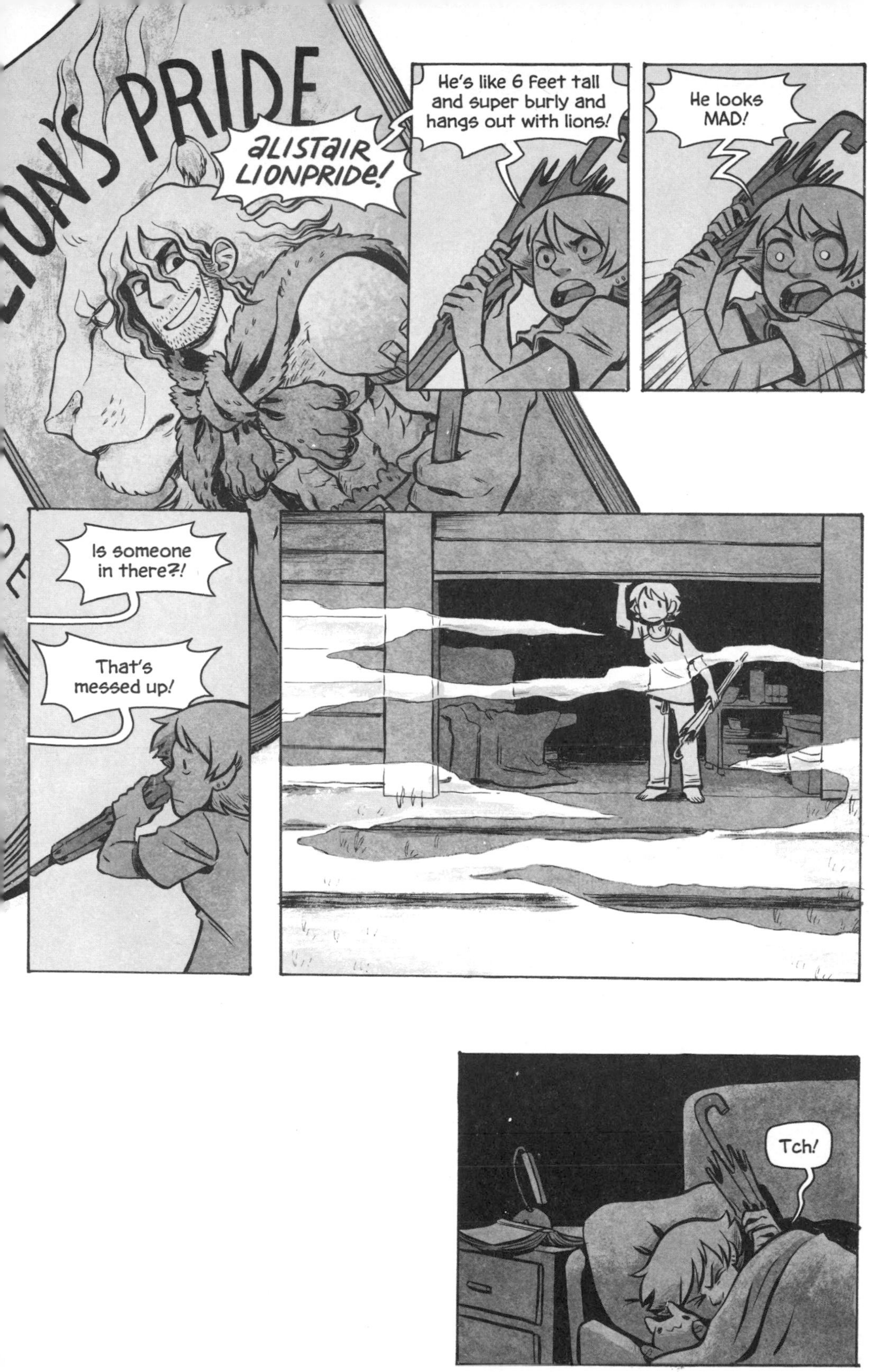
LION'S PRIDE
ALISTAIR LIONPRIDE!
He's like 6 feet tall and super burly and hangs out with lions!
He looks MAD!
Is someone in there?!
That's messed up!
Tch!

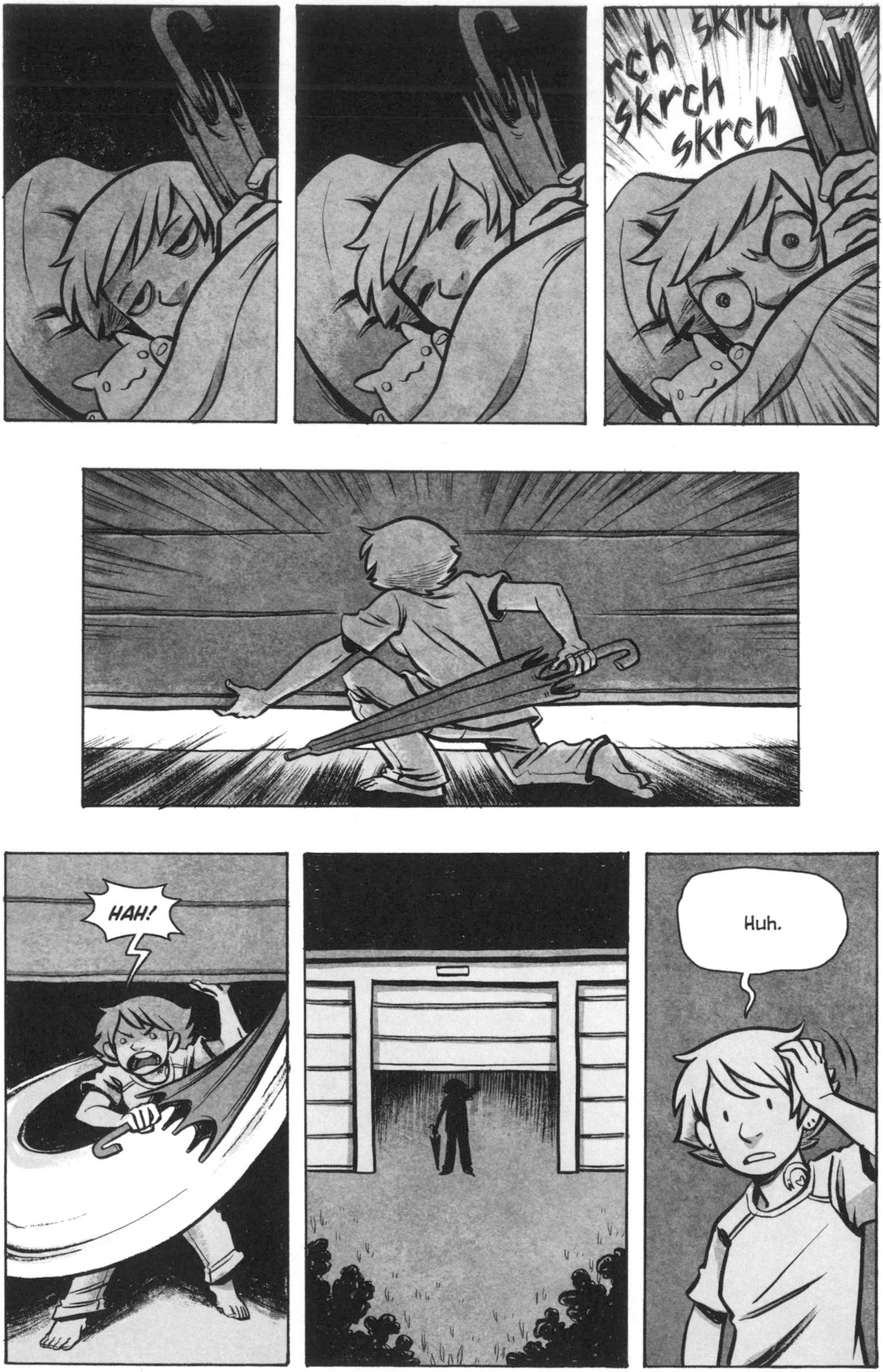
skrch
skrch
skrch
skrch
HAH!
Huh.

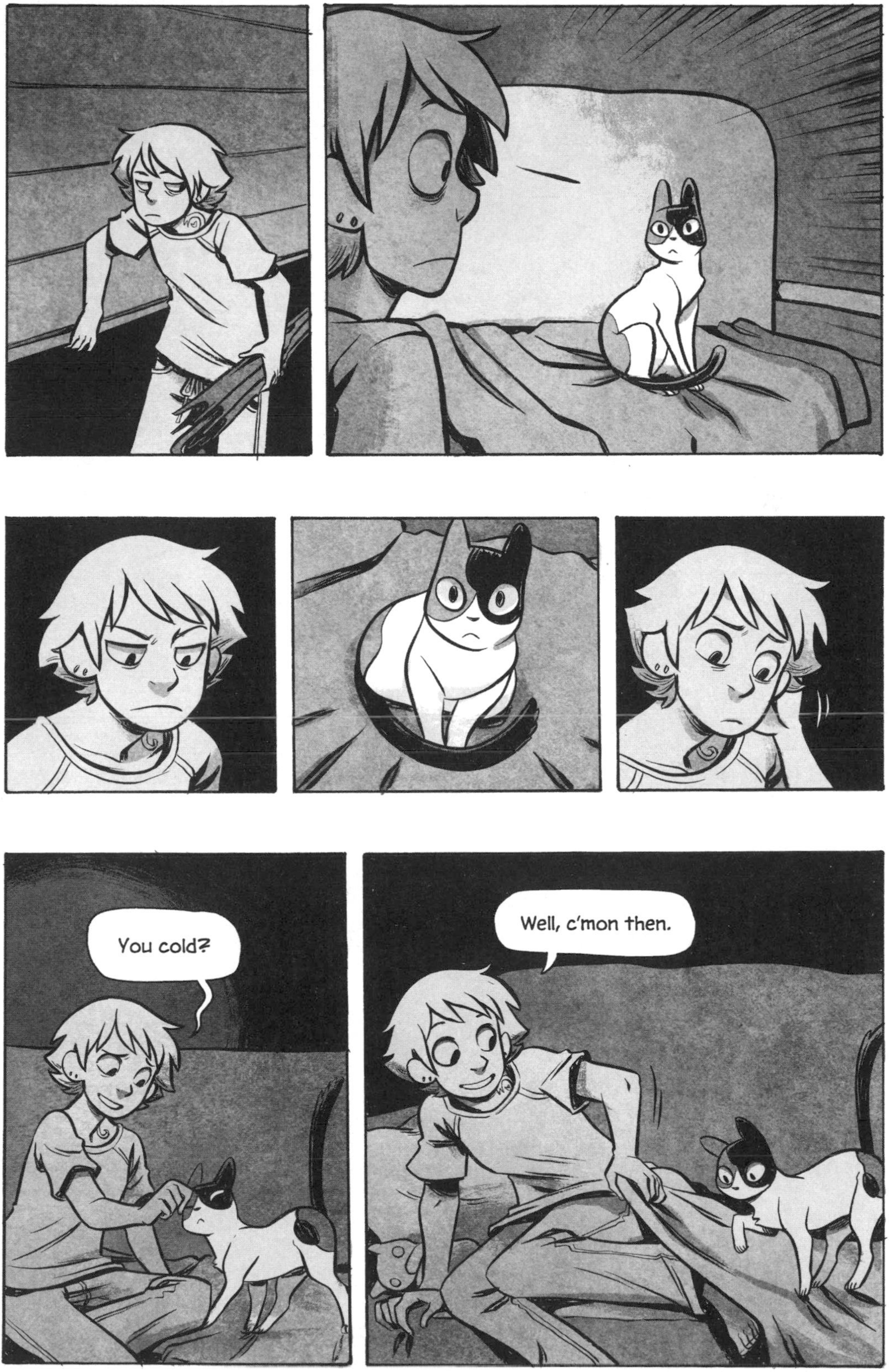
You cold?
Well, c'mon then.

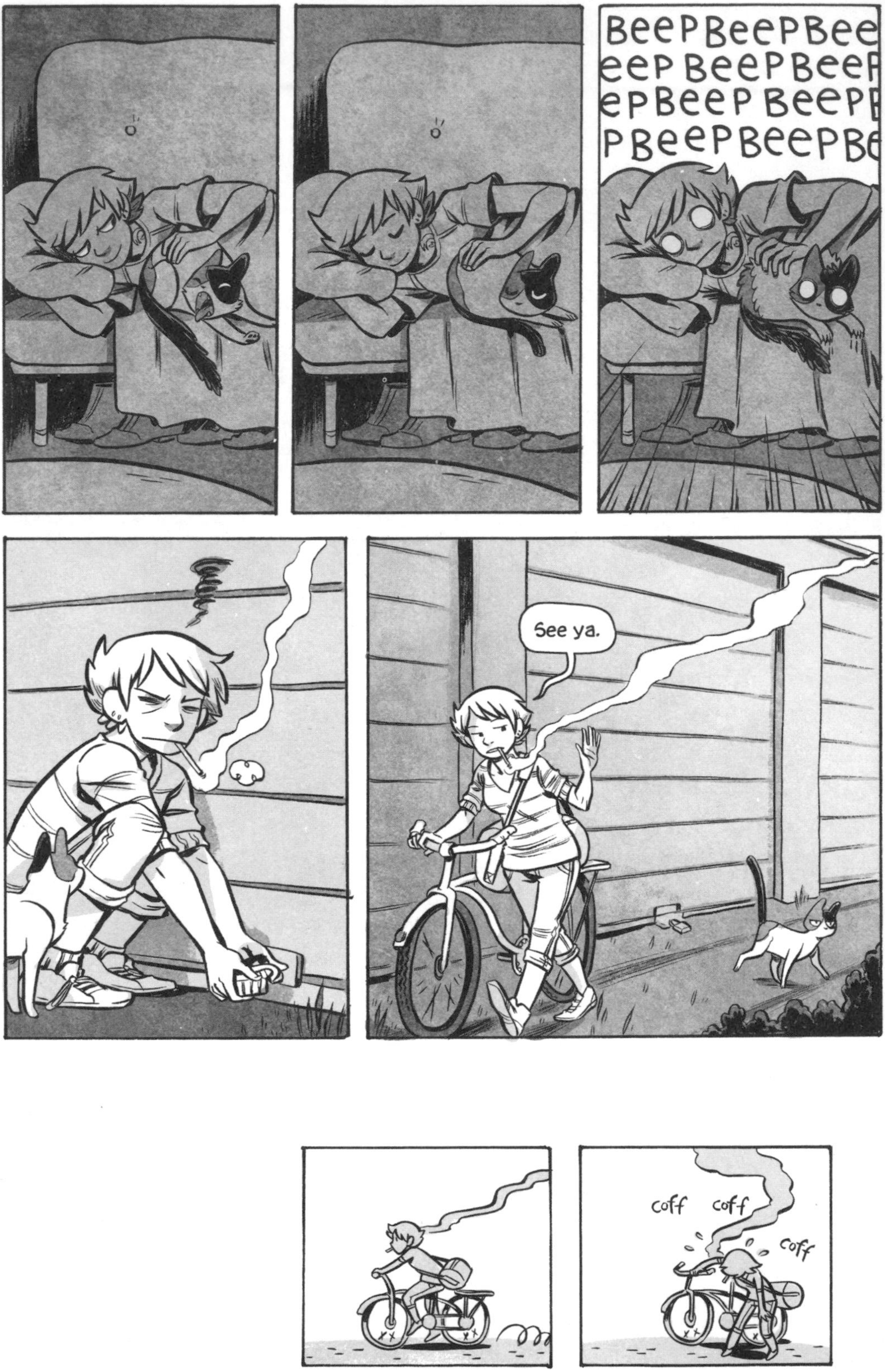
BeeP BeeP Bee
eeP BeeP BeeP
eP BeeP BeeP B
P BeeP BeeP Be
See ya.
coff coff
coff

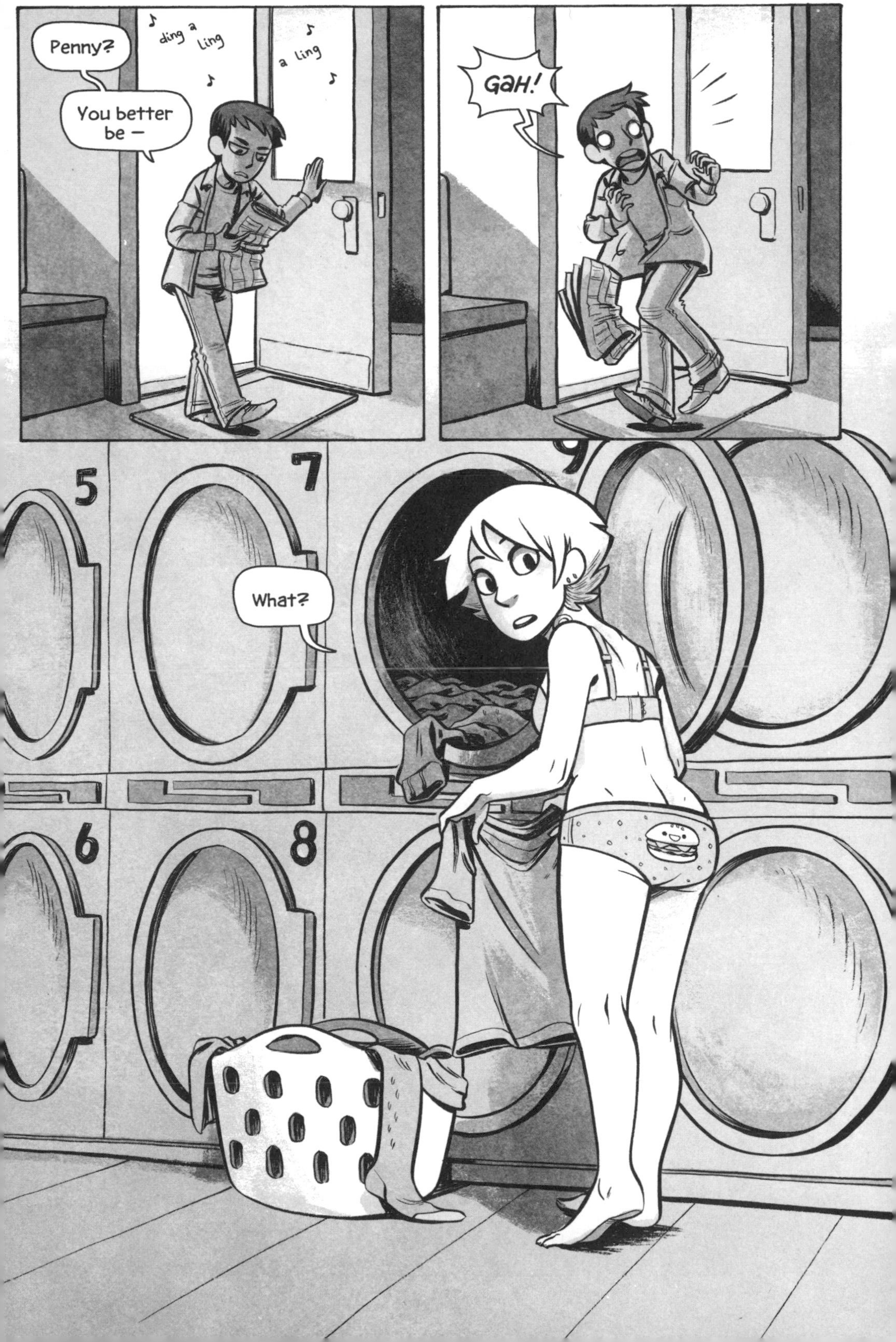
Penny?
You better be —
ding a ling
a ling
GAH!
5
7
9
What?
6
8

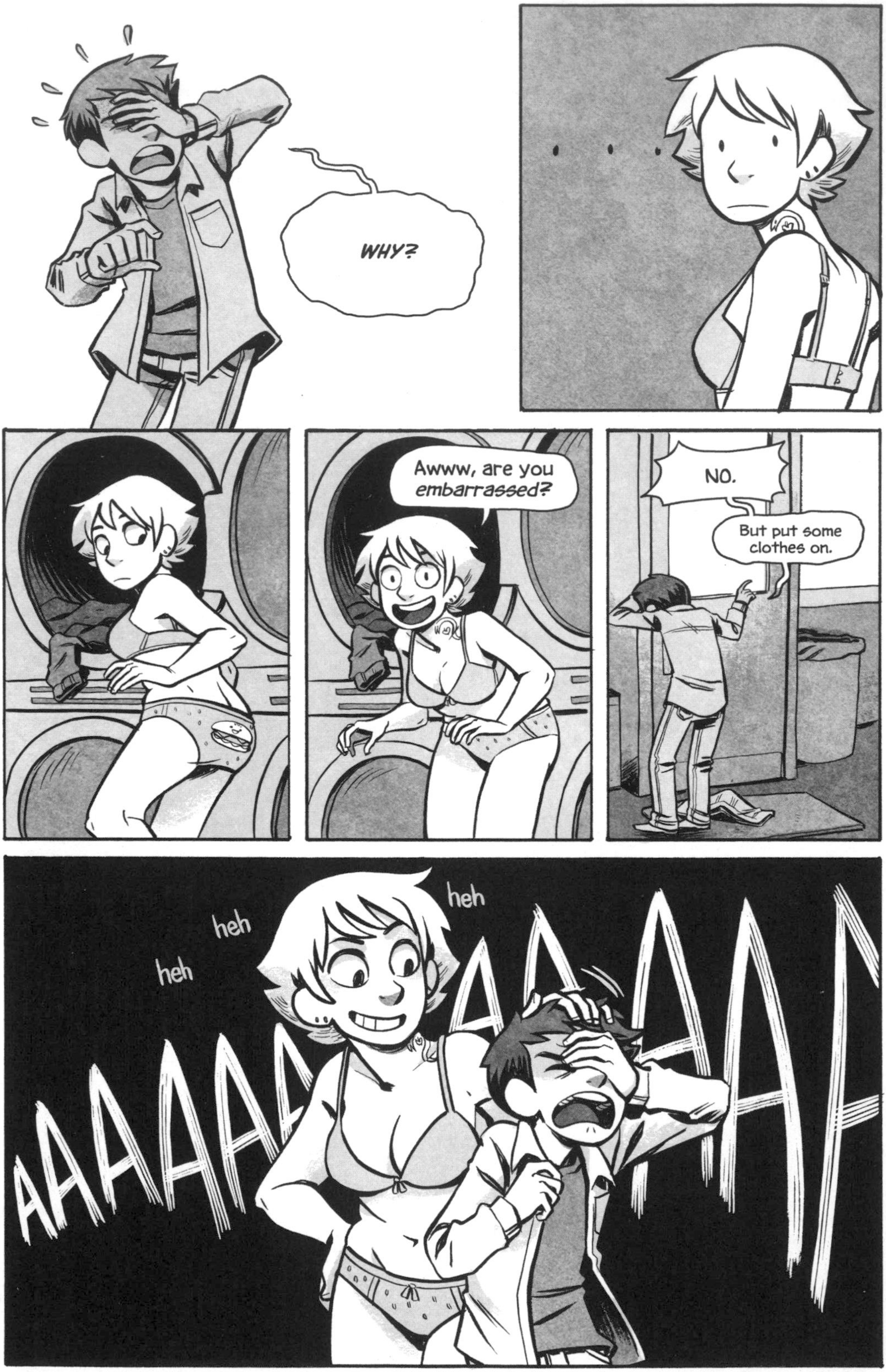
WHY?
. . .
Awww, are you *embarrassed*?
NO.
But put some clothes on.
heh
heh
heh
AAAAAAAAAAAAAA

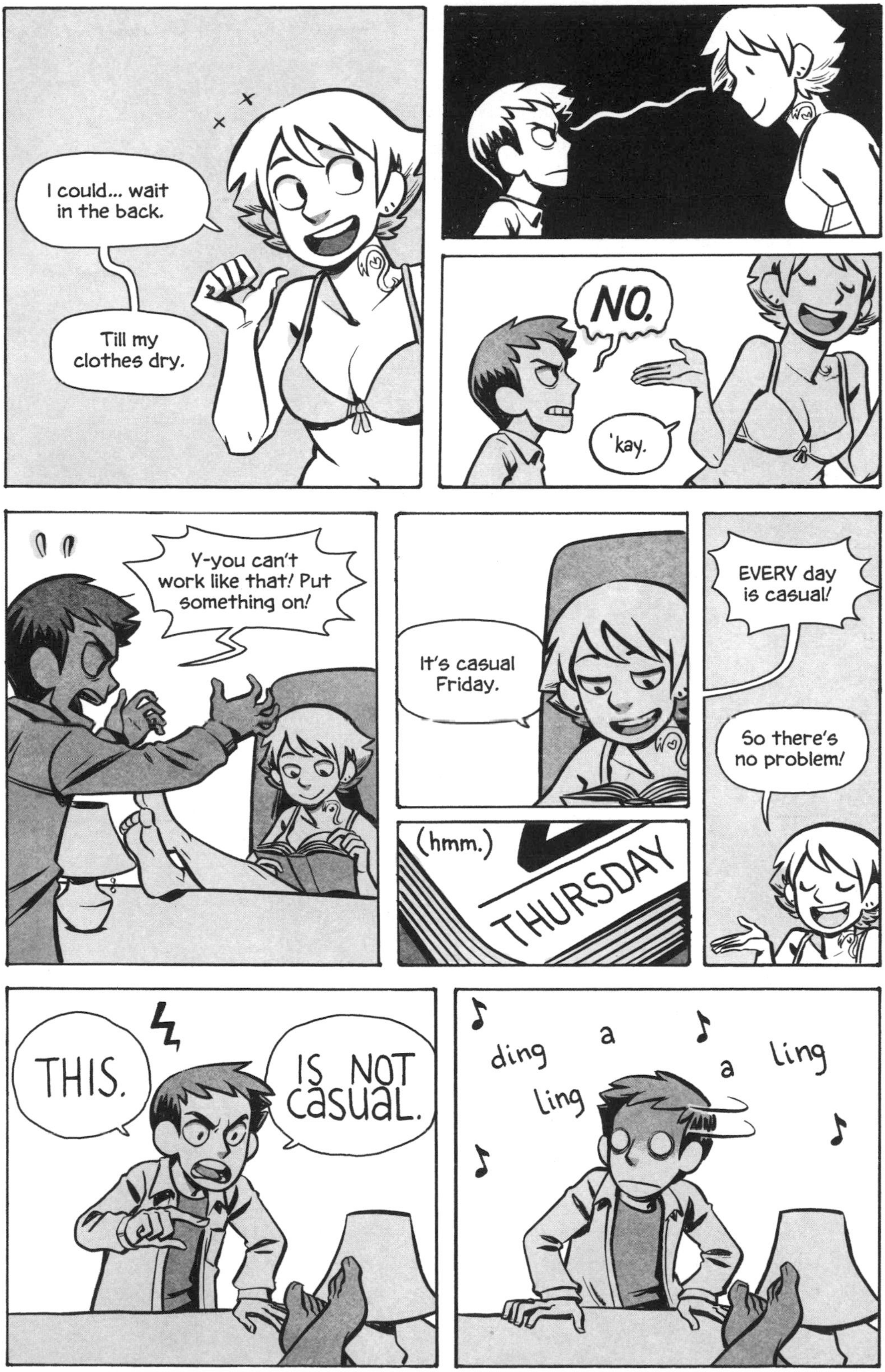
I could... wait in the back.
Till my clothes dry.
NO.
'kay.
Y-you can't work like that! Put something on!
It's casual Friday.
(hmm.)
THURSDAY
EVERY day is casual!
So there's no problem!
THIS.
IS NOT casual.
ding a ling a ling

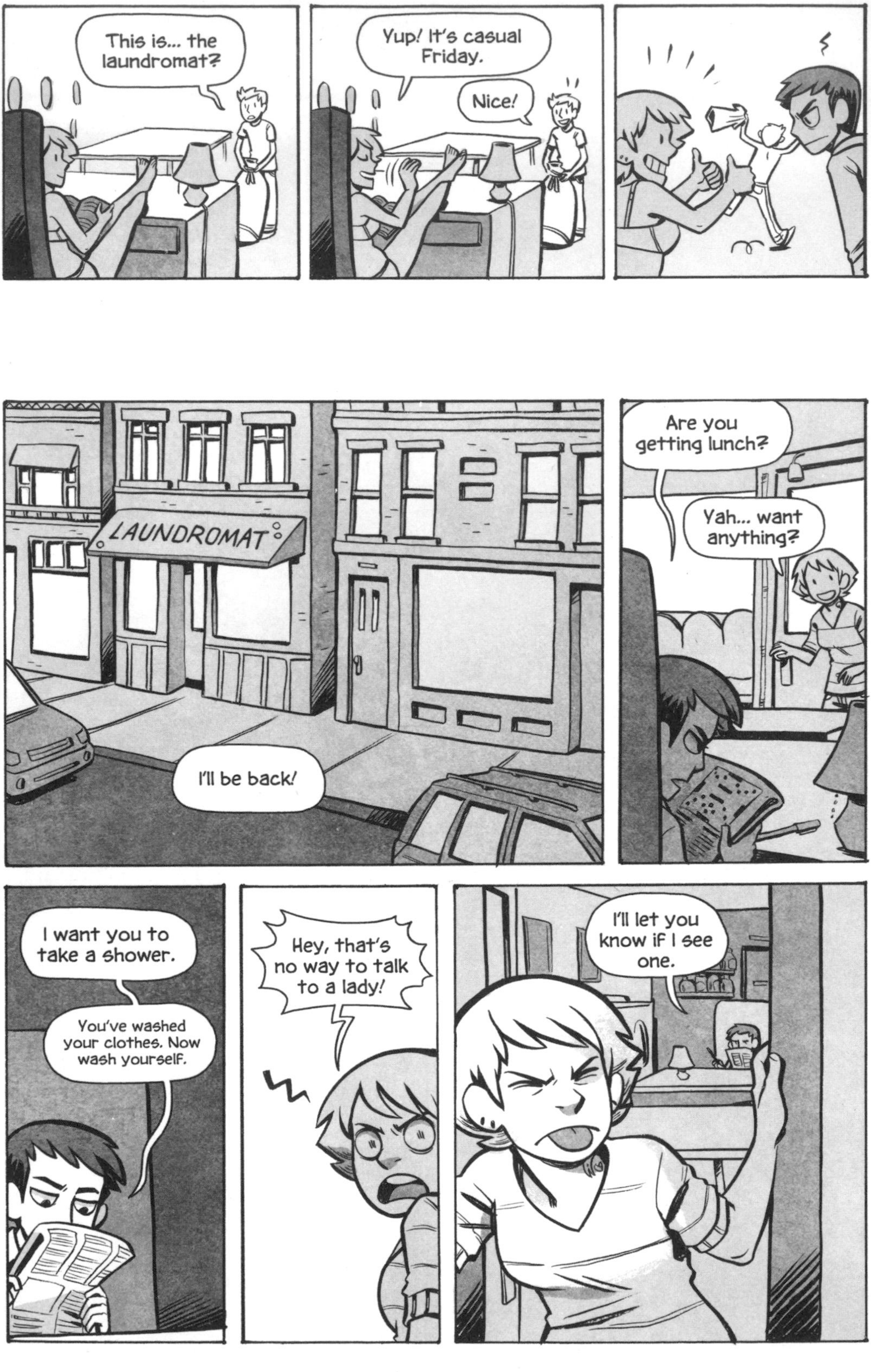
This is... the laundromat?
Yup! It's casual Friday.
Nice!
LAUNDROMAT
I'll be back!
Are you getting lunch?
Yah... want anything?
I want you to take a shower.
You've washed your clothes. Now wash yourself.
Hey, that's no way to talk to a lady!
I'll let you know if I see one.

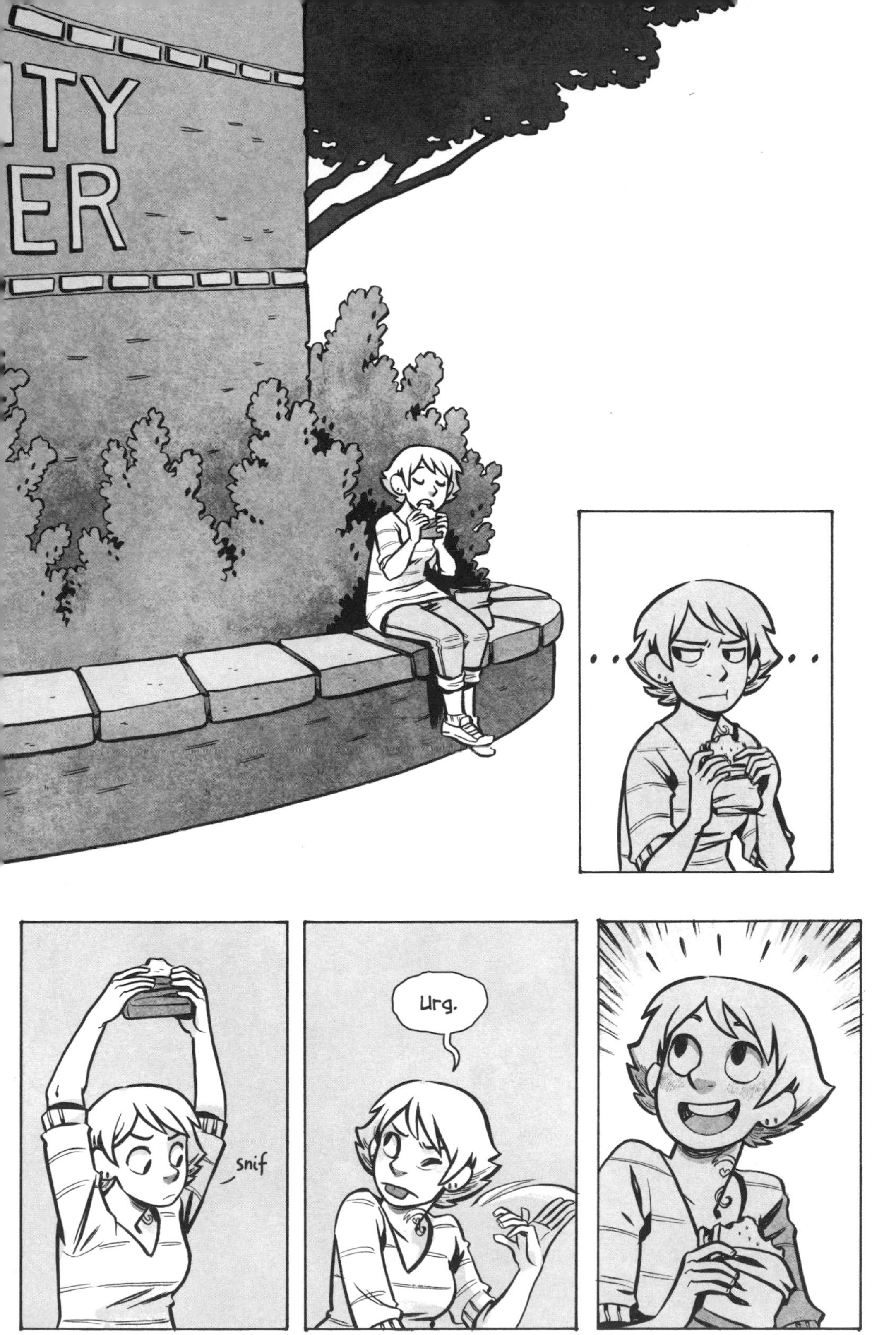
TY
ER
snif
Urg.

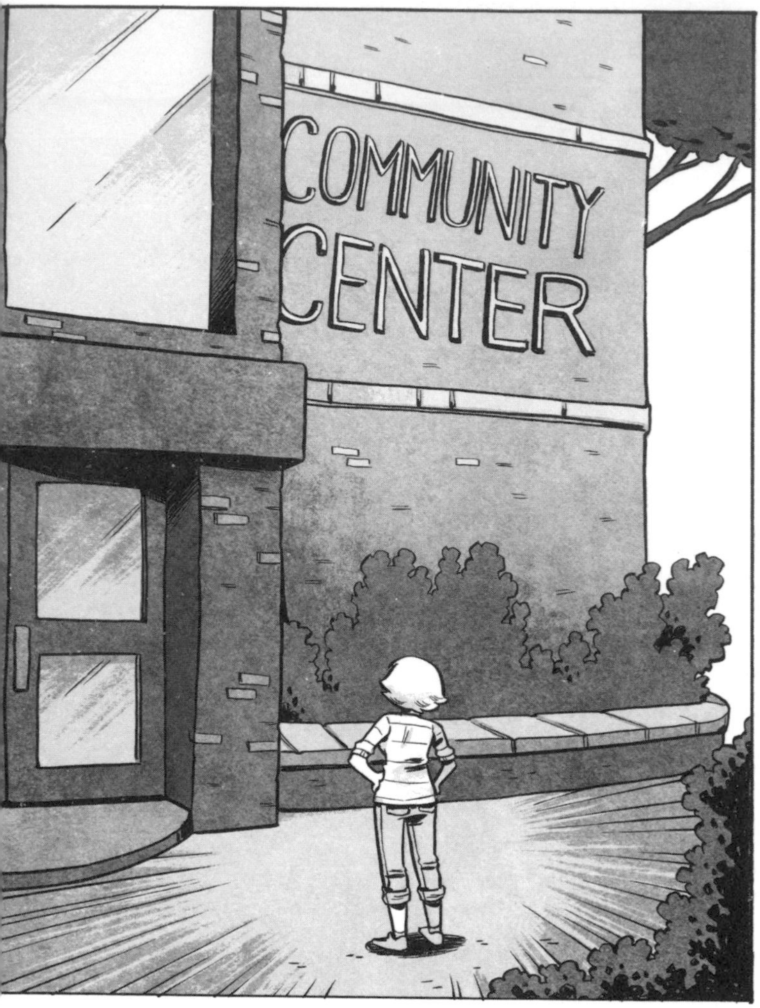
COMMUNITY
CENTER

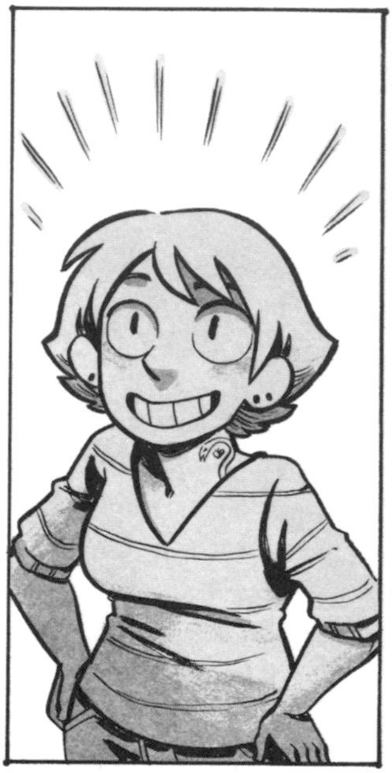

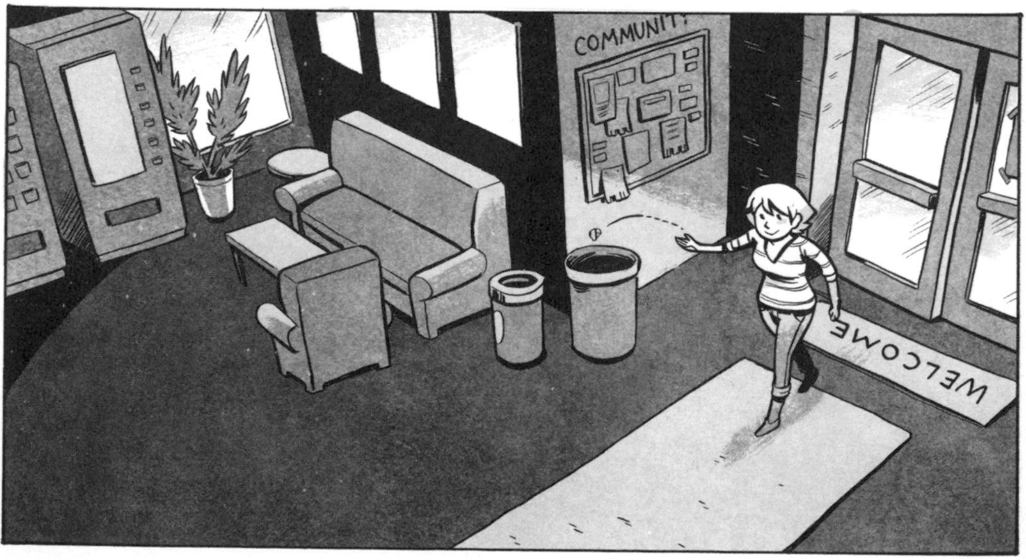
WELCOME

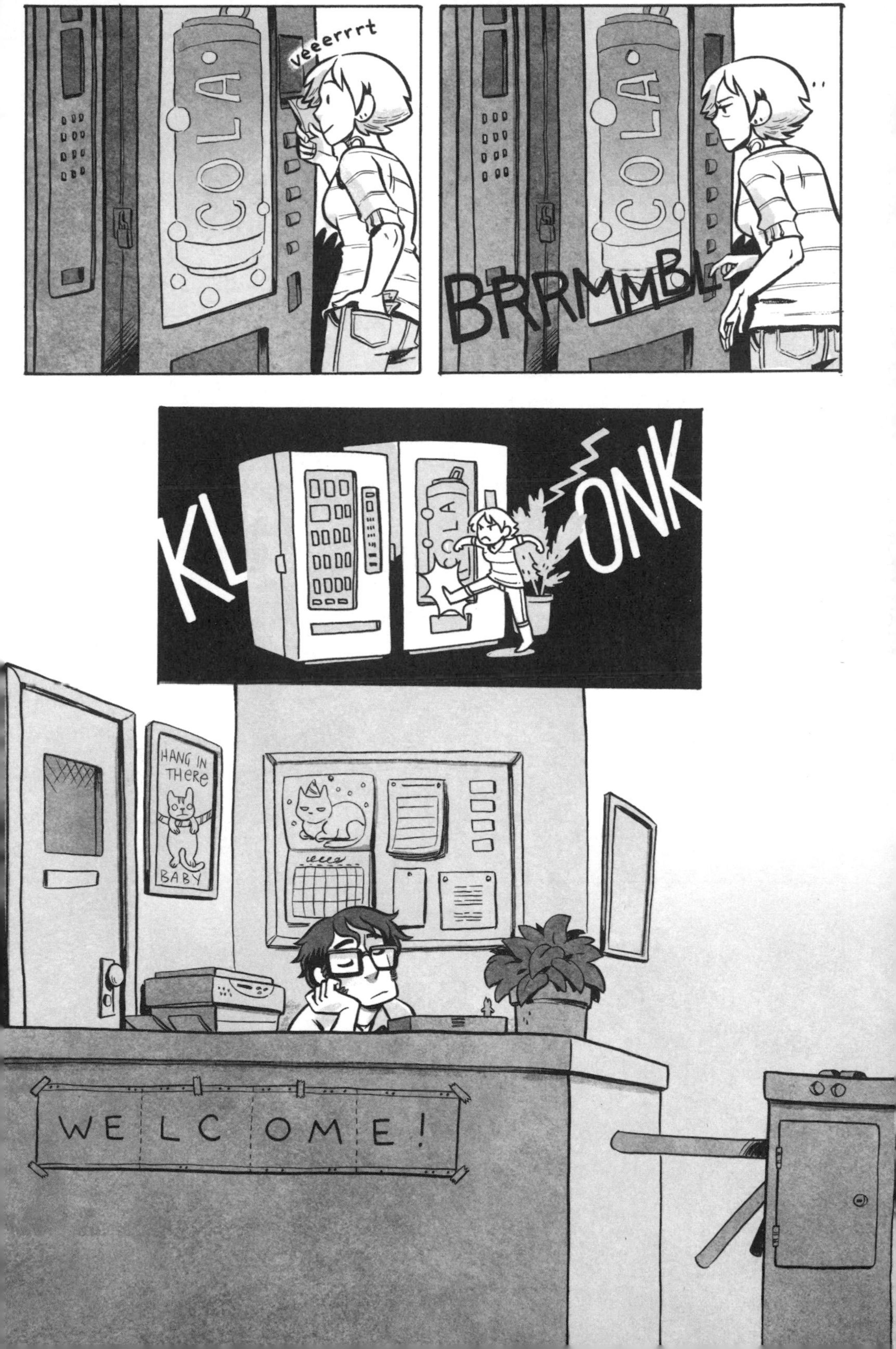
veeerrrt
COLA
COLA
..
BRRMMBL
KL
ONK
COLA
HANG IN THERE
BABY
WELCOME!

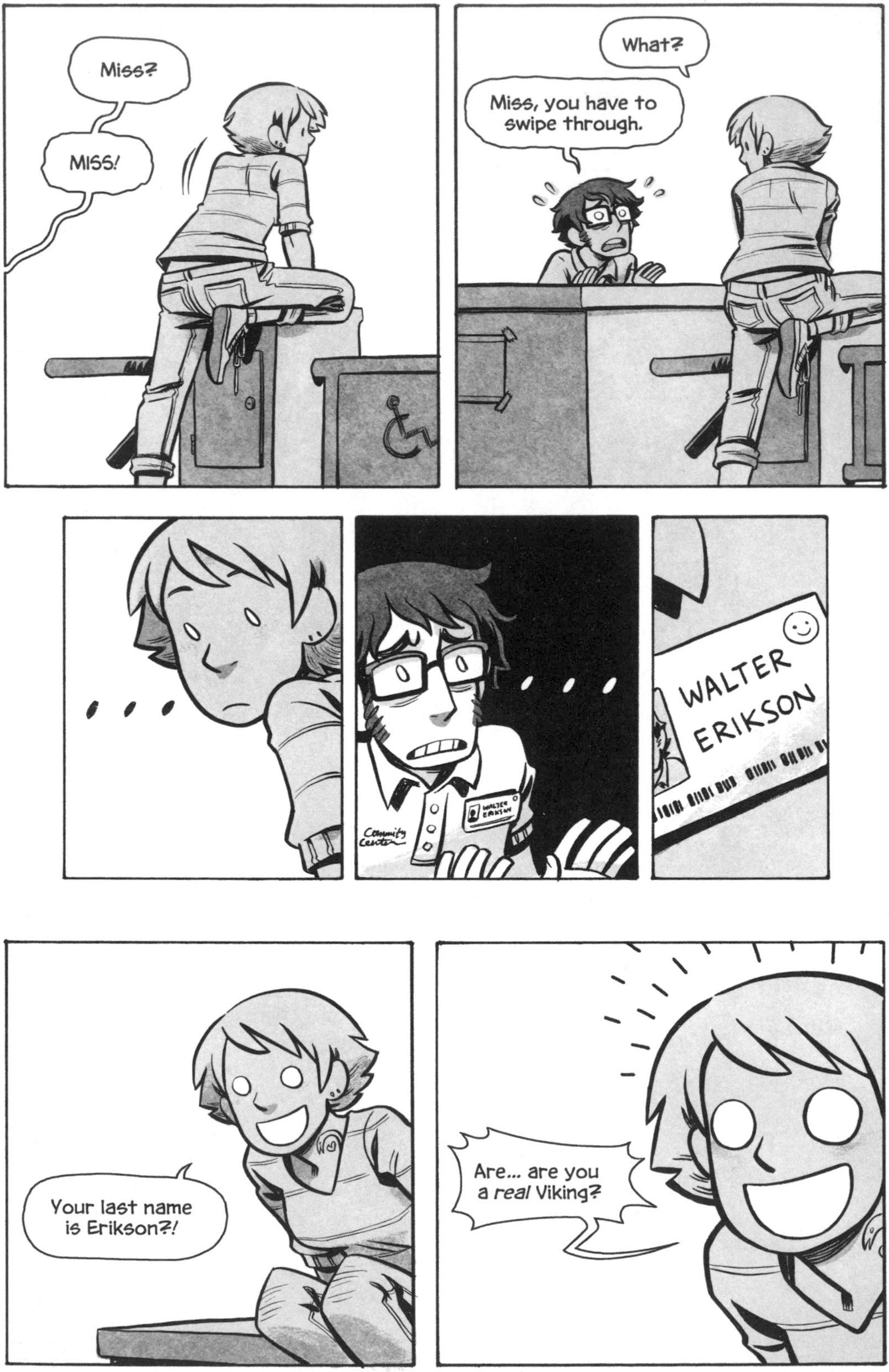
Miss?
MISS!
What?
Miss, you have to swipe through.
. . .
. . .
WALTER ERIKSON
Your last name is Erikson?!
Are... are you a *real* Viking?

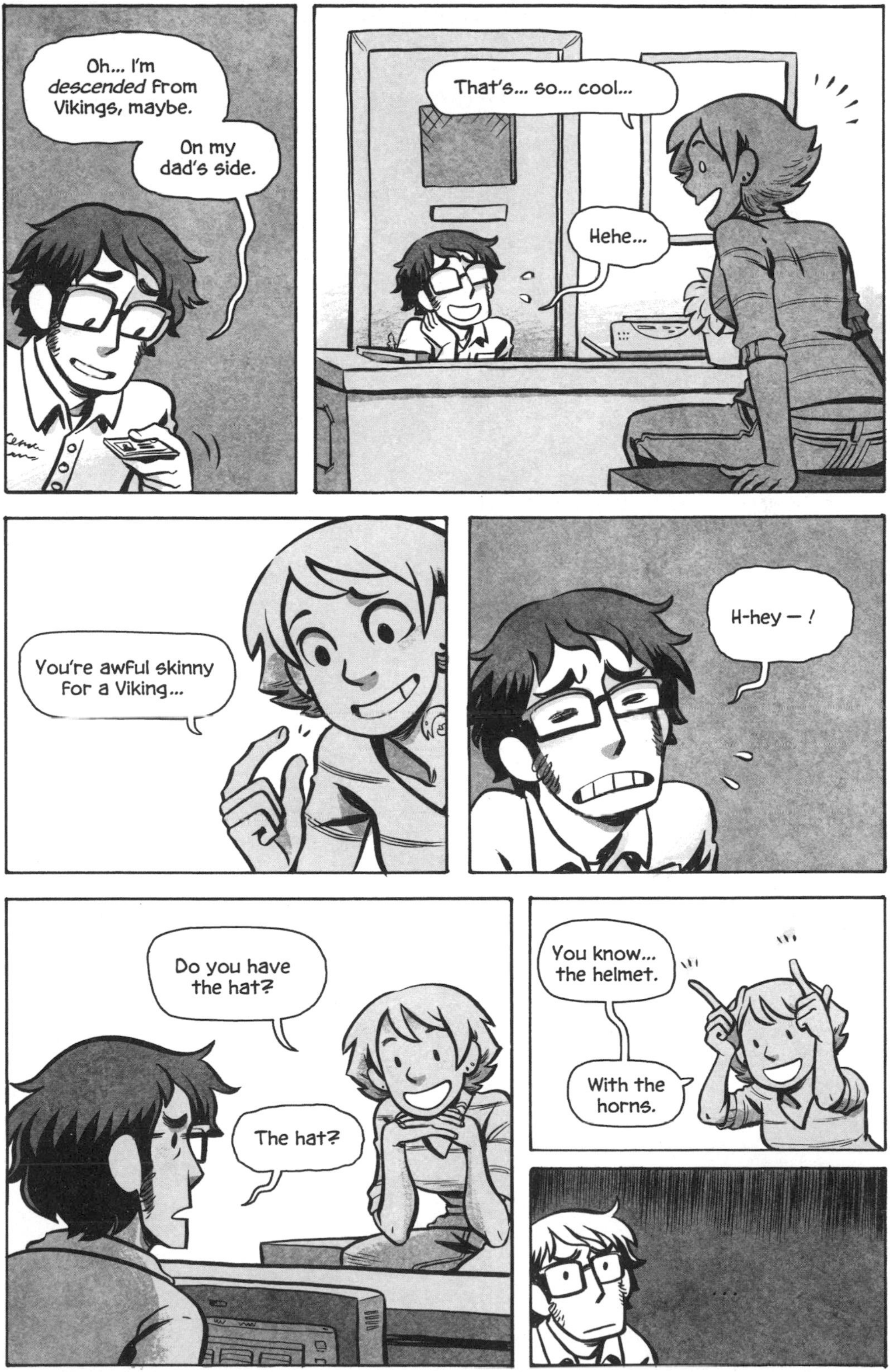
Oh... I'm *descended* from Vikings, maybe.
On my dad's side.
That's... so... cool...
Hehe...
You're awful skinny for a Viking...
H-hey — !
Do you have the hat?
The hat?
You know... the helmet.
With the horns.
...

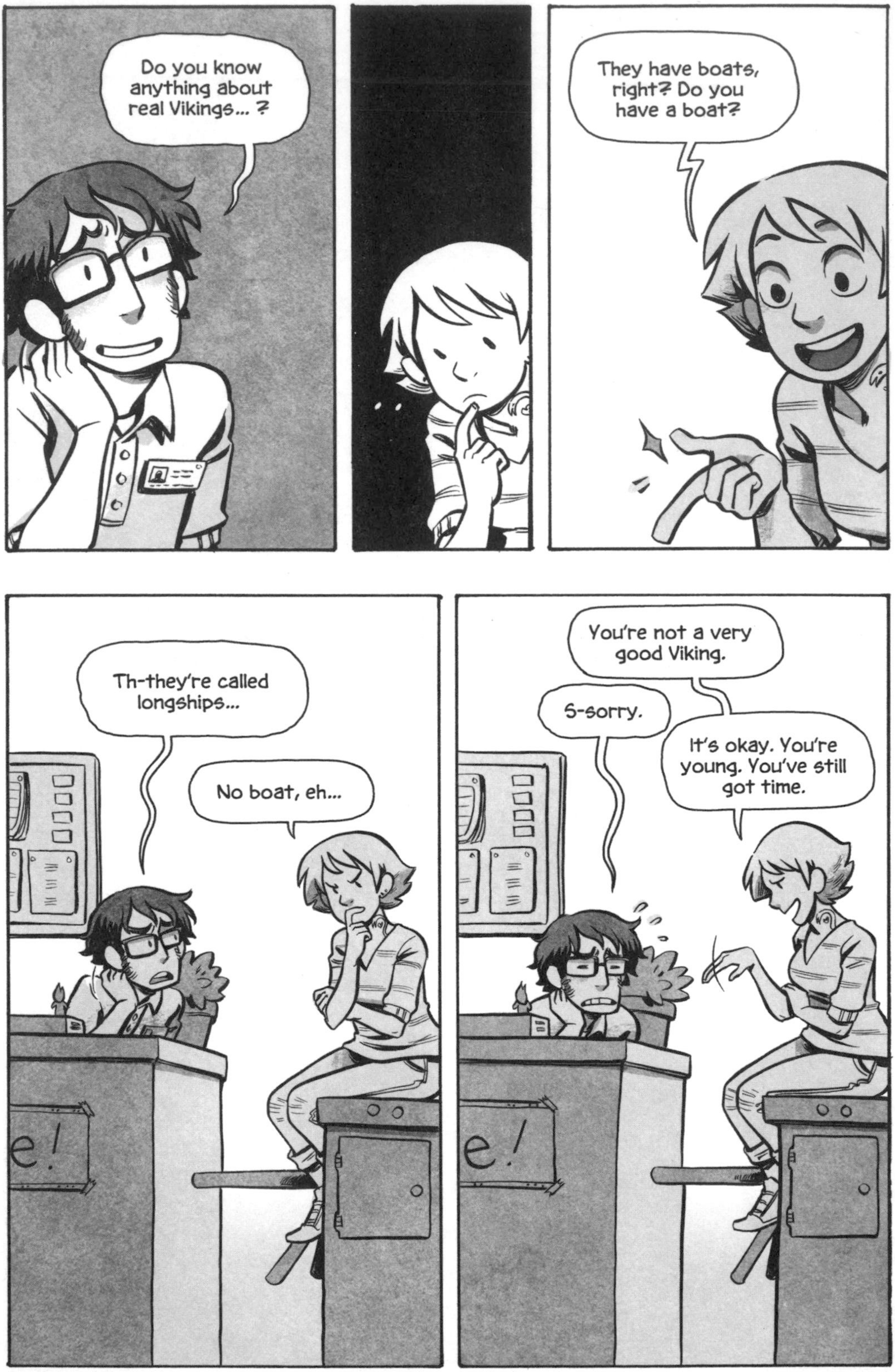
Do you know anything about real Vikings... ?
They have boats, right? Do you have a boat?
Th-they're called longships...
No boat, eh...
You're not a very good Viking.
S-sorry.
It's okay. You're young. You've still got time.

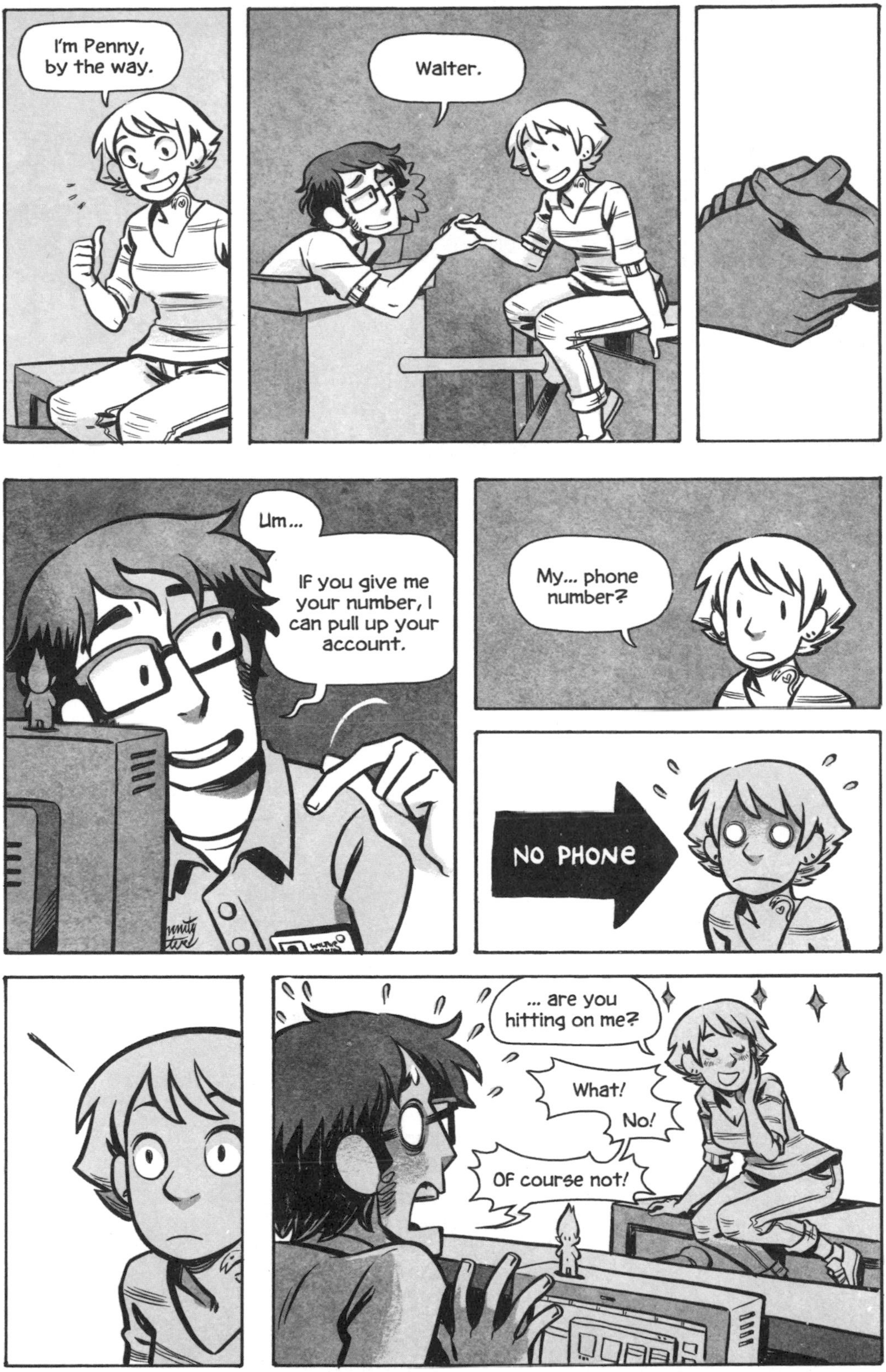
I'm Penny, by the way.
Walter.
Um...
If you give me your number, I can pull up your account.
My... phone number?
NO PHONE
... are you hitting on me?
What!
No!
Of course not!

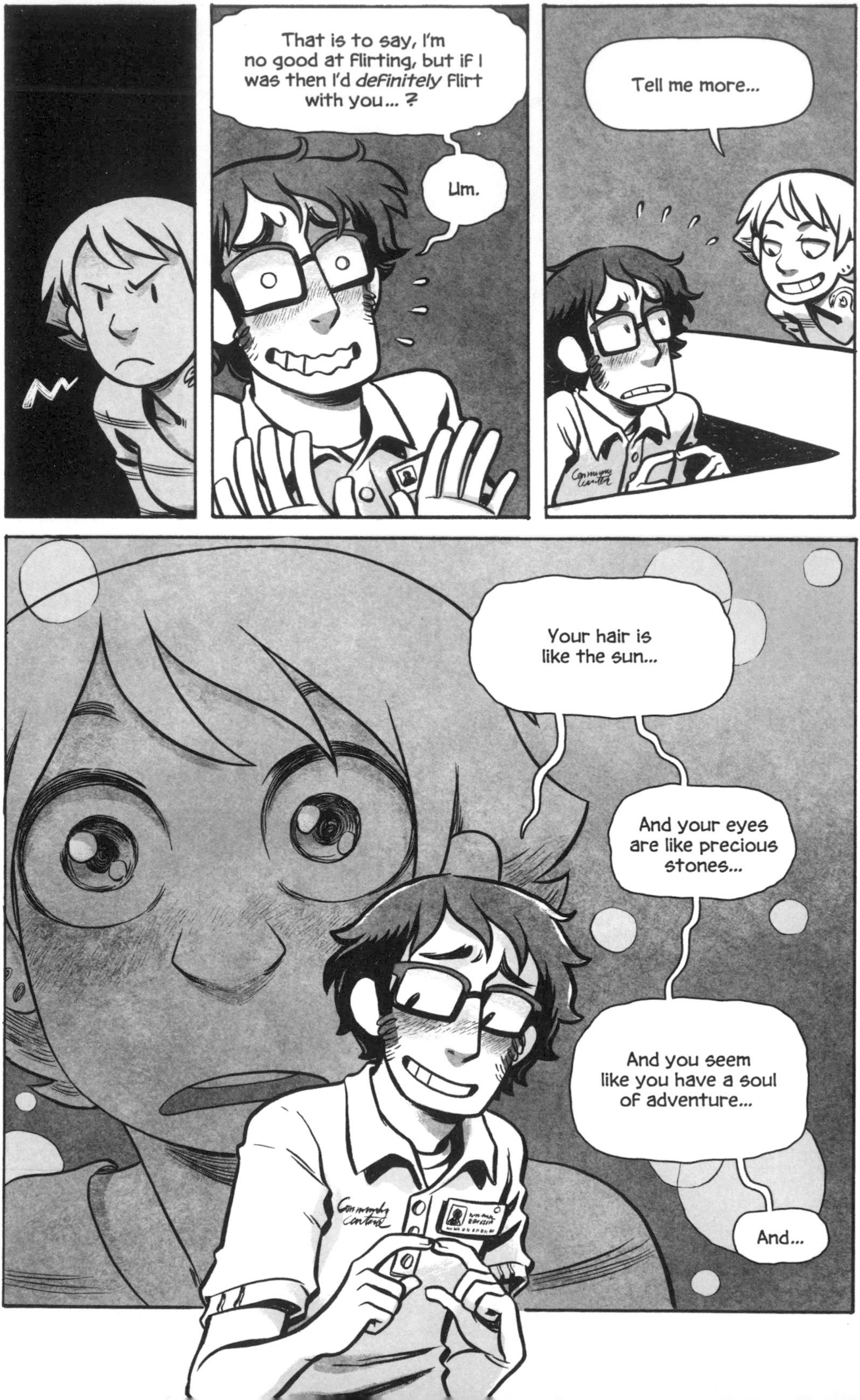
That is to say, I'm no good at flirting, but if I was then I'd *definitely* flirt with you... ?
Um.
Tell me more...
Your hair is like the sun...
And your eyes are like precious stones...
And you seem like you have a soul of adventure...
And...

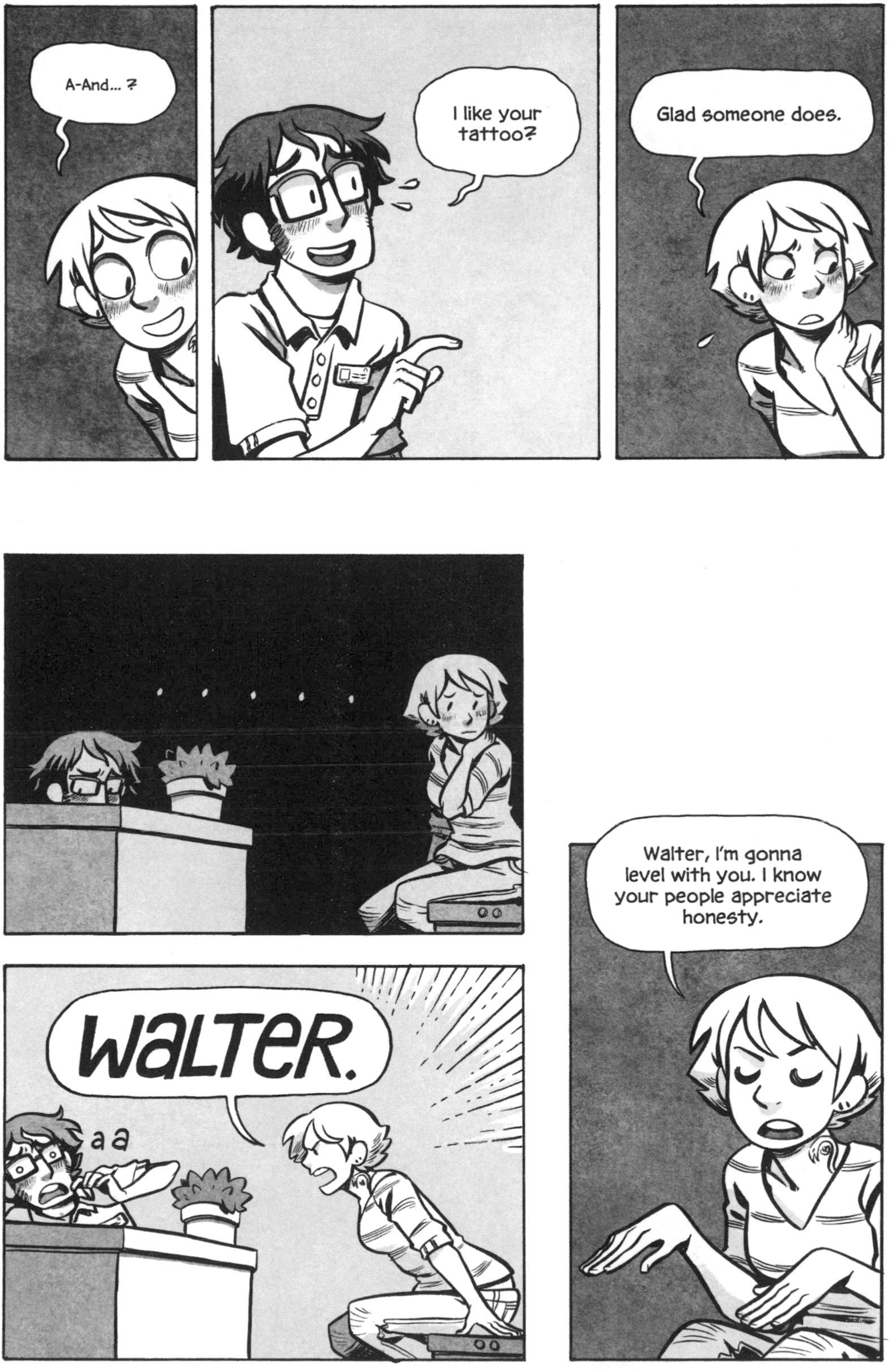
A-And... ?
I like your tattoo?
Glad someone does.
Walter, I'm gonna level with you. I know your people appreciate honesty.
WALTER.
aa

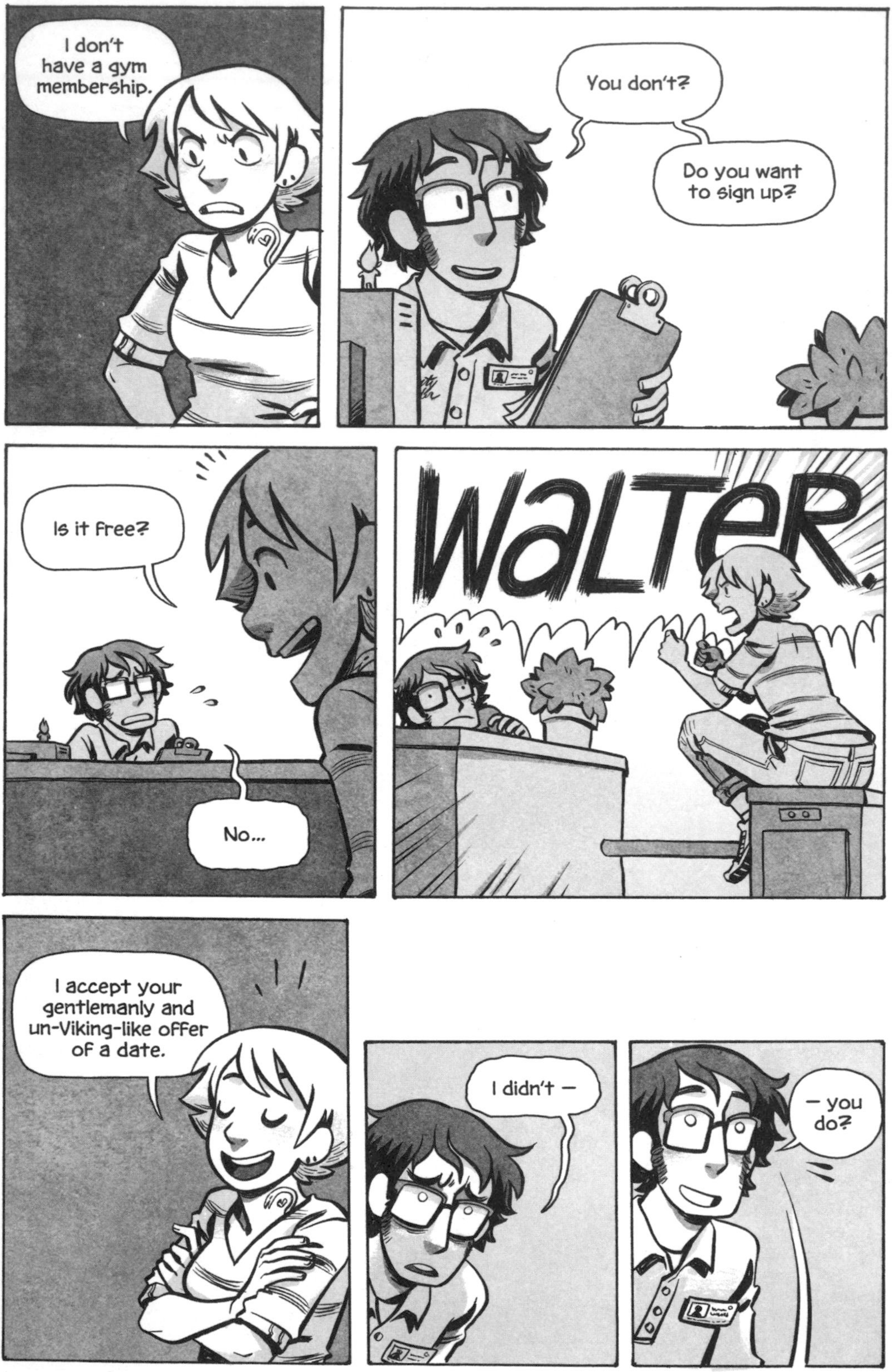

I don't have a gym membership.
You don't?
Do you want to sign up?
Is it free?
No...
WALTER.
I accept your gentlemanly and un-Viking-like offer of a date.
I didn't —
— you do?

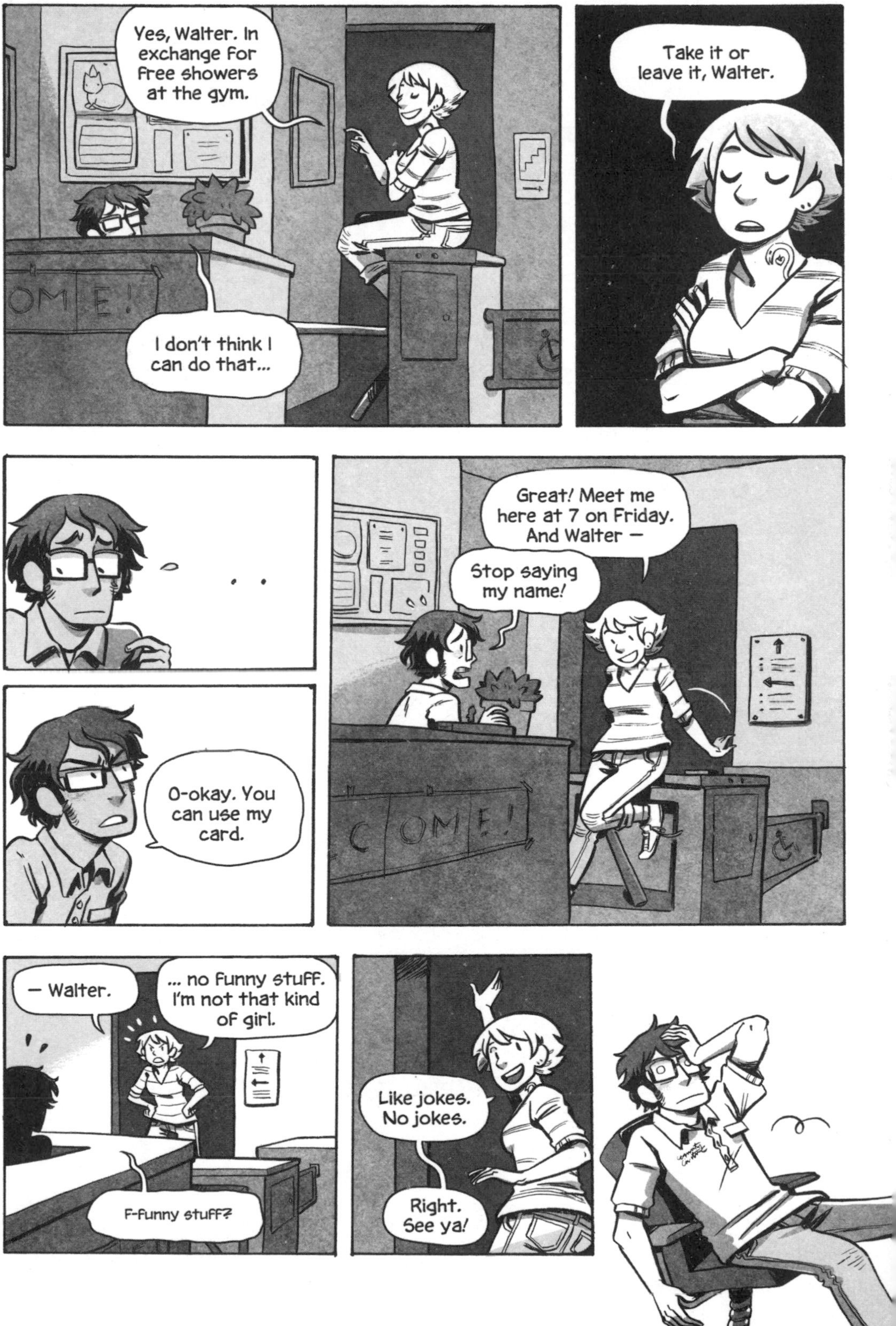
Yes, Walter. In exchange for free showers at the gym.
I don't think I can do that...
Take it or leave it, Walter.
. .
O-okay. You can use my card.
Great! Meet me here at 7 on Friday. And Walter —
Stop saying my name!
— Walter.
... no funny stuff. I'm not that kind of girl.
F-funny stuff?
Like jokes. No jokes.
Right. See ya!

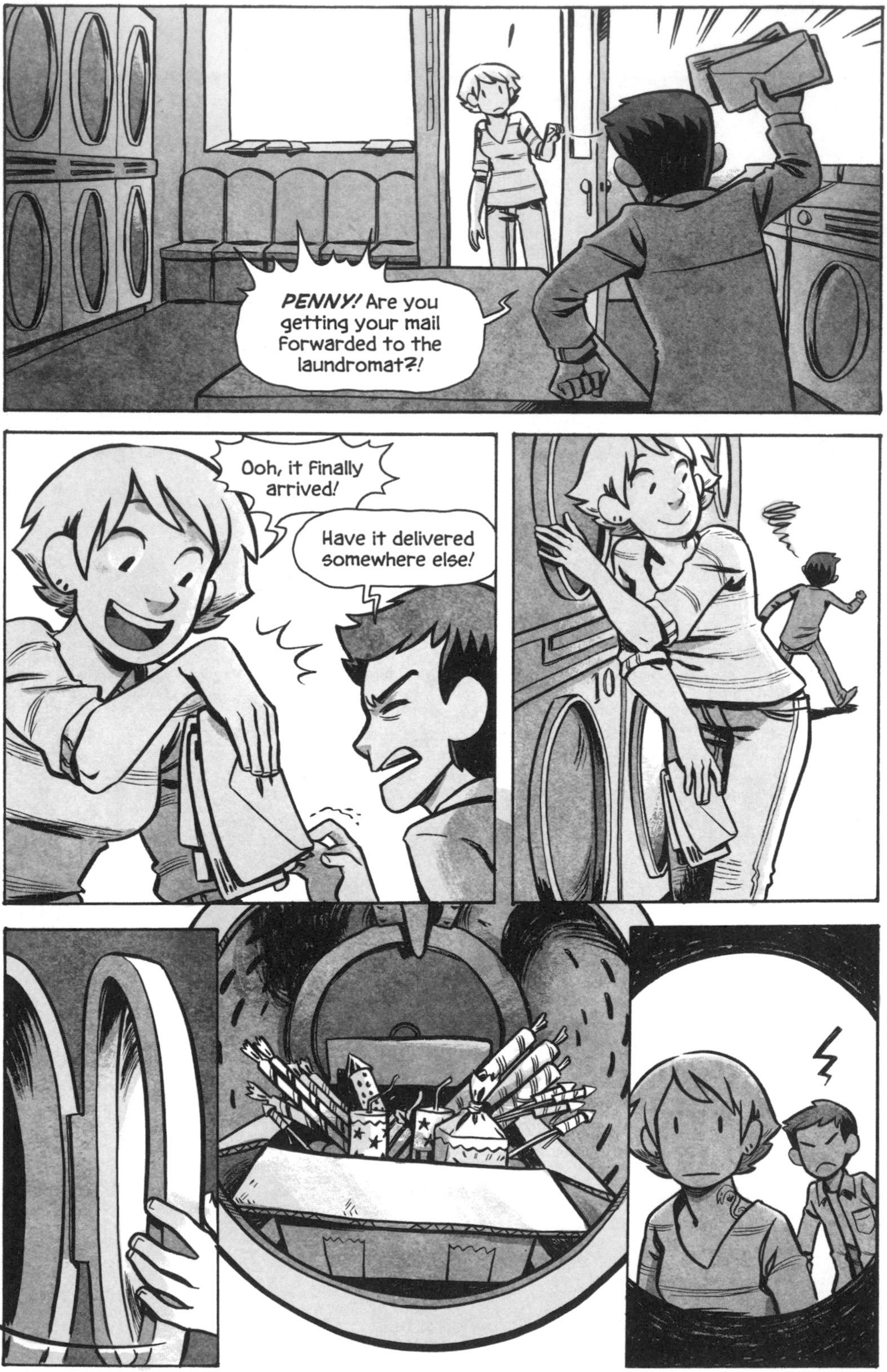
PENNY! Are you getting your mail forwarded to the laundromat?!
Ooh, it finally arrived!
Have it delivered somewhere else!
10

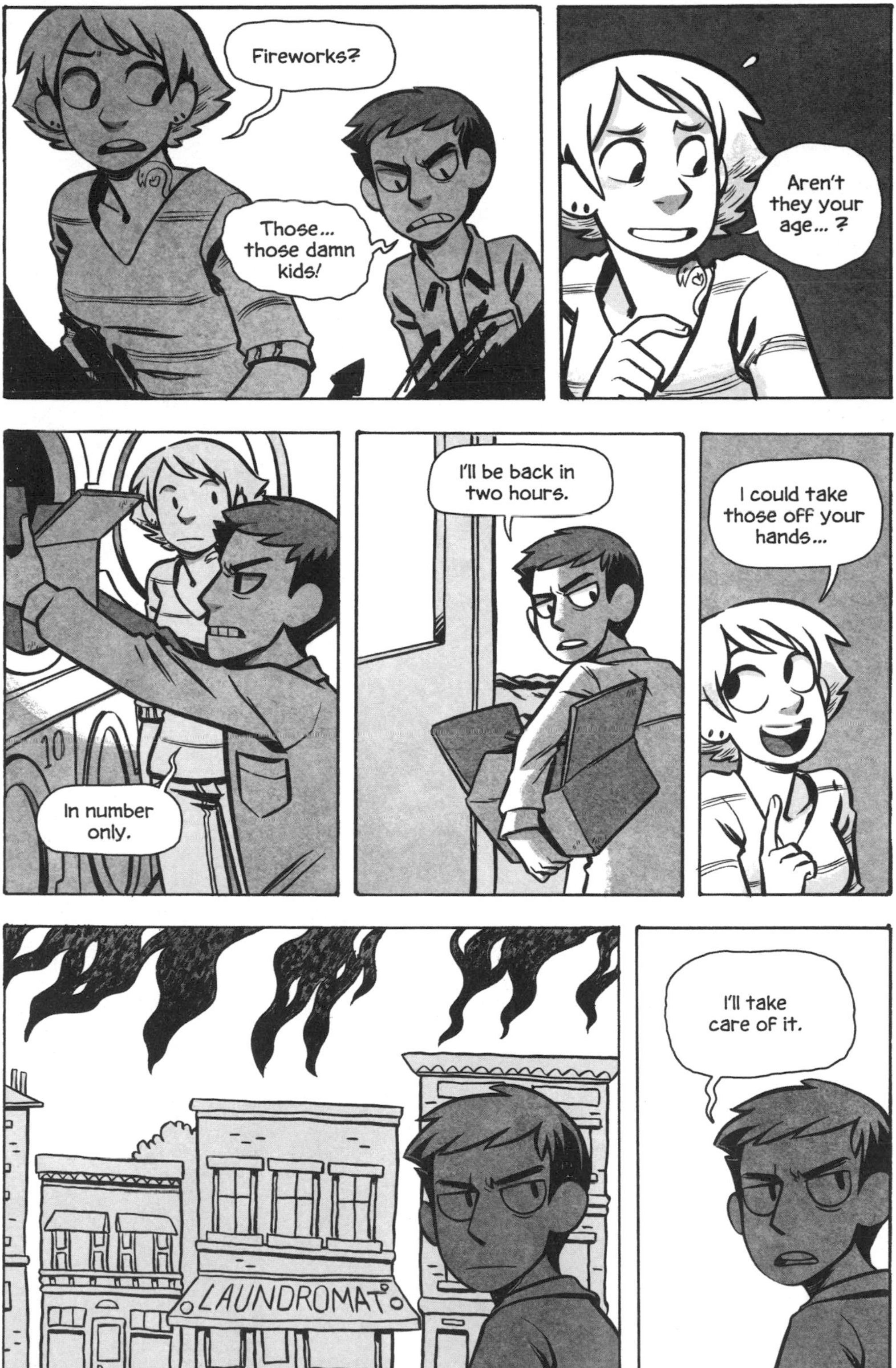
Fireworks?
Those... those damn kids!
Aren't they your age... ?
In number only.
I'll be back in two hours.
I could take those off your hands...
LAUNDROMAT
I'll take care of it.

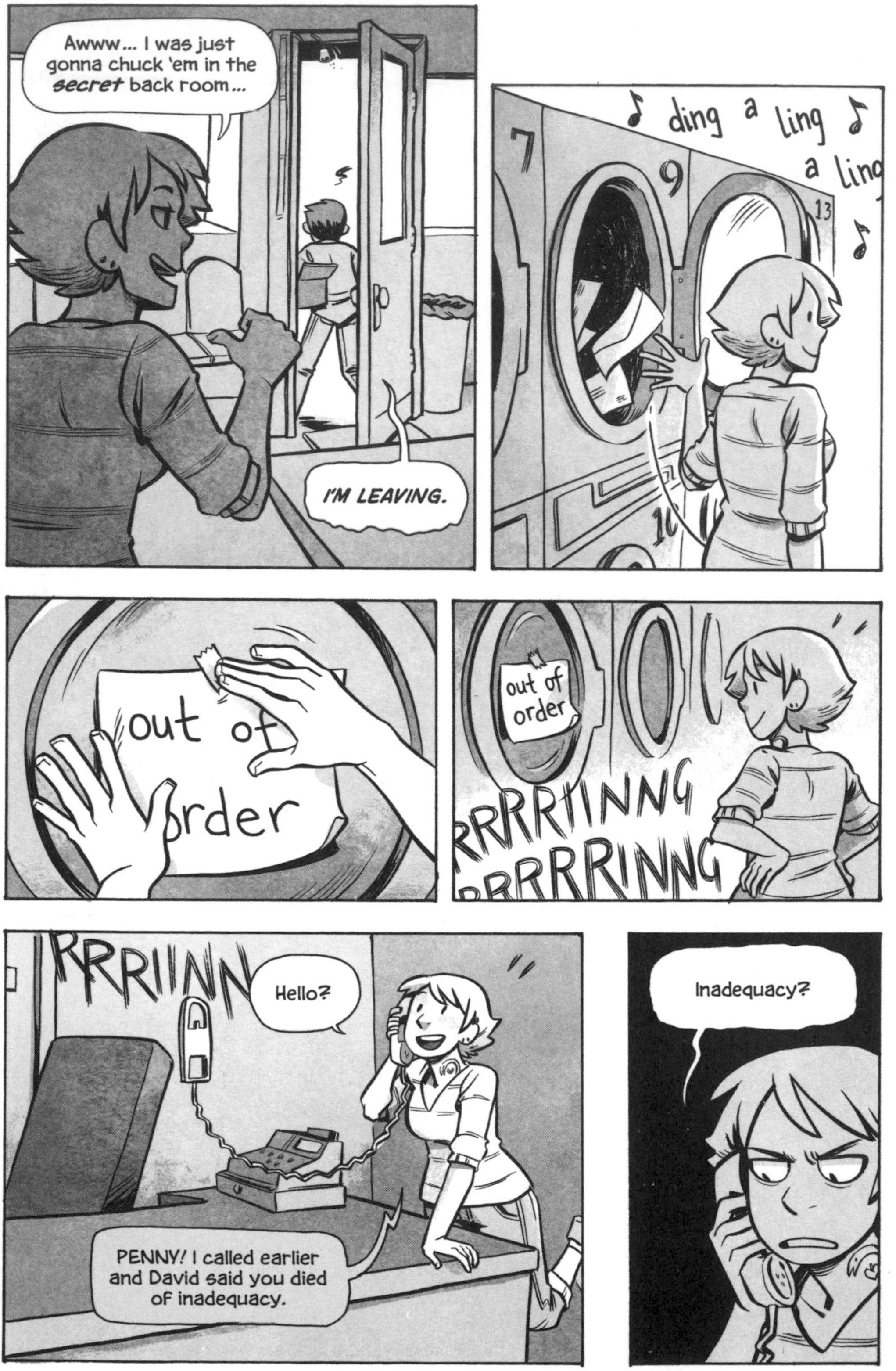

Awww... I was just gonna chuck 'em in the *secret* back room...
I'M LEAVING.
ding a ling a ling
out of order
out of order
RRRRIINNG
RRRRRINNG
RRRIINN
Hello?
PENNY! I called earlier and David said you died of inadequacy.
Inadequacy?

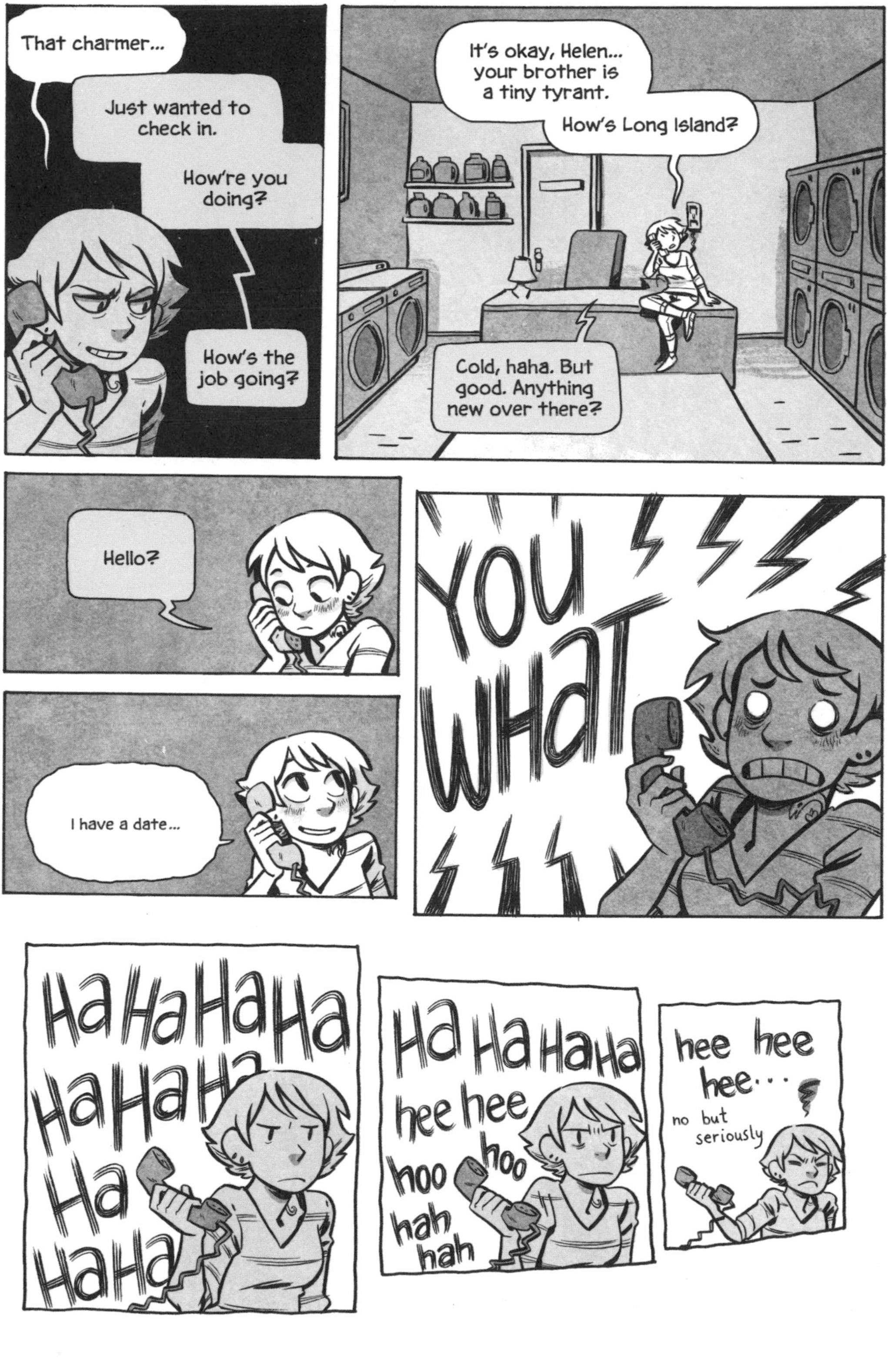
That charmer...
Just wanted to check in.
How're you doing?
How's the job going?
It's okay, Helen... your brother is a tiny tyrant.
How's Long Island?
Cold, haha. But good. Anything new over there?
Hello?
I have a date...
YOU WHAT
HaHaHaHaHa
HaHaHaHa
Ha
HaHa
HaHaHaHaHa
hee hee
hoo
hoo
hah
hah
hee hee
hee...
no but seriously

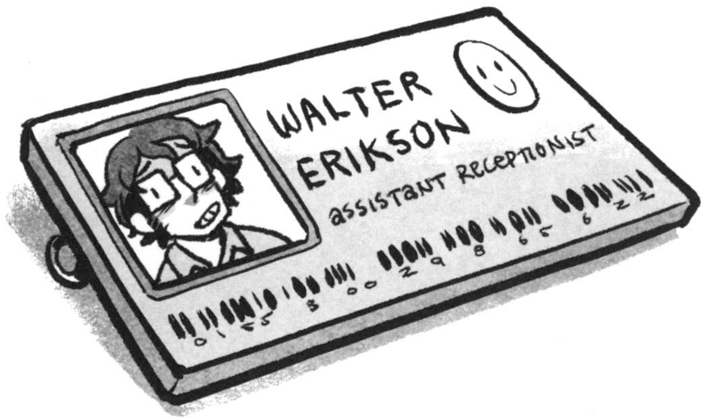
WALTER
ERIKSON
ASSISTANT RECEPTIONIST

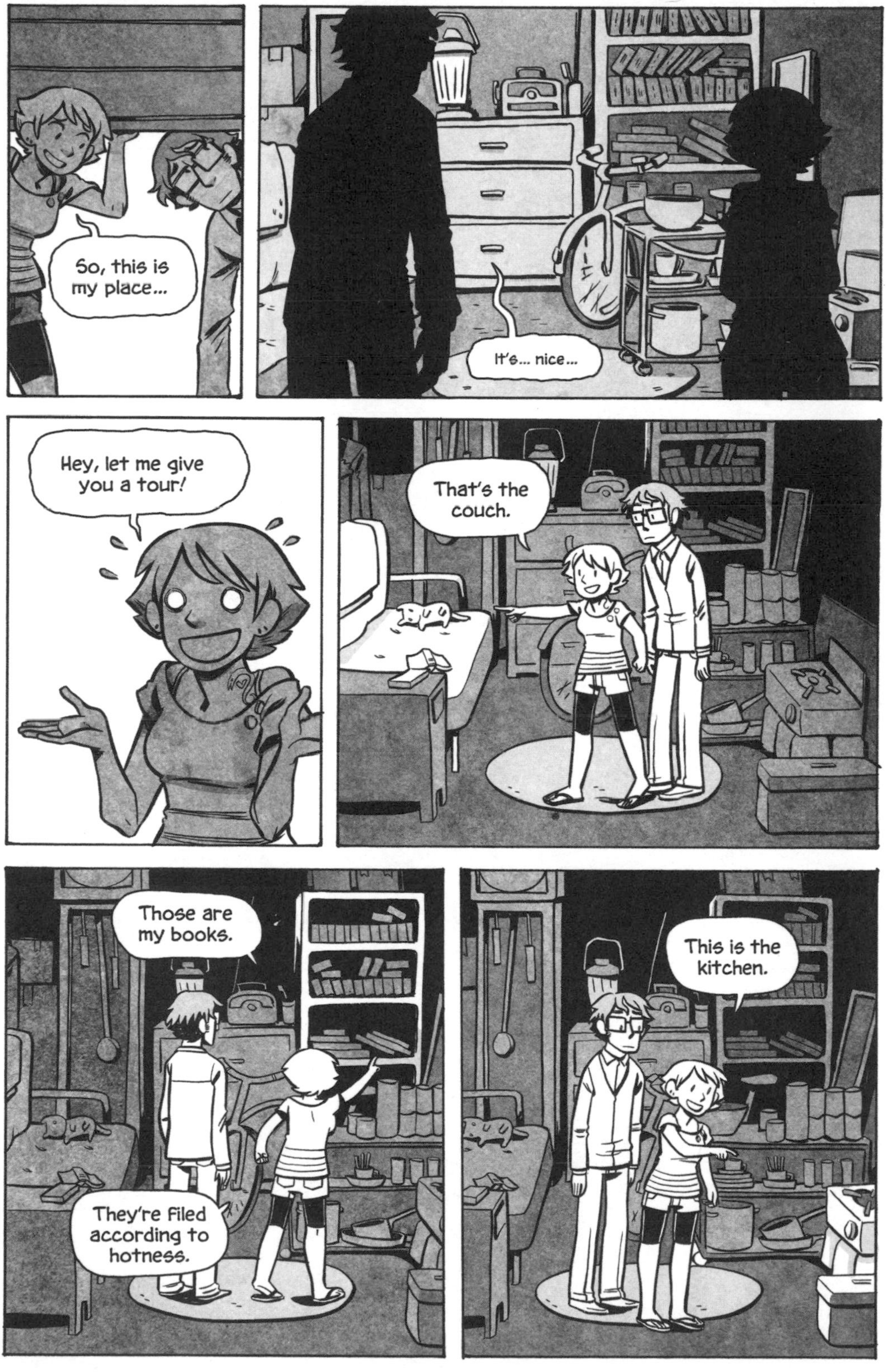
So, this is my place...
It's... nice...
Hey, let me give you a tour!
That's the couch.
Those are my books.
They're filed according to hotness.
This is the kitchen.

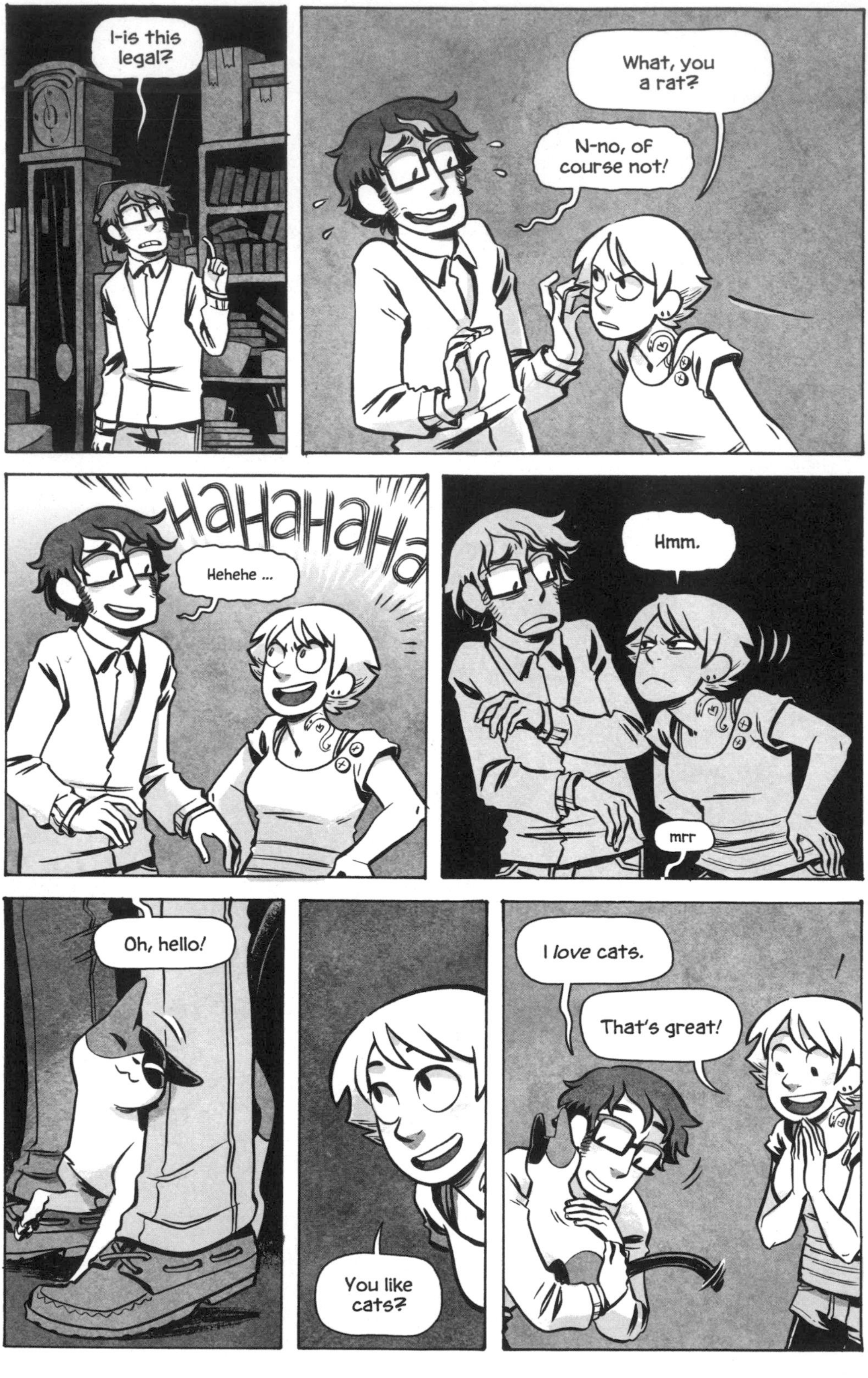

I-is this legal?
What, you a rat?
N-no, of course not!
HaHaHaHaHa
Hehehe ...
Hmm.
mrr
Oh, hello!
You like cats?
I love cats.
That's great!

This is Boyfriend.

You named your cat Boyfriend?

Boyfriend *is* my boyfriend.

You know... Boyfriend's actually more of a Girlfriend.

Huh?

Calicos are usually girls. Like 99% of the time.

I mean, she *could* be a he, but there are pretty much only two *extremely* rare ways for a calico to be male.

THIS SET THE TONE FOR THE REST OF THE EVENING

Well, the gene for fur coloration travels on the X chromosome and females have two X chromosomes, so they can have something called co-dominant alleles,

which causes the tortoise shell orange and black mottling, but males only have one X chromosome, so they can only have one fur color unless something genetically unusual causes a male cat to have two X chromosomes,

ither being that when the zygote was fertilized, the sperm had both an X *and* Y chromosome, producin male cat with two X and c romosomes, or Klinefelt yndrome, or the cat coul a chimera, which is caus hen an embryo consume he or more other embryo a different color genot in the producing a single with two or re dist sets of gene nform and sing a e ma ration ey i e chromoso

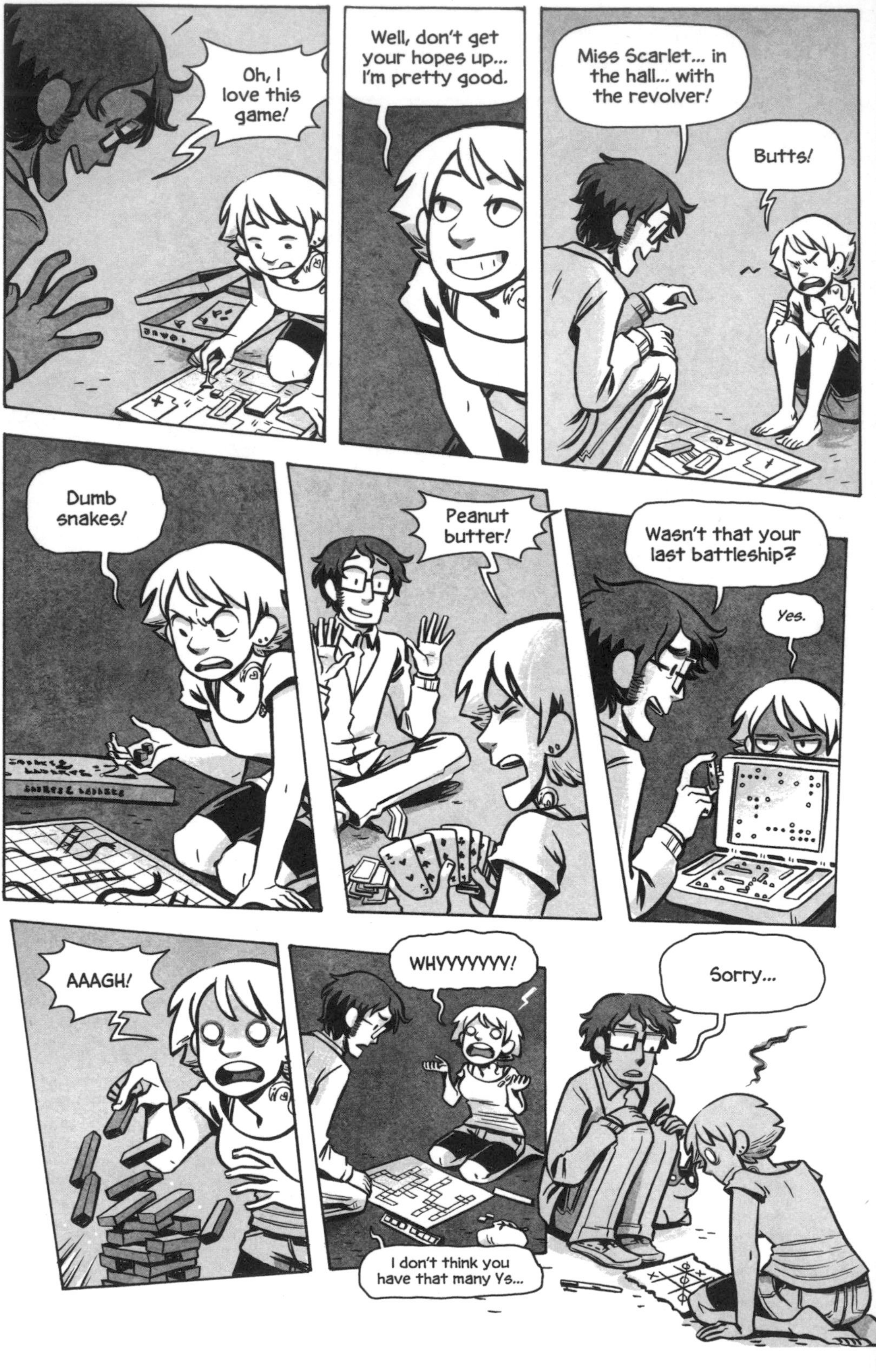

Oh, I love this game!
Well, don't get your hopes up... I'm pretty good.
Miss Scarlet... in the hall... with the revolver!
Butts!
Dumb snakes!
Peanut butter!
Wasn't that your last battleship?
Yes.
AAAGH!
WHYYYYYYY!
I don't think you have that many Ys...
Sorry...

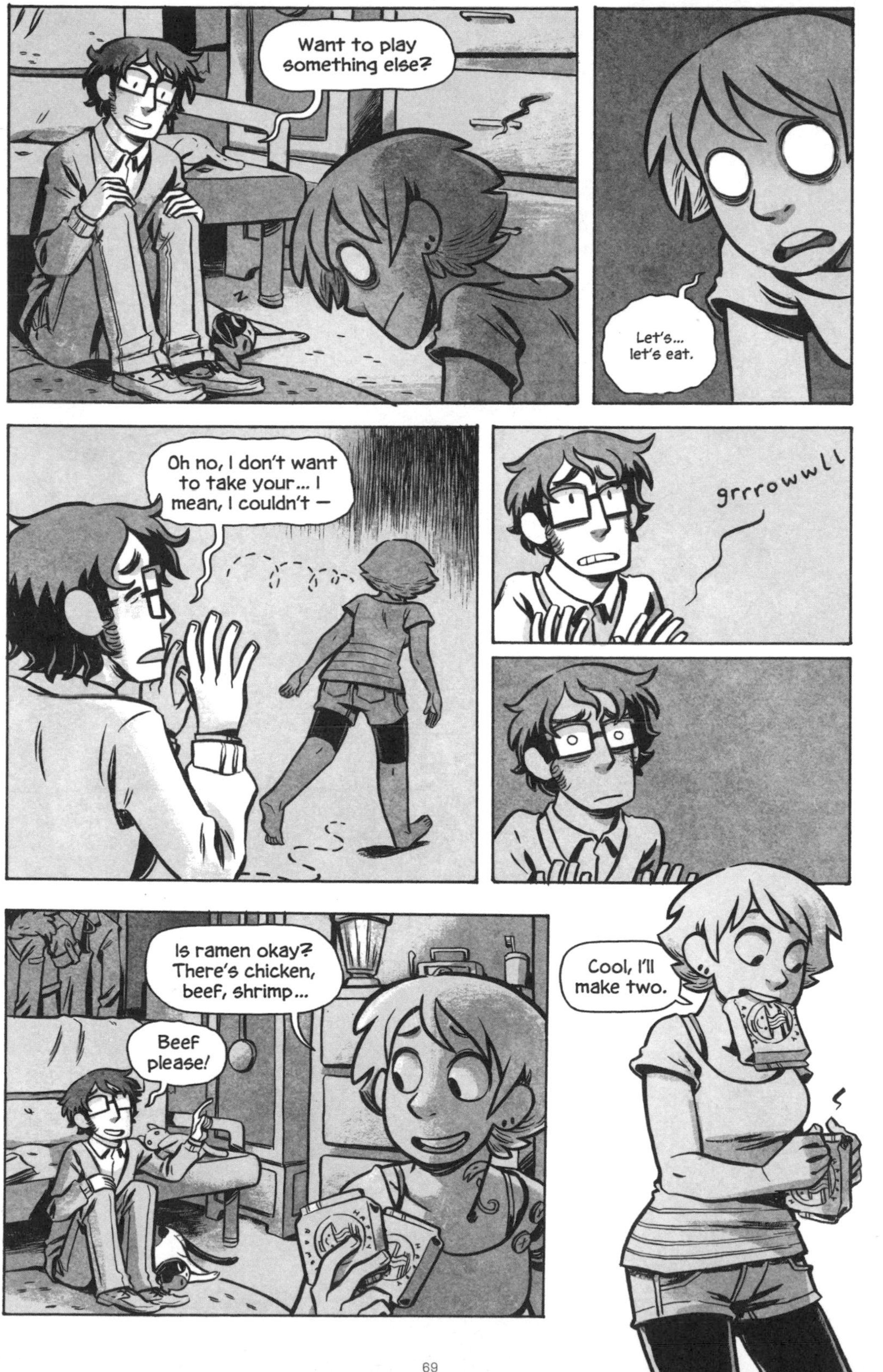
Want to play something else?
Let's... let's eat.
Oh no, I don't want to take your... I mean, I couldn't —
grrrowwll
Is ramen okay? There's chicken, beef, shrimp...
Beef please!
Cool, I'll make two.

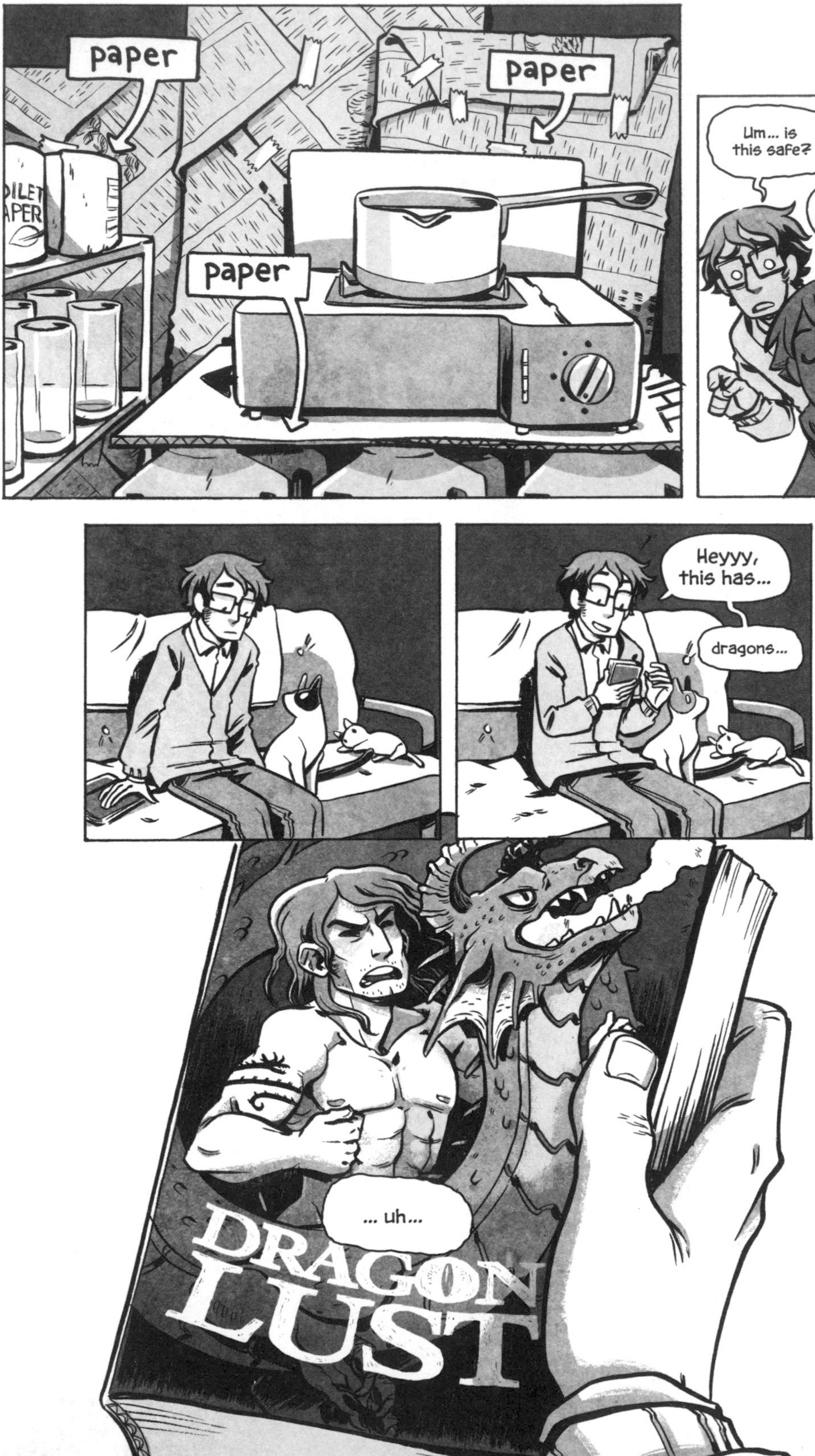

paper
paper
paper
TOILET PAPER
Um... is this safe?
Shhh.
Heyyy, this has...
dragons...
... uh...
DRAGON LUST

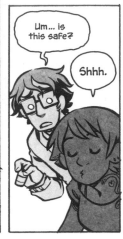

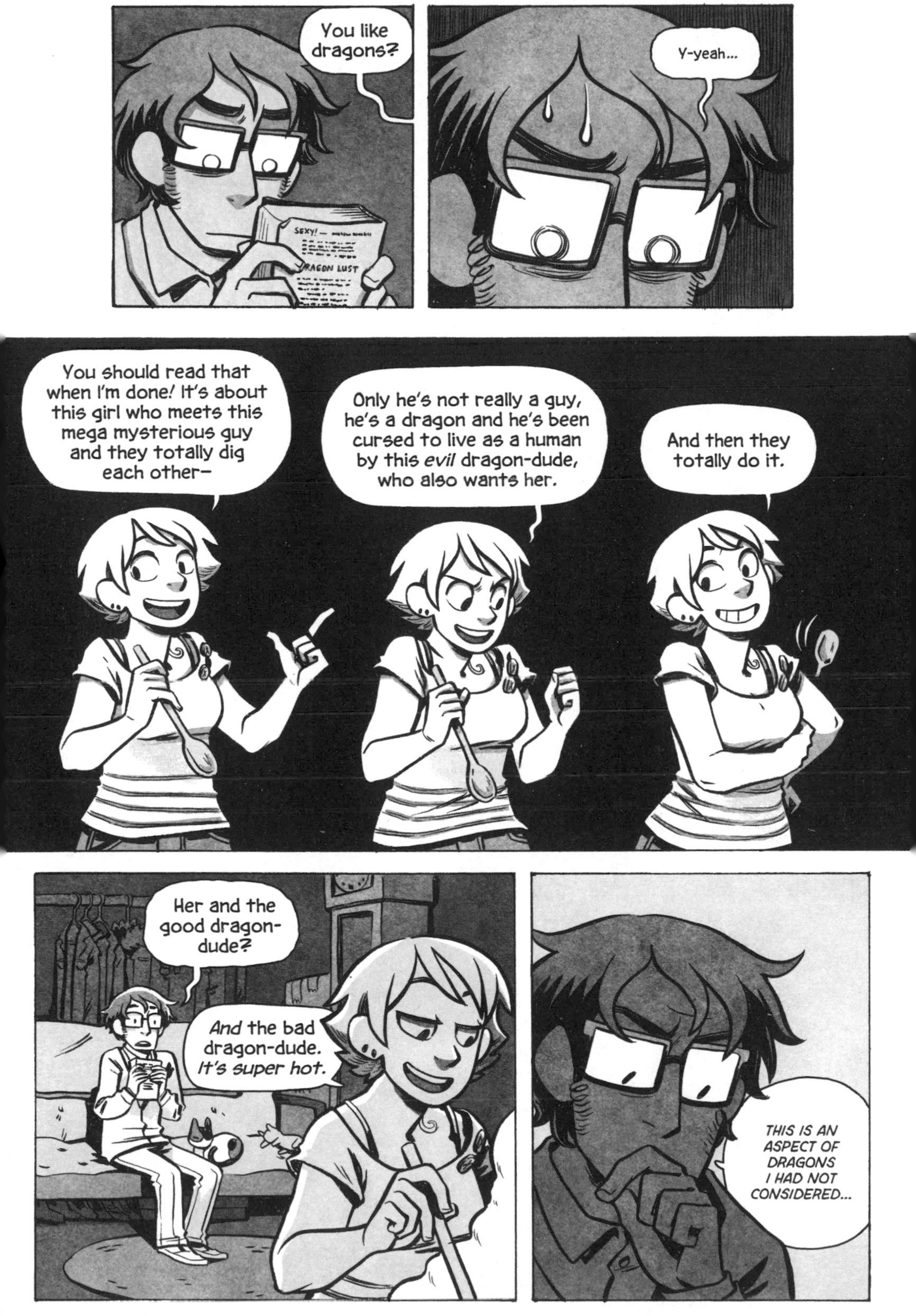
You like dragons?
SEXY!
DRAGON LUST
Y-yeah...
You should read that when I'm done! It's about this girl who meets this mega mysterious guy and they totally dig each other–
Only he's not really a guy, he's a dragon and he's been cursed to live as a human by this *evil* dragon-dude, who also wants her.
And then they totally do it.
Her and the good dragon-dude?
And the bad dragon-dude. *It's super hot.*
THIS IS AN ASPECT OF DRAGONS I HAD NOT CONSIDERED...

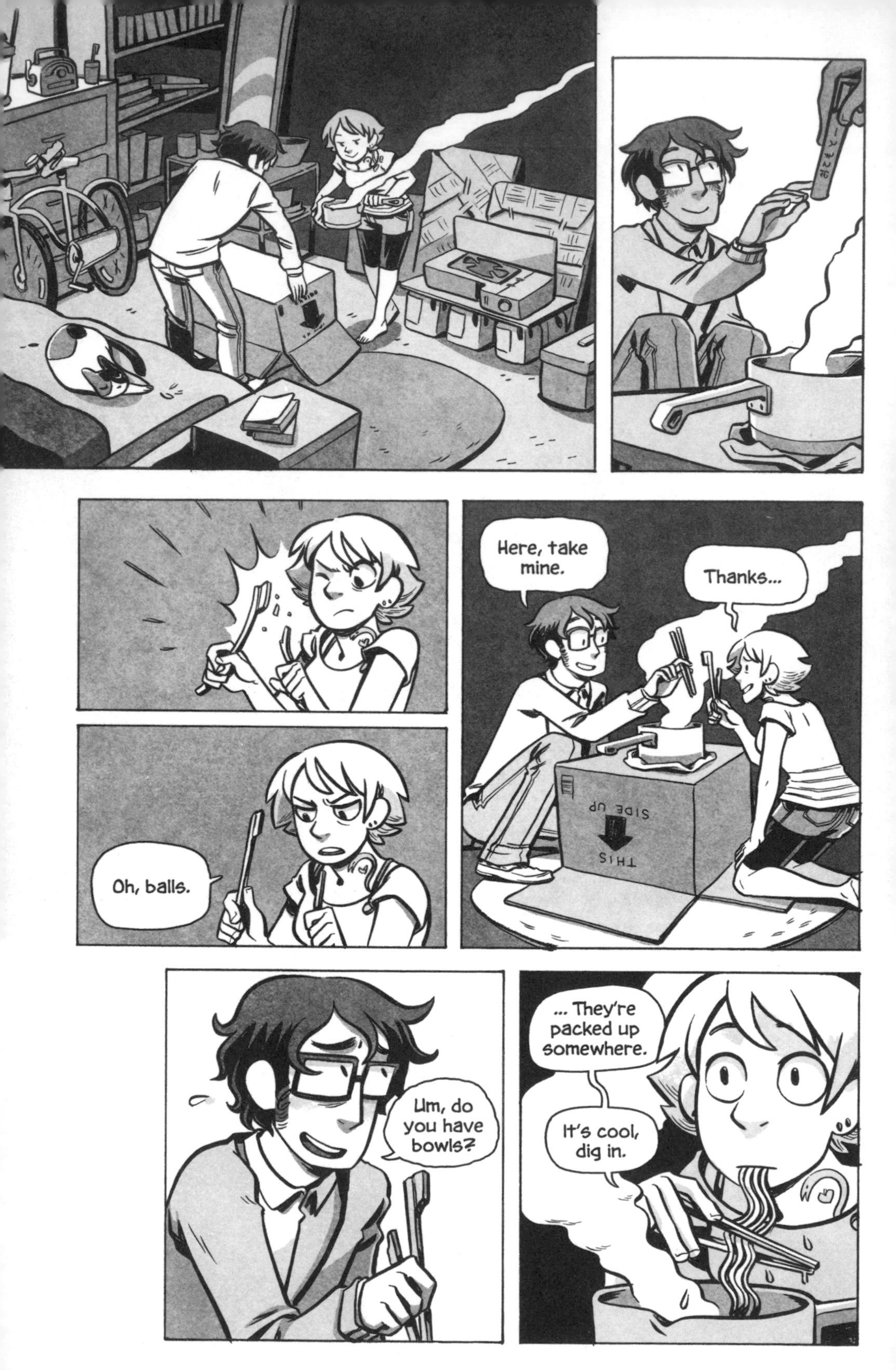
Oh, balls.
Here, take mine.
Thanks...
THIS SIDE UP
Um, do you have bowls?
... They're packed up somewhere.
It's cool, dig in.

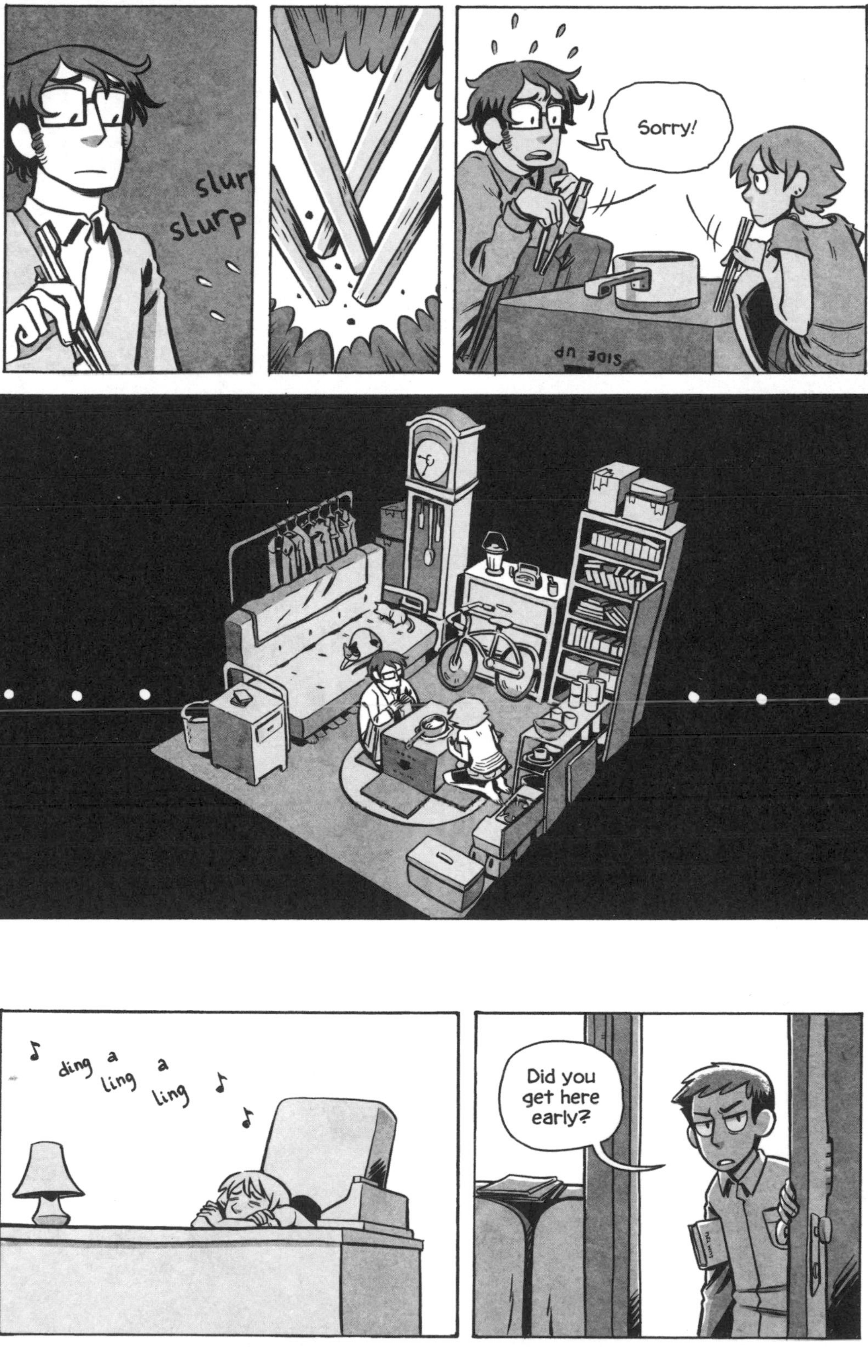
slur
slurp
Sorry!
SIDE UP
ding a ling a ling
Did you get here early?

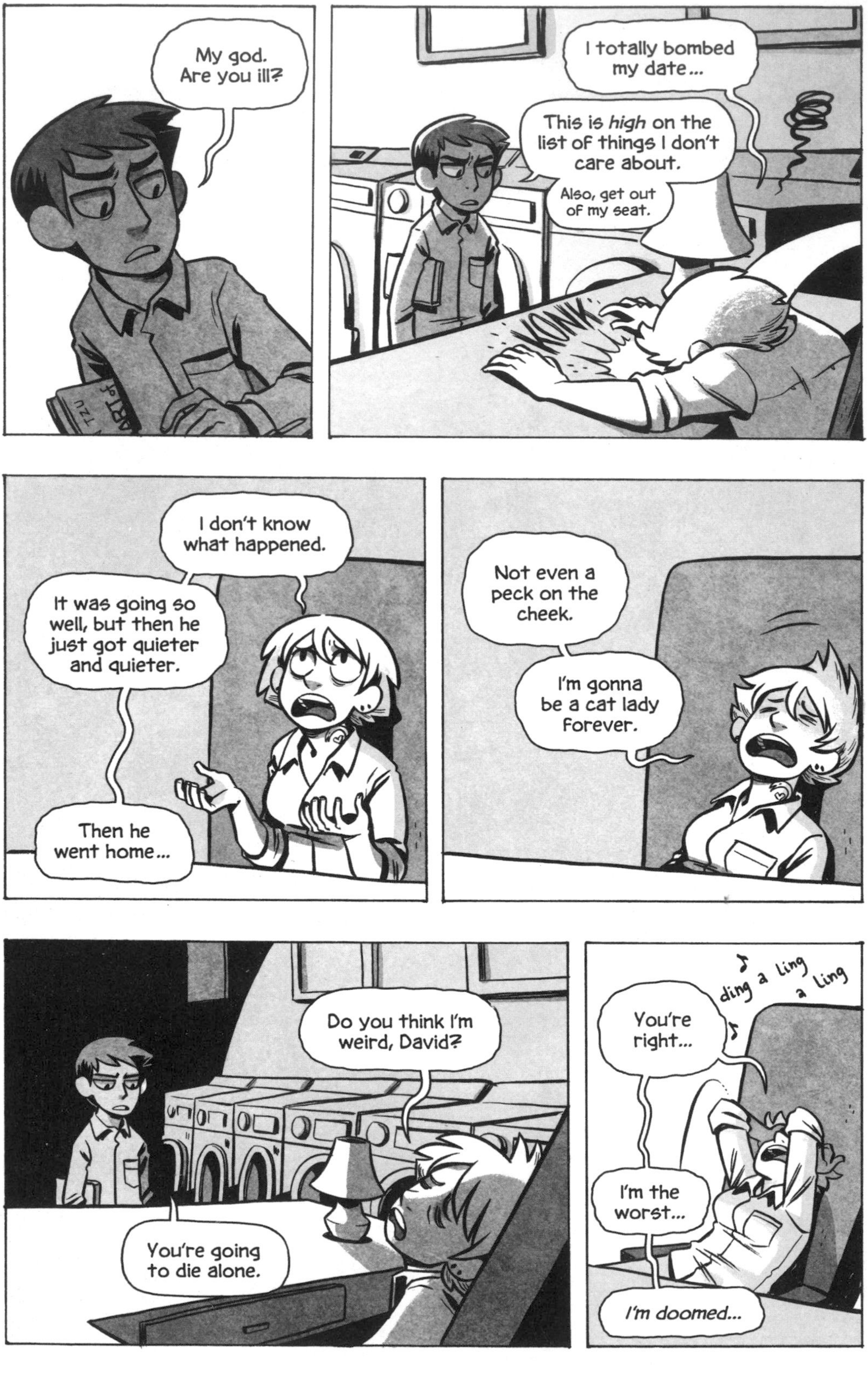

My god. Are you ill?
I totally bombed my date...
This is *high* on the list of things I don't care about.
Also, get out of my seat.
KONK
ART of
TZU
I don't know what happened.
It was going so well, but then he just got quieter and quieter.
Then he went home...
Not even a peck on the cheek.
I'm gonna be a cat lady forever.
Do you think I'm weird, David?
You're going to die alone.
ding a ling a ling
You're right...
I'm the worst...
I'm doomed...

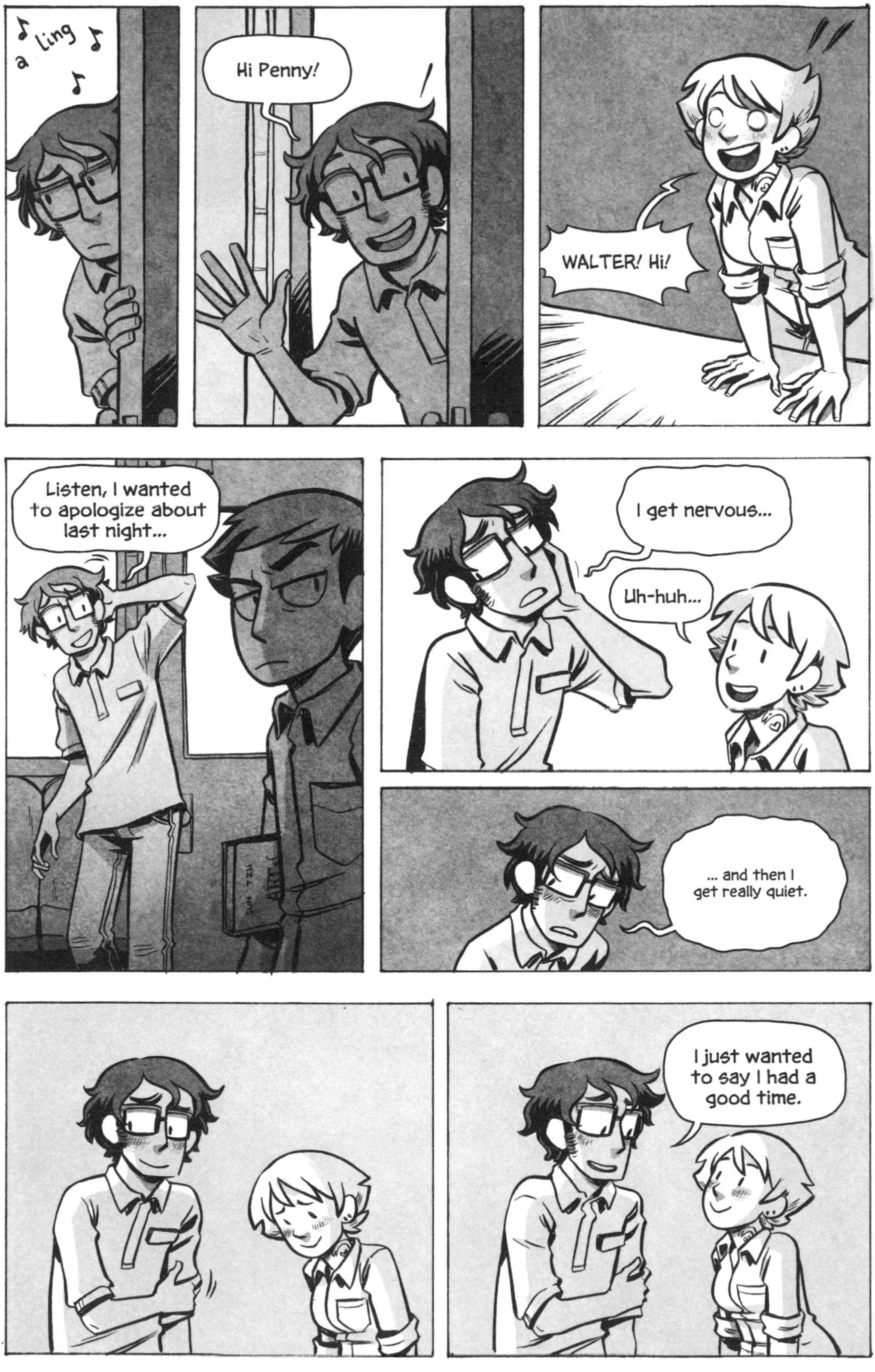

a ling
Hi Penny!
WALTER! Hi!
Listen, I wanted to apologize about last night...
I get nervous...
Uh-huh...
... and then I get really quiet.
I just wanted to say I had a good time.

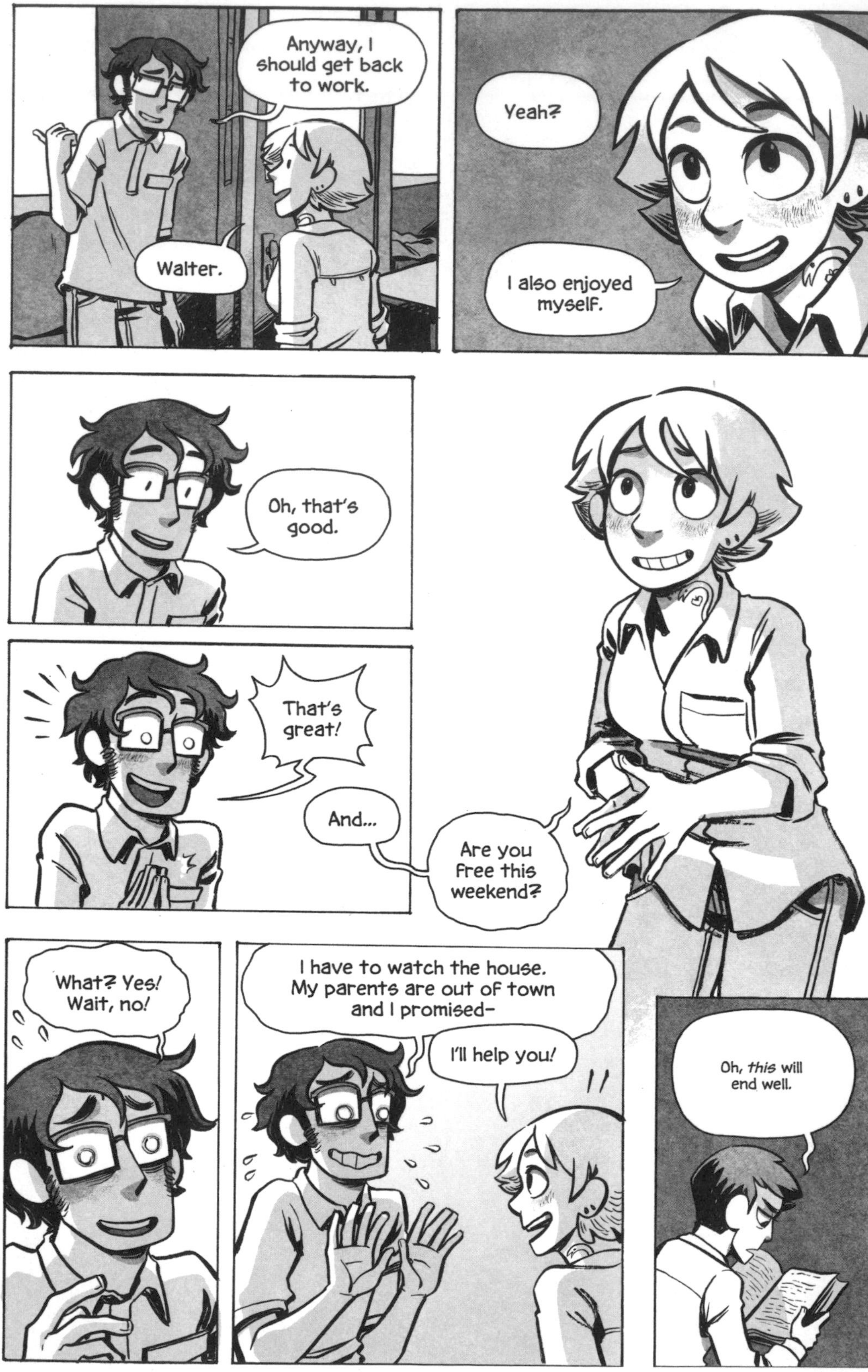
Anyway, I should get back to work.
Walter.
Yeah?
I also enjoyed myself.
Oh, that's good.
That's great!
And...
Are you free this weekend?
What? Yes! Wait, no!
I have to watch the house. My parents are out of town and I promised-
I'll help you!
Oh, *this* will end well.

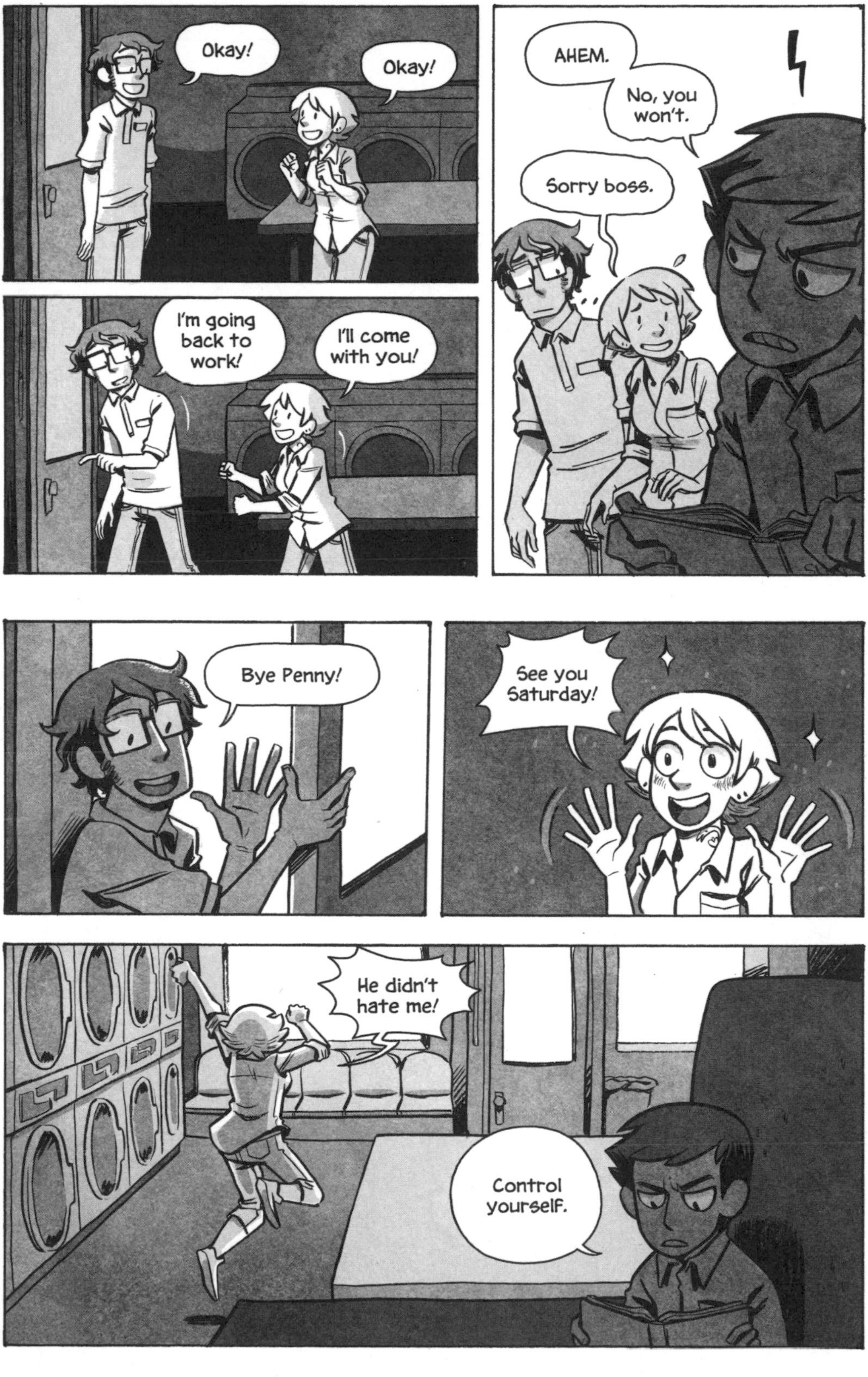
Okay!
Okay!
I'm going back to work!
I'll come with you!
AHEM.
No, you won't.
Sorry boss.
Bye Penny!
See you Saturday!
He didn't hate me!
Control yourself.

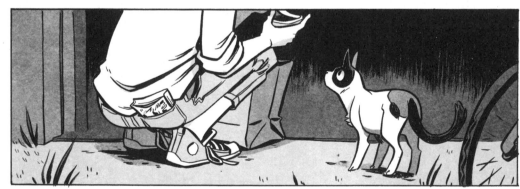

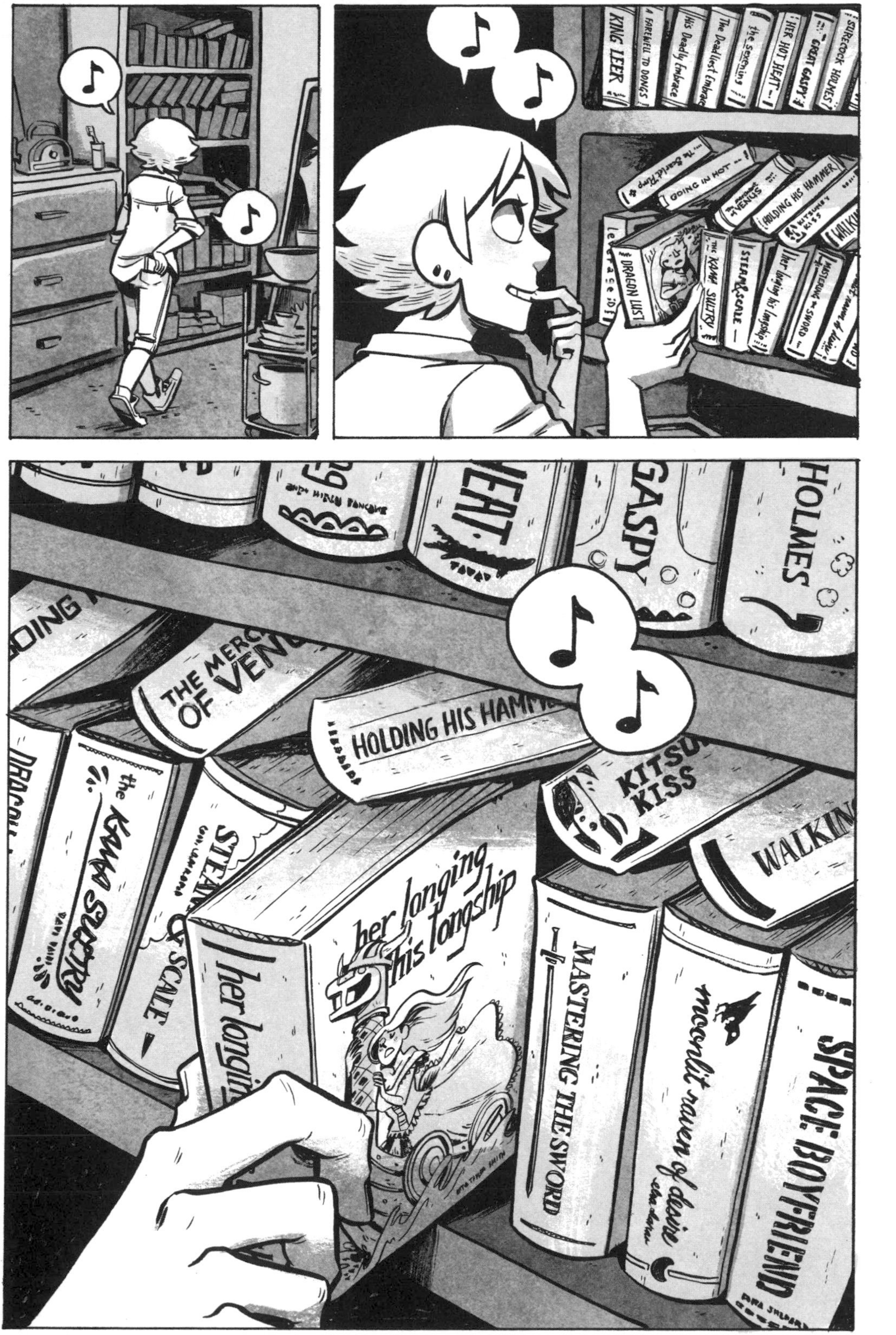

KING LEER
A FAREWELL TO DONGS
His Deadly Embrace
The Deadliest Embrace
the SEXPhins
HER HOT HEAT
GREAT GASPY
SHERLOCK HOLMES
GOING IN HOT
VENUS
HOLDING HIS HAMMER
KITSUNEY KISS
DRAGON LUST
the KAMA SULTRY
STEAM & SCALE
her longing his longship
MASTERING THE SWORD
HOLMES
GASPY
HEAT
THE MERC
OF VEN
HOLDING HIS HAM
KITSU
KISS
WALKIN
the KAMA SULTRY
SCALE
her longing
her longing
this longship
MASTERING THE SWORD
moonlit raven of desire
SPACE BOYFRIEND

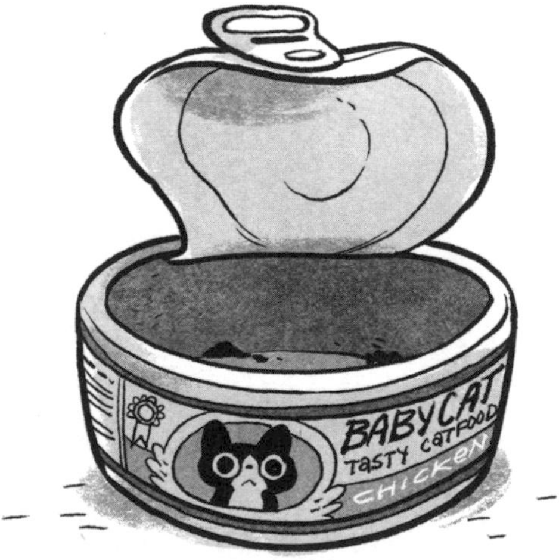
BABYCAT
TASTY CATFOOD
CHICKEN

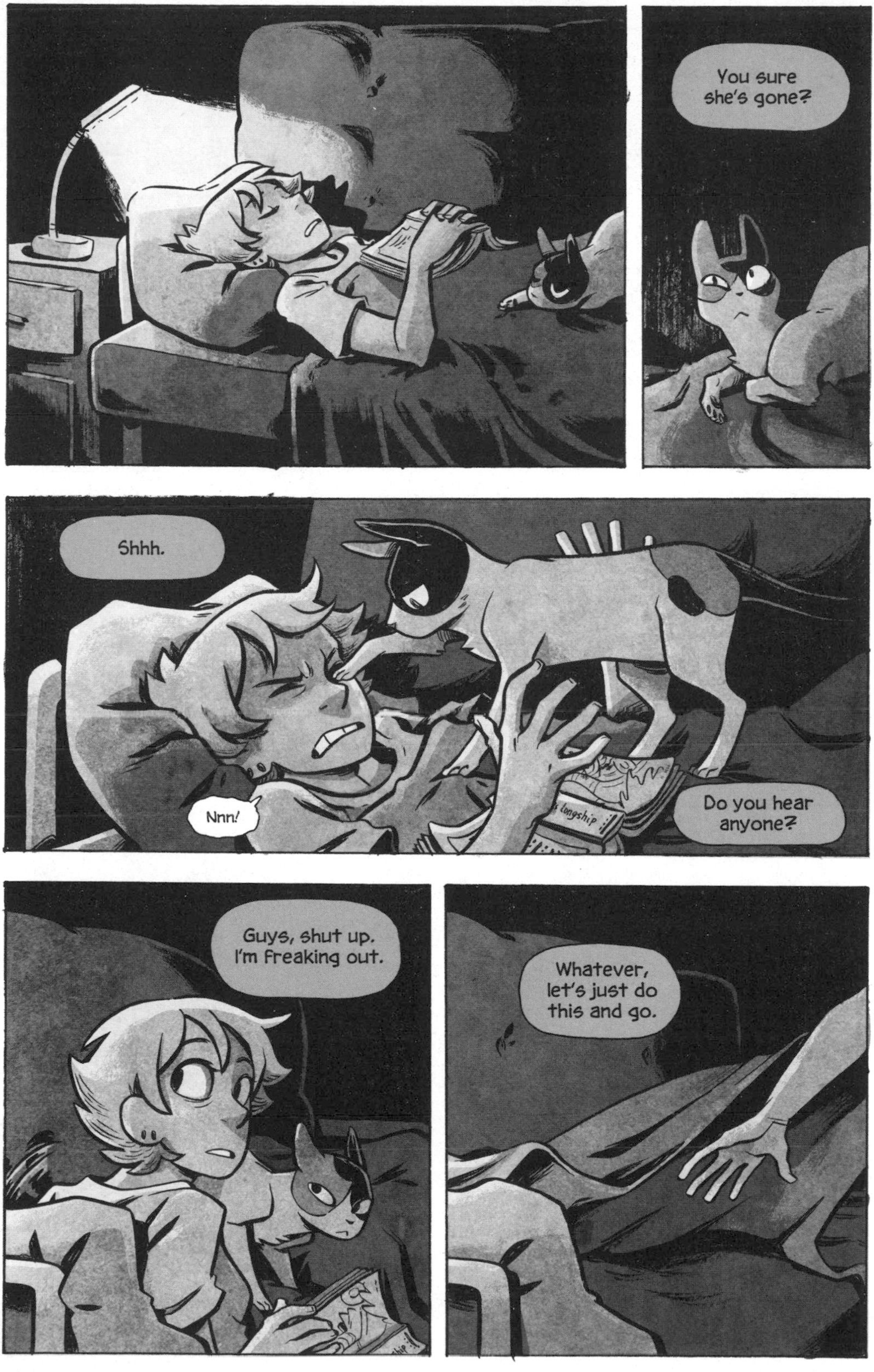
You sure she's gone?
Shhh.
Nnn!
Do you hear anyone?
longship
Guys, shut up. I'm freaking out.
Whatever, let's just do this and go.

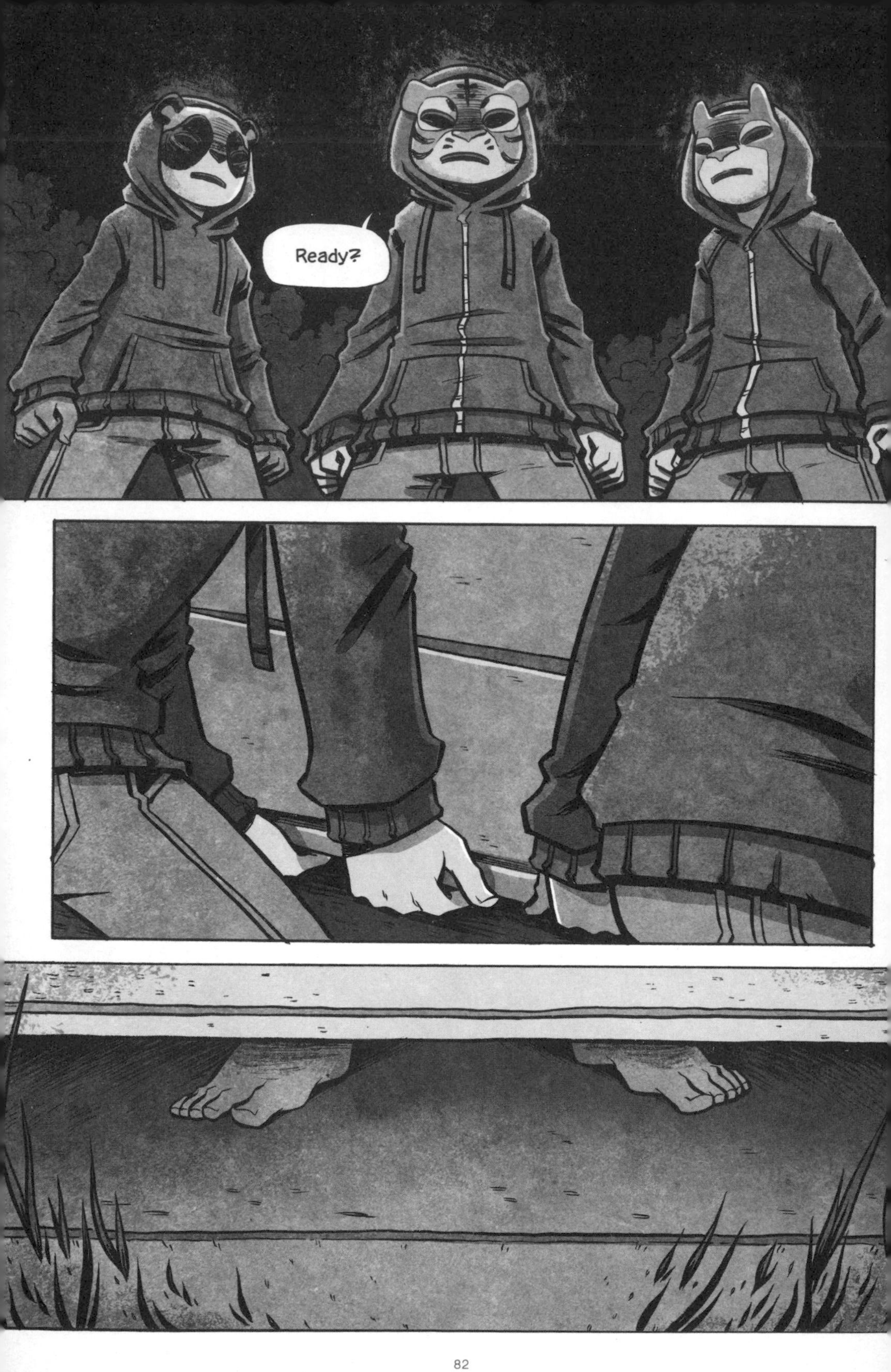
Ready?

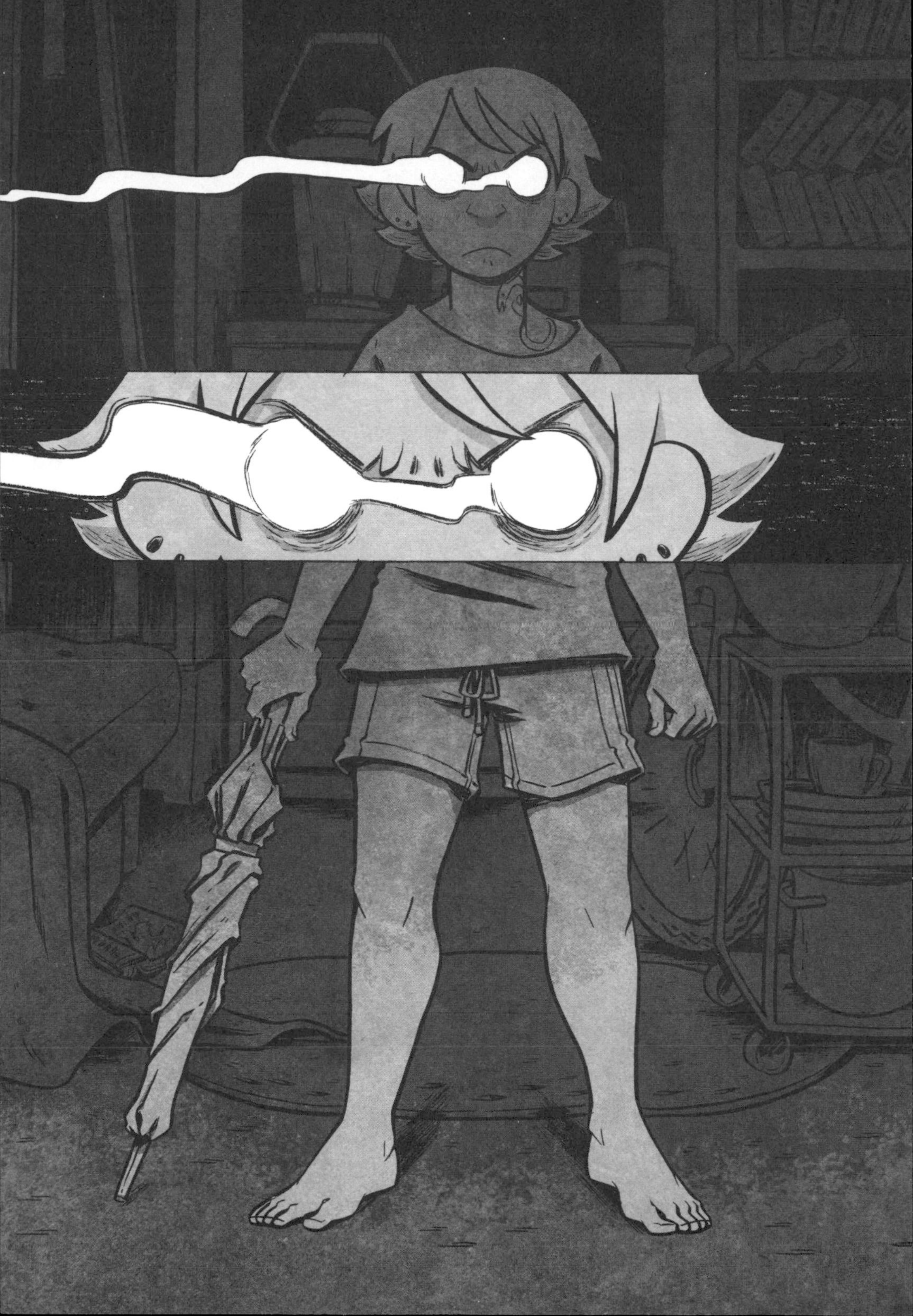

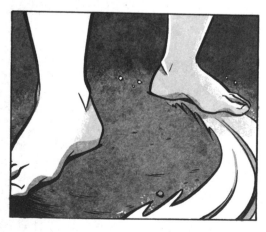

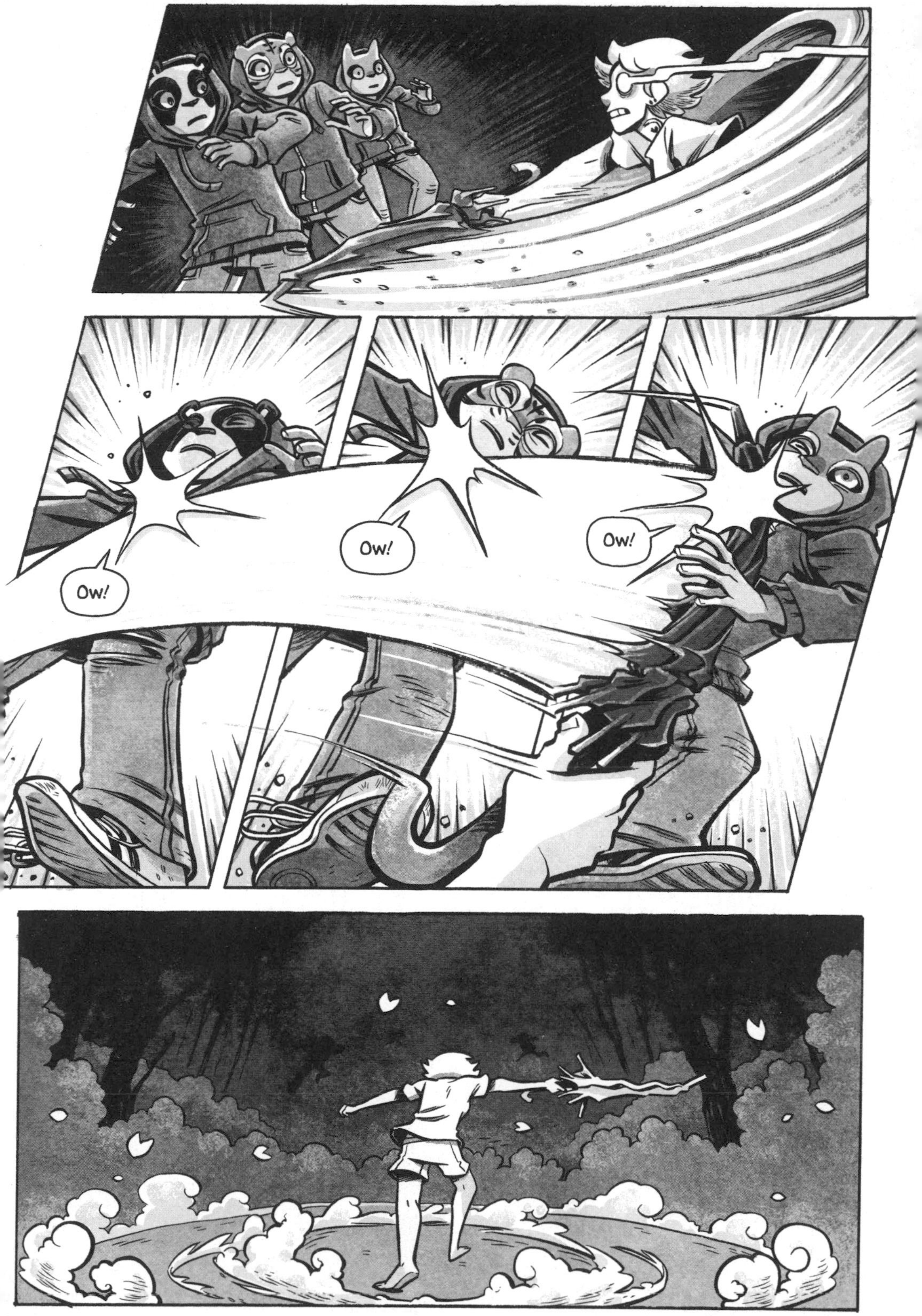
Ow!
Ow!
Ow!

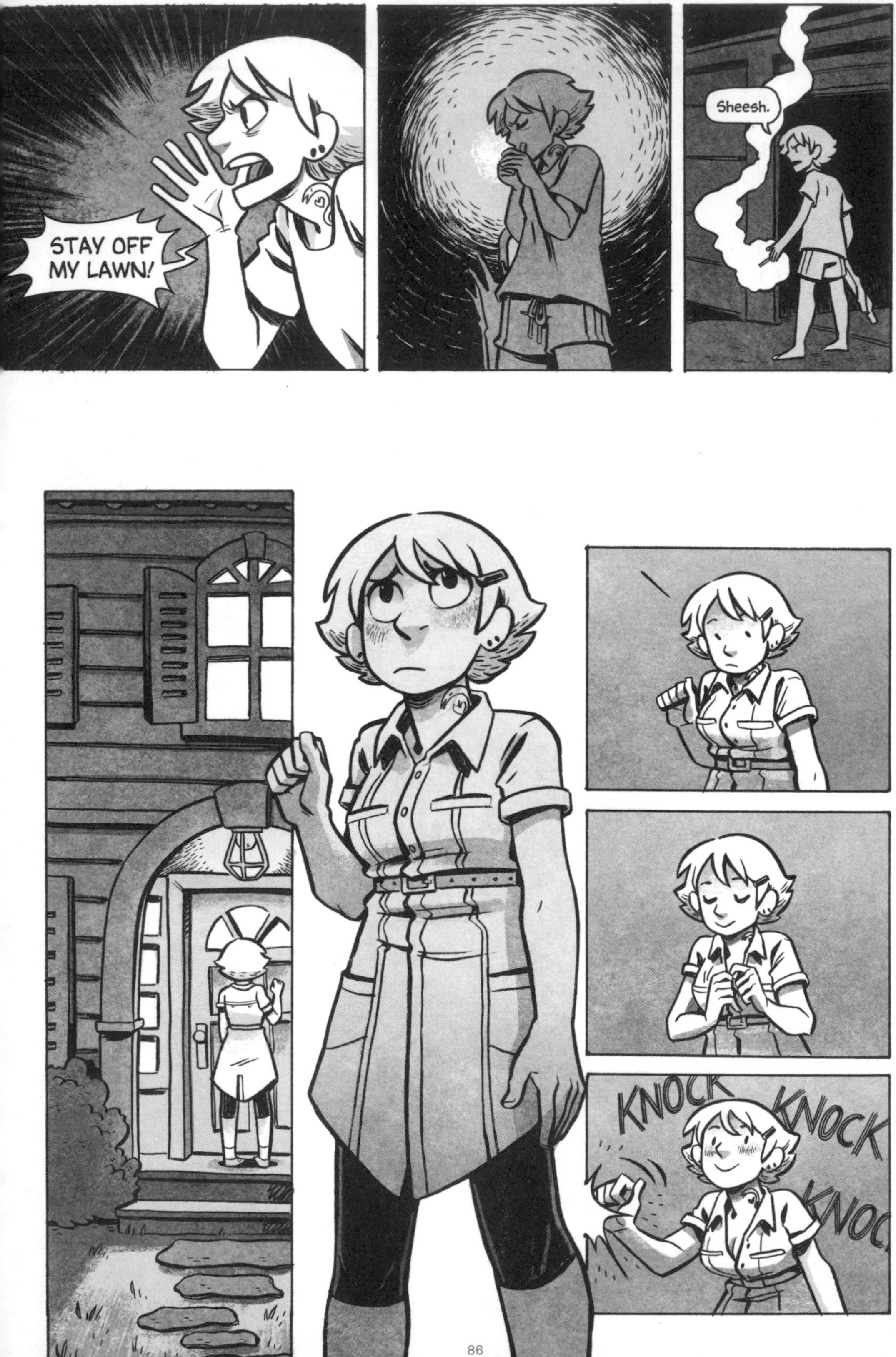
STAY OFF MY LAWN!
Sheesh.
KNOCK
KNOCK
KNOCK

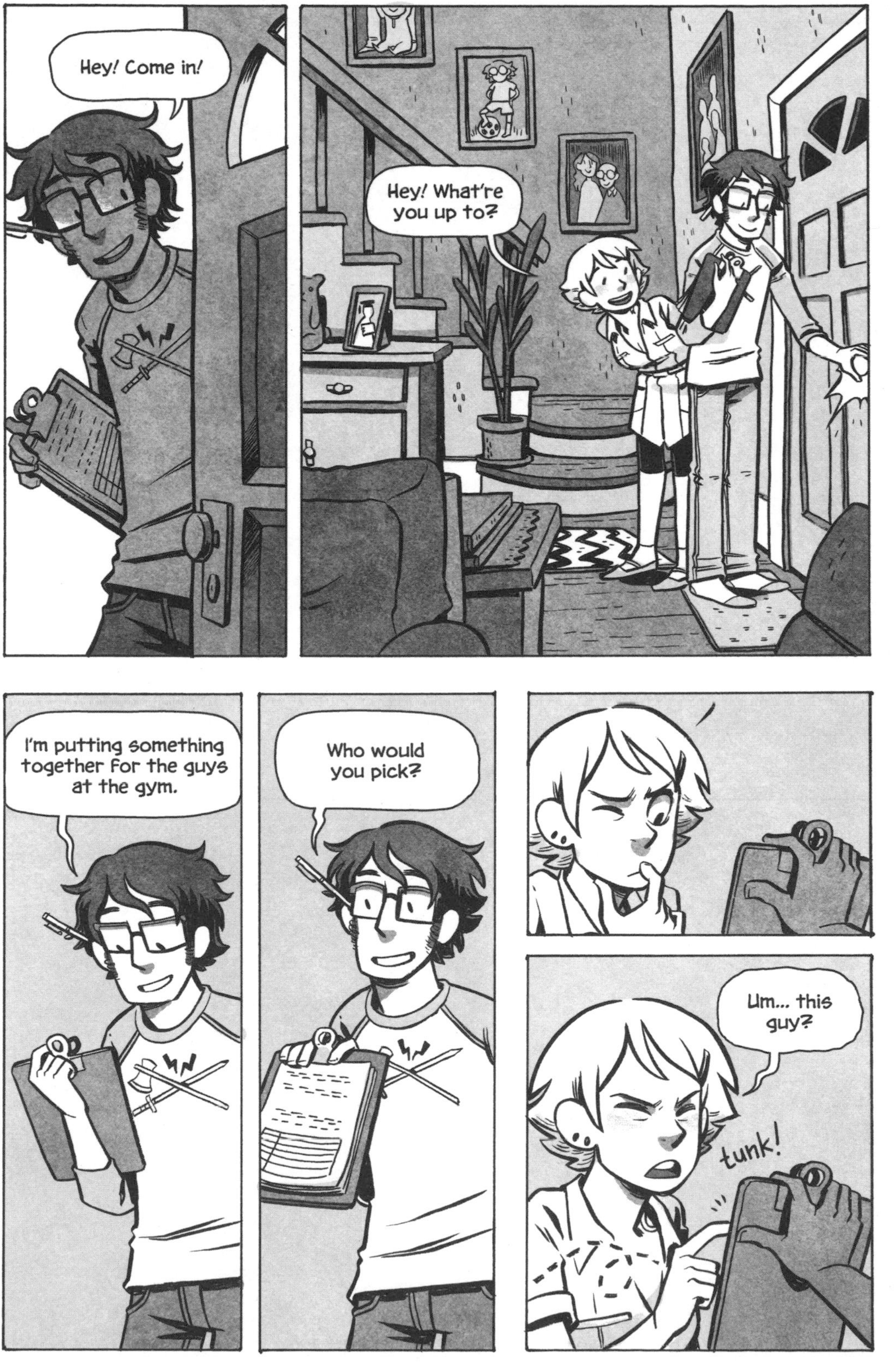
Hey! Come in!
Hey! What're you up to?
I'm putting something together for the guys at the gym.
Who would you pick?
Um... this guy?
tunk!

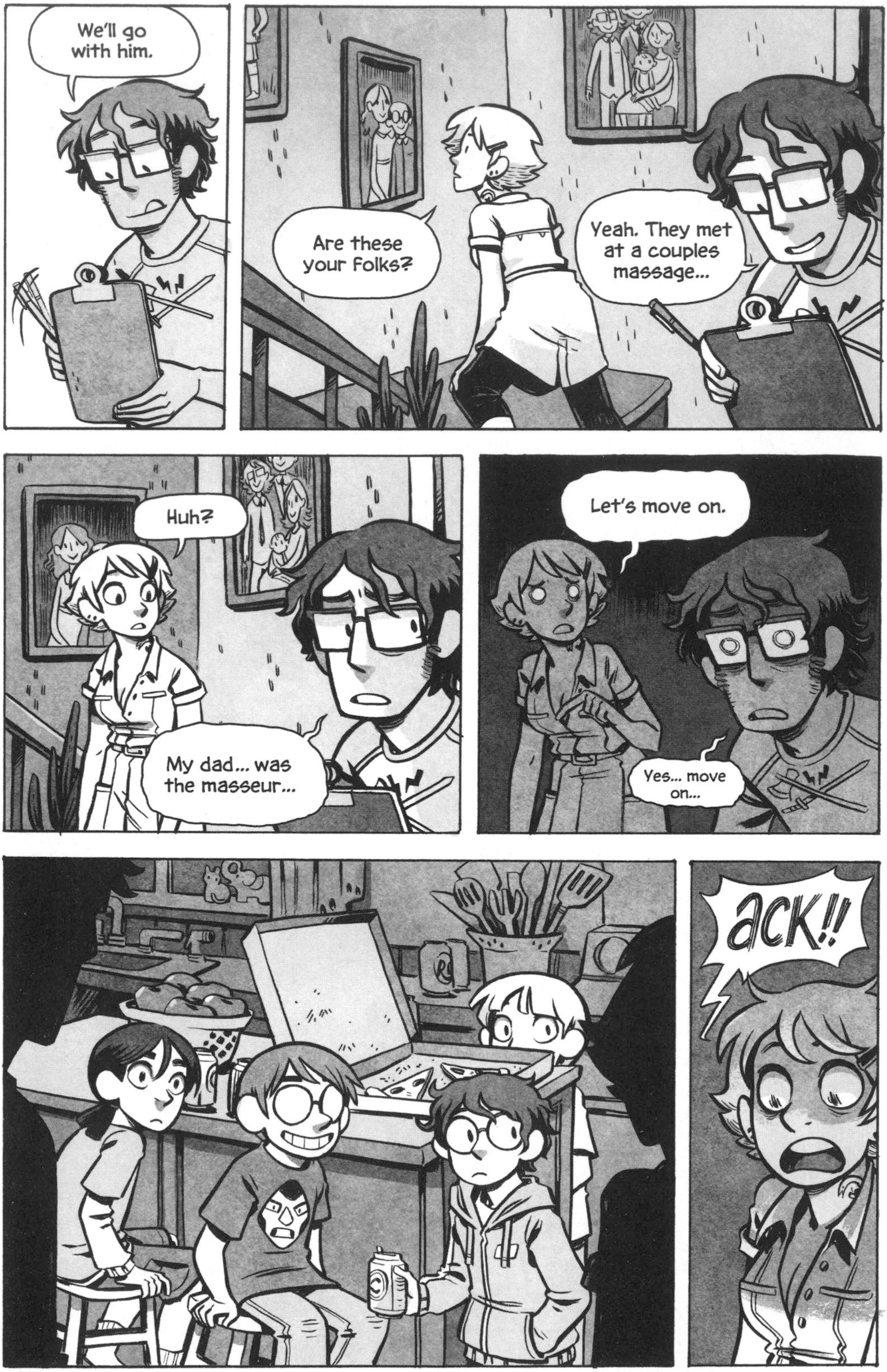
We'll go with him.
Are these your folks?
Yeah. They met at a couples massage...
Huh?
My dad... was the masseur...
Let's move on.
Yes... move on...
ack!!

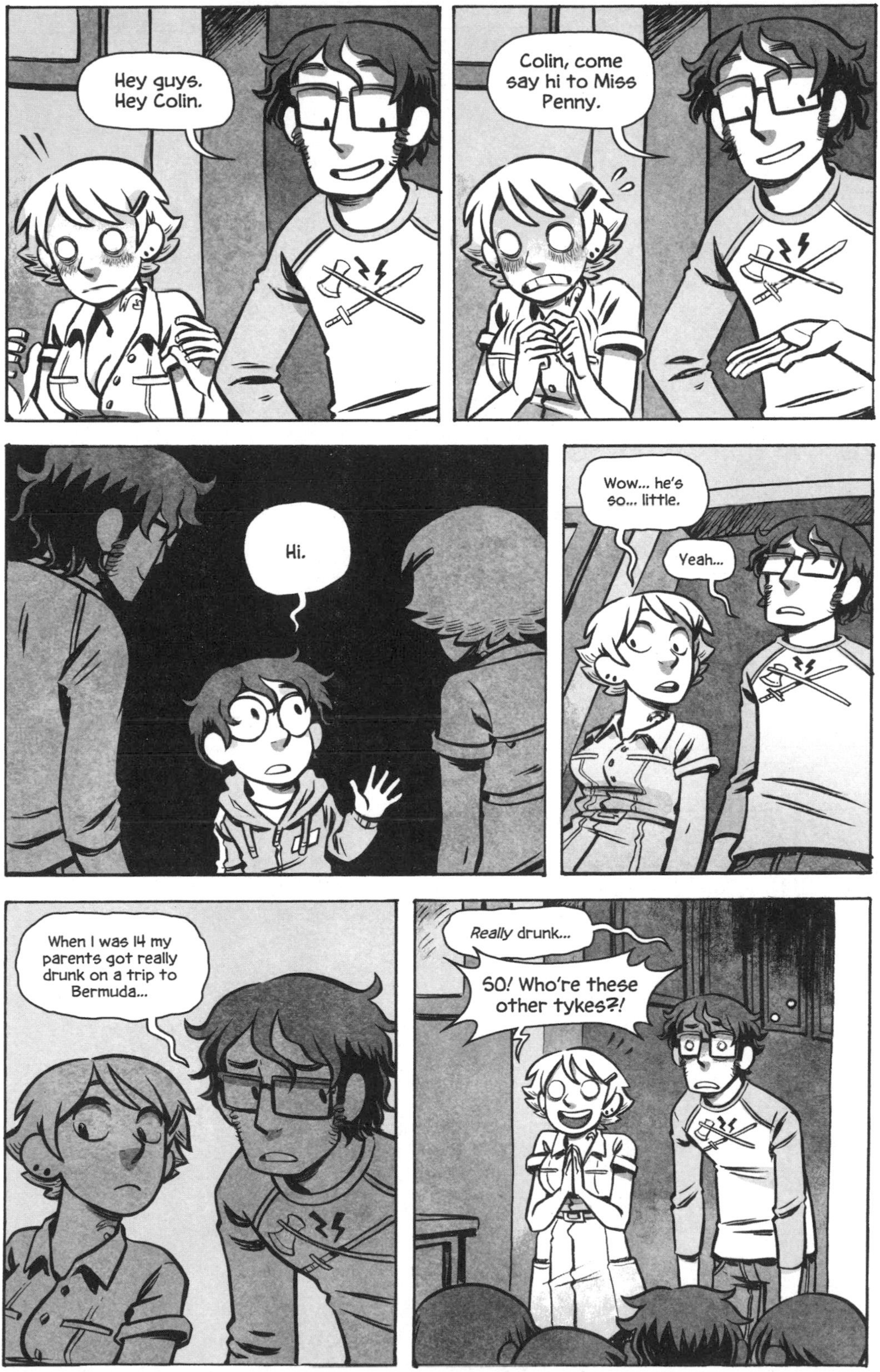

Hey guys.
Hey Colin.
Colin, come say hi to Miss Penny.
Hi.
Wow... he's so... little.
Yeah...
When I was 14 my parents got really drunk on a trip to Bermuda...
Really drunk...
SO! Who're these other tykes?!

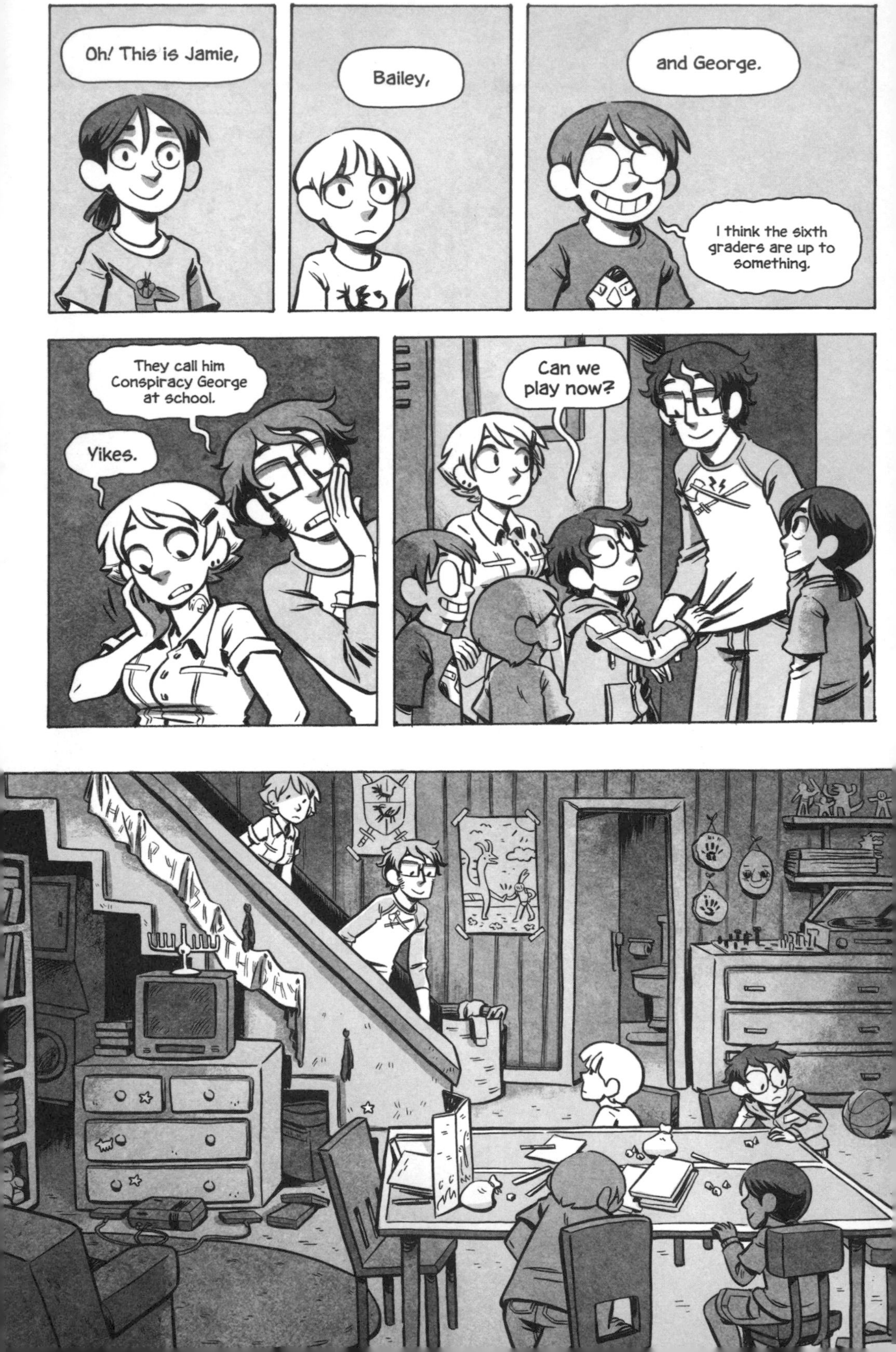
Oh! This is Jamie,
Bailey,
and George.
I think the sixth graders are up to something.
They call him Conspiracy George at school.
Yikes.
Can we play now?

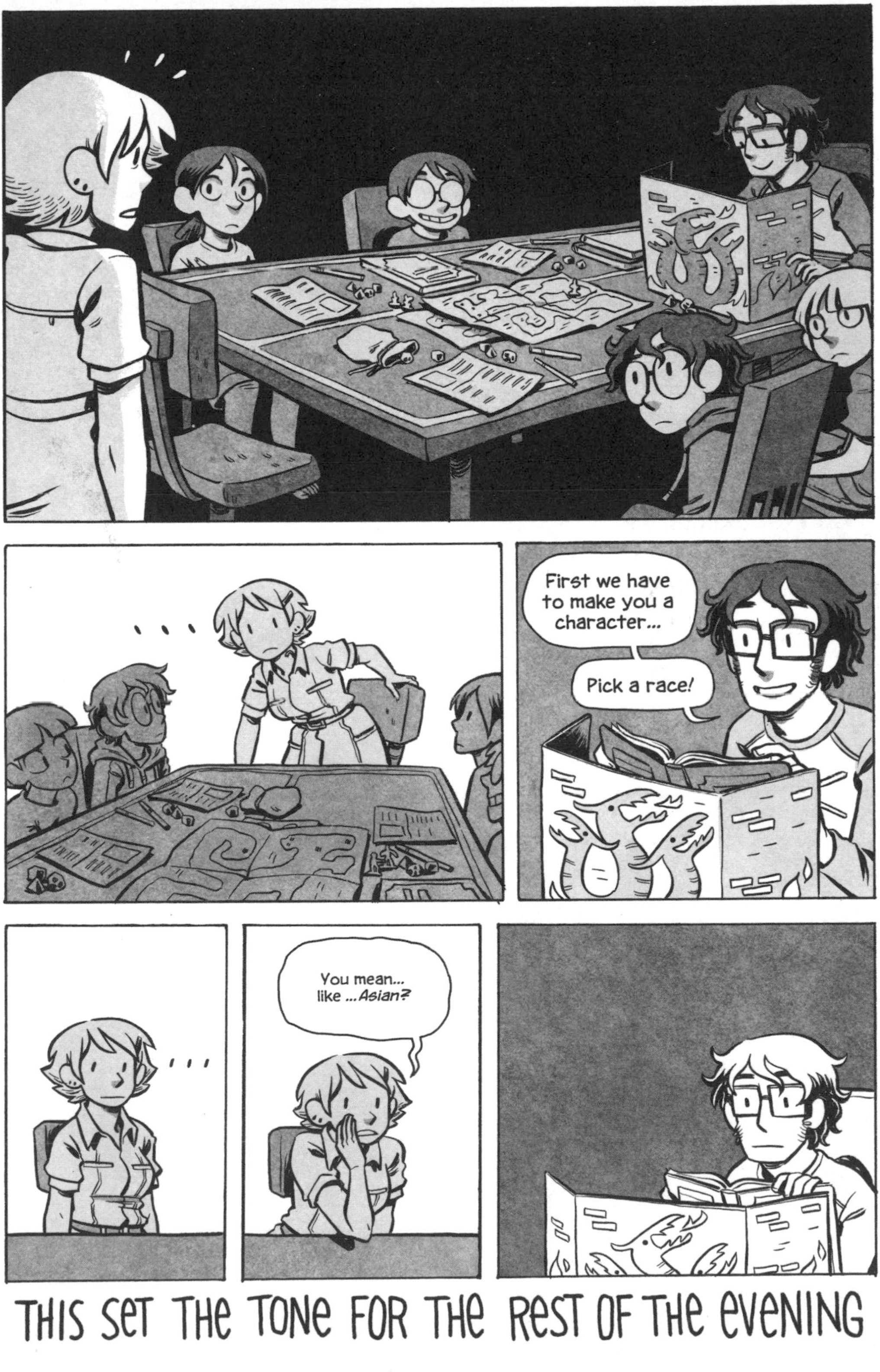
First we have to make you a character...
Pick a race!
You mean... like ...Asian?
THIS SET THE TONE FOR THE REST OF THE EVENING

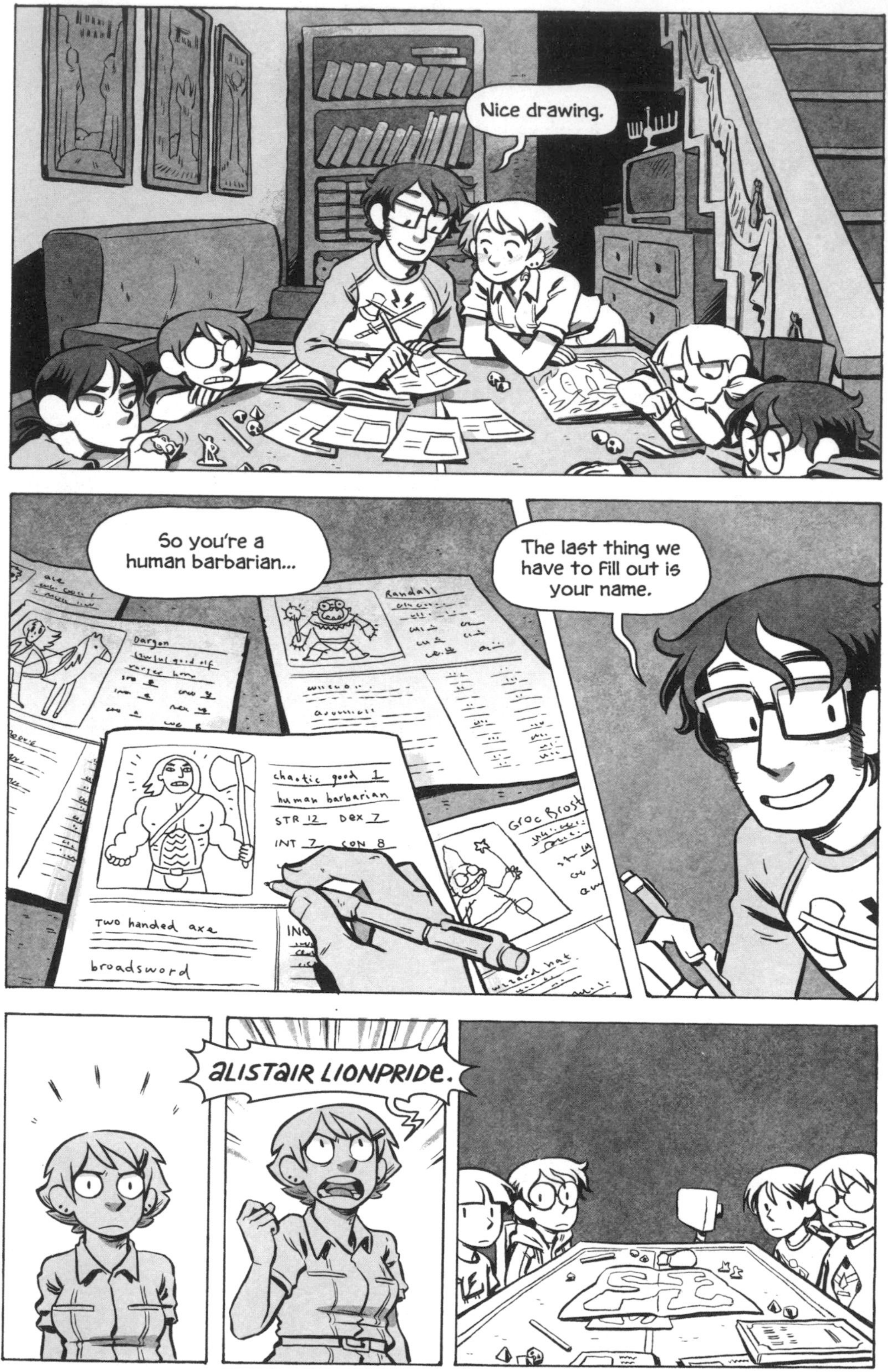
Nice drawing.
So you're a human barbarian...
The last thing we have to fill out is your name.
Randall
Dargon
chaotic good 1
human barbarian
STR 12 DEX 7
INT 7 CON 8
Two handed axe
broadsword
Groc Brost
wizard hat
ALISTAIR LIONPRIDE.

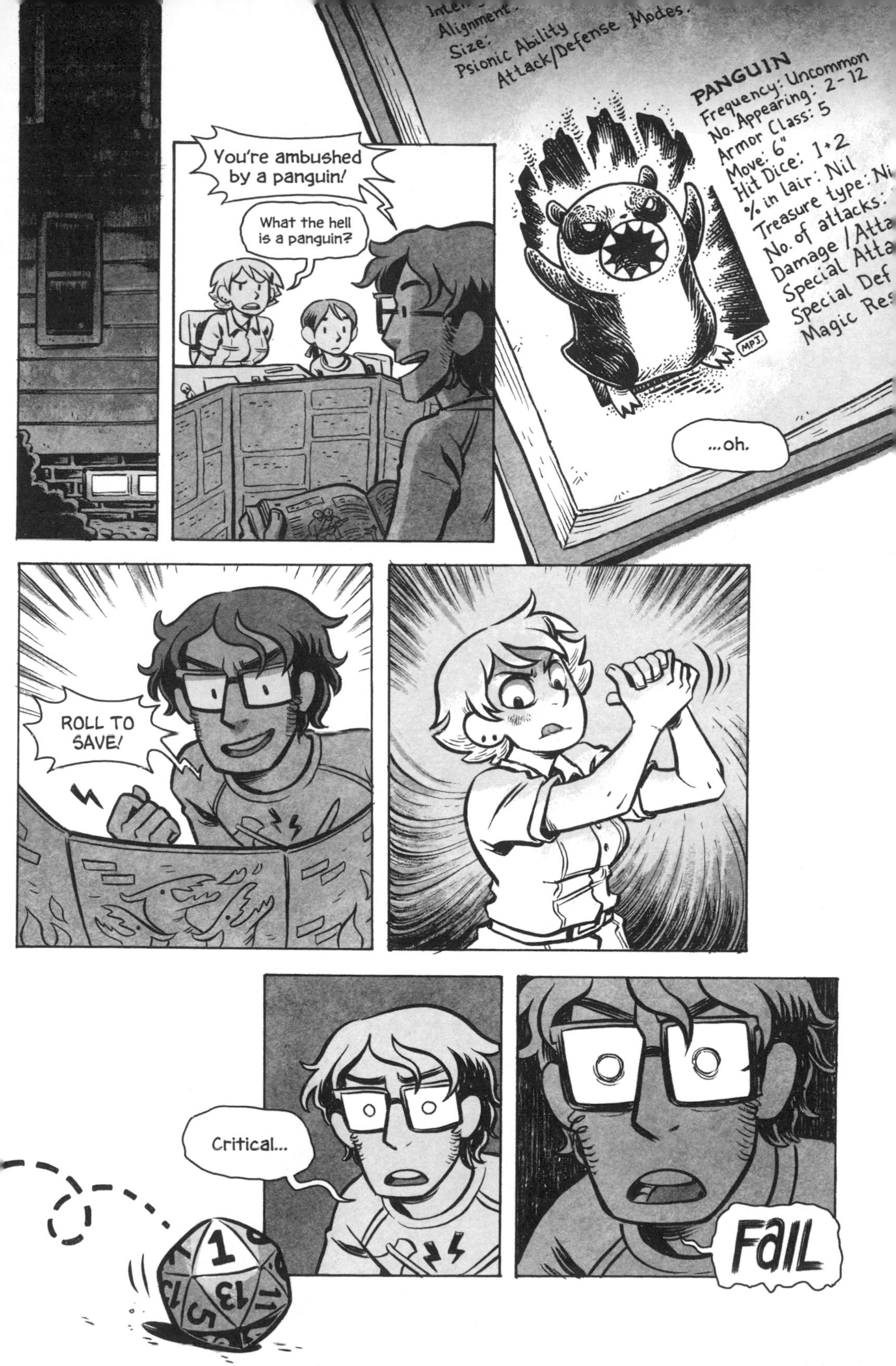
Alignment:
Size:
Psionic Ability
Attack/Defense Modes:
You're ambushed by a panguin!
What the hell is a panguin?
PANGUIN
Frequency: Uncommon
No. Appearing: 2-12
Armor Class: 5
Move: 6"
Hit Dice: 1+2
% in lair: Nil
Treasure type: Ni
No. of attacks:
Damage/Atta
Special Atta
Special Def
Magic Res
...oh.
ROLL TO SAVE!
Critical...
FAIL

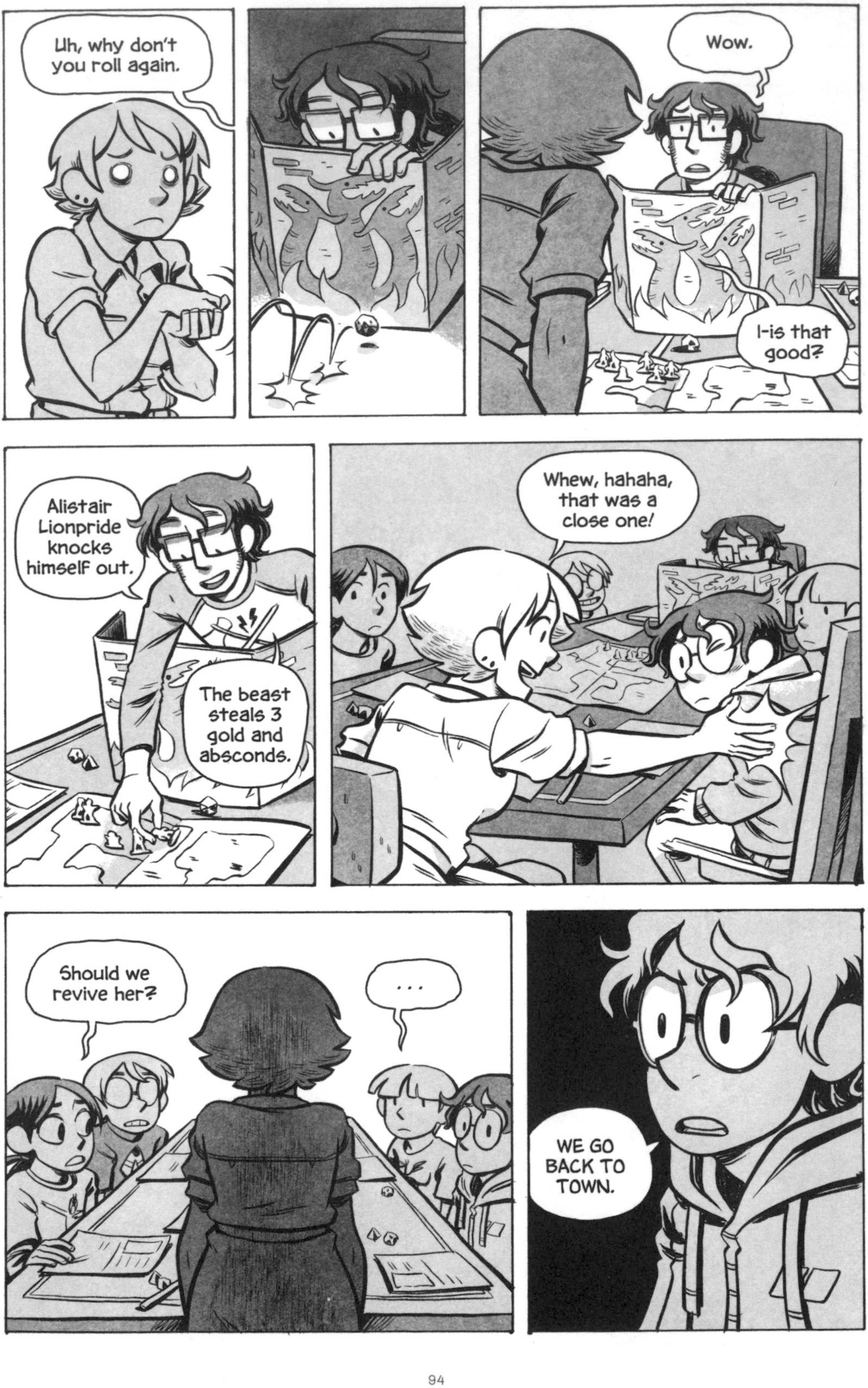

Uh, why don't you roll again.
Wow.
I-is that good?
Alistair Lionpride knocks himself out.
The beast steals 3 gold and absconds.
Whew, hahaha, that was a close one!
Should we revive her?
...
WE GO BACK TO TOWN.

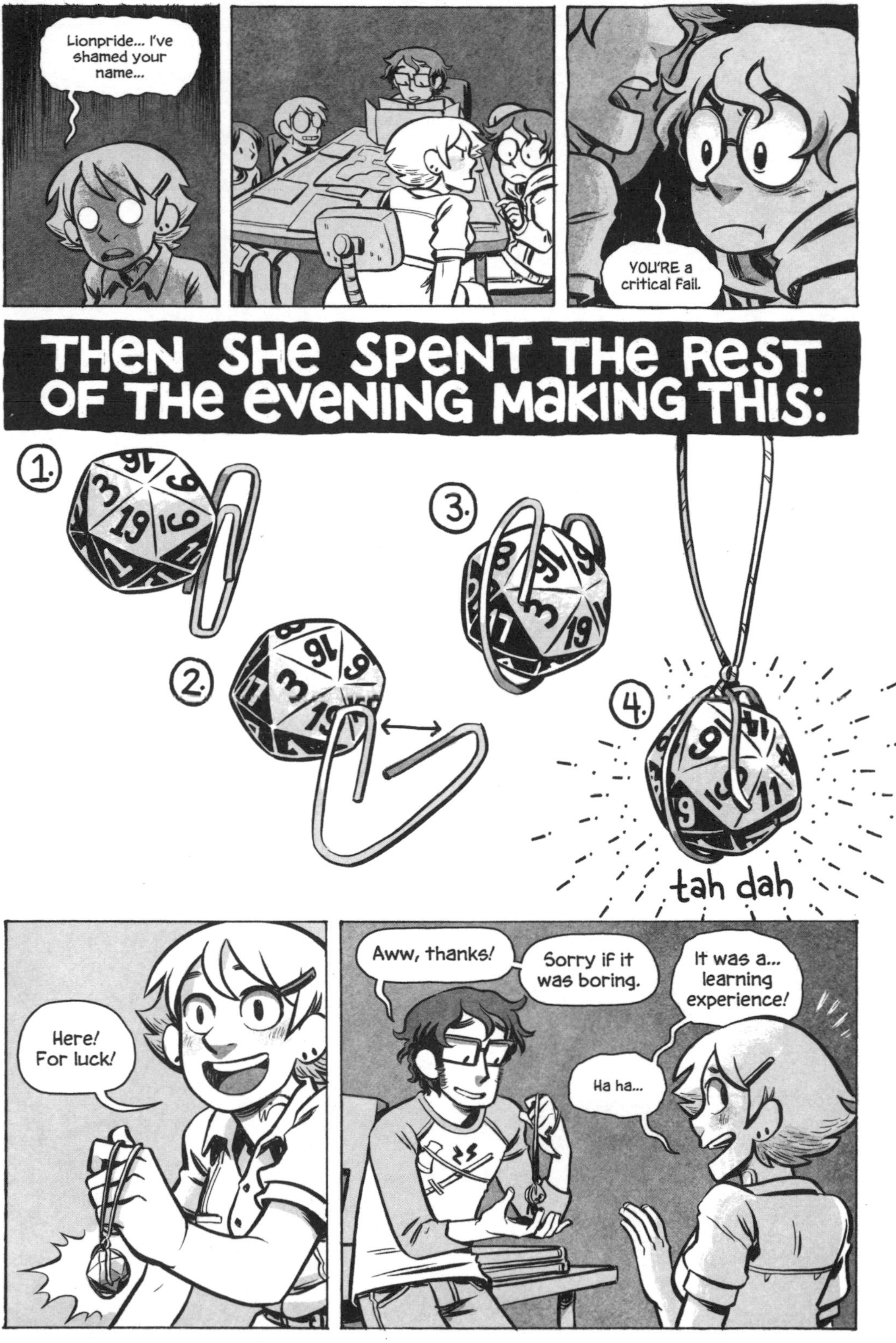
Lionpride... I've shamed your name...
YOU'RE a critical fail.
THEN SHE SPENT THE REST OF THE EVENING MAKING THIS:
1.
2.
3.
4.
tah dah
Here! For luck!
Aww, thanks!
Sorry if it was boring.
It was a... learning experience!
Ha ha...

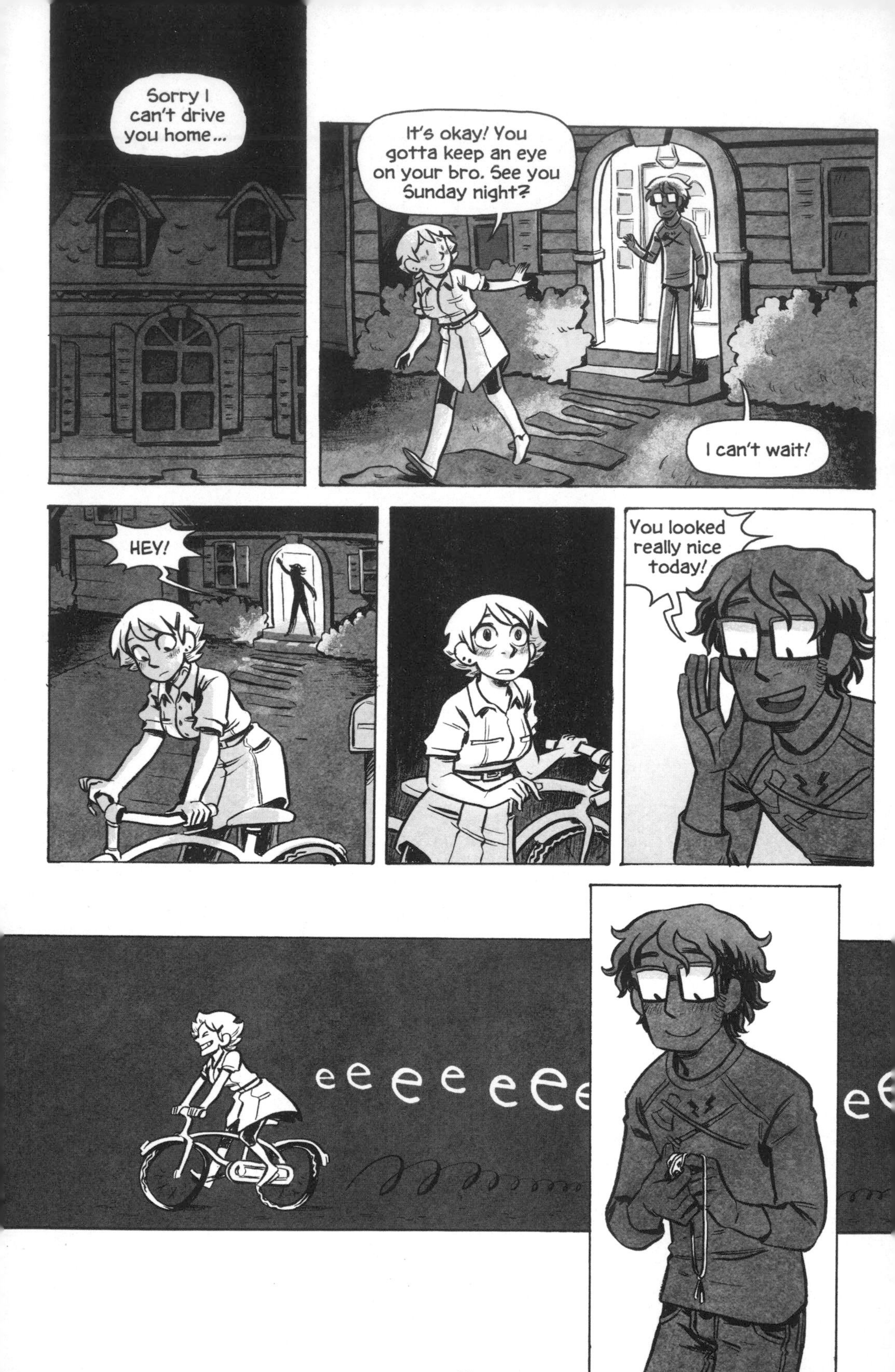
Sorry I can't drive you home...
It's okay! You gotta keep an eye on your bro. See you Sunday night?
I can't wait!
HEY!
You looked really nice today!
eeeeeeeee

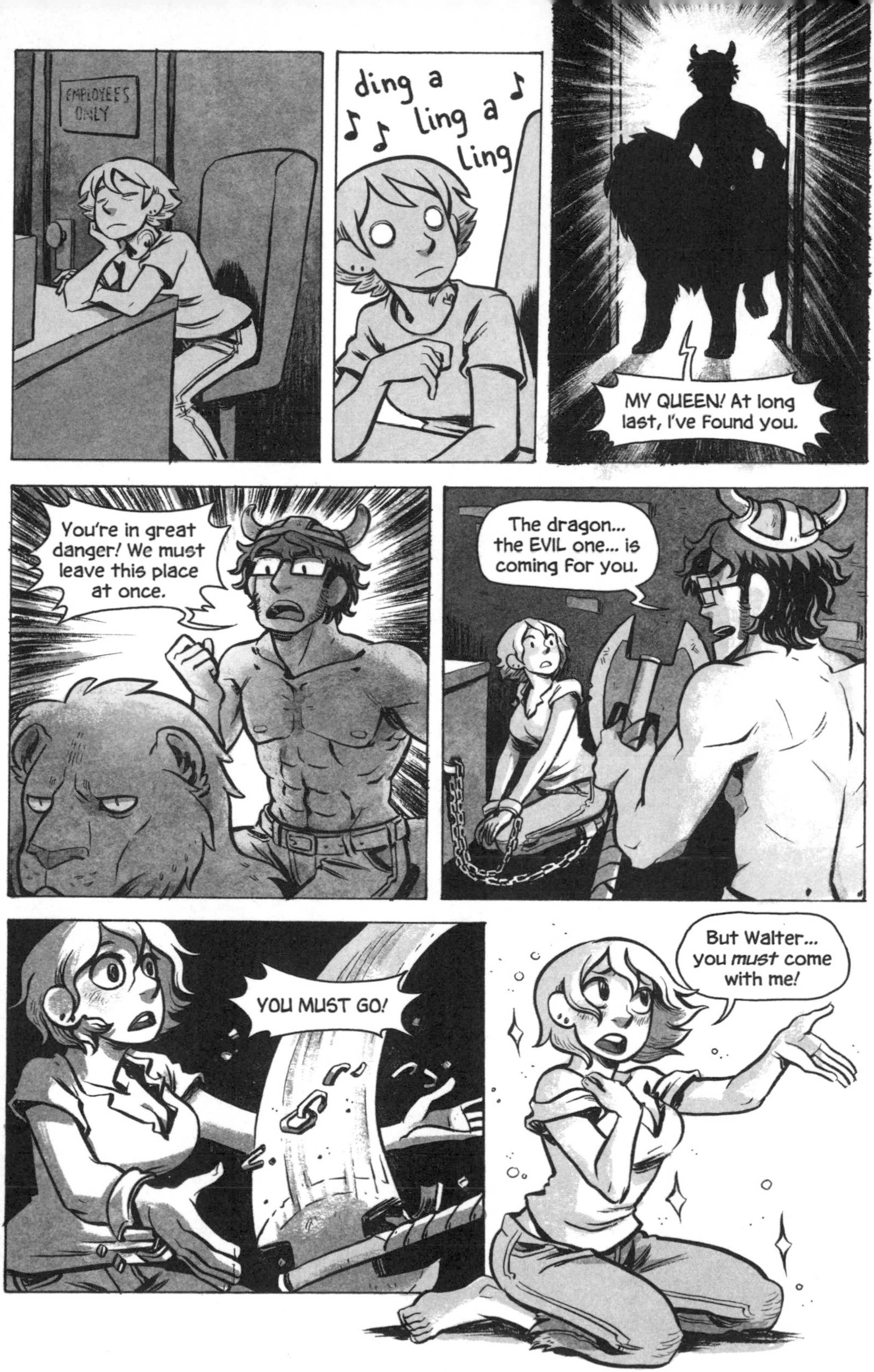
EMPLOYEES ONLY
ding a ling a ling
MY QUEEN! At long last, I've Found you.
You're in great danger! We must leave this place at once.
The dragon... the EVIL one... is coming for you.
YOU MUST GO!
But Walter... you *must* come with me!

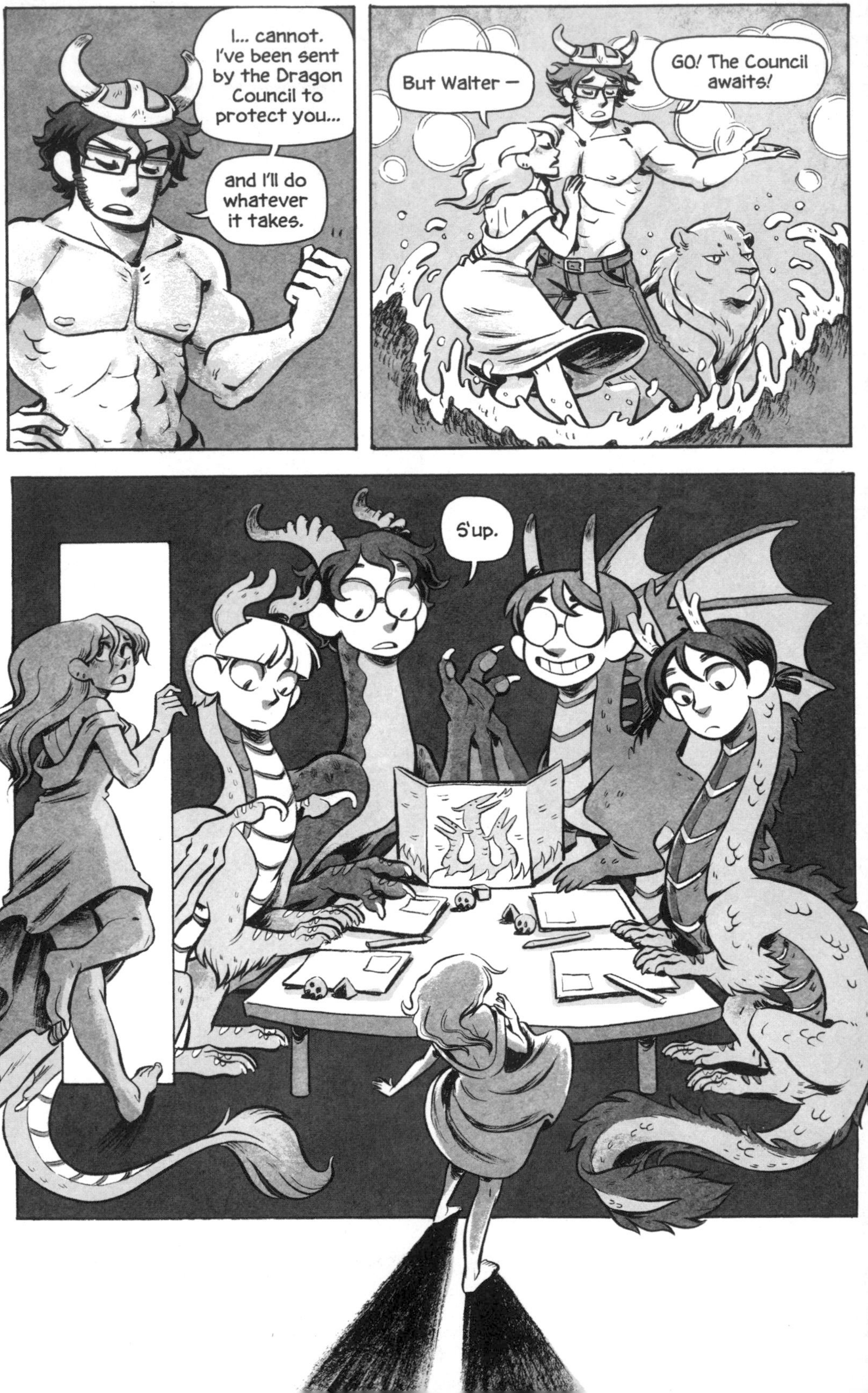

I... cannot. I've been sent by the Dragon Council to protect you...
and I'll do whatever it takes.
But Walter —
GO! The Council awaits!
S'up.

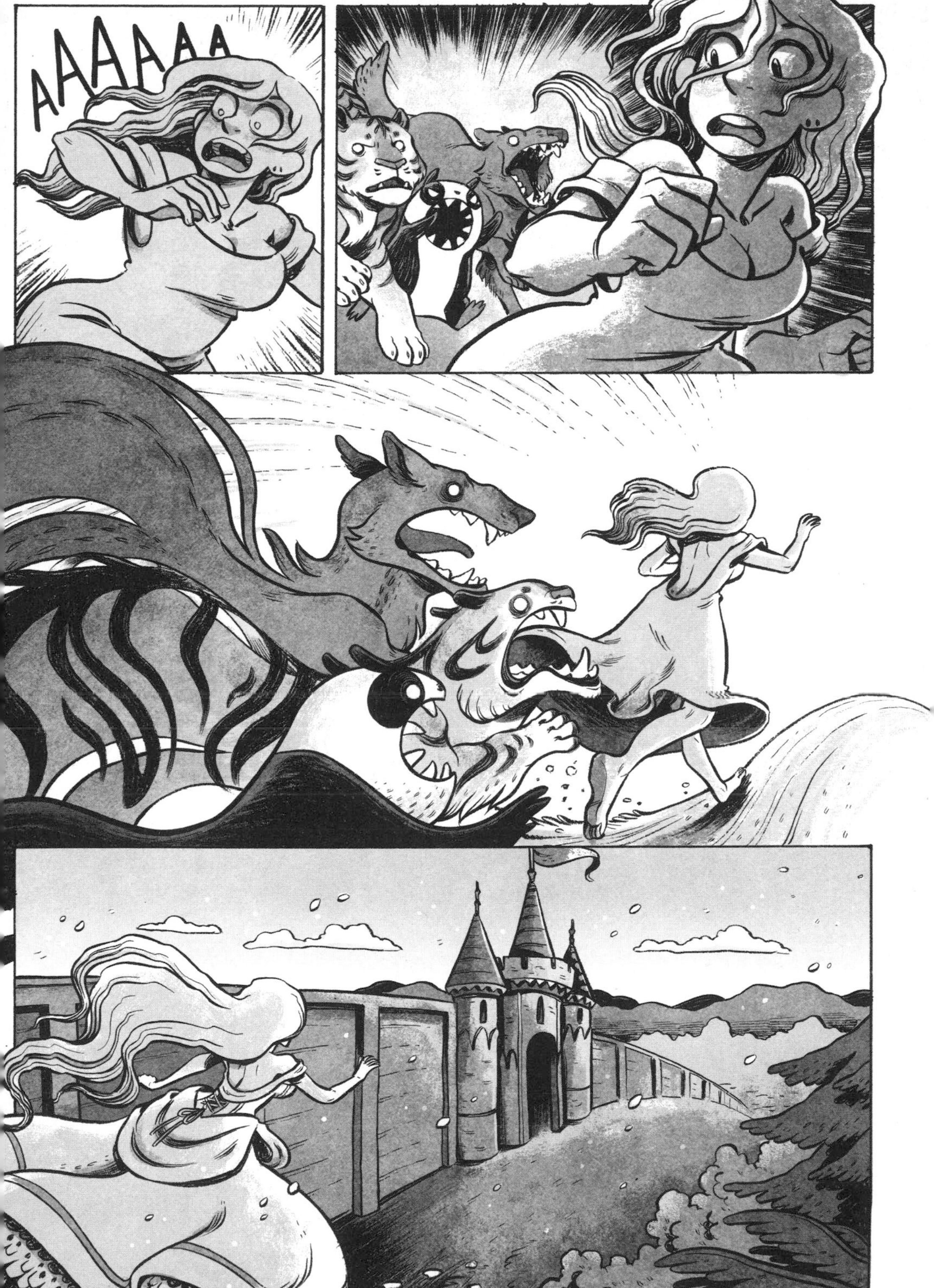
AAAAAA

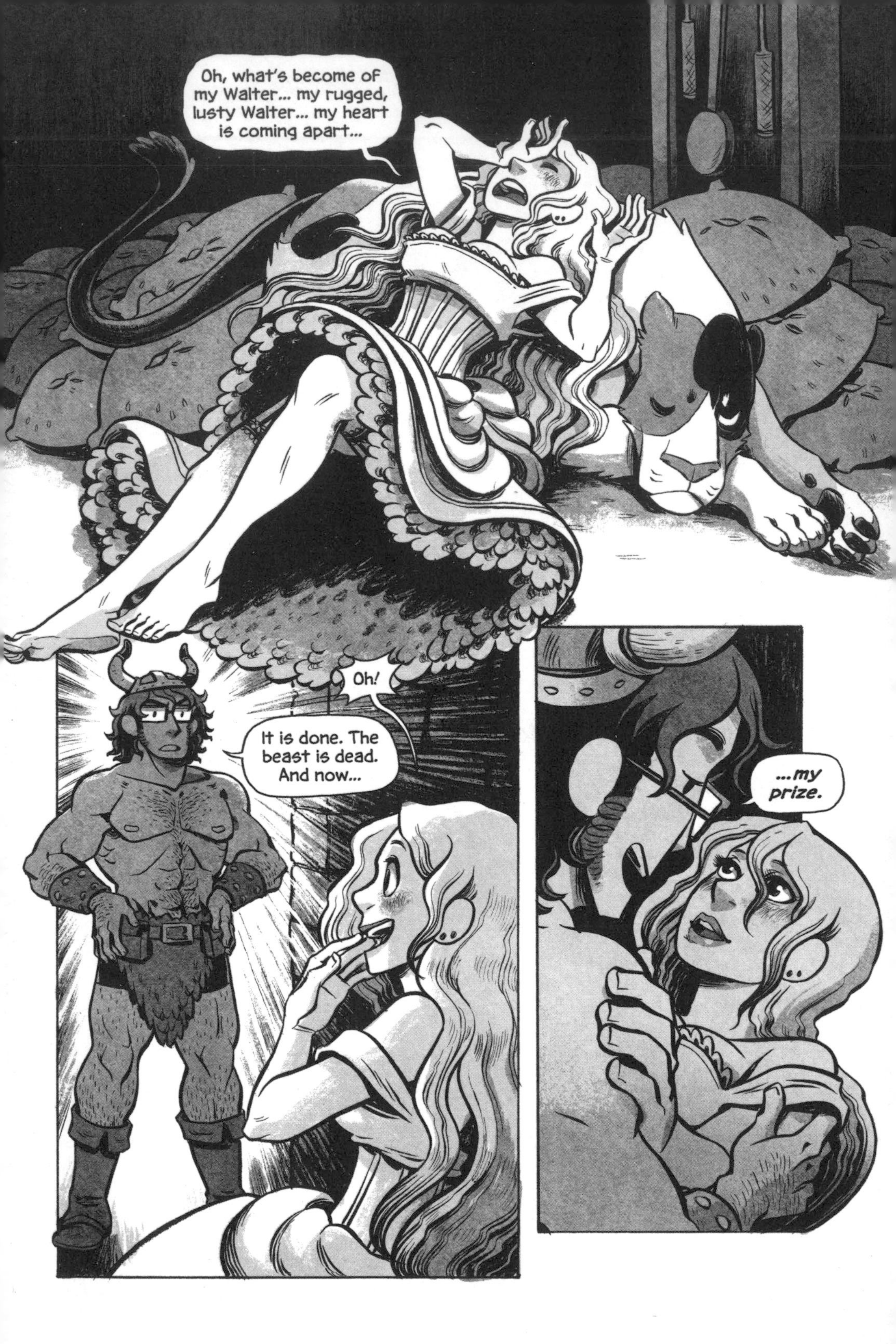
Oh, what's become of my Walter... my rugged, lusty Walter... my heart is coming apart...
Oh!
It is done. The beast is dead. And now...
...my prize.

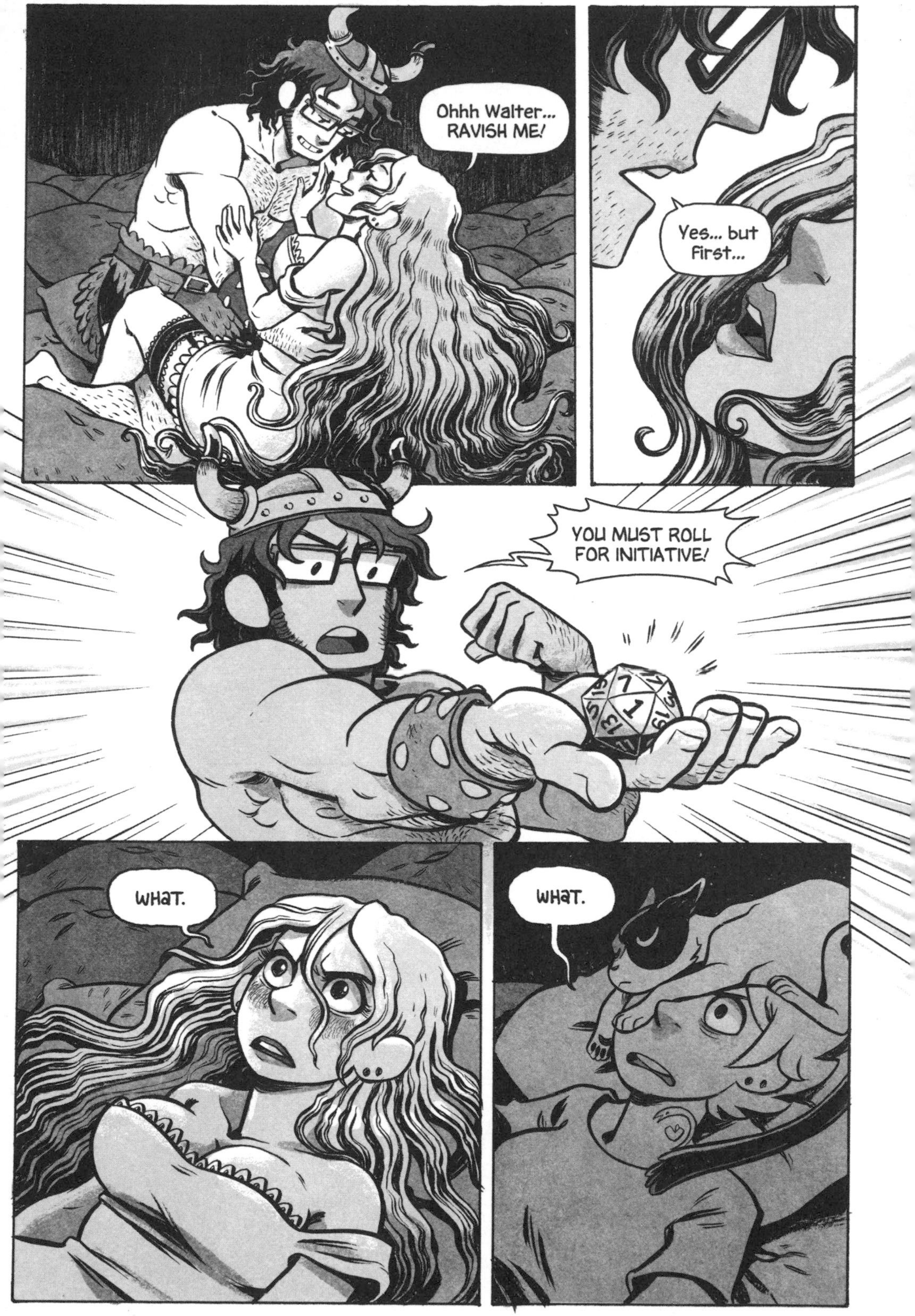
Ohhh Walter... RAVISH ME!
Yes... but first...
YOU MUST ROLL FOR INITIATIVE!
WHAT.
WHAT.

DRAW YOUR CHARACTER HERE!

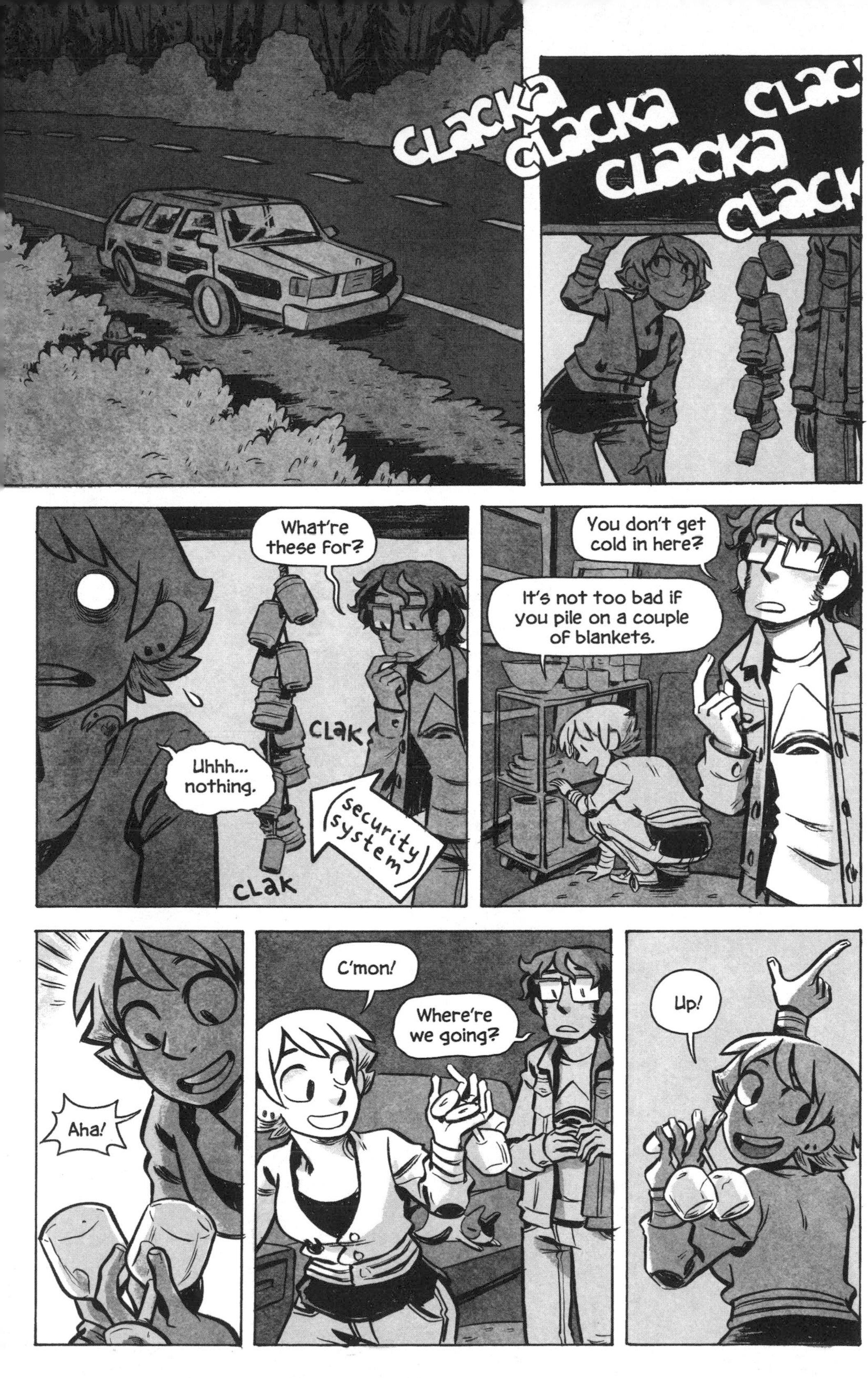
CLACKA CLACKA CLACKA CLACKA CLACK CLACK
What're these for?
Uhhh... nothing.
CLAK
CLAK
security system
You don't get cold in here?
It's not too bad if you pile on a couple of blankets.
Aha!
C'mon!
Where're we going?
Up!

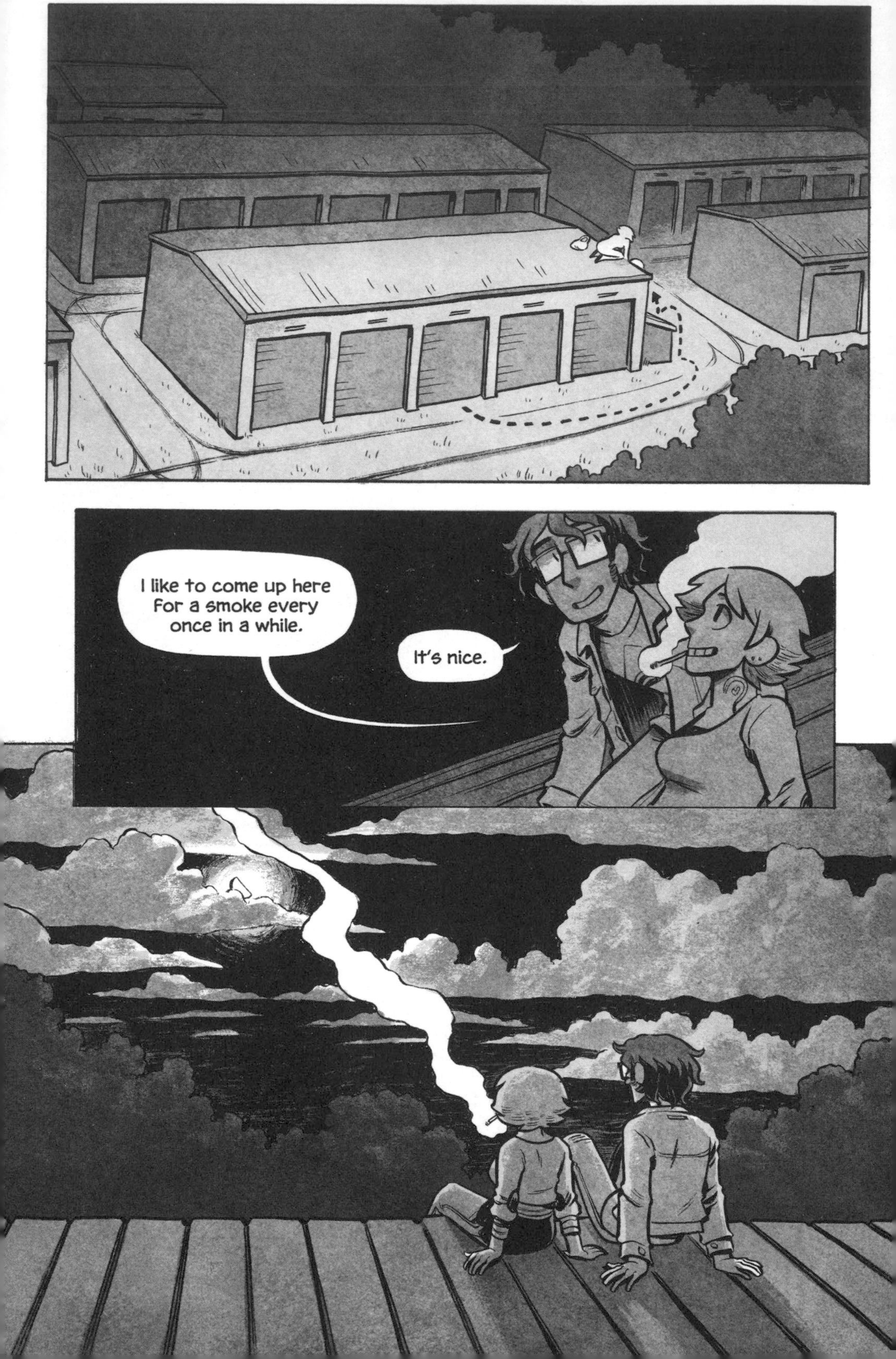
I like to come up here for a smoke every once in a while.
It's nice.

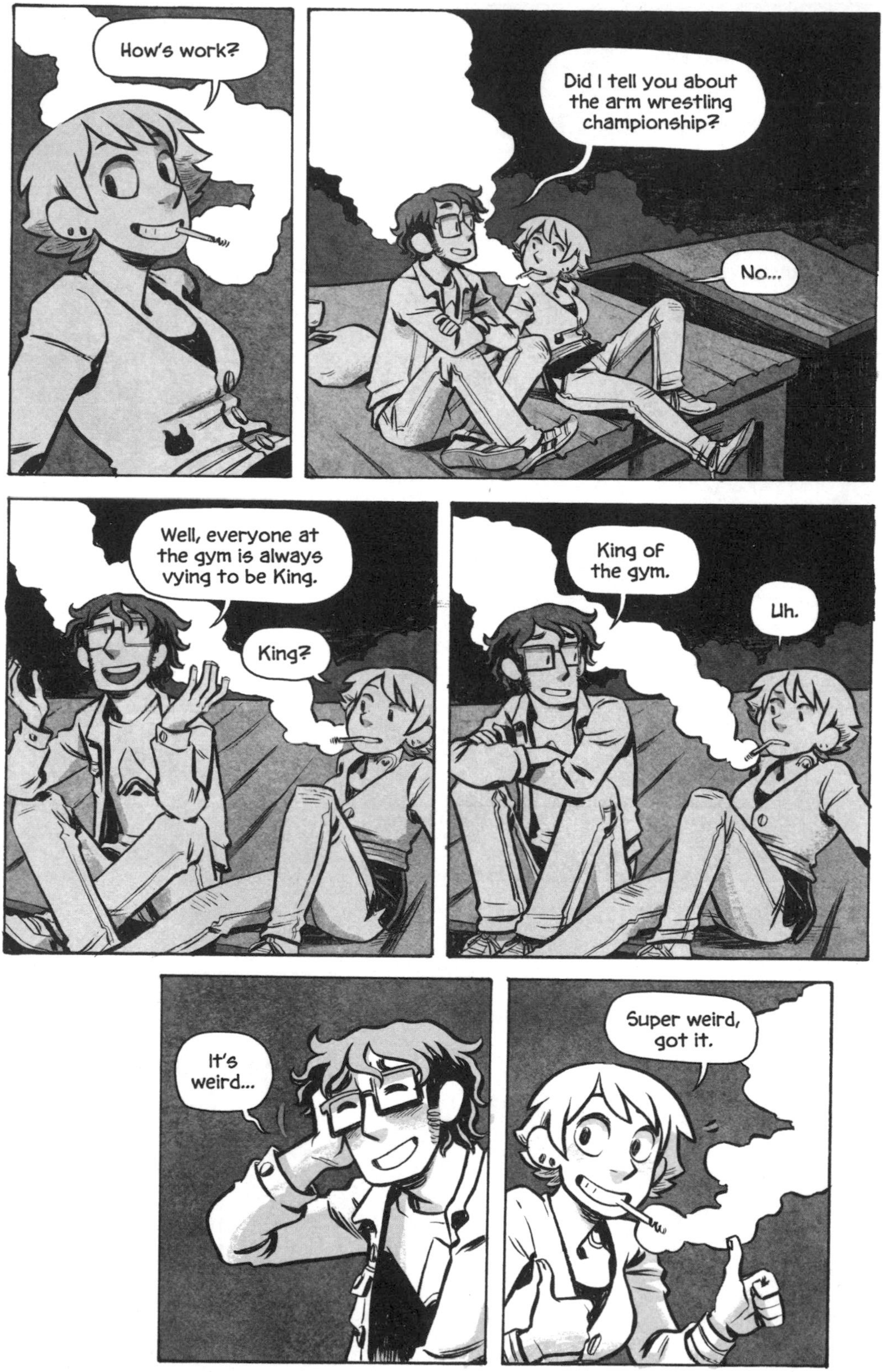
How's work?
Did I tell you about the arm wrestling championship?
No...
Well, everyone at the gym is always vying to be King.
King?
King of the gym.
Uh.
It's weird...
Super weird, got it.

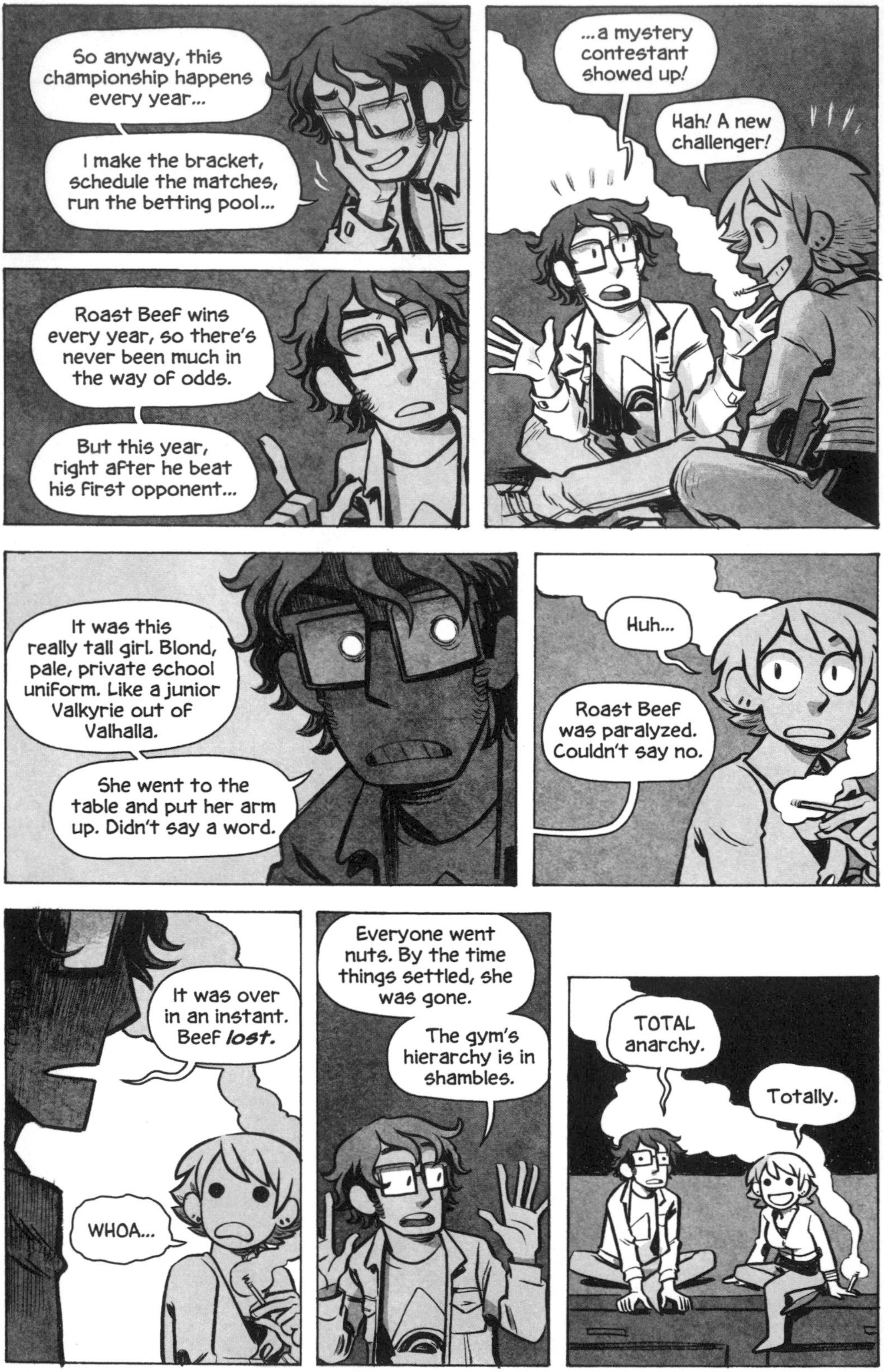
So anyway, this championship happens every year...
I make the bracket, schedule the matches, run the betting pool...
...a mystery contestant showed up!
Hah! A new challenger!
Roast Beef wins every year, so there's never been much in the way of odds.
But this year, right after he beat his first opponent...
It was this really tall girl. Blond, pale, private school uniform. Like a junior Valkyrie out of Valhalla.
She went to the table and put her arm up. Didn't say a word.
Huh...
Roast Beef was paralyzed. Couldn't say no.
It was over in an instant. Beef *lost.*
WHOA...
Everyone went nuts. By the time things settled, she was gone.
The gym's hierarchy is in shambles.
TOTAL anarchy.
Totally.

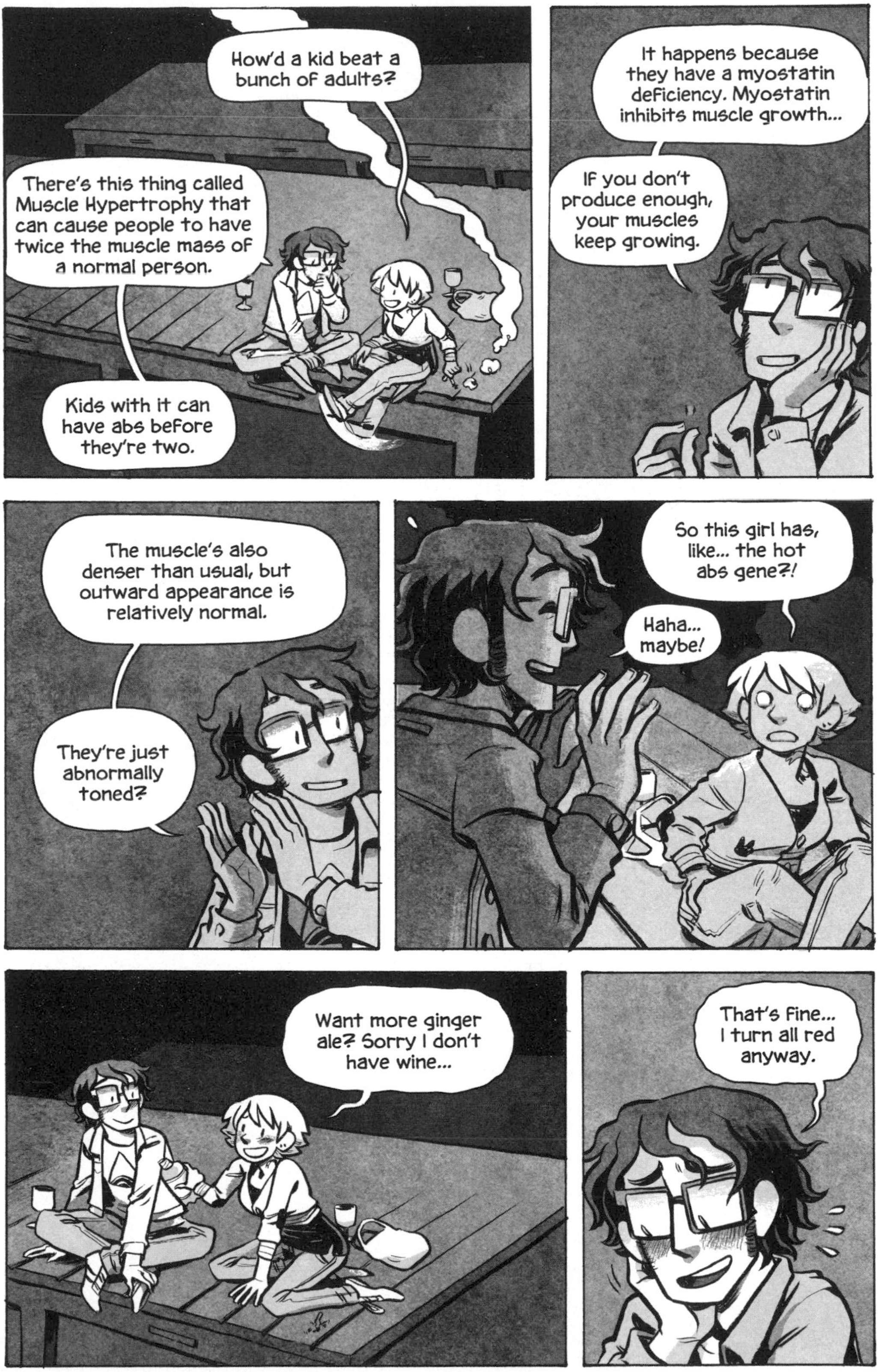
How'd a kid beat a bunch of adults?
There's this thing called Muscle Hypertrophy that can cause people to have twice the muscle mass of a normal person.
Kids with it can have abs before they're two.
It happens because they have a myostatin deficiency. Myostatin inhibits muscle growth...
If you don't produce enough, your muscles keep growing.
The muscle's also denser than usual, but outward appearance is relatively normal.
They're just abnormally toned?
So this girl has, like... the hot abs gene?!
Haha... maybe!
Want more ginger ale? Sorry I don't have wine...
That's fine... I turn all red anyway.

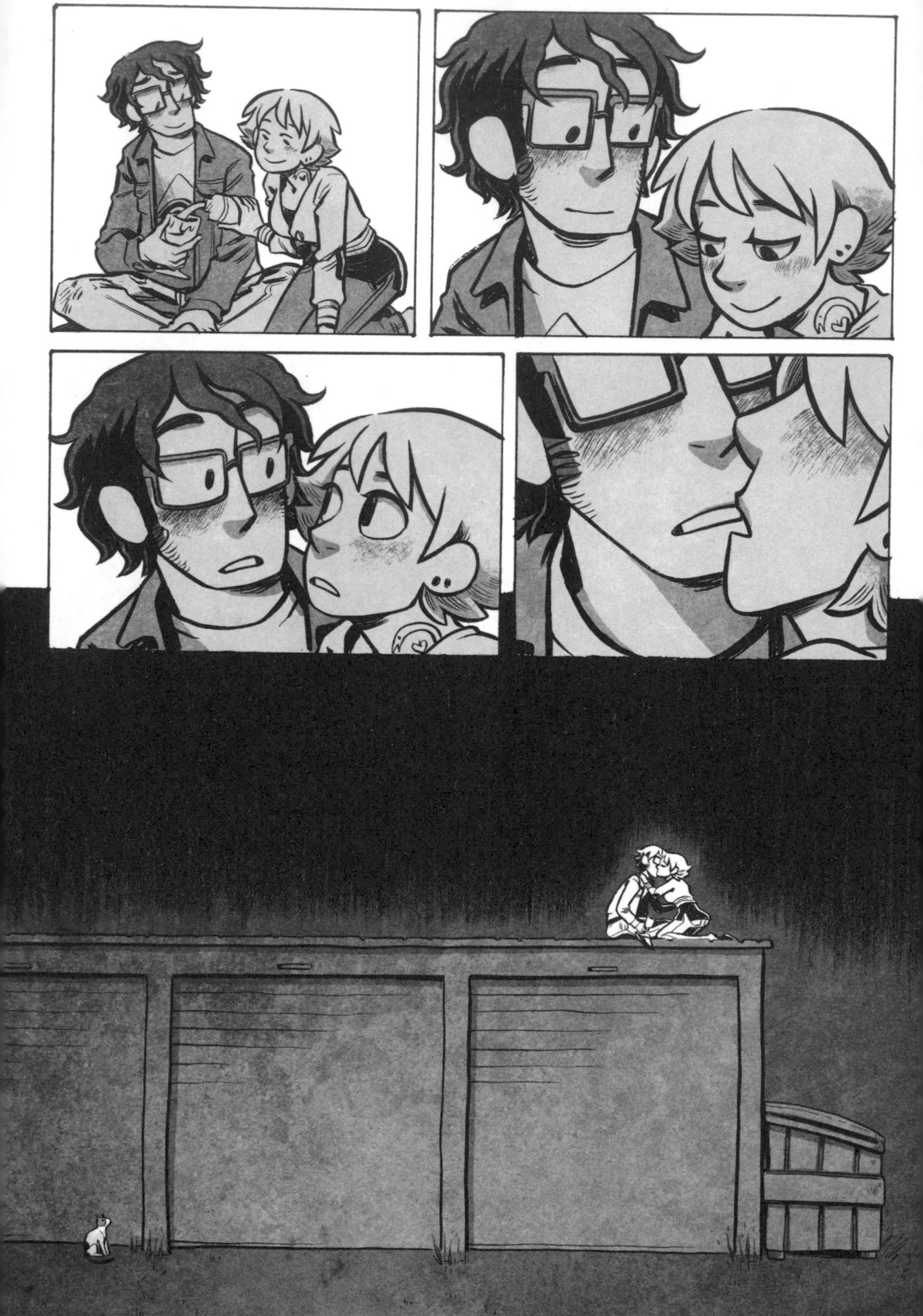

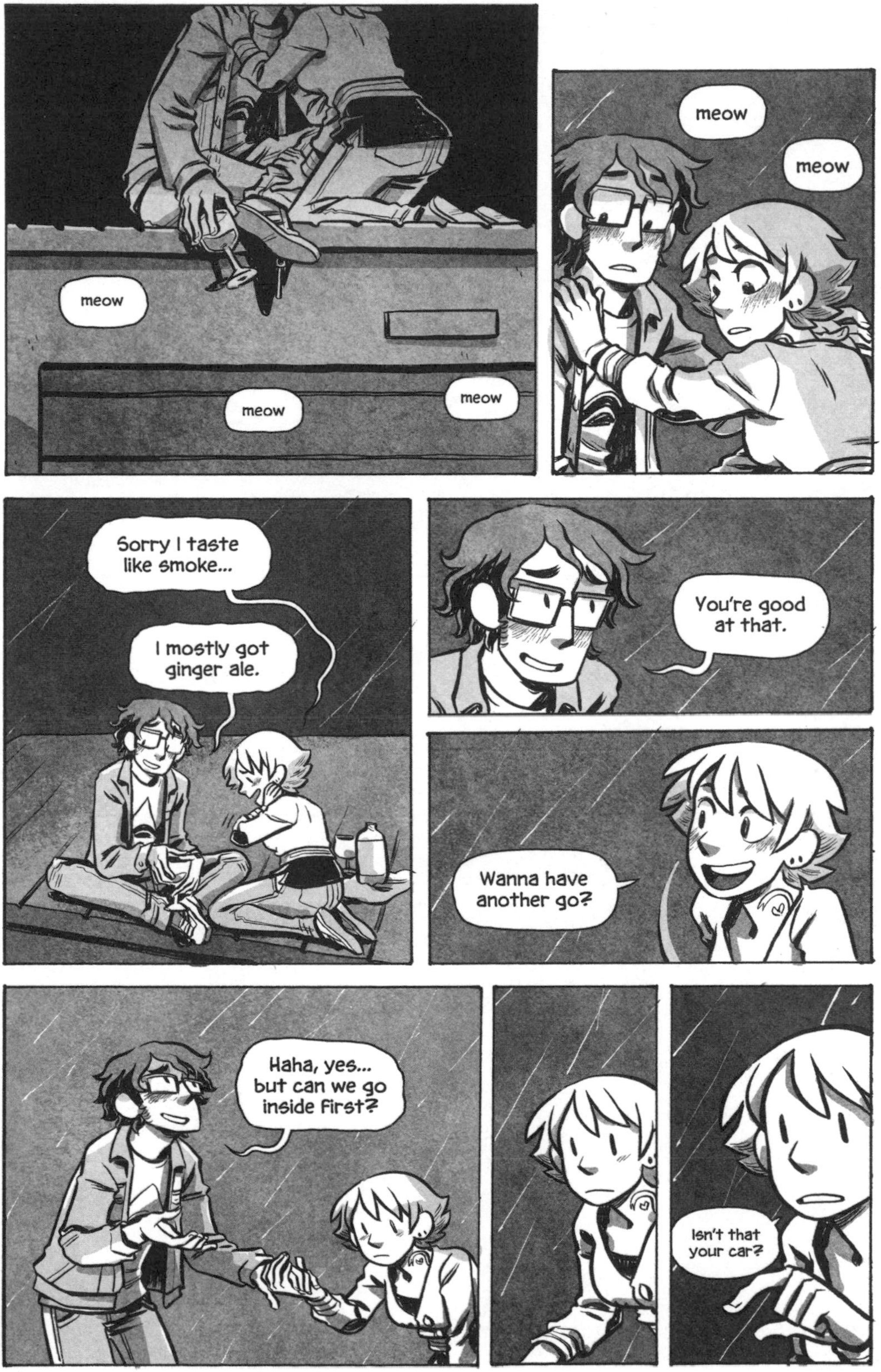
meow
meow
meow
meow
meow
Sorry I taste like smoke...
I mostly got ginger ale.
You're good at that.
Wanna have another go?
Haha, yes... but can we go inside first?
Isn't that your car?

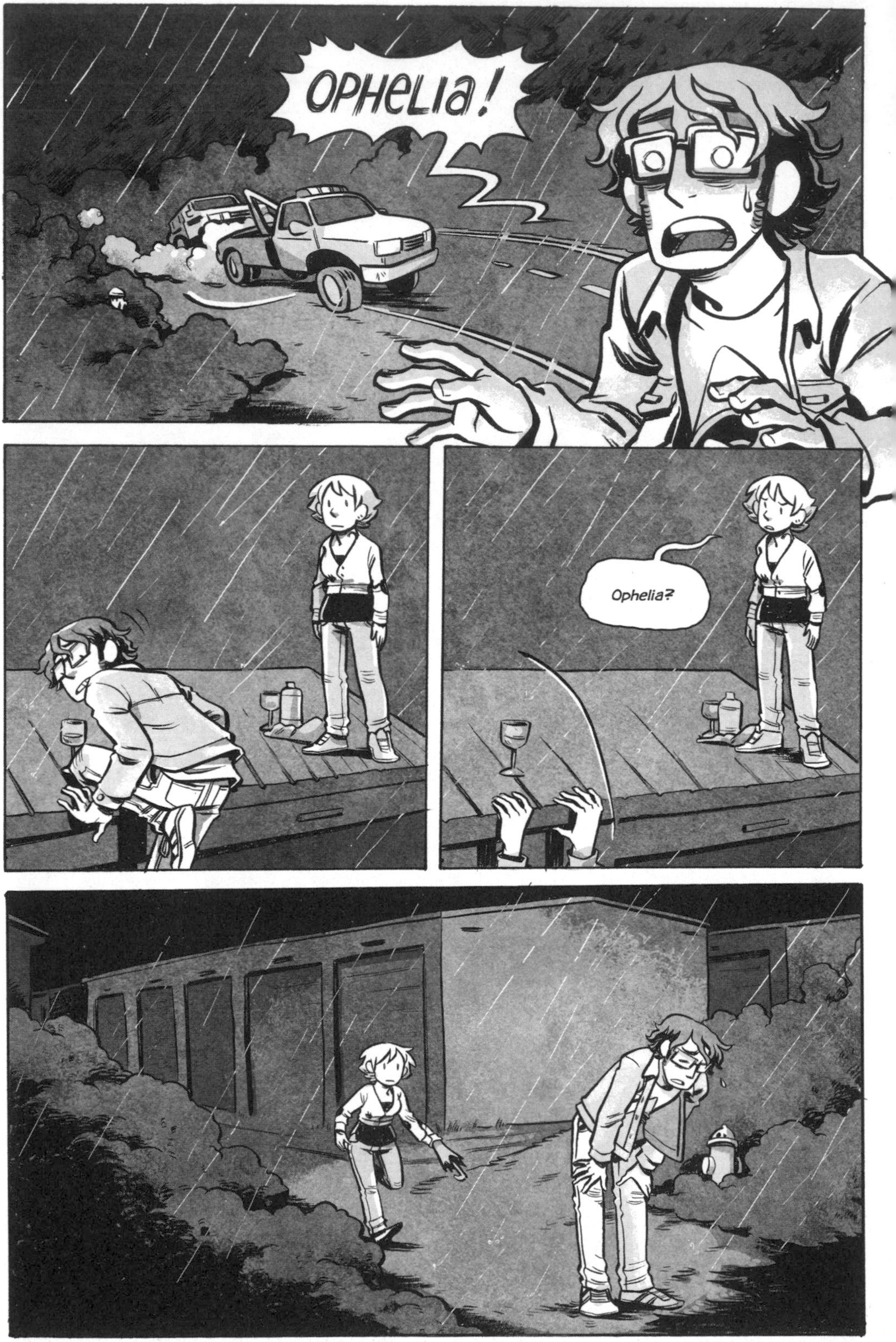
OPHELIA!
Ophelia?

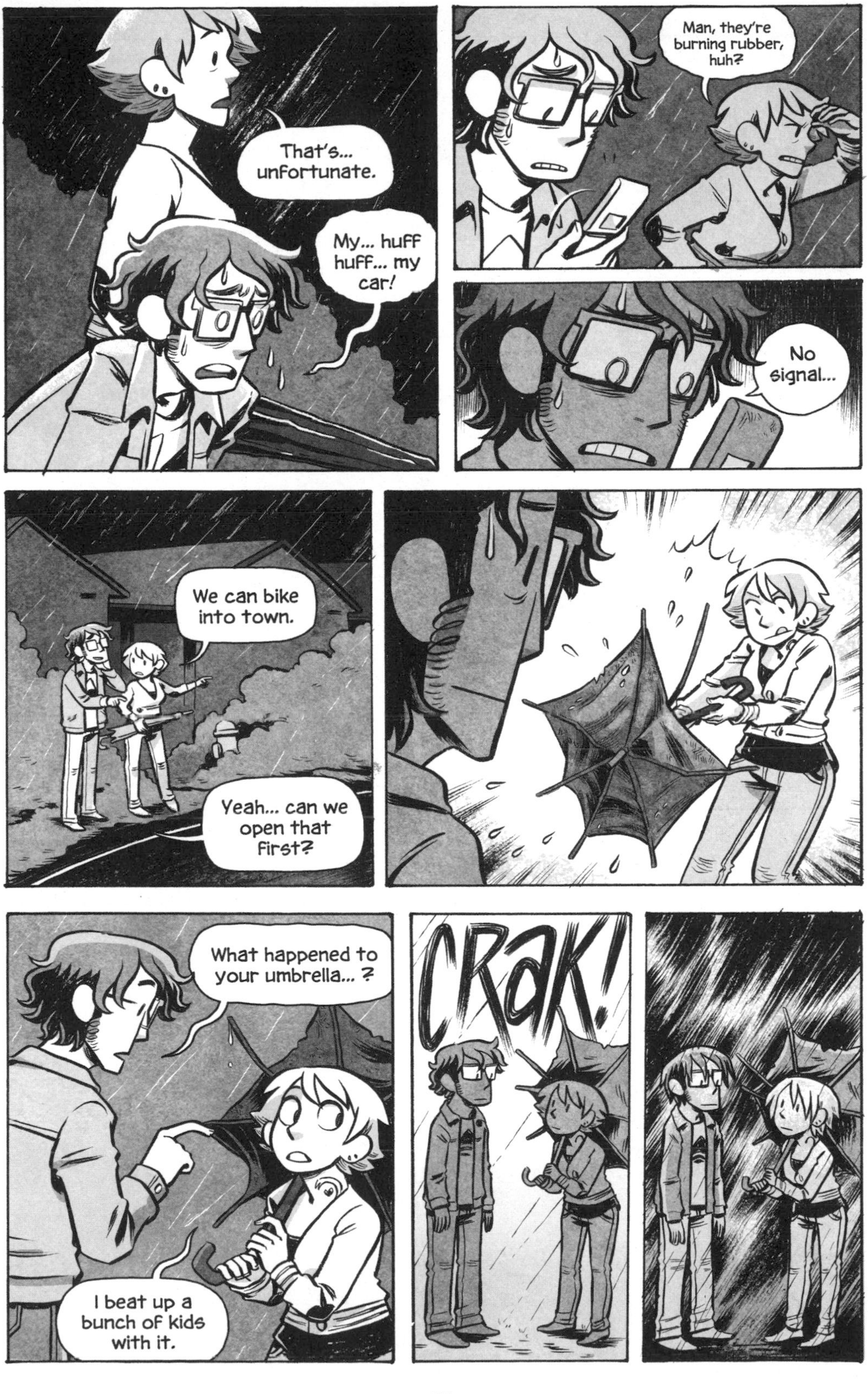
That's... unfortunate.
My... huff huff... my car!
Man, they're burning rubber, huh?
No signal...
We can bike into town.
Yeah... can we open that first?
What happened to your umbrella... ?
I beat up a bunch of kids with it.
CRAK!

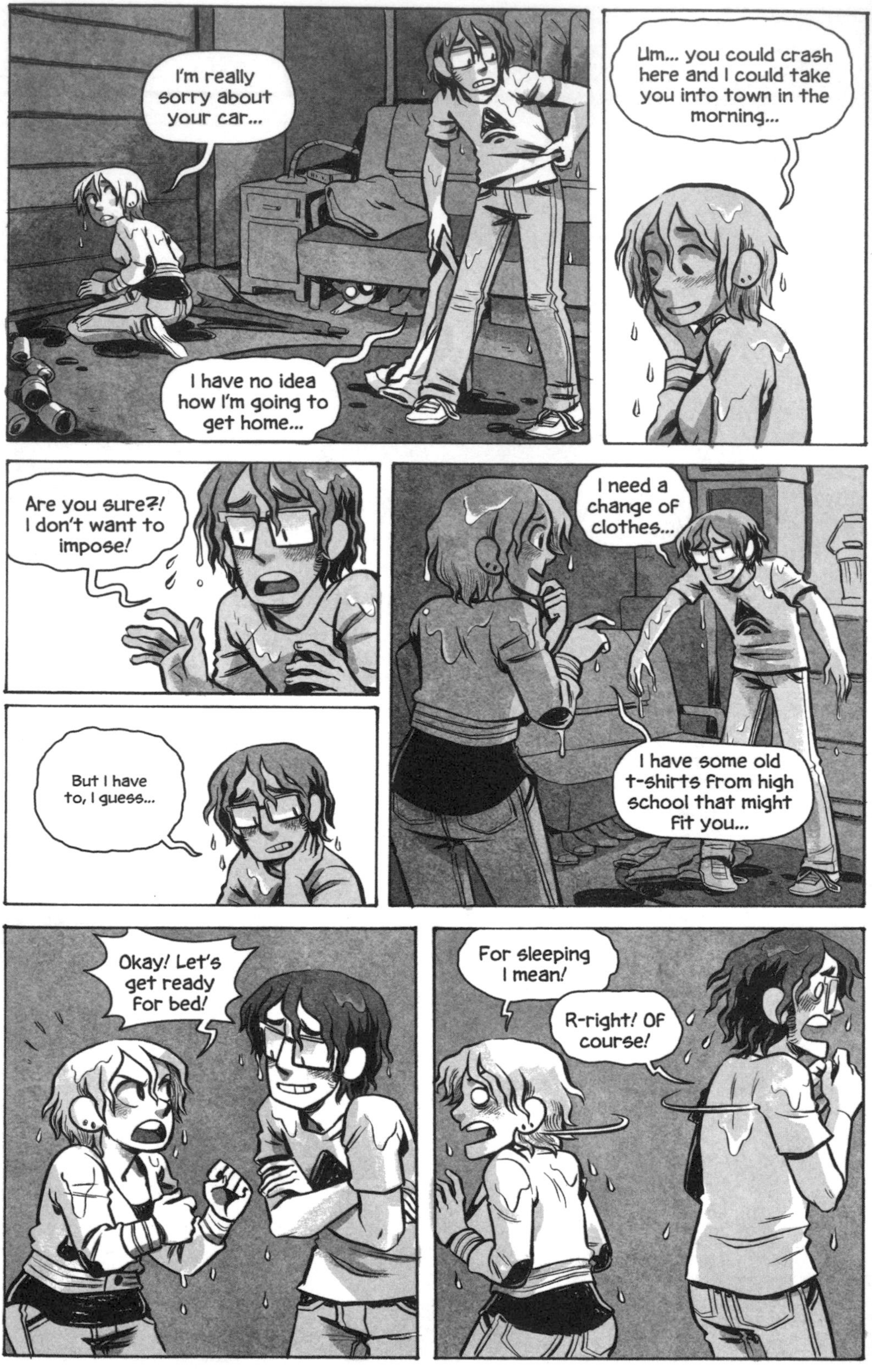
I'm really sorry about your car...
I have no idea how I'm going to get home...
Um... you could crash here and I could take you into town in the morning...
Are you sure?! I don't want to impose!
But I have to, I guess...
I need a change of clothes...
I have some old t-shirts from high school that might fit you...
Okay! Let's get ready for bed!
For sleeping I mean!
R-right! Of course!

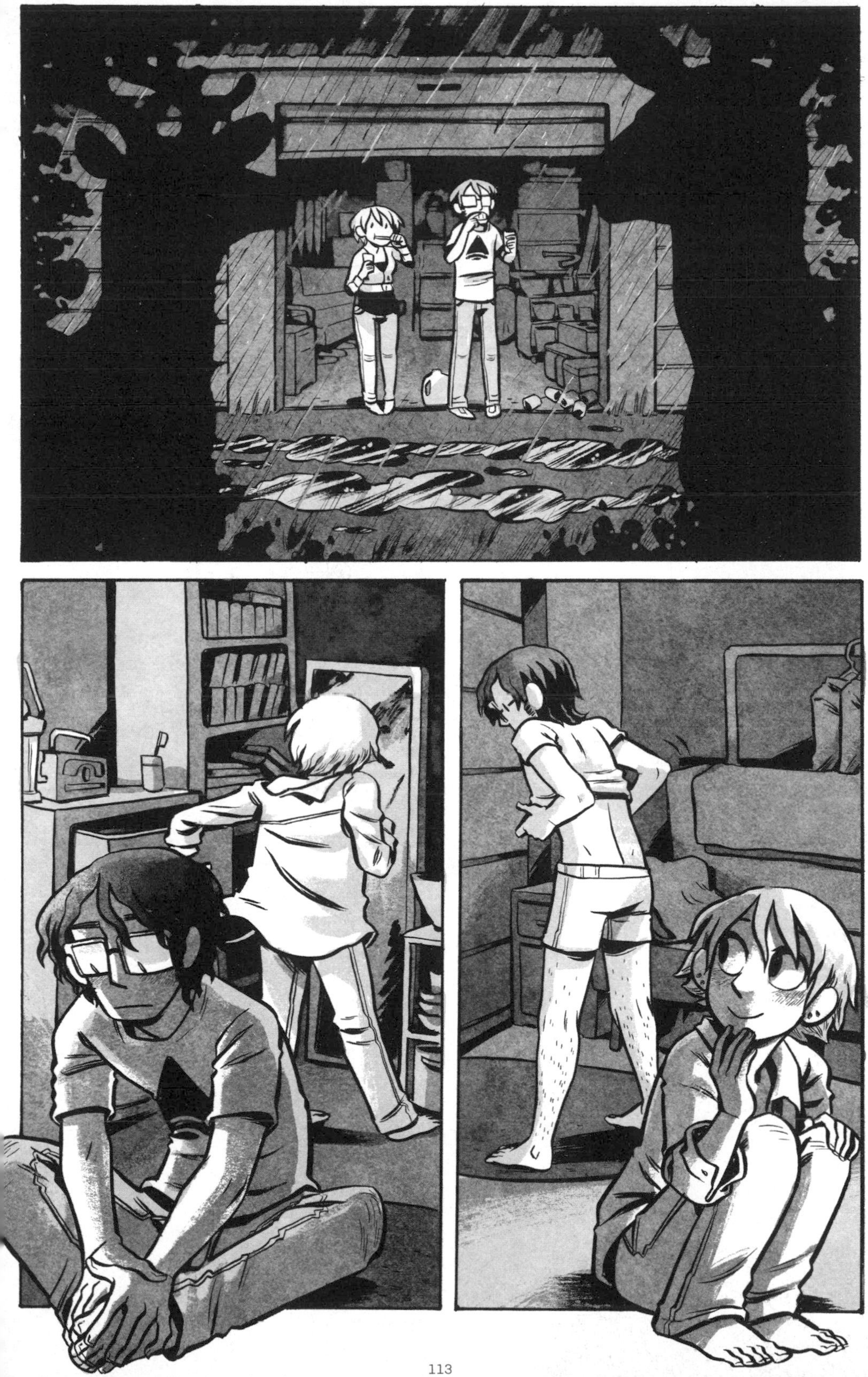

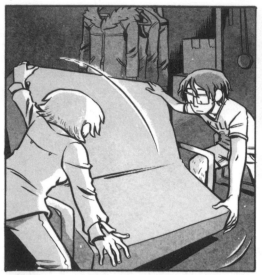

I only have one pillow, sooo...

G'night, Walter.

Night, Penny.

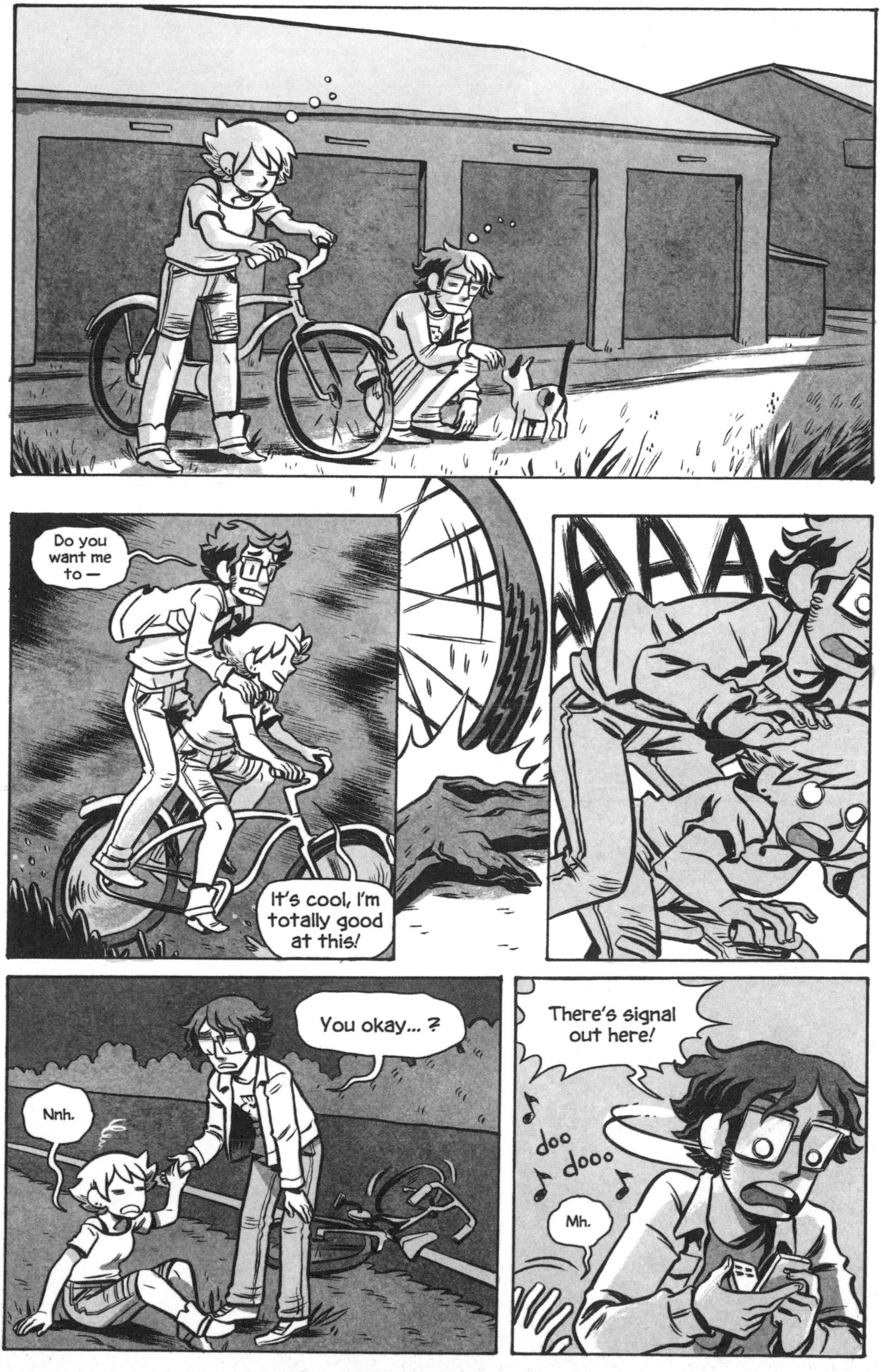

Do you want me to —
It's cool, I'm totally good at this!
AAAA
You okay... ?
Nnh.
There's signal out here!
doo dooo
Mh.

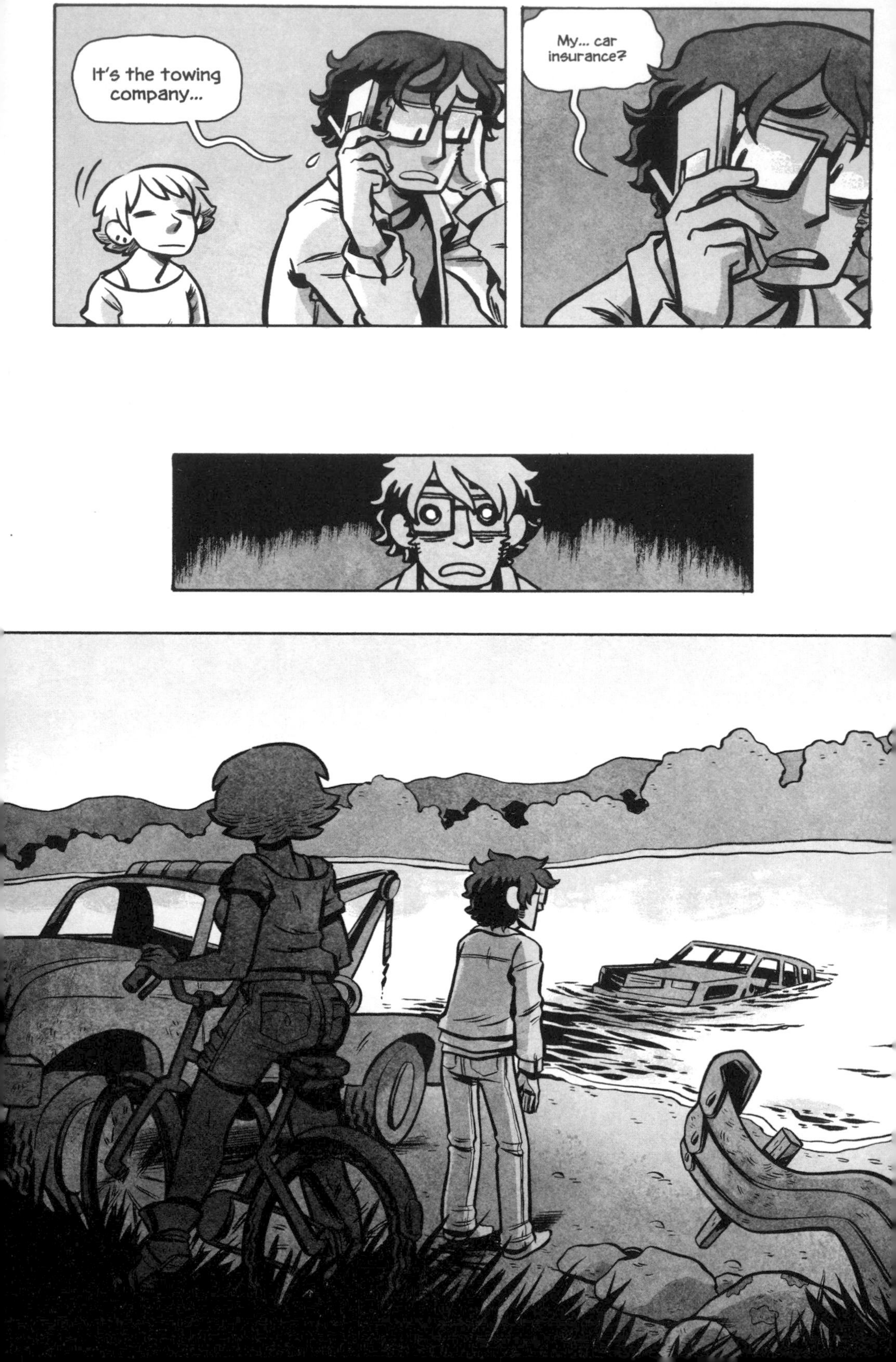
It's the towing company...
My... car insurance?

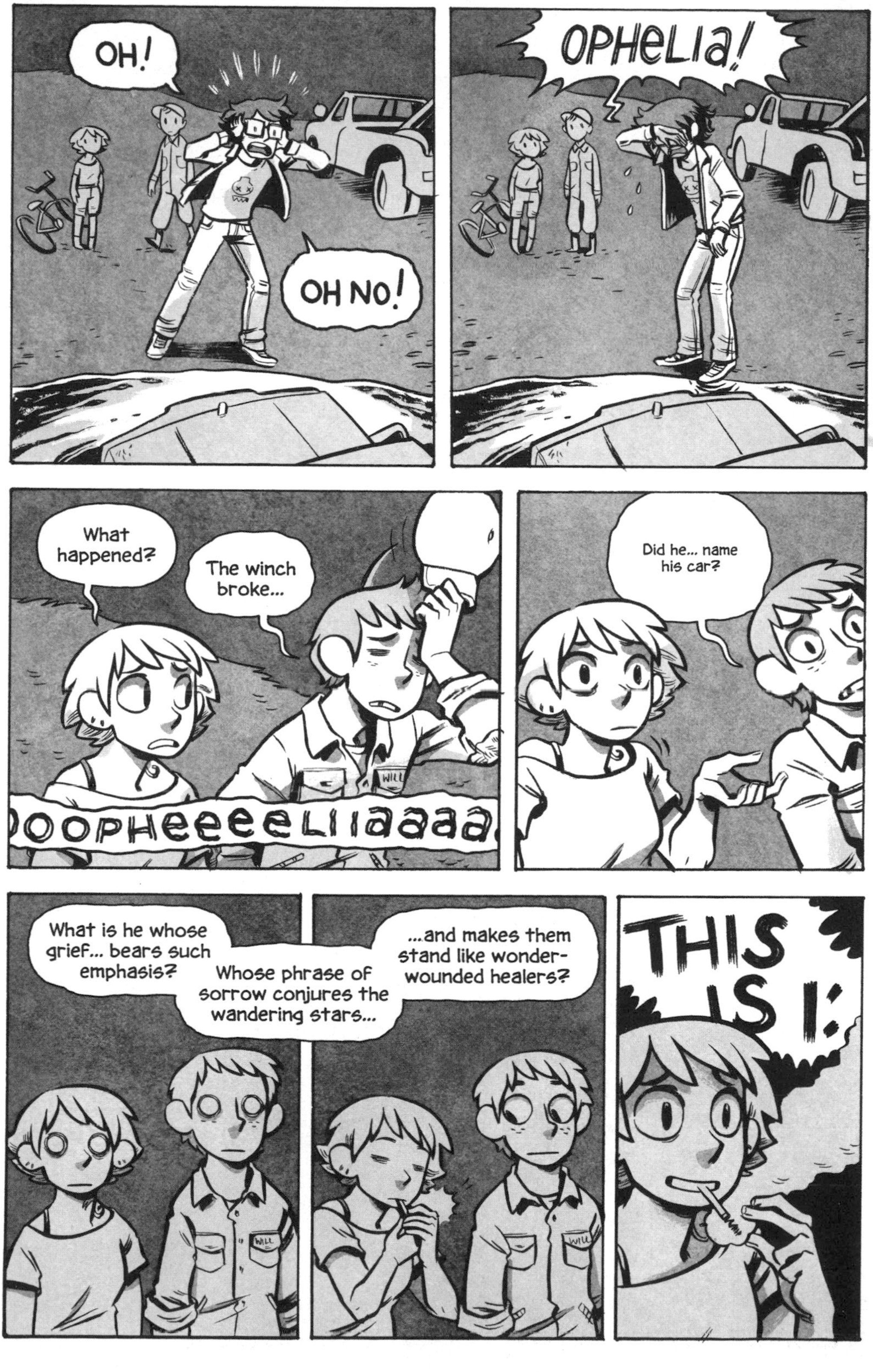
OH!
OH NO!
OPHELIA!
What happened?
The winch broke...
OOPHEEEELIIAAAA
Did he... name his car?
What is he whose grief... bears such emphasis?
Whose phrase of sorrow conjures the wandering stars...
...and makes them stand like wonder-wounded healers?
THIS IS I:

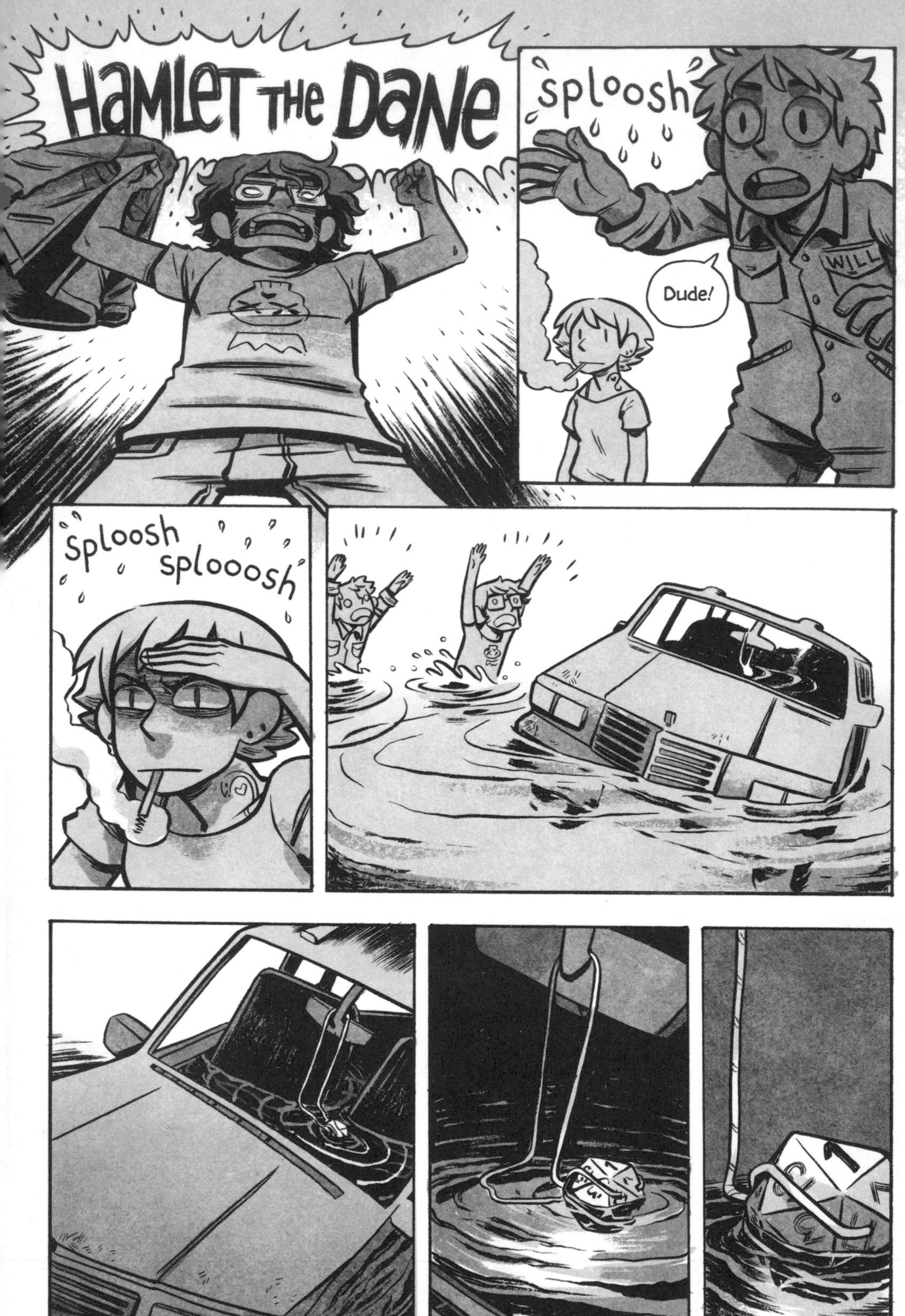
HAMLET THE DANE
sploosh
WILL
Dude!
sploosh
sploooosh

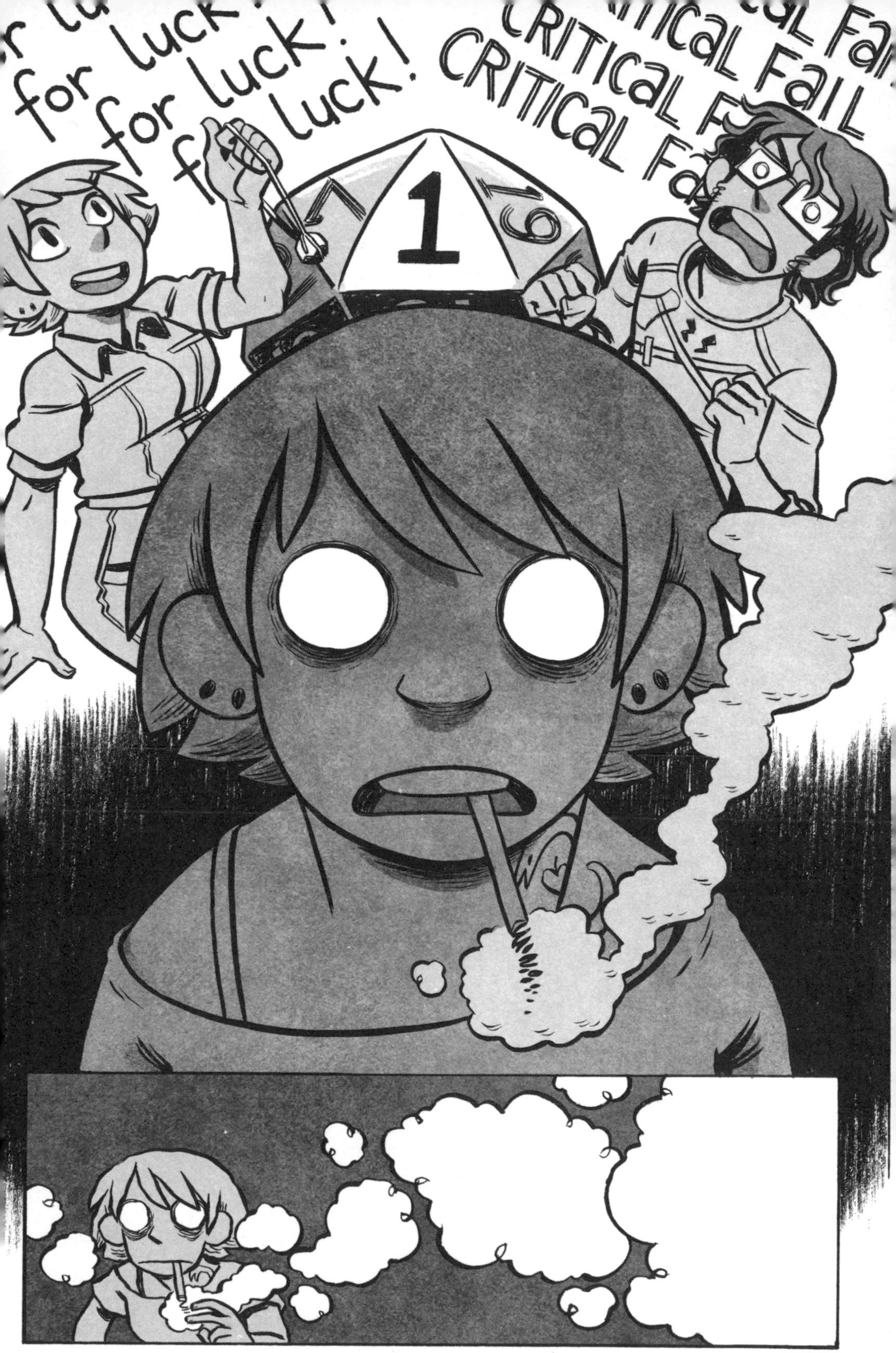
for luck!
for luck!
for luck!
for luck!
CRITICAL FAIL
CRITICAL FAIL
CRITICAL FAIL
1

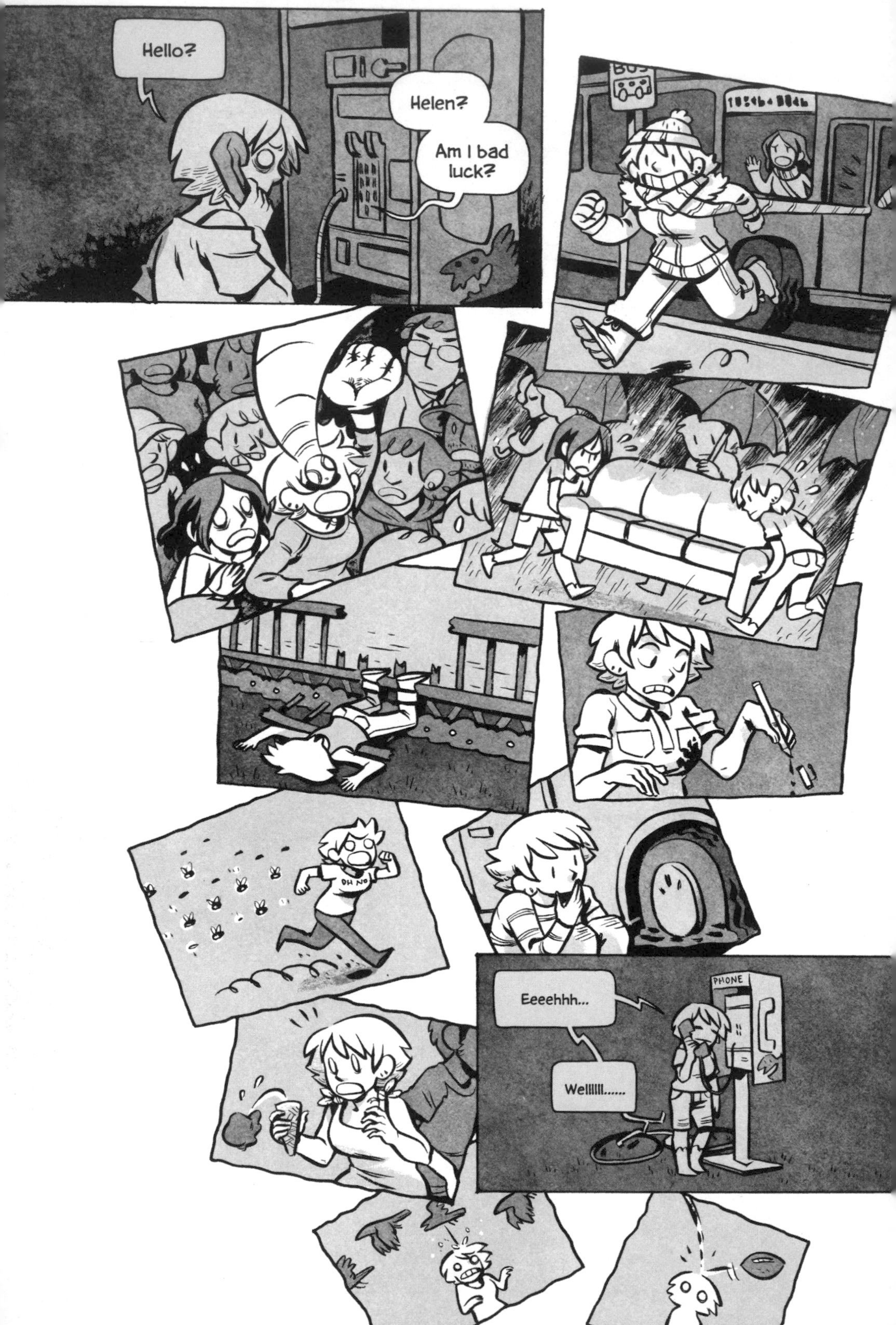
Hello?
Helen?
Am I bad luck?
BUS
OH NO
PHONE
Eeeehhh...
Welllll......

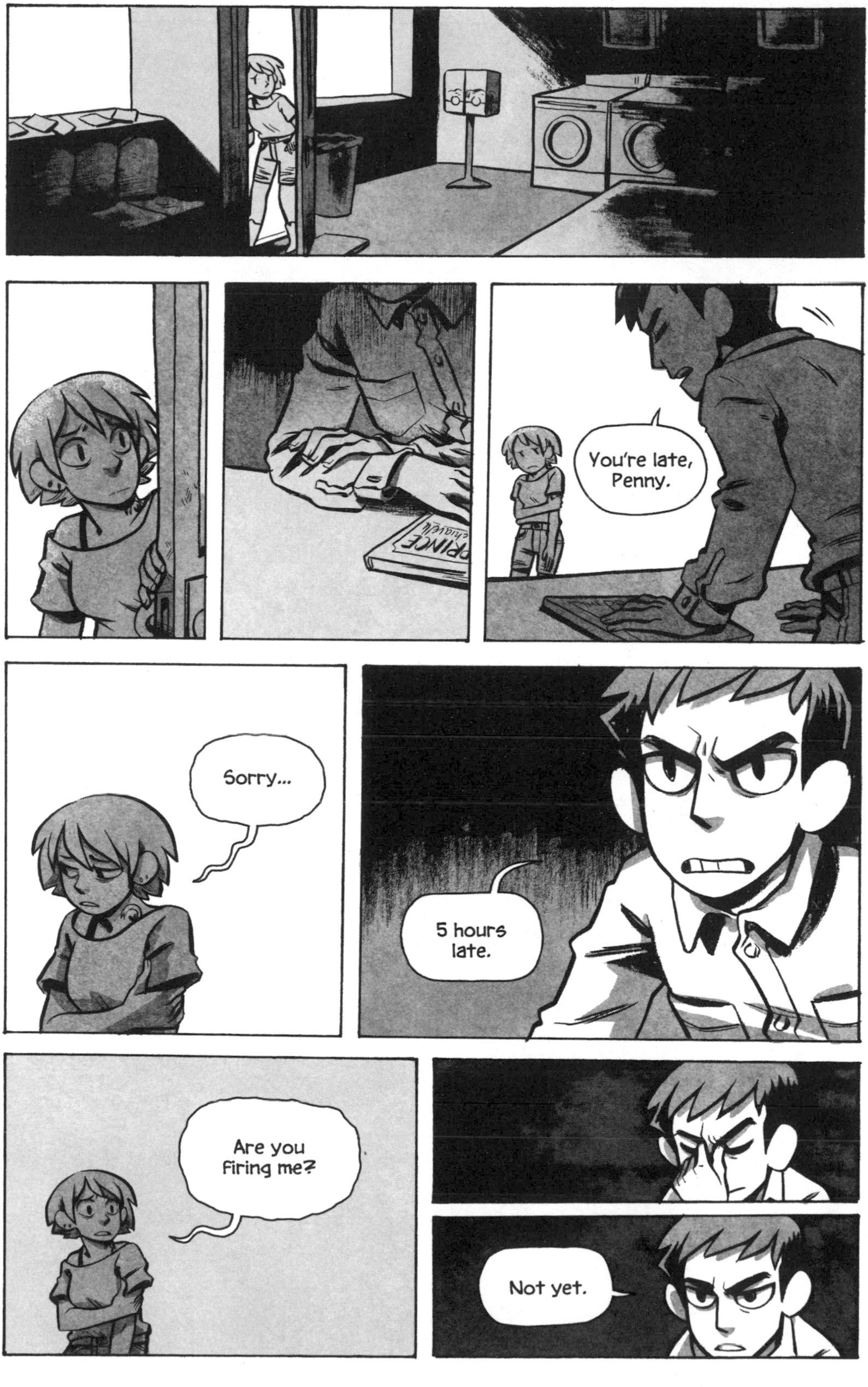
PRINCE
You're late, Penny.
Sorry...
5 hours late.
Are you firing me?
Not yet.

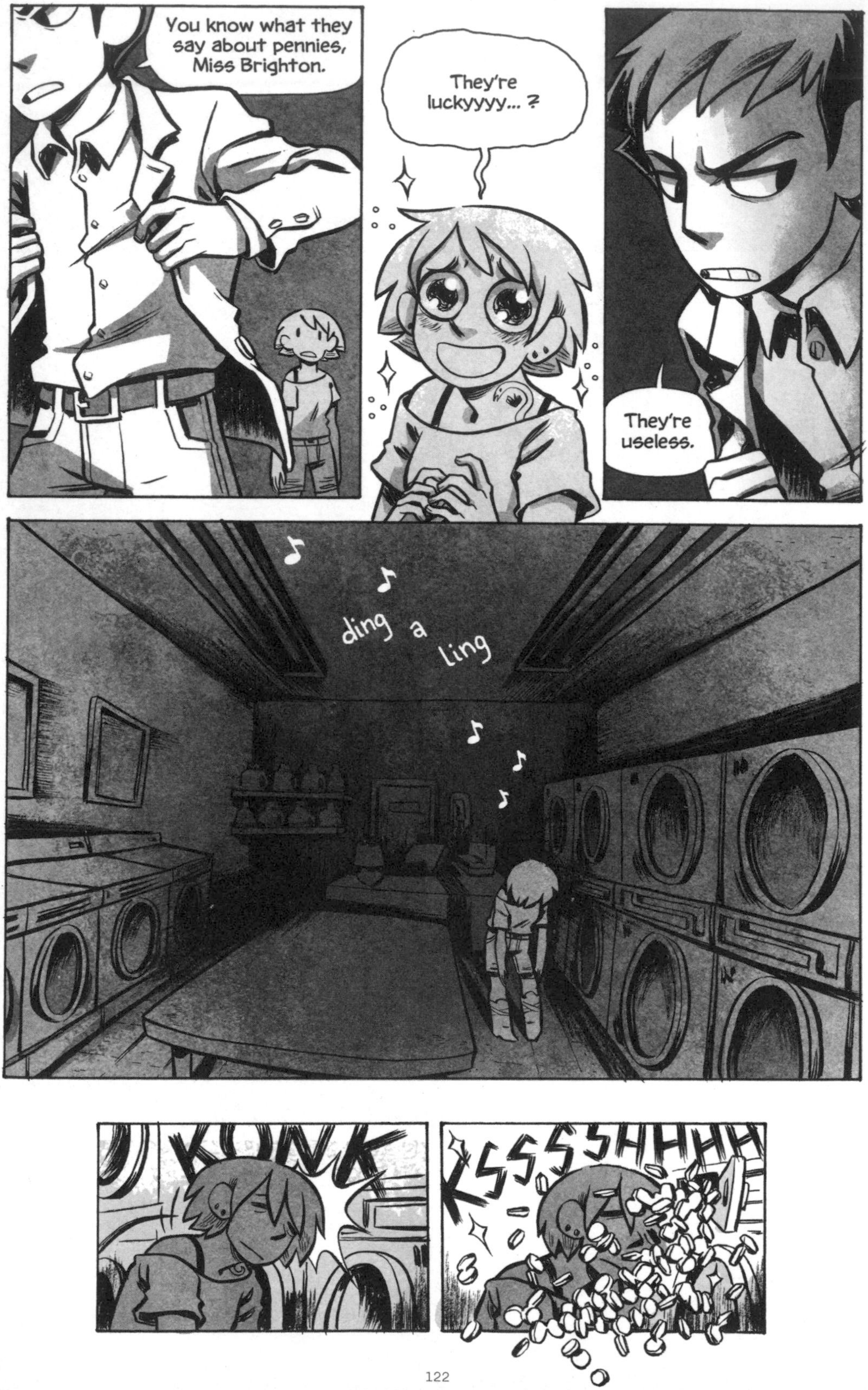
You know what they say about pennies, Miss Brighton.
They're luckyyyy... ?
They're useless.
ding a ling
KONK
KSSSSHHHH

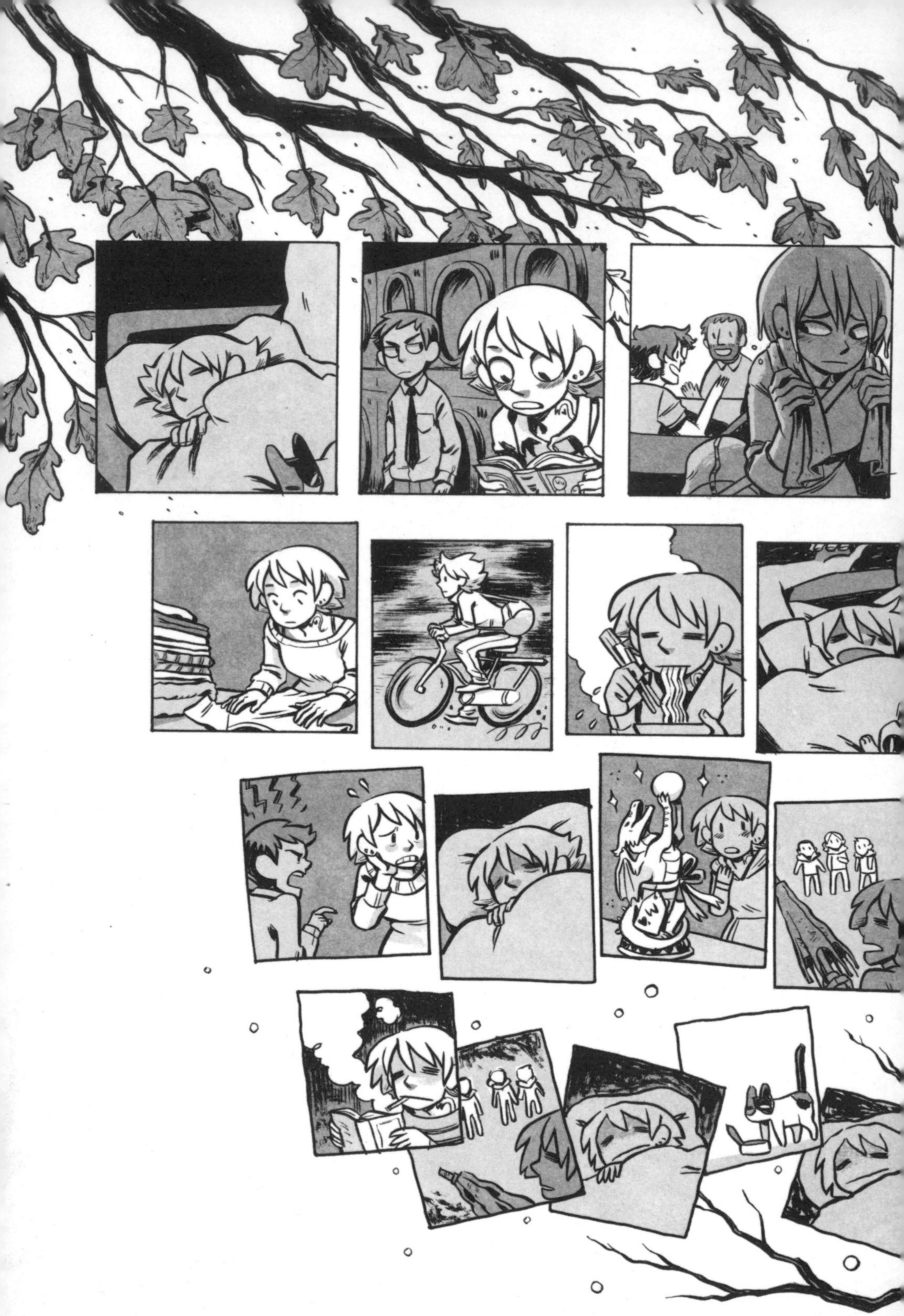

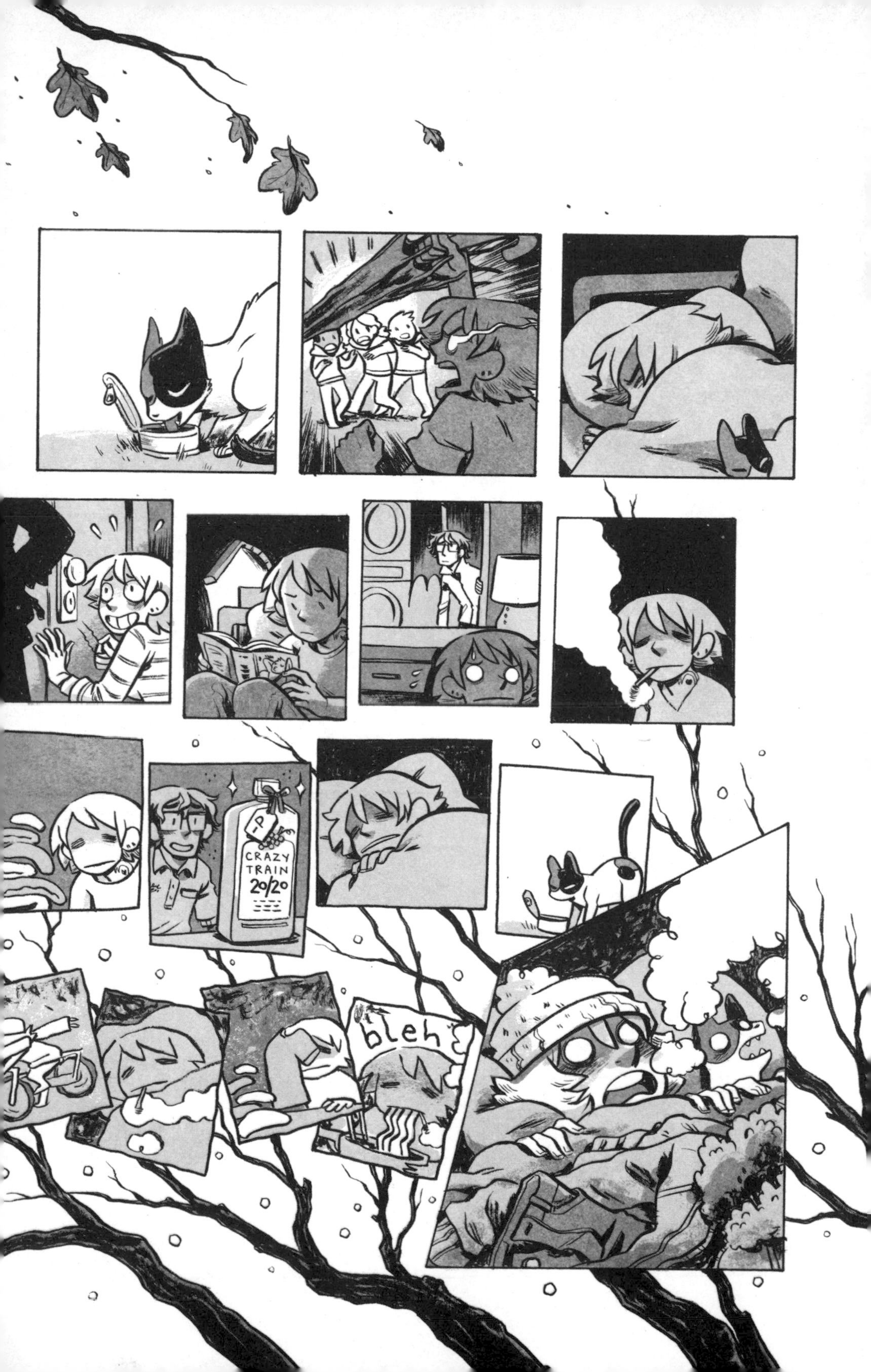
CRAZY TRAIN 20/20
bleh

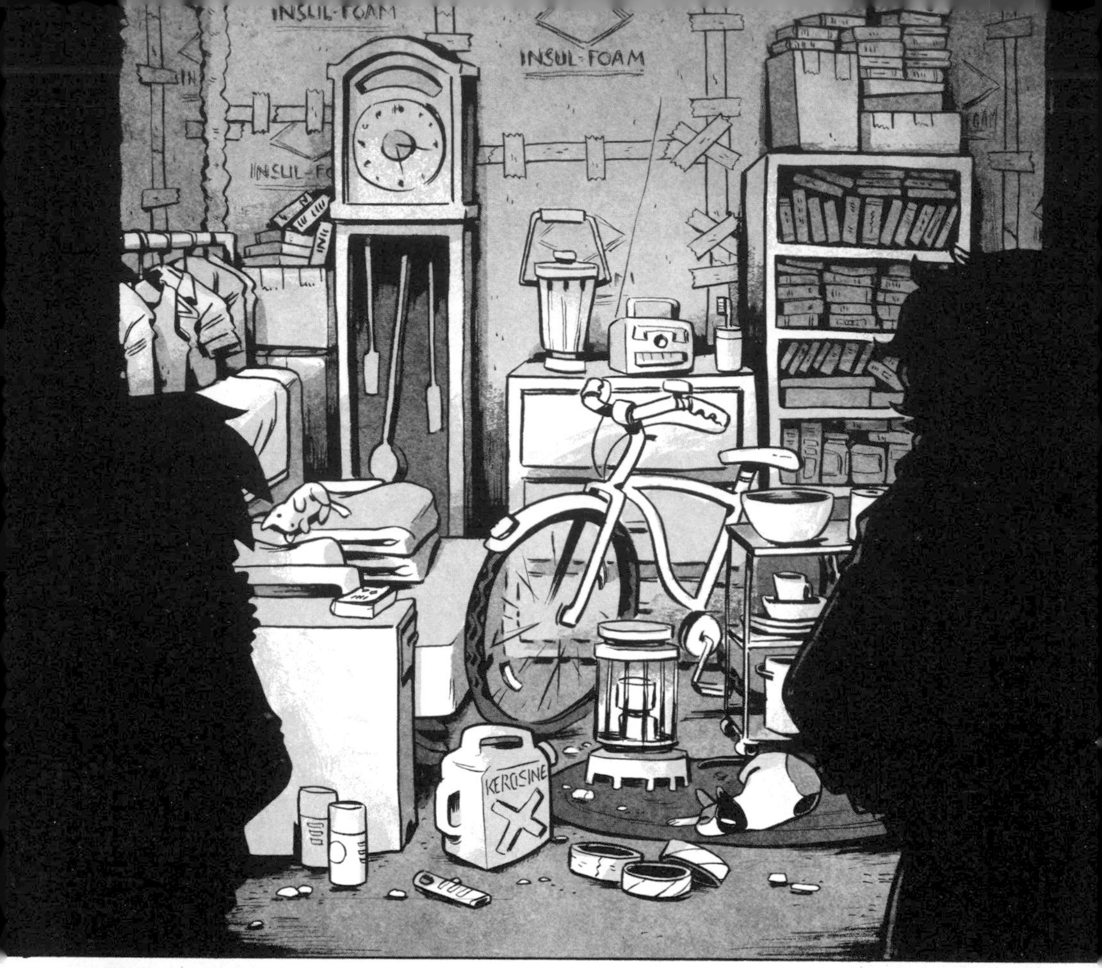
INSUL-FOAM
INSUL-FOAM
INSUL-FOAM
KEROSINE

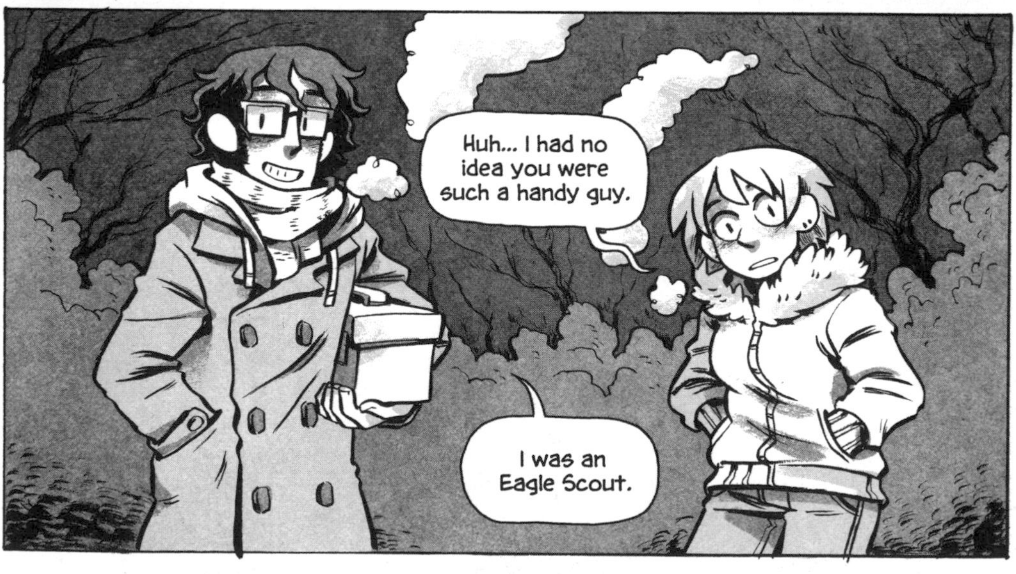
Huh... I had no idea you were such a handy guy.
I was an Eagle Scout.

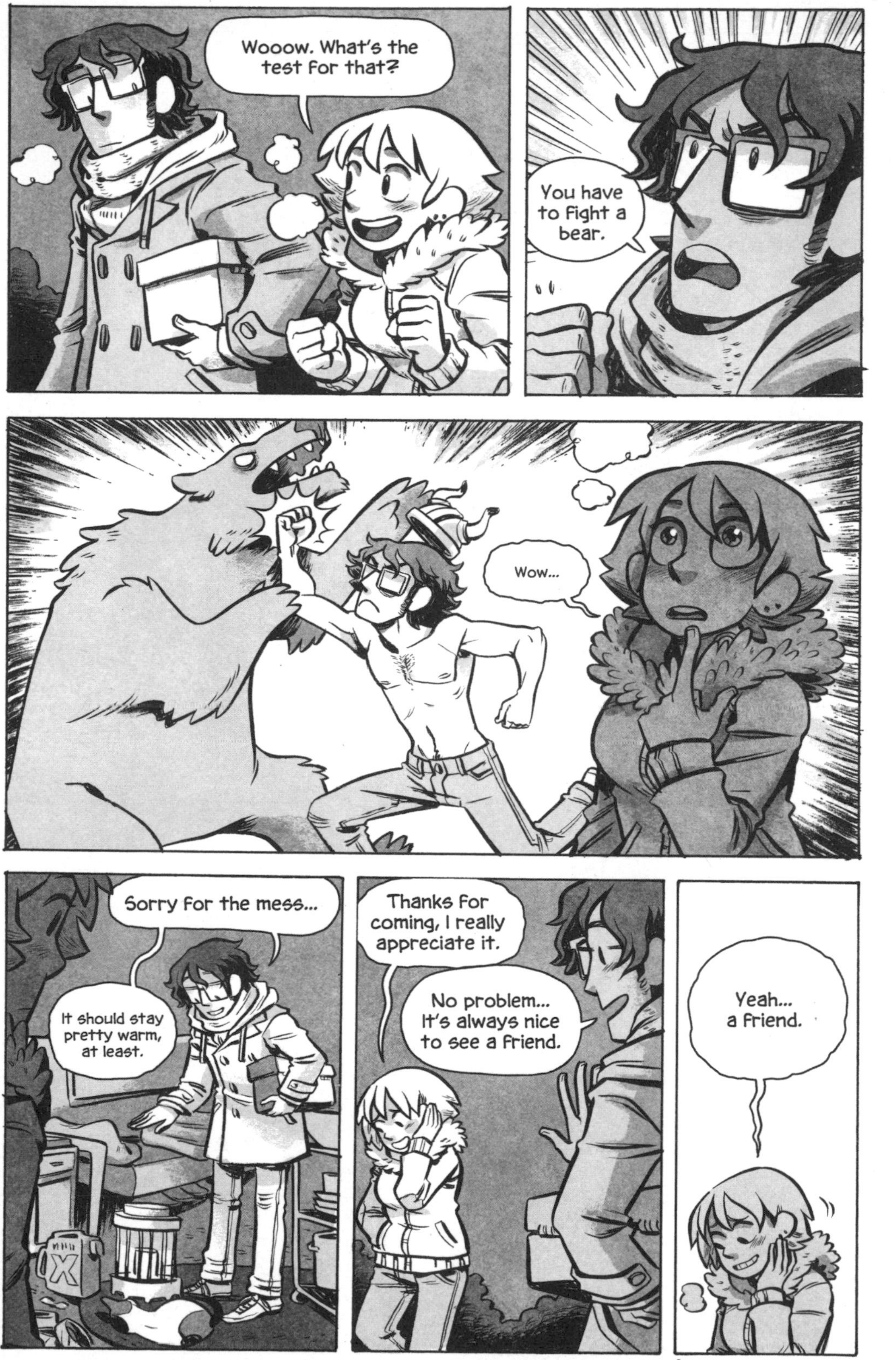
Wooow. What's the test for that?
You have to fight a bear.
Wow...
Sorry for the mess...
It should stay pretty warm, at least.
Thanks for coming, I really appreciate it.
No problem... It's always nice to see a friend.
Yeah... a friend.

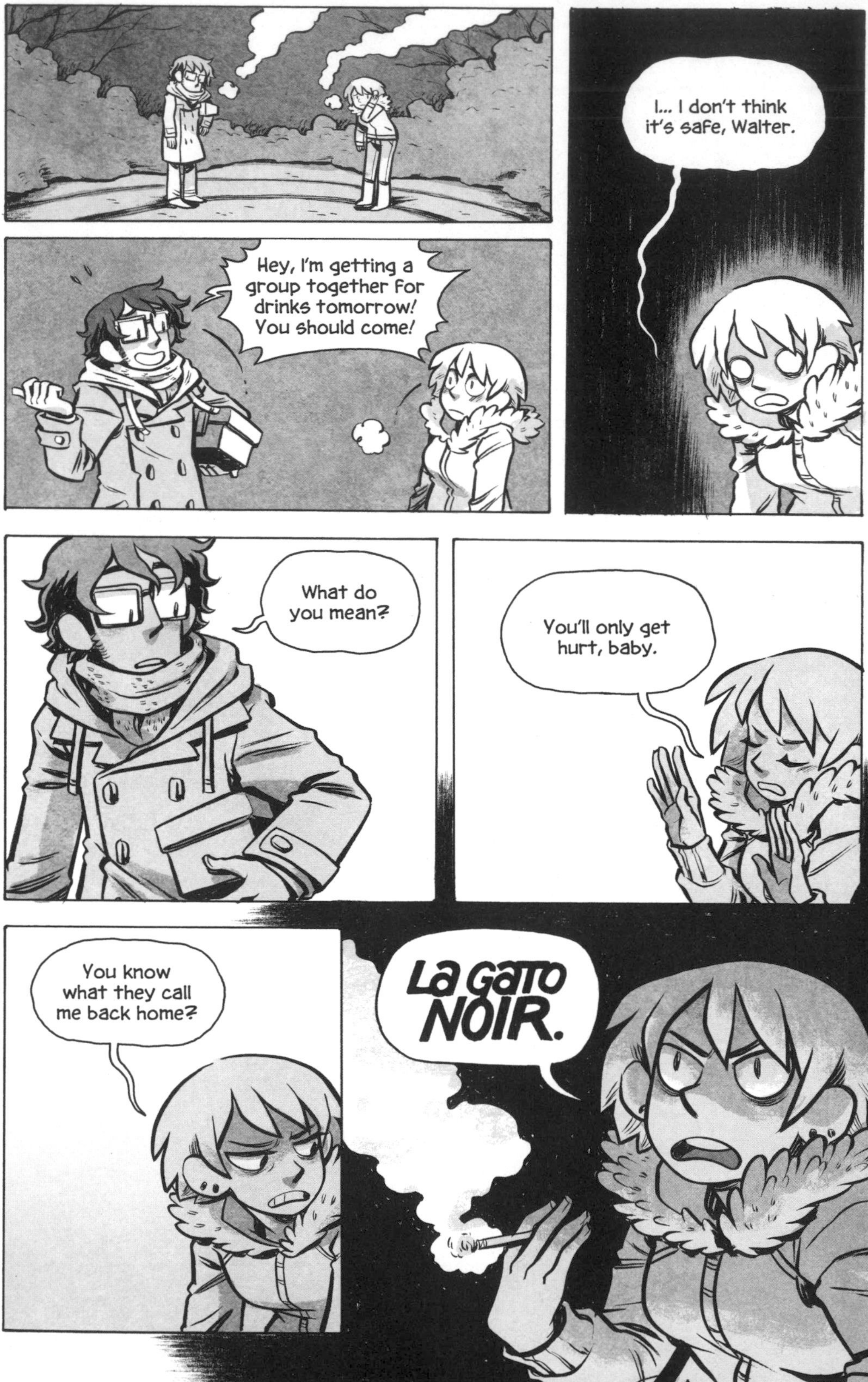
Hey, I'm getting a group together for drinks tomorrow! You should come!
I... I don't think it's safe, Walter.
What do you mean?
You'll only get hurt, baby.
You know what they call me back home?
LA GATO NOIR.

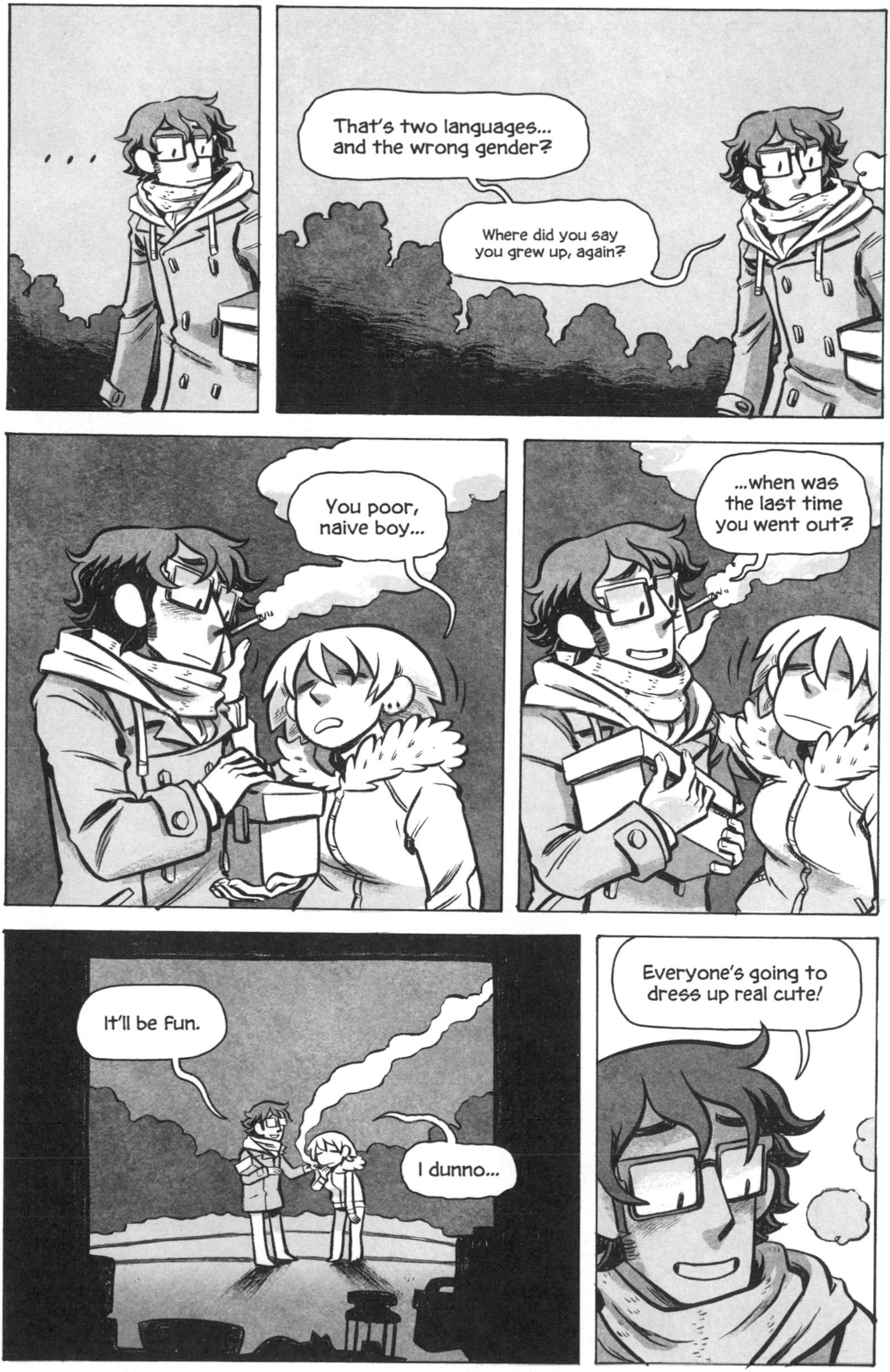
...
That's two languages... and the wrong gender?
Where did you say you grew up, again?
You poor, naive boy...
...when was the last time you went out?
It'll be fun.
I dunno...
Everyone's going to dress up real cute!

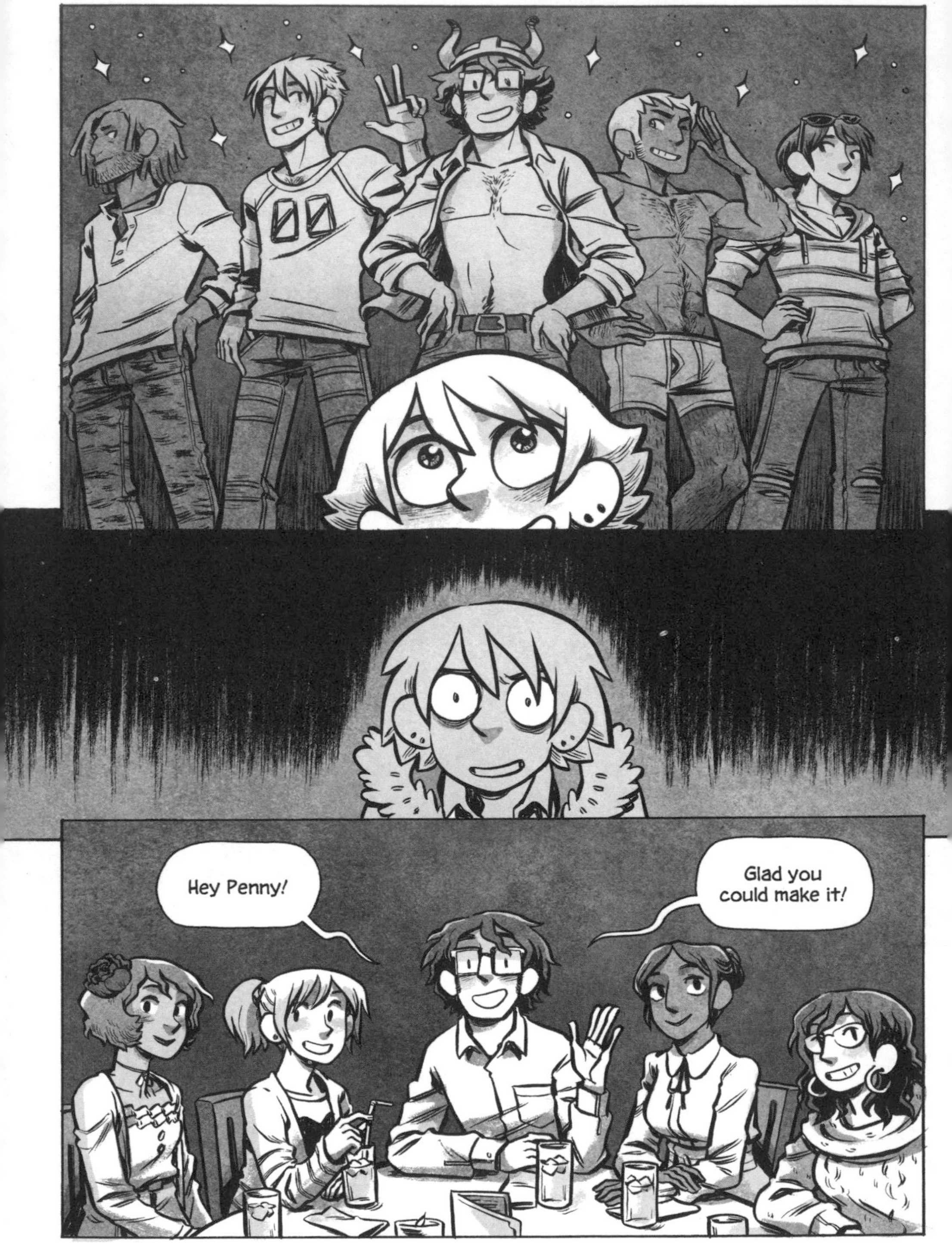
Hey Penny!
Glad you could make it!
THIS SET THE TONE FOR THE REST OF THE EVENING

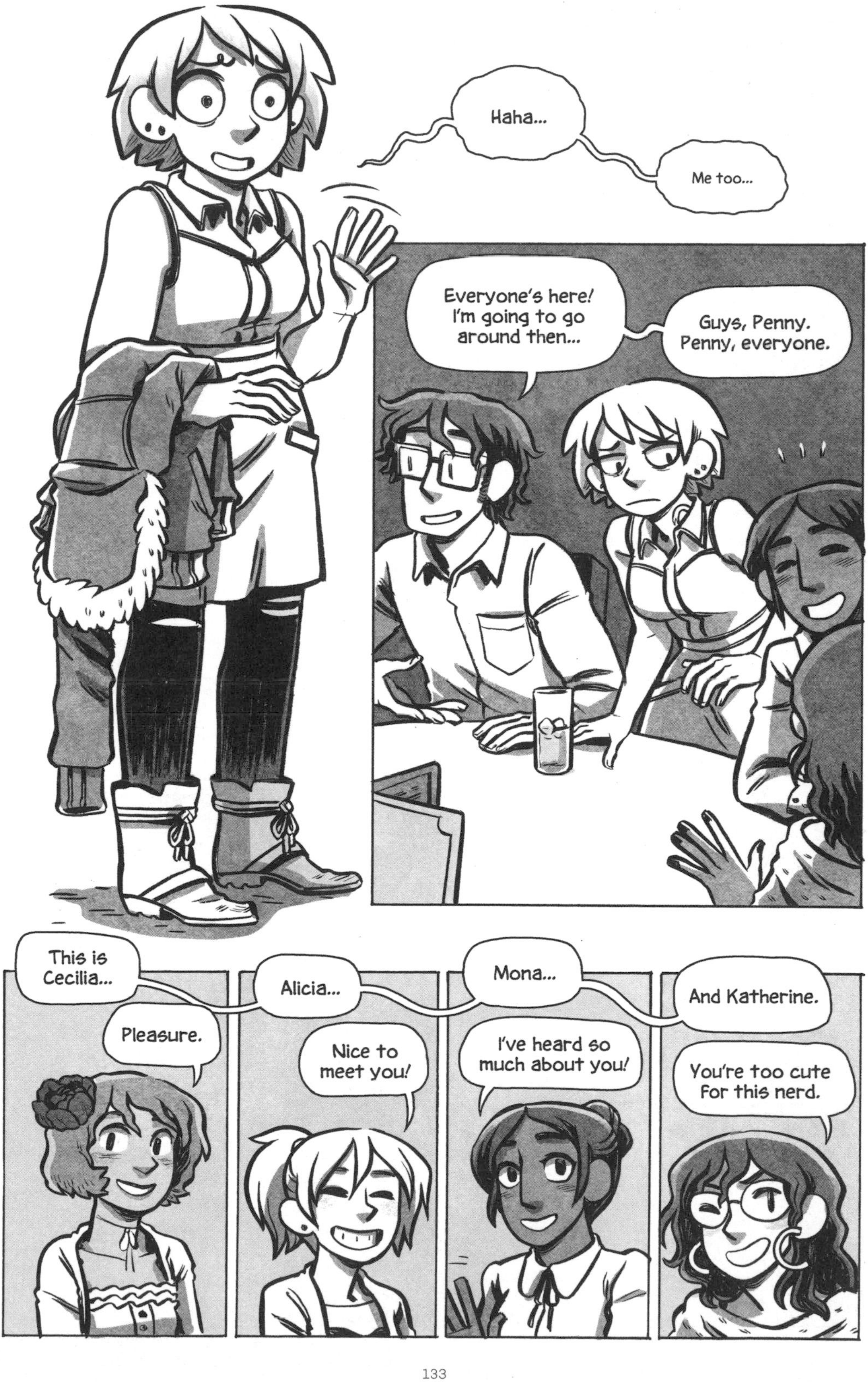

Haha...
Me too...
Everyone's here! I'm going to go around then...
Guys, Penny. Penny, everyone.
This is Cecilia...
Pleasure.
Alicia...
Nice to meet you!
Mona...
I've heard so much about you!
And Katherine.
You're too cute for this nerd.

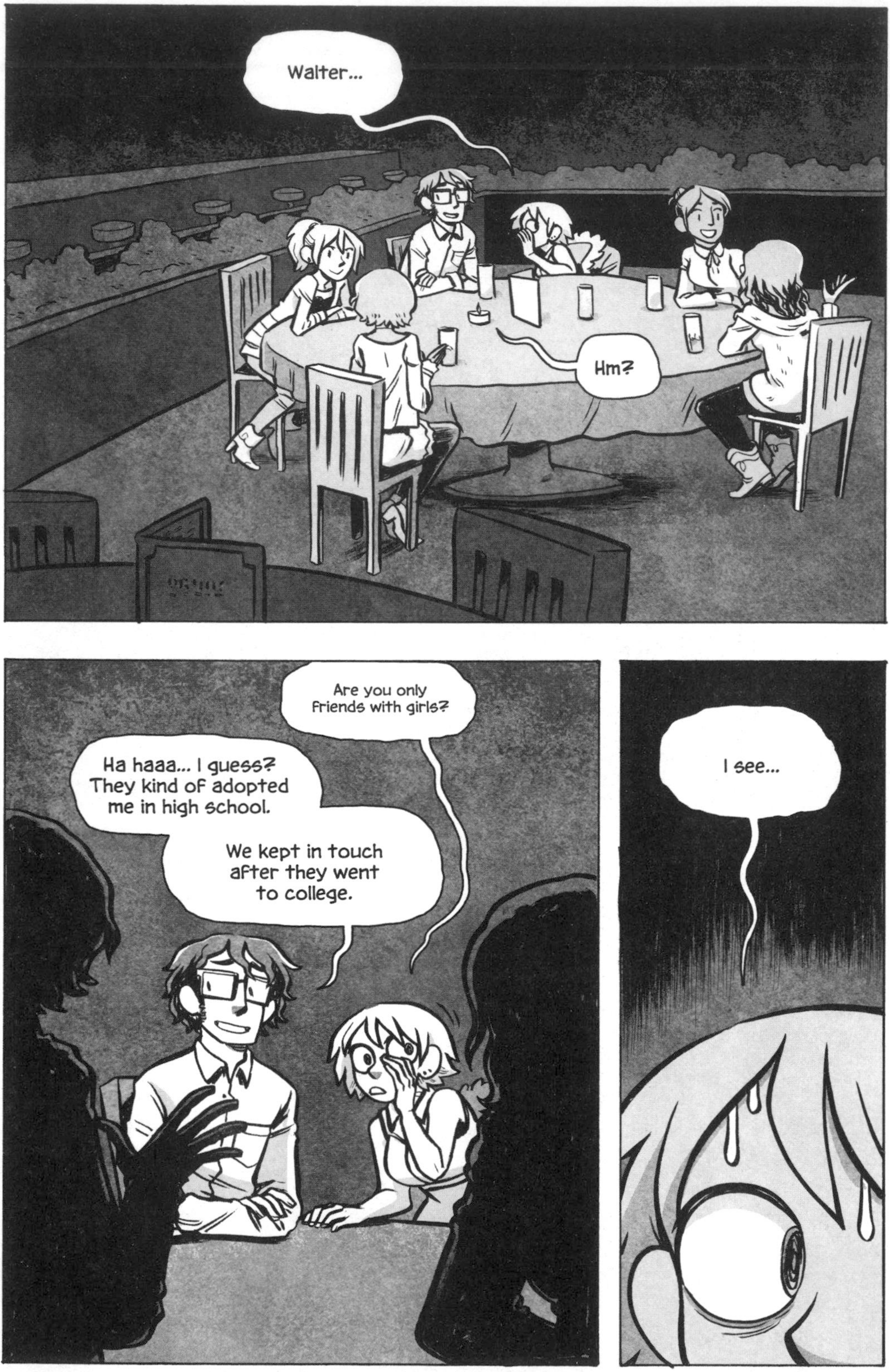
Walter...
Hm?
Are you only friends with girls?
Ha haaa... I guess? They kind of adopted me in high school.
We kept in touch after they went to college.
I see...

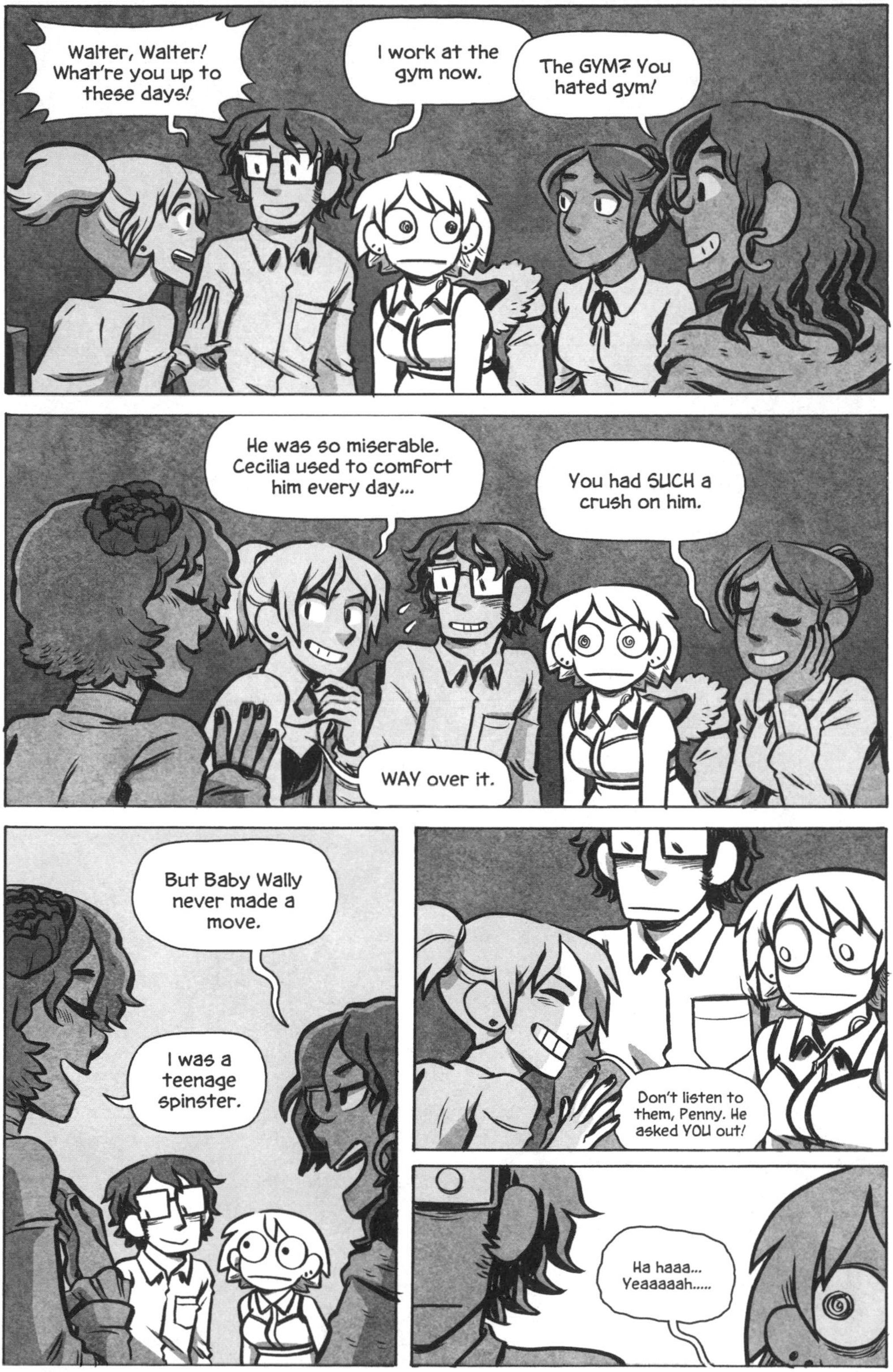

Walter, Walter! What're you up to these days!
I work at the gym now.
The GYM? You hated gym!
He was so miserable. Cecilia used to comfort him every day...
You had SUCH a crush on him.
WAY over it.
But Baby Wally never made a move.
I was a teenage spinster.
Don't listen to them, Penny. He asked YOU out!
Ha haaa... Yeaaaaah.....

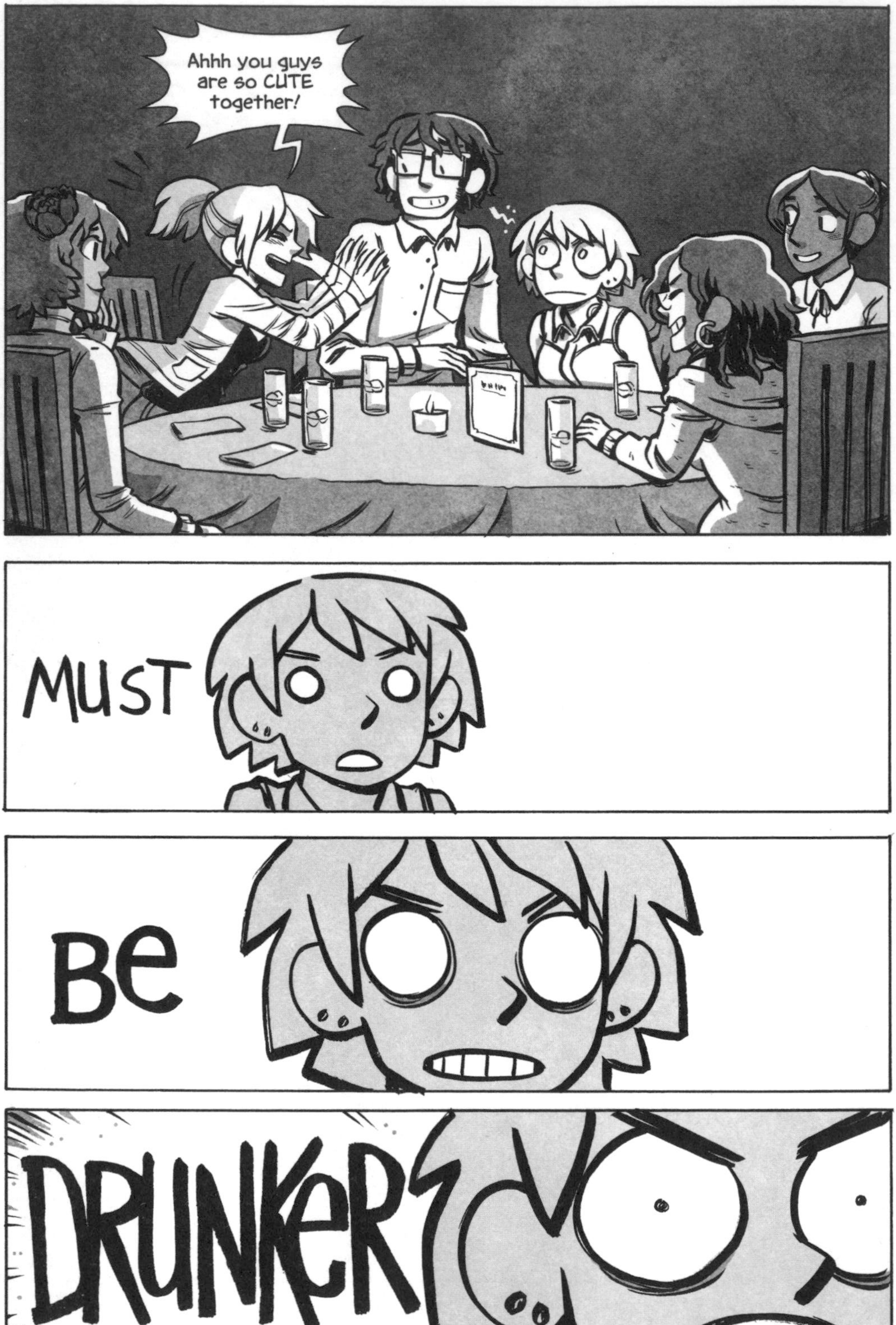
Ahhh you guys are so CUTE together!
MUST
BE
DRUNKER

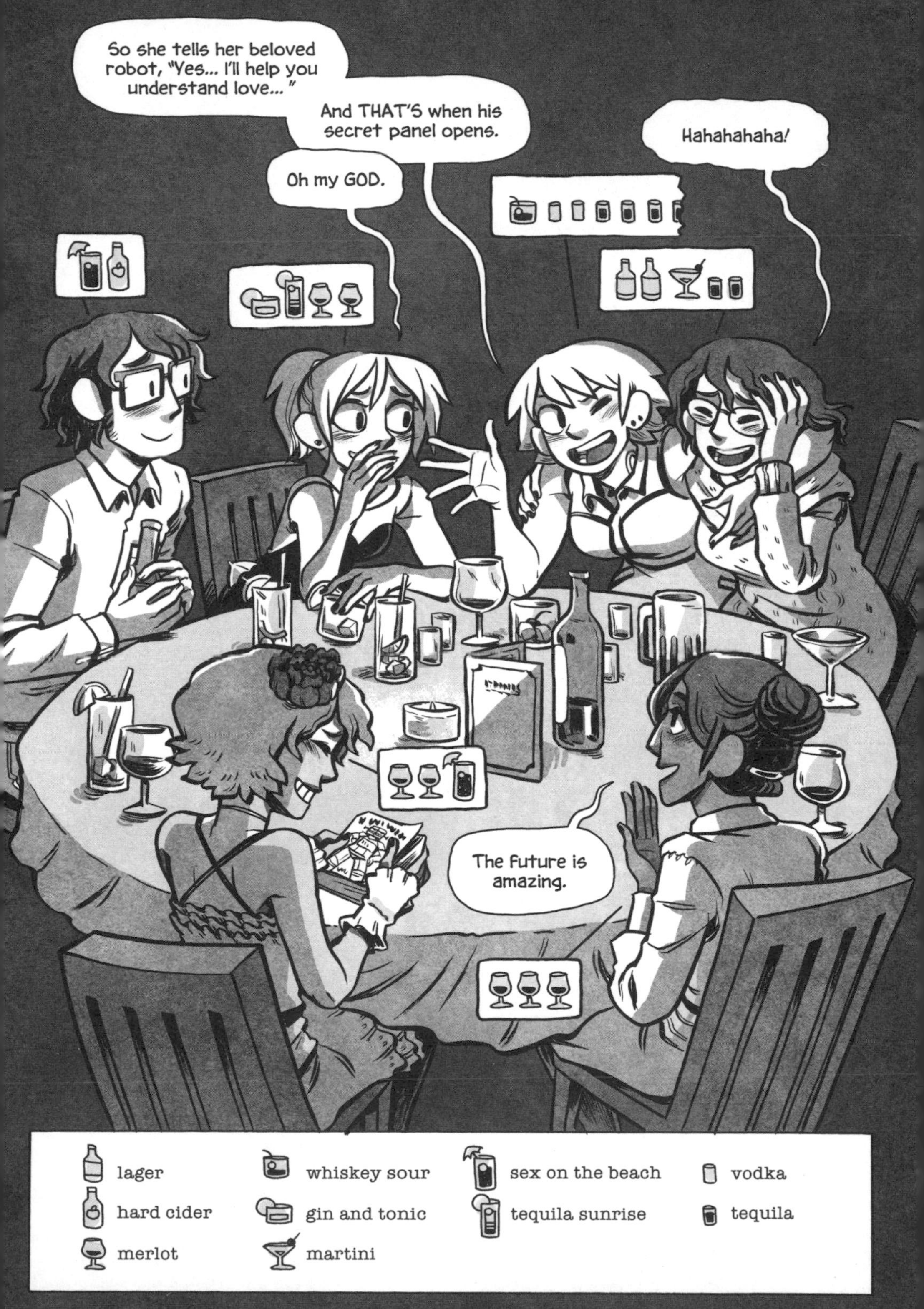
So she tells her beloved robot, "Yes... I'll help you understand love..."
And THAT'S when his secret panel opens.
Hahahahaha!
Oh my GOD.
The future is amazing.
lager
hard cider
merlot
whiskey sour
gin and tonic
martini
sex on the beach
tequila sunrise
vodka
tequila

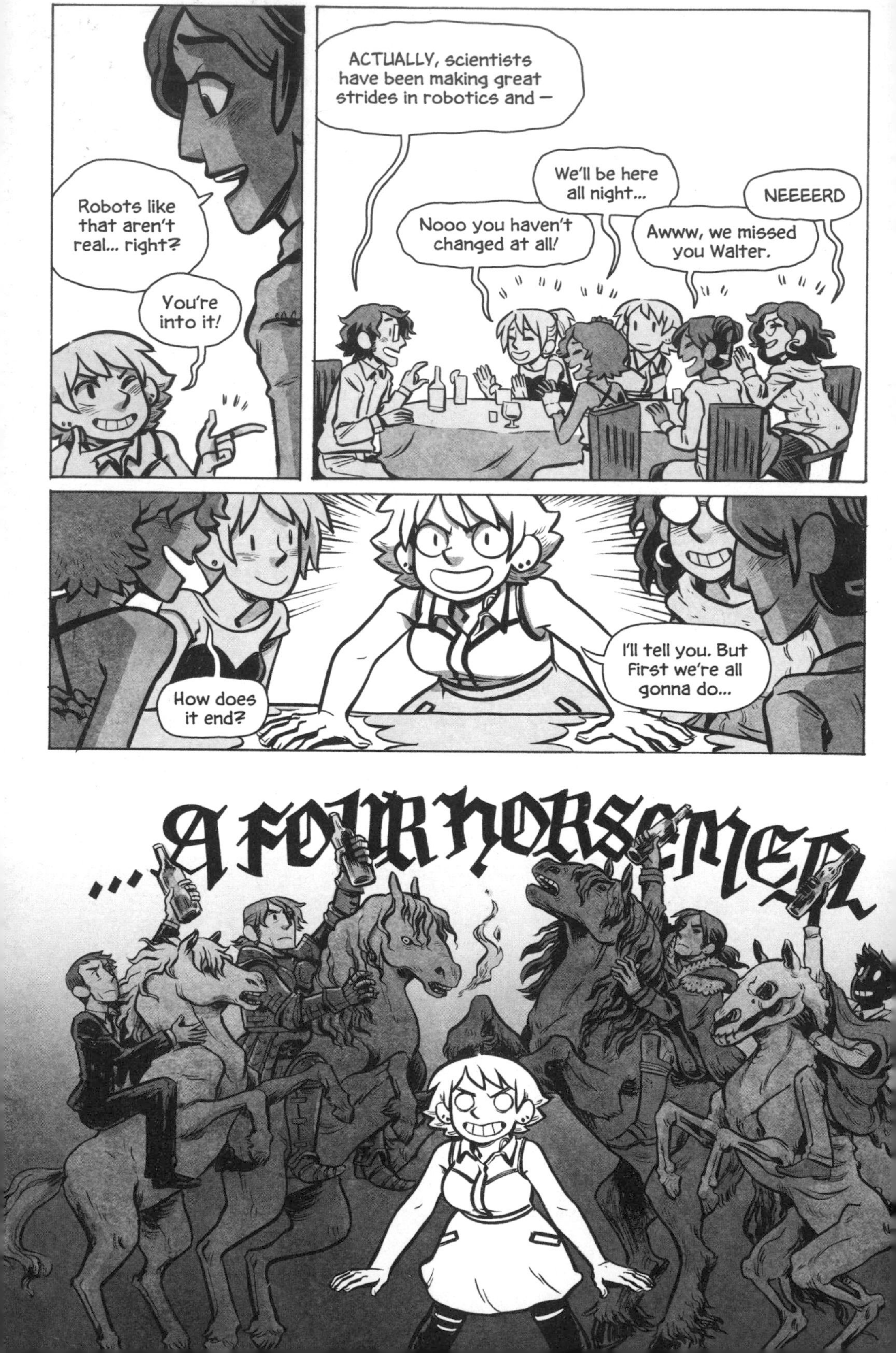
Robots like that aren't real... right?
You're into it!
ACTUALLY, scientists have been making great strides in robotics and —
Nooo you haven't changed at all!
We'll be here all night...
Awww, we missed you Walter.
NEEEERD
How does it end?
I'll tell you. But first we're all gonna do...
...A FOUR HORSEMEN

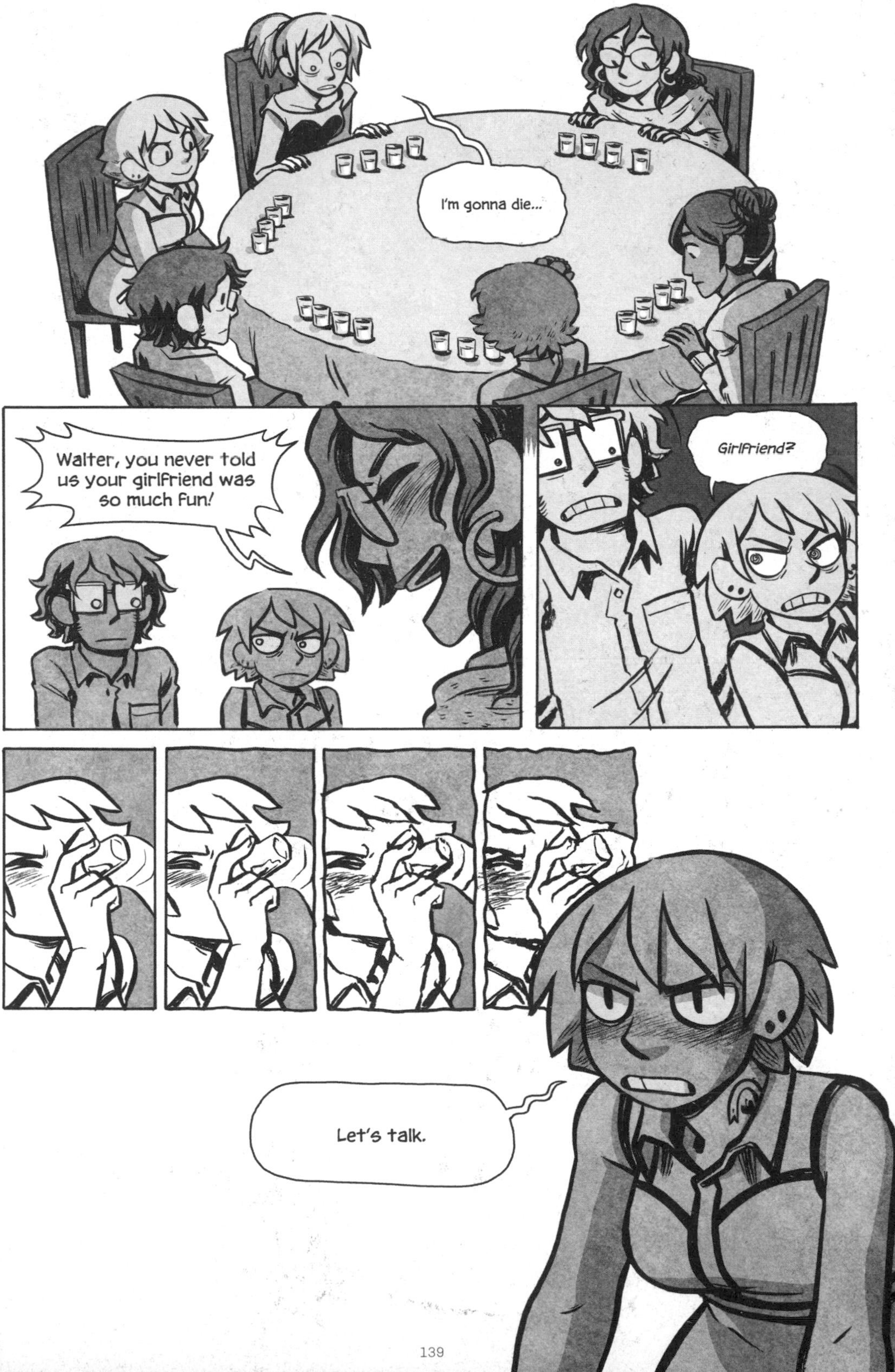
I'm gonna die...
Walter, you never told us your girlfriend was so much fun!
Girlfriend?
Let's talk.

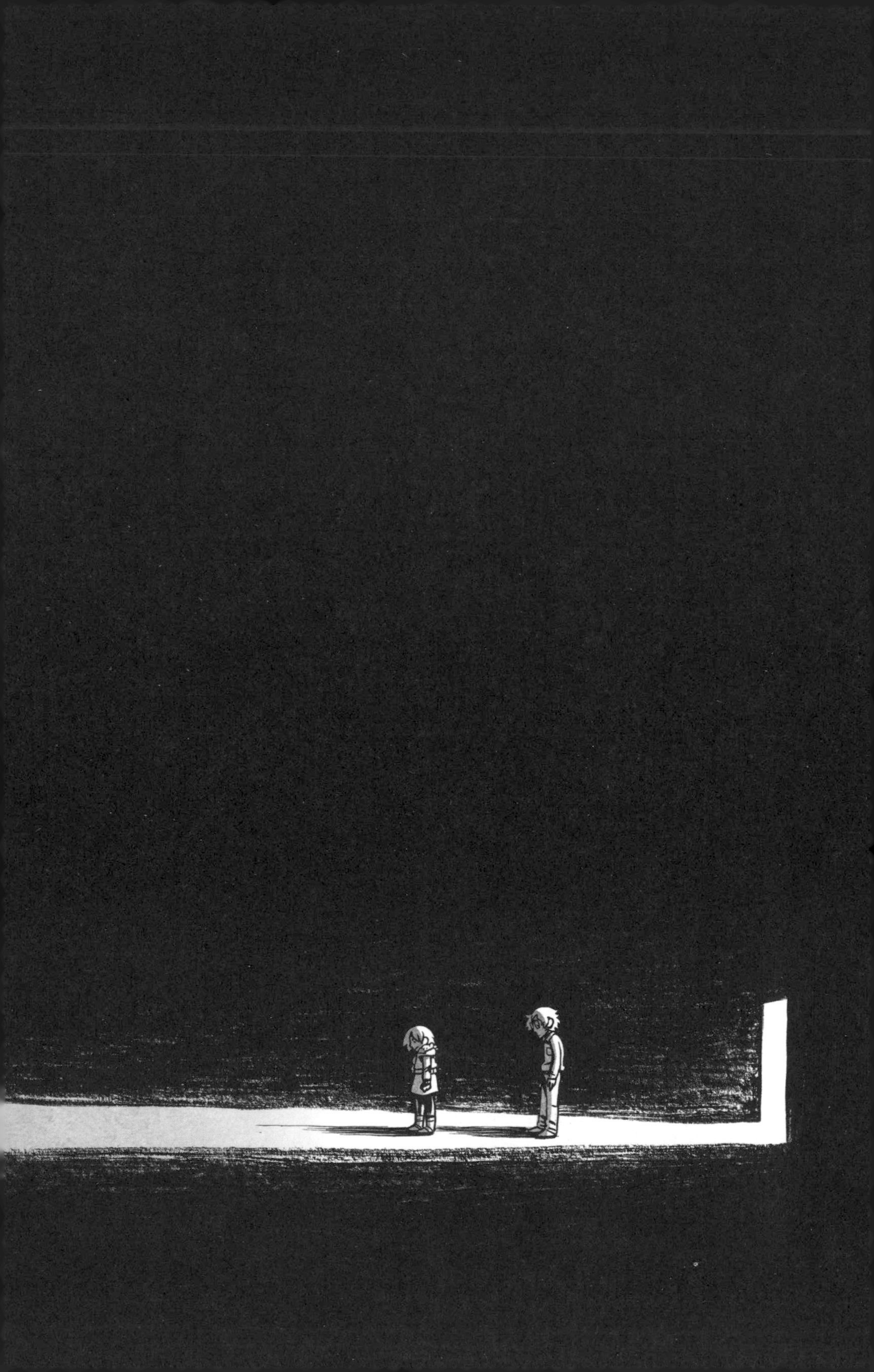

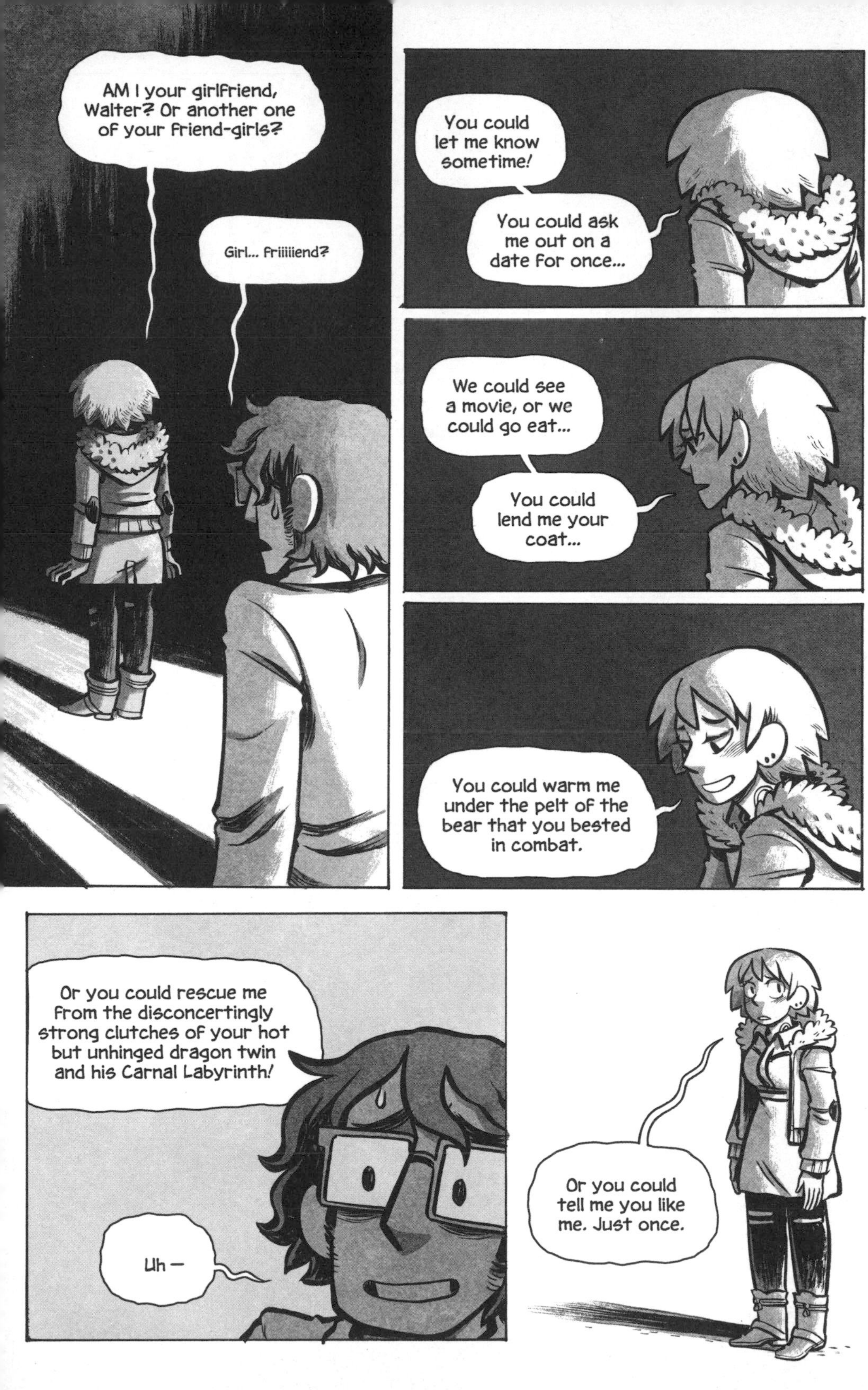
AM I your girlfriend, Walter? Or another one of your friend-girls?
Girl... Friiiiiend?
You could let me know sometime!
You could ask me out on a date for once...
We could see a movie, or we could go eat...
You could lend me your coat...
You could warm me under the pelt of the bear that you bested in combat.
Or you could rescue me from the disconcertingly strong clutches of your hot but unhinged dragon twin and his Carnal Labyrinth!
Uh —
Or you could tell me you like me. Just once.

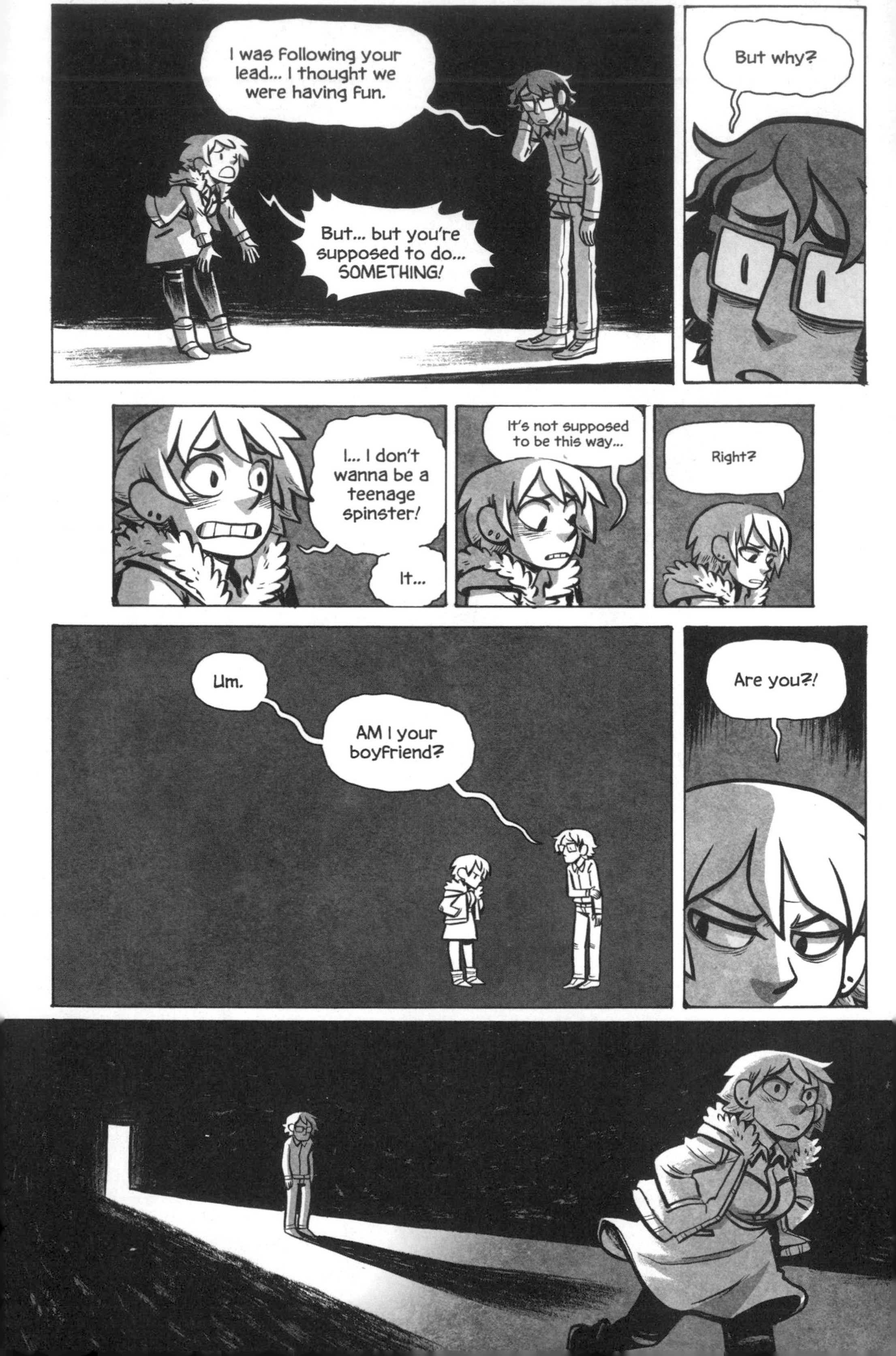
I was following your lead... I thought we were having fun.
But... but you're supposed to do... SOMETHING!
But why?
I... I don't wanna be a teenage spinster!
It...
It's not supposed to be this way...
Right?
Um.
AM I your boyfriend?
Are you?!

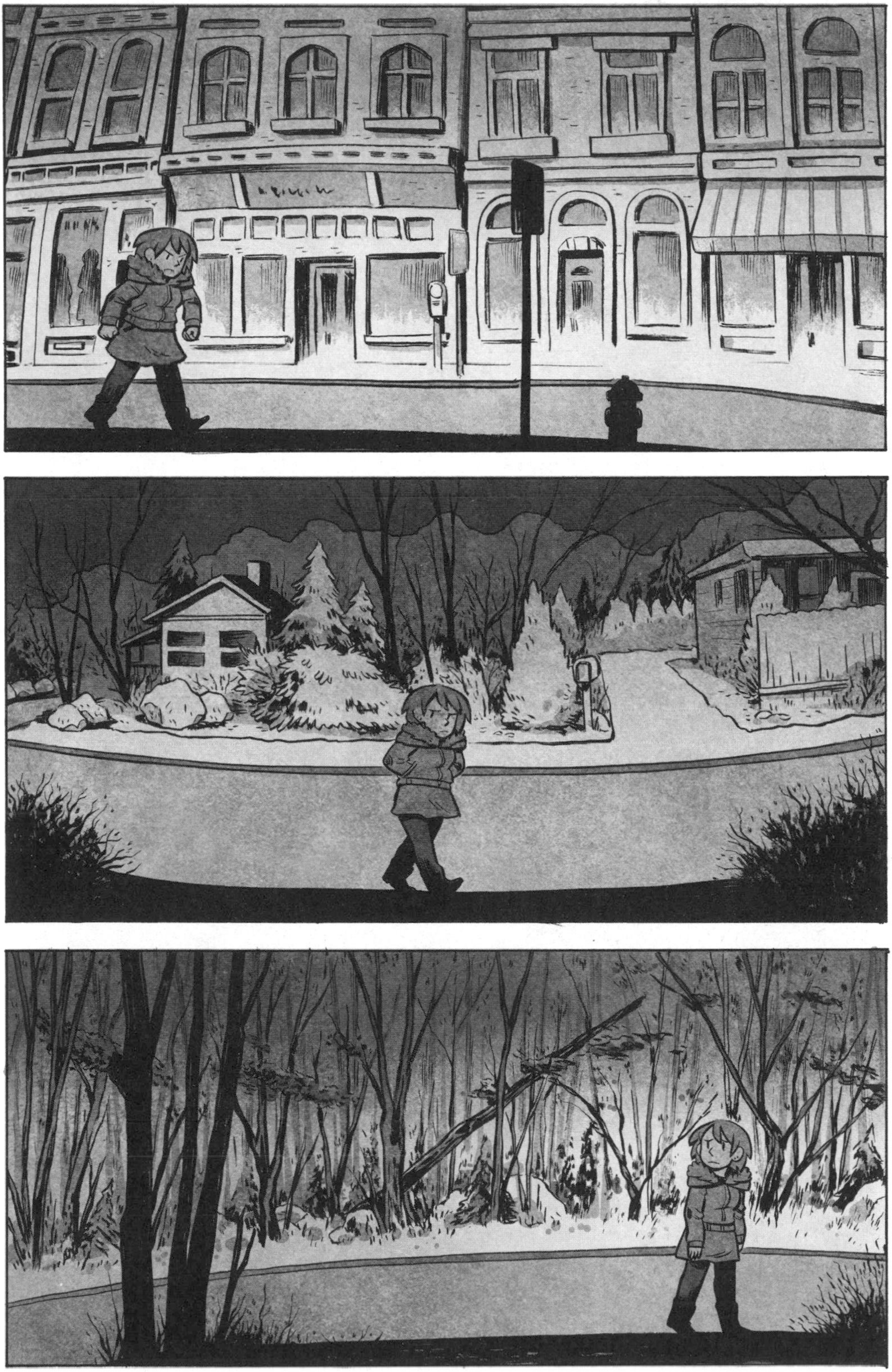

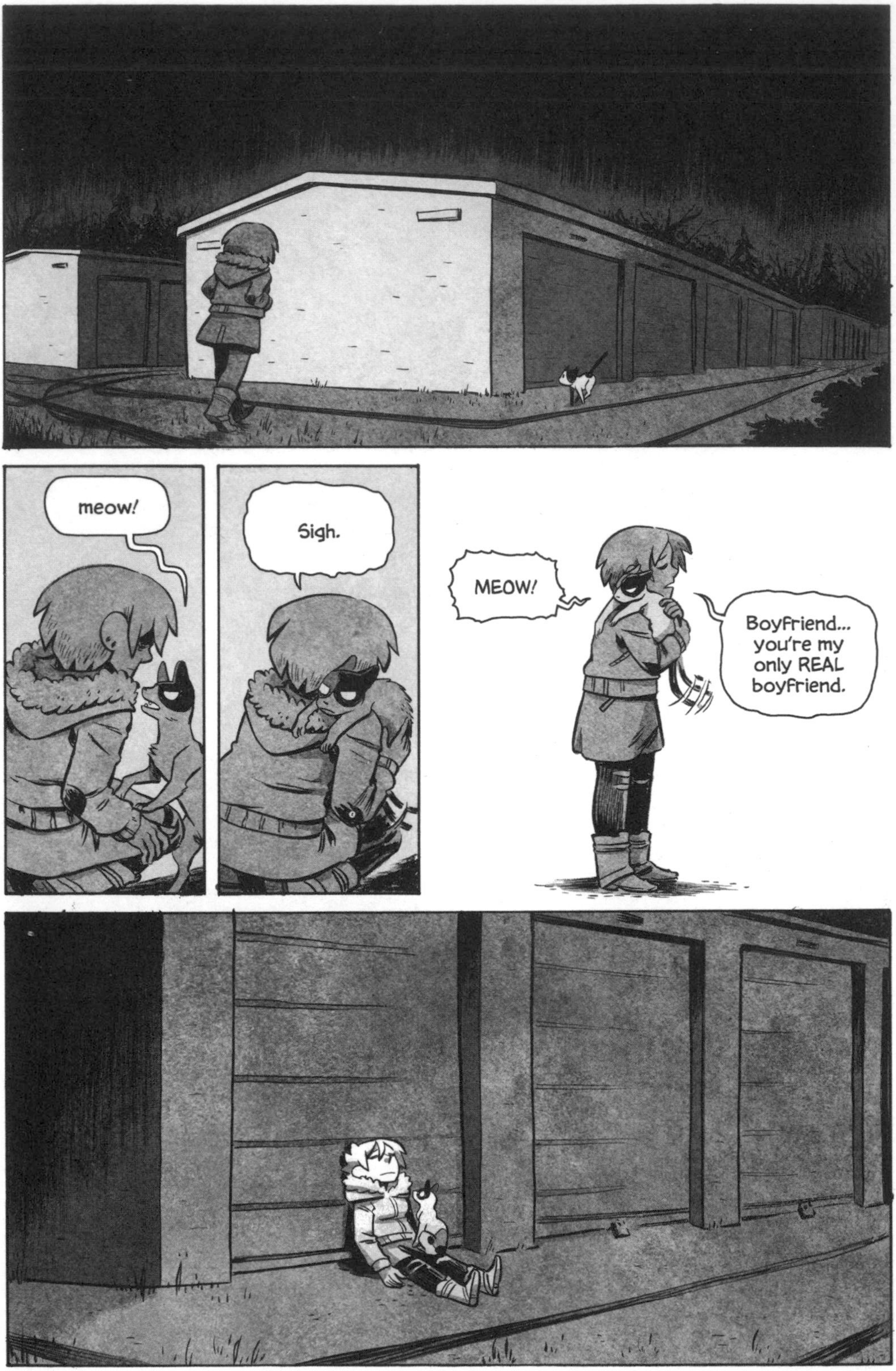
meow!
Sigh.
MEOW!
Boyfriend... you're my only REAL boyfriend.

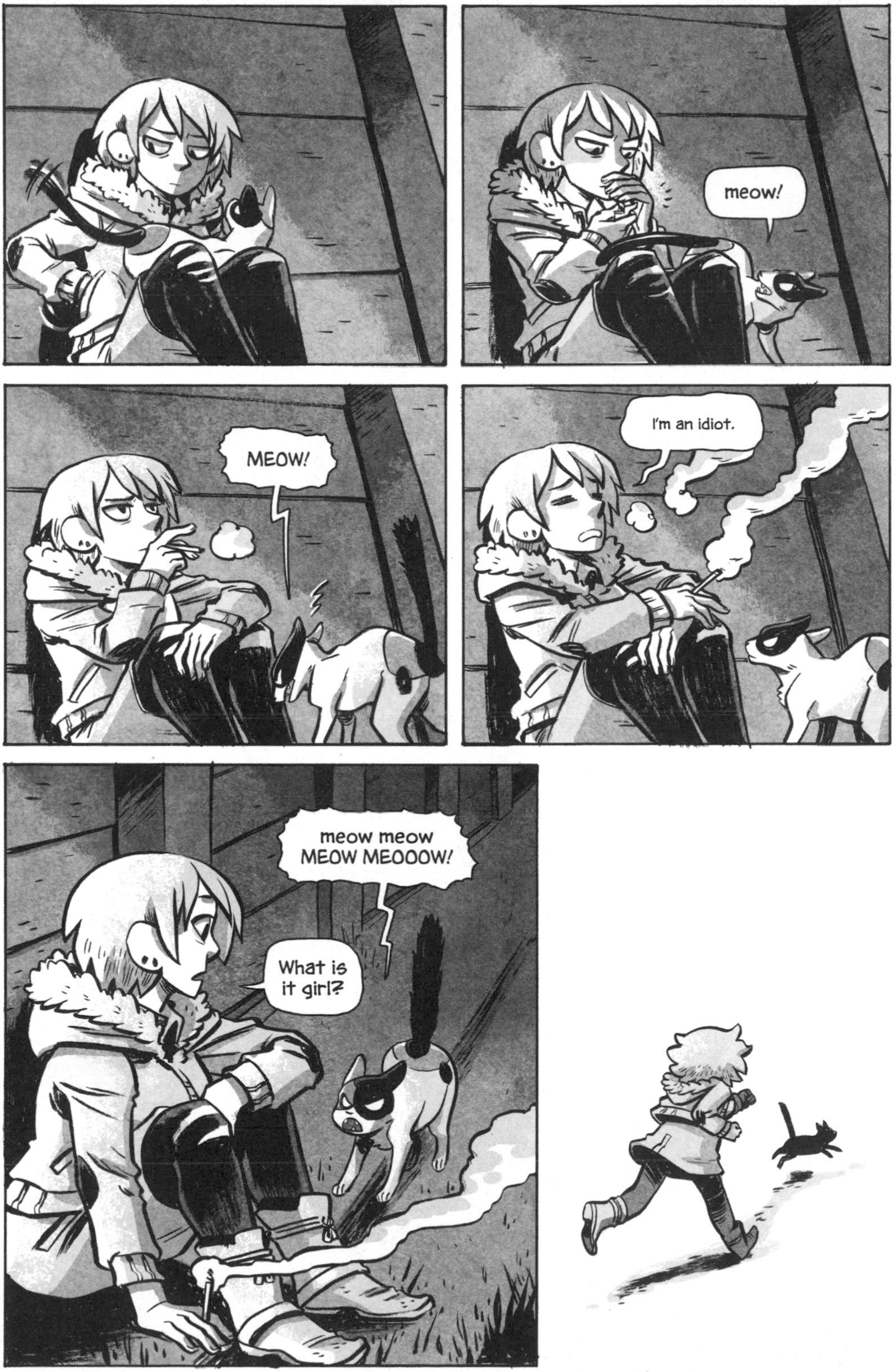
meow!
MEOW!
I'm an idiot.
meow meow
MEOW MEOOOW!
What is
it girl?

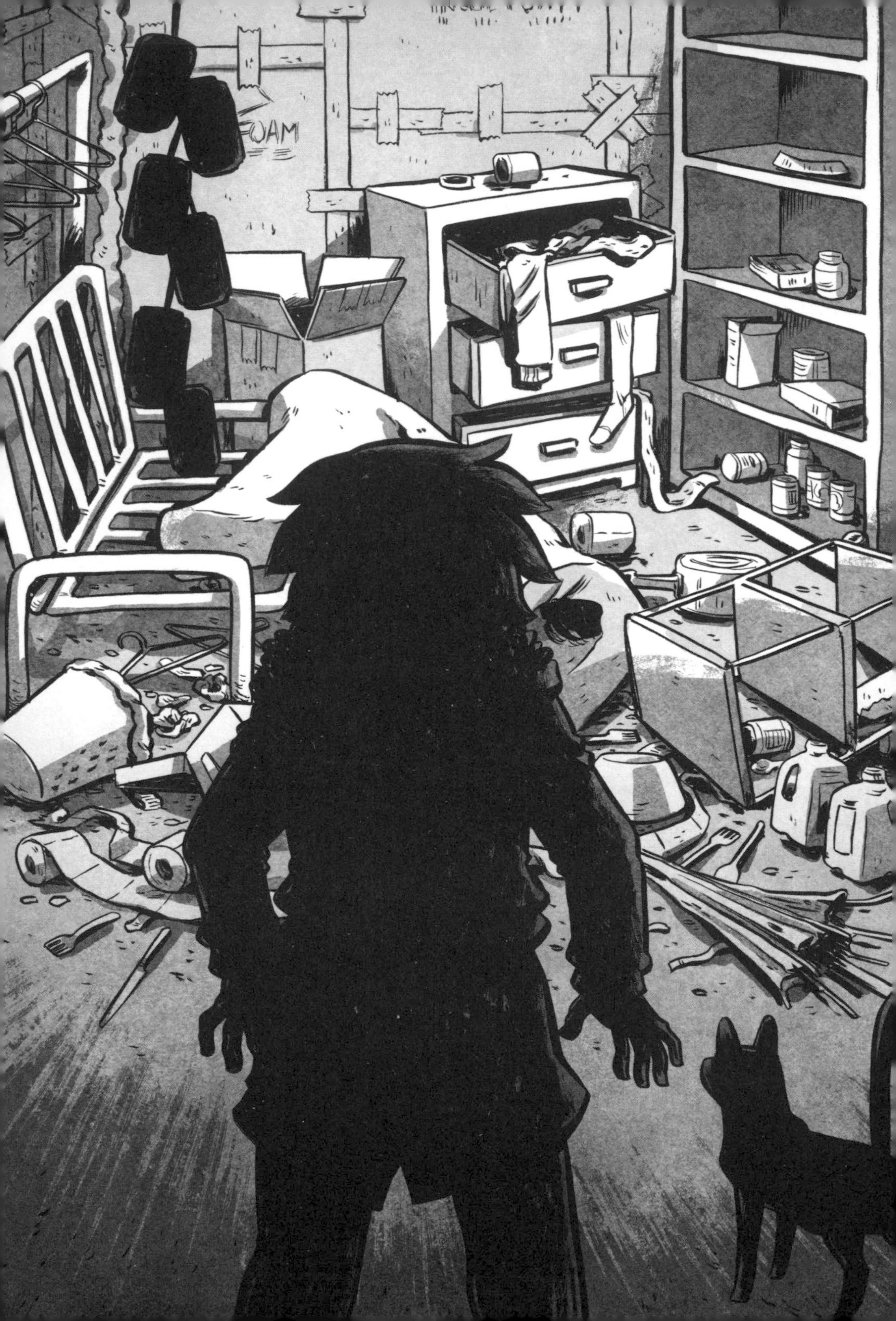
FOAM

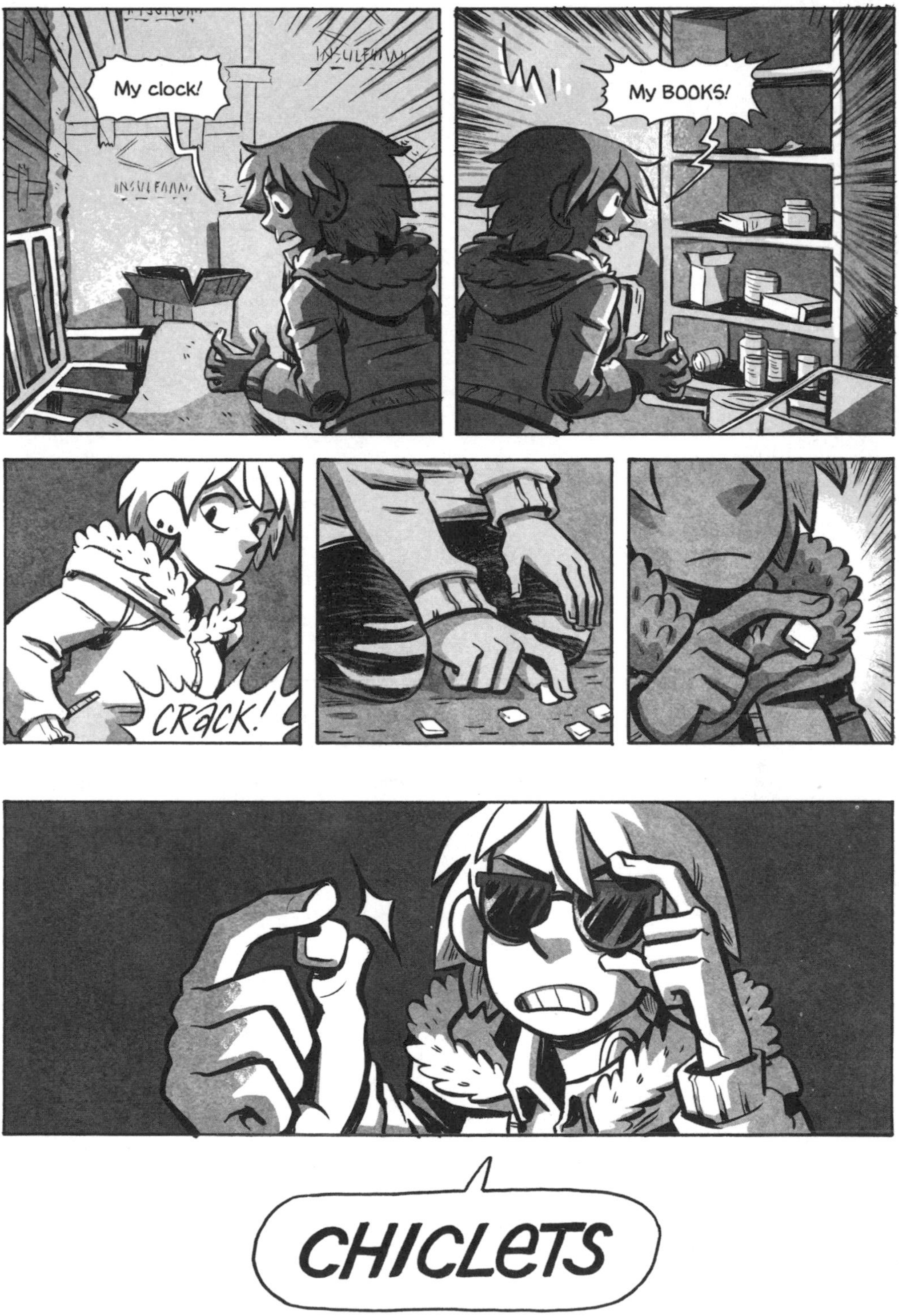
My clock!
My BOOKS!
CRACK!
CHICLETS

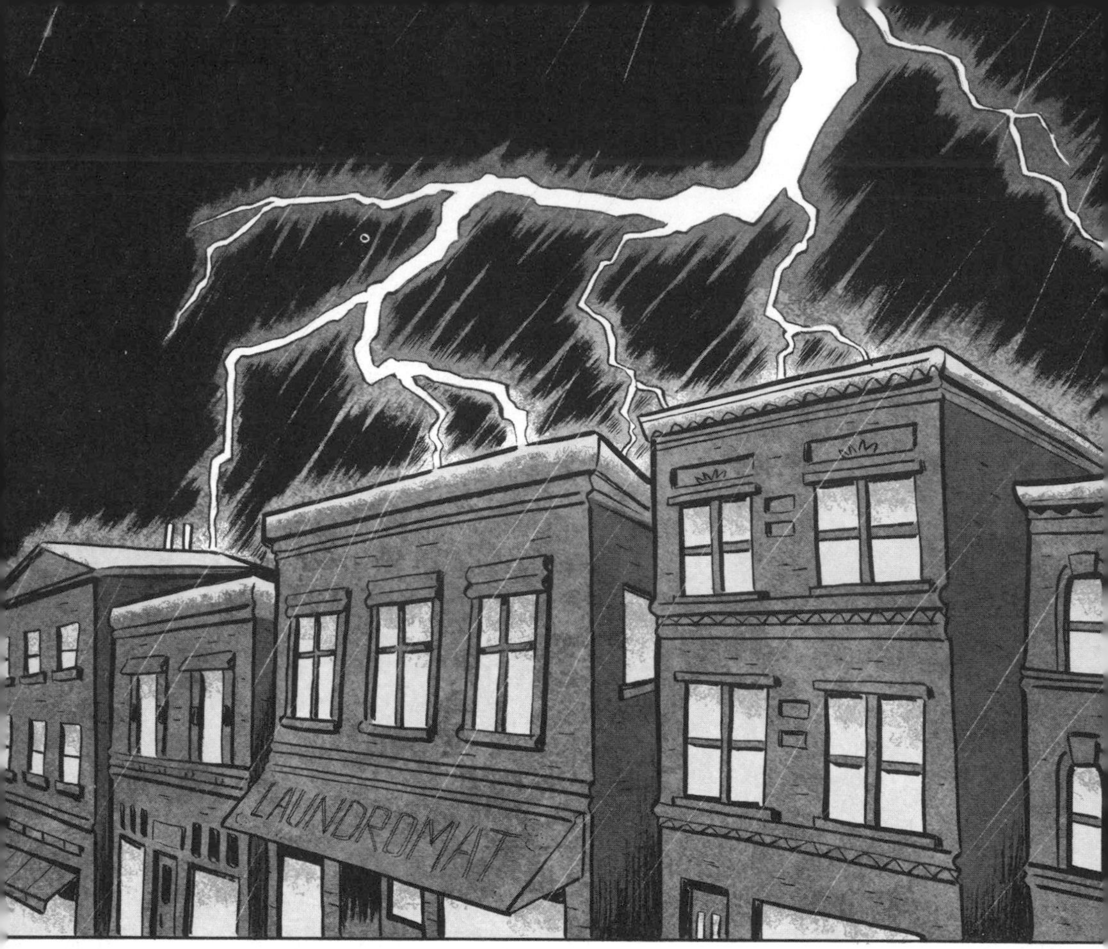
LAUNDROMAT

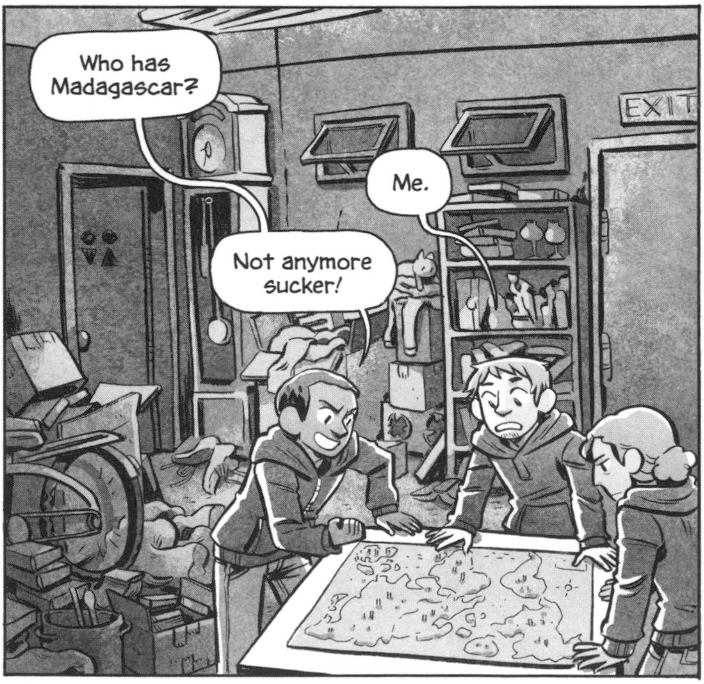
Who has Madagascar?
EXIT
Me.
Not anymore sucker!

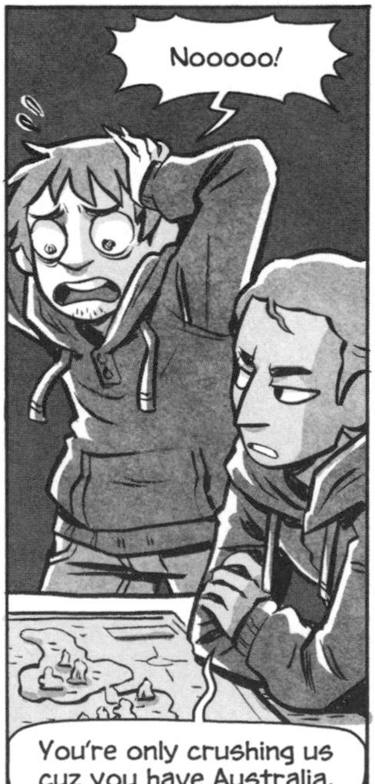
Nooooo!
You're only crushing us cuz you have Australia.

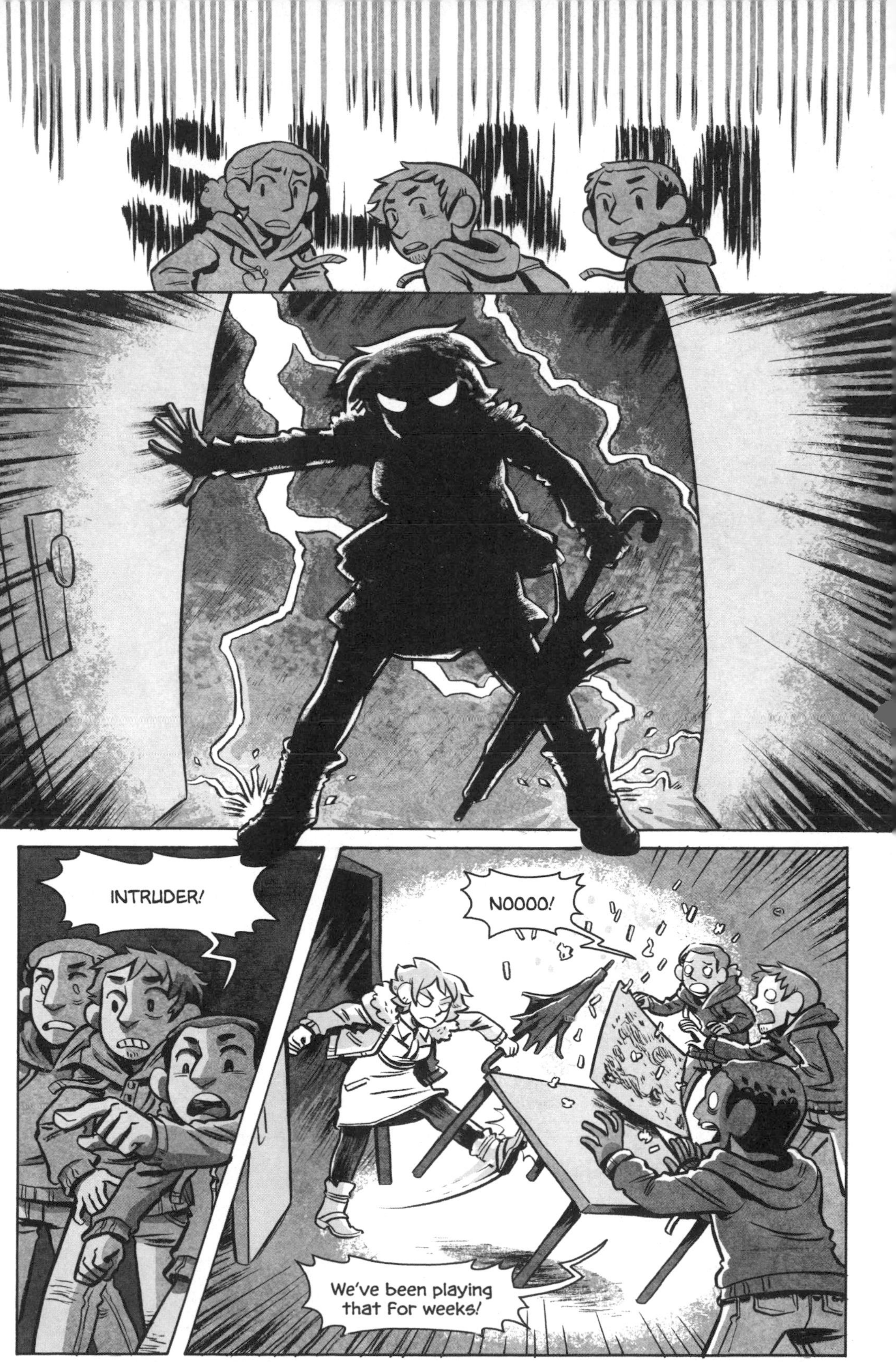
SLAM
INTRUDER!
NOOOO!
We've been playing that for weeks!

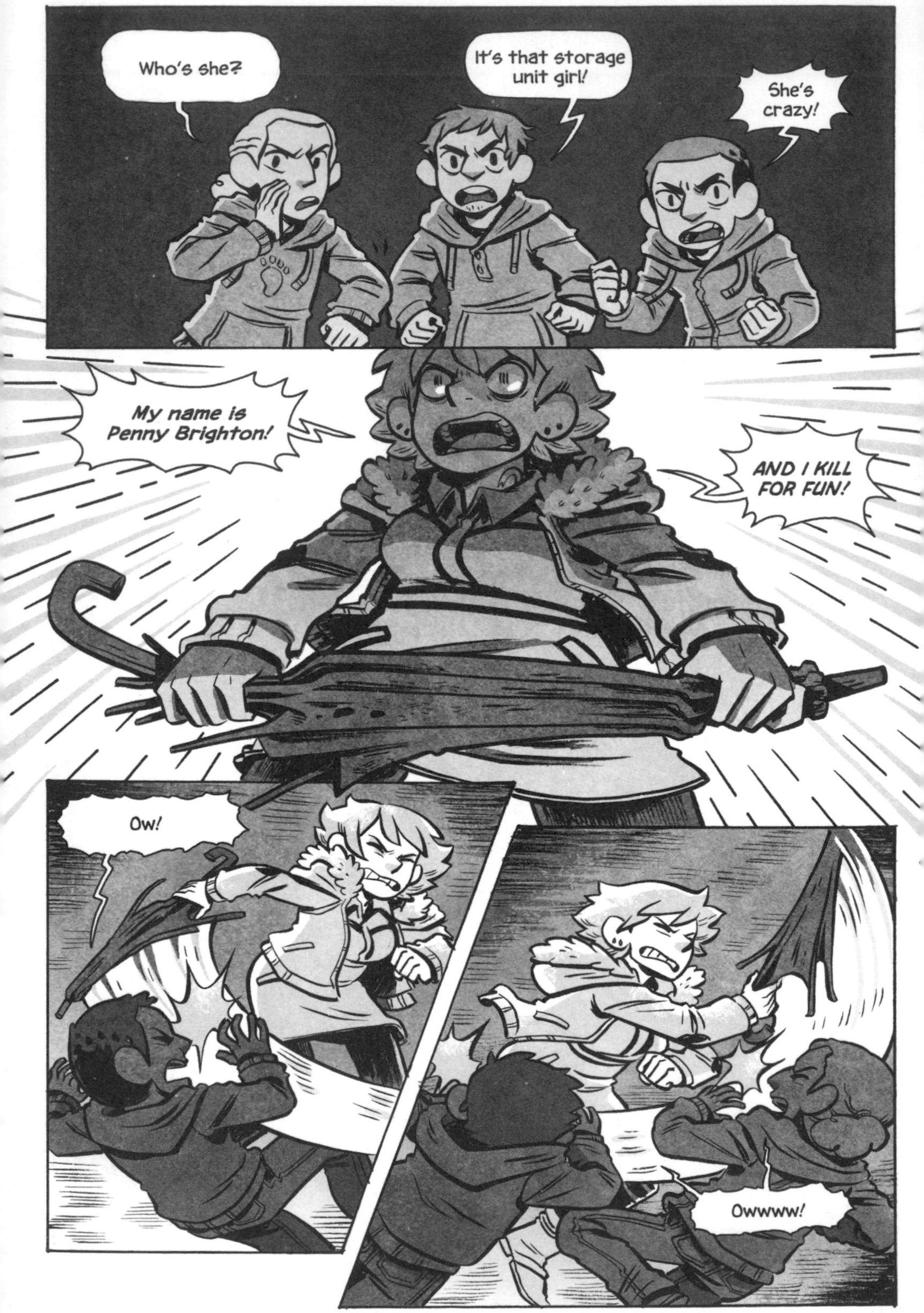
Who's she?
It's that storage unit girl!
She's crazy!
My name is Penny Brighton!
AND I KILL FOR FUN!
Ow!
Owwww!

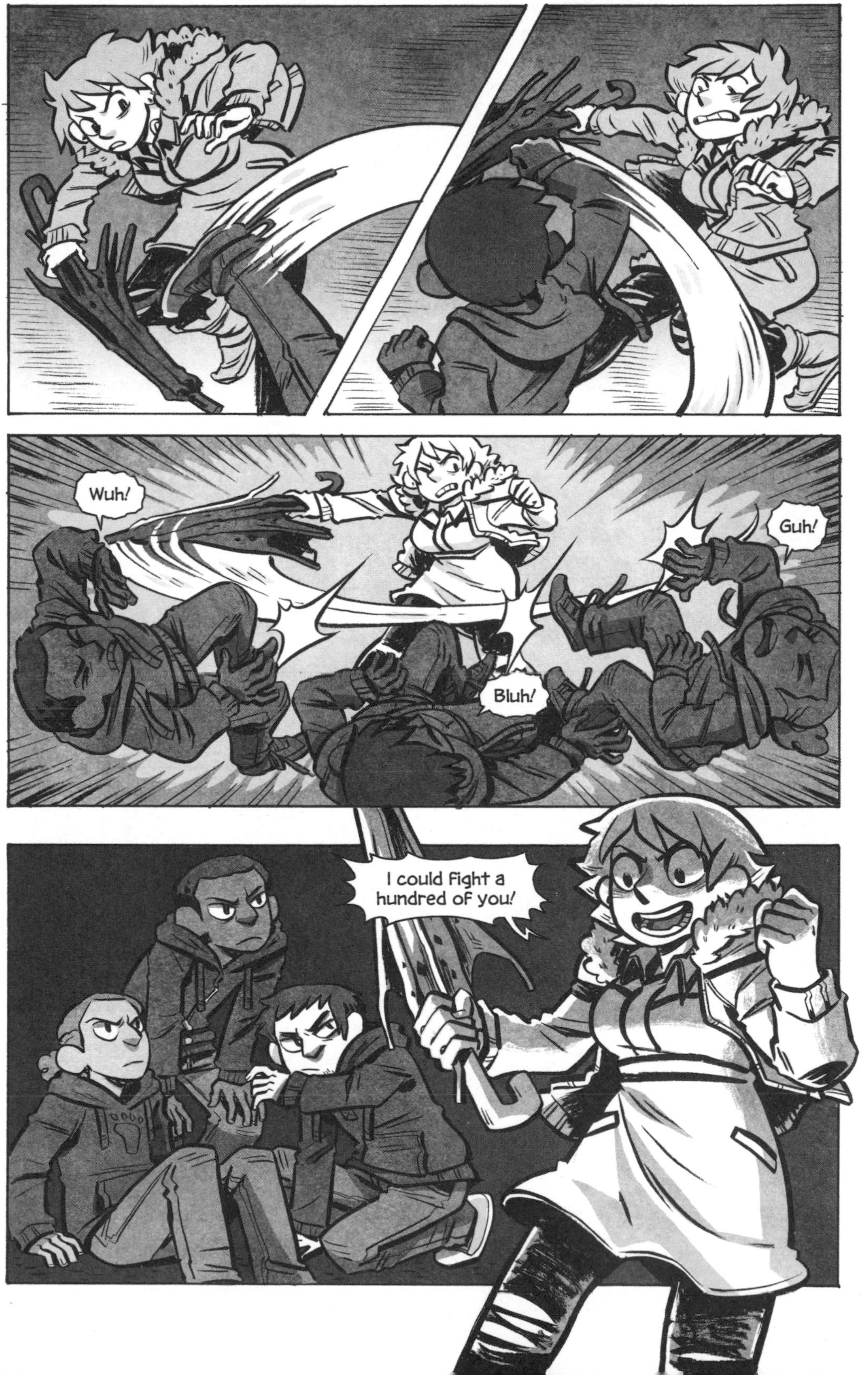
Wuh!
Guh!
Bluh!
I could fight a hundred of you!

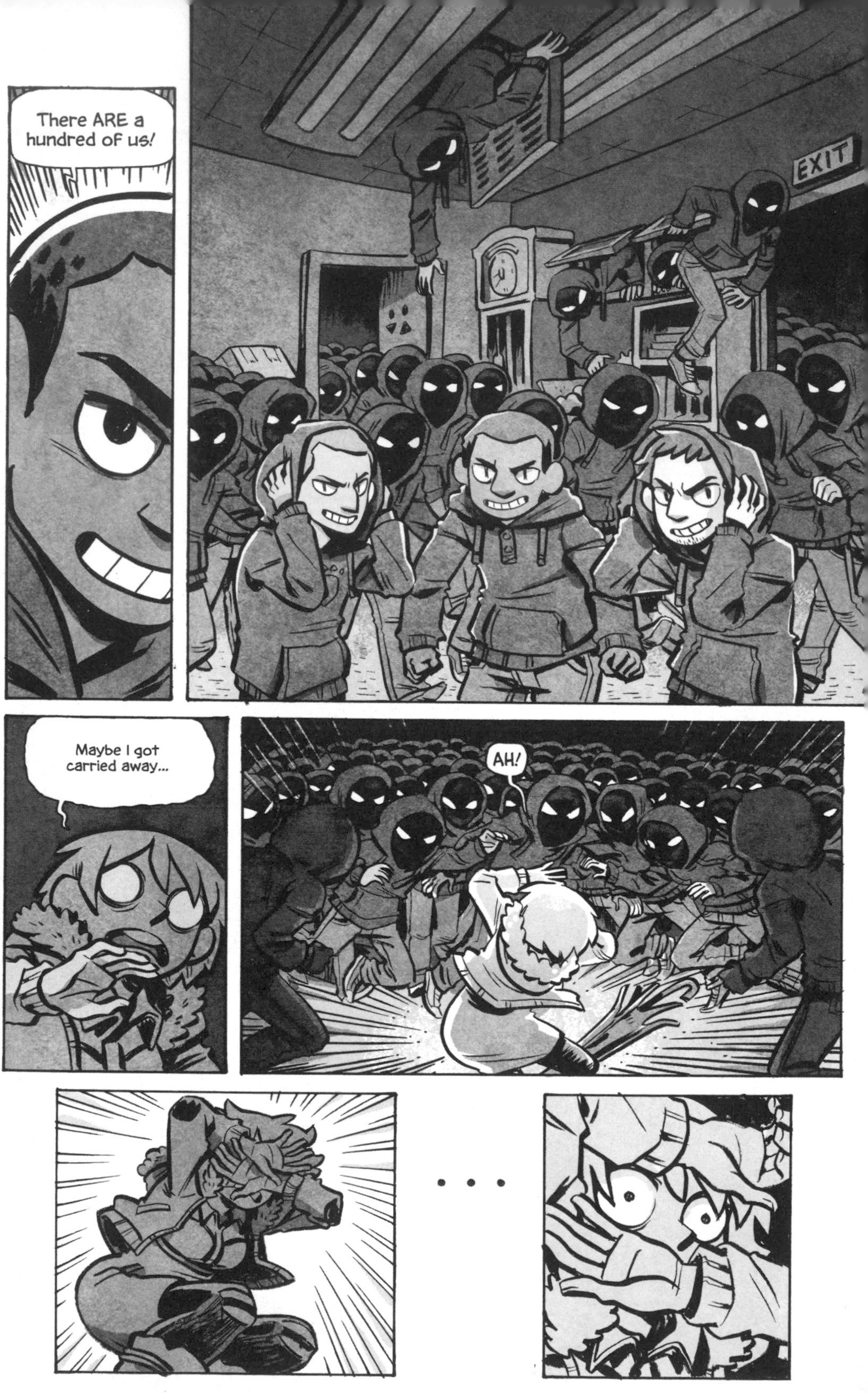
There ARE a hundred of us!
EXIT
Maybe I got carried away...
AH!
• • •

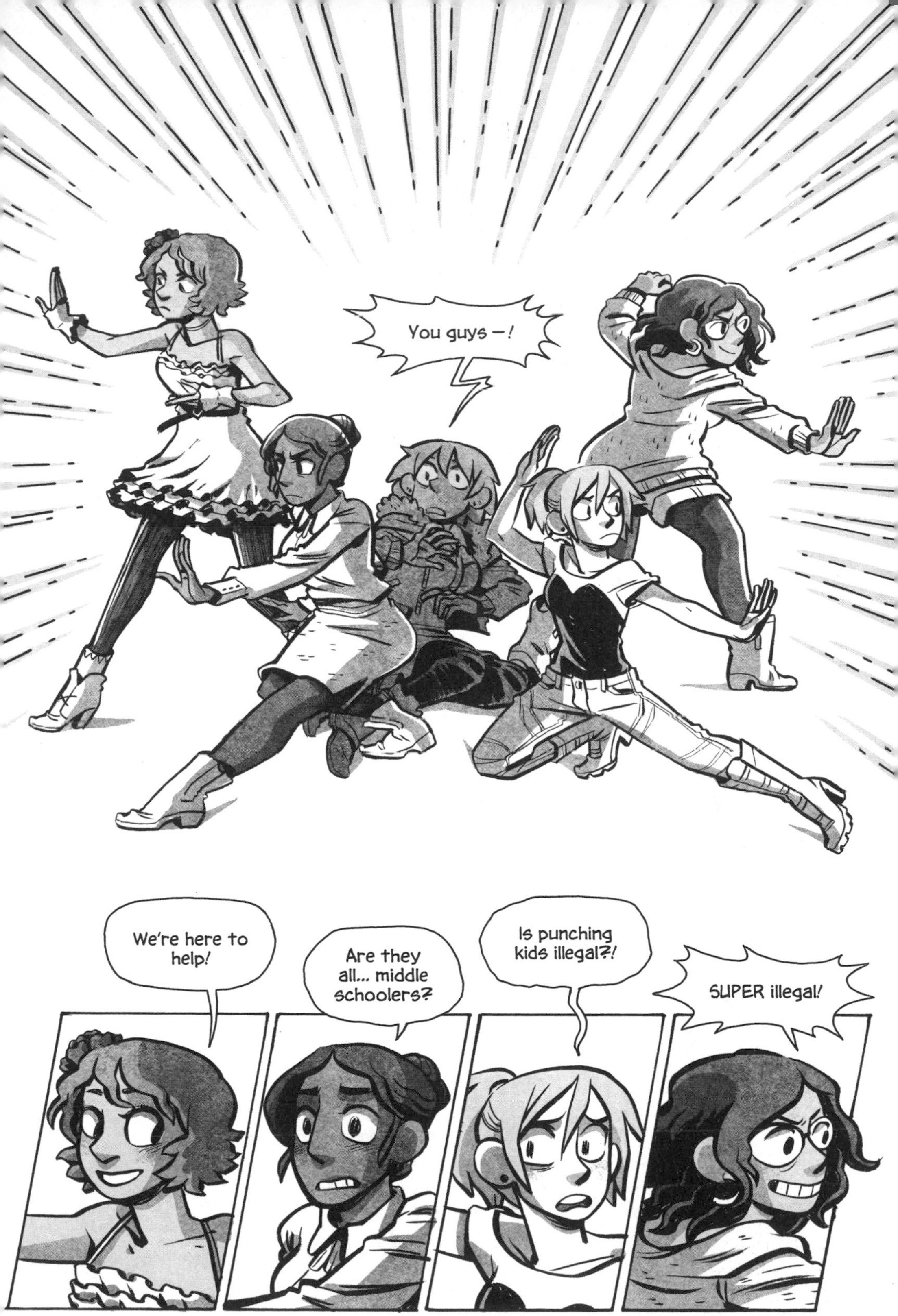
You guys —!
We're here to help!
Are they all... middle schoolers?
Is punching kids illegal?!
SUPER illegal!

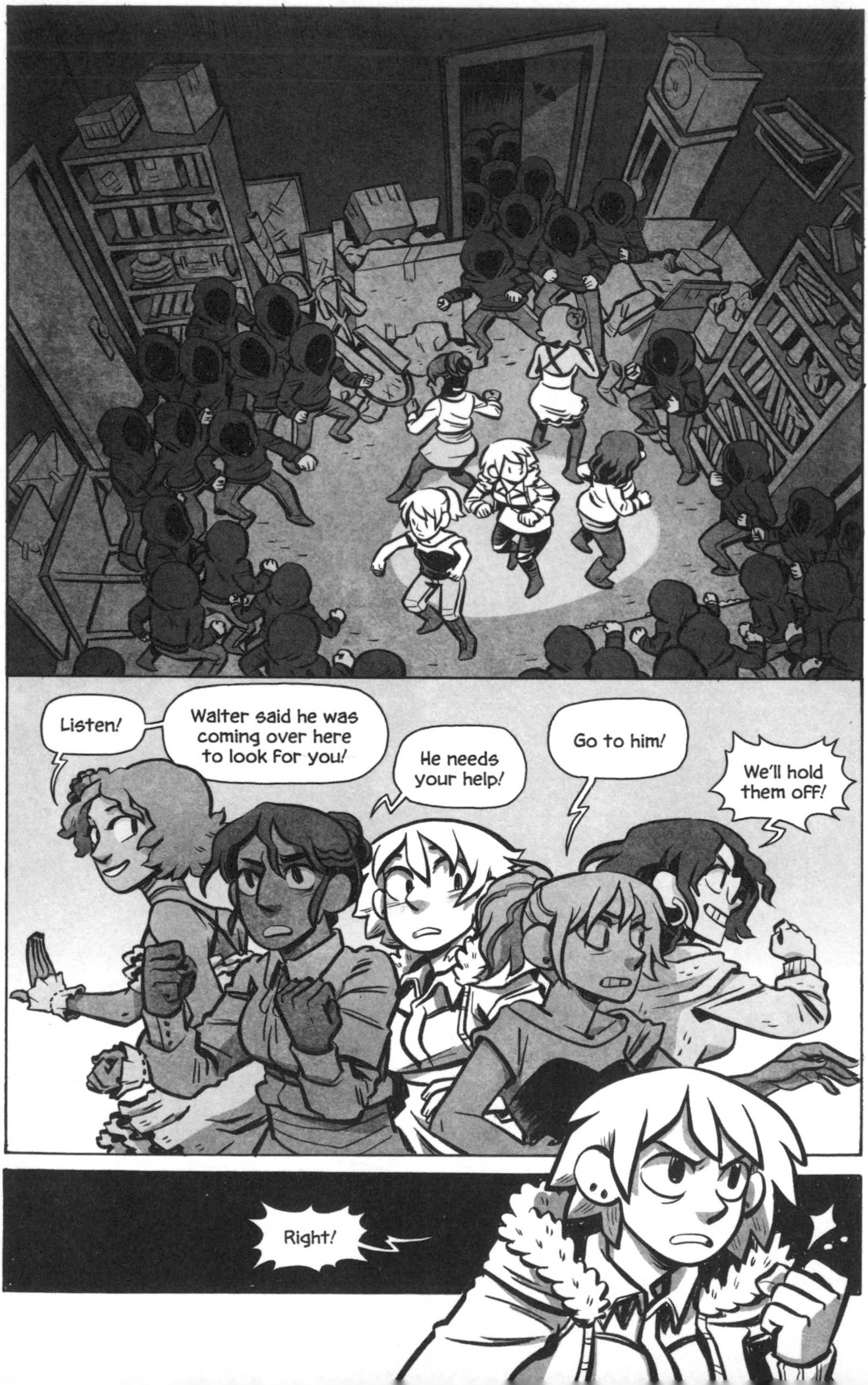
Listen!
Walter said he was coming over here to look for you!
He needs your help!
Go to him!
We'll hold them off!
Right!

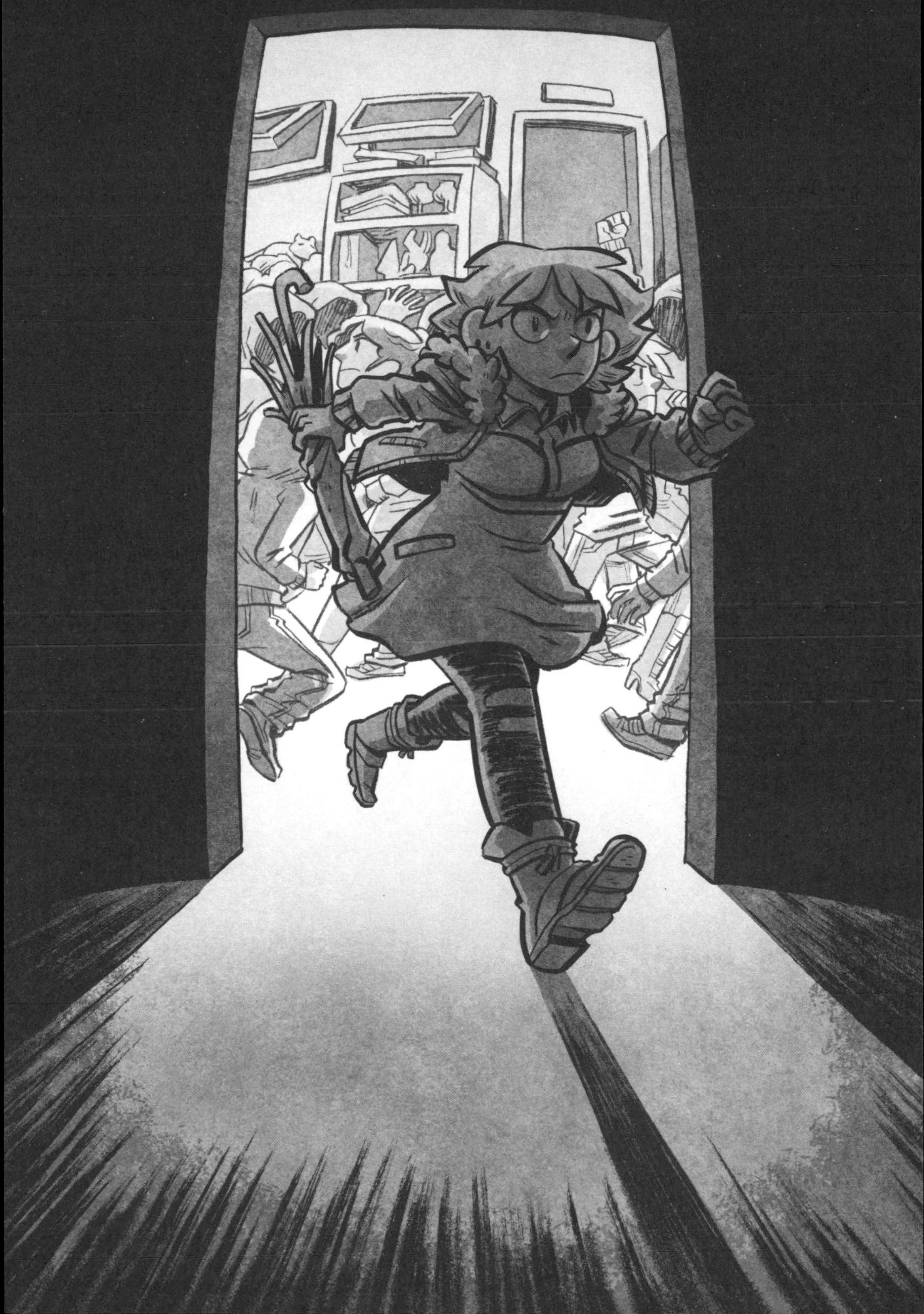

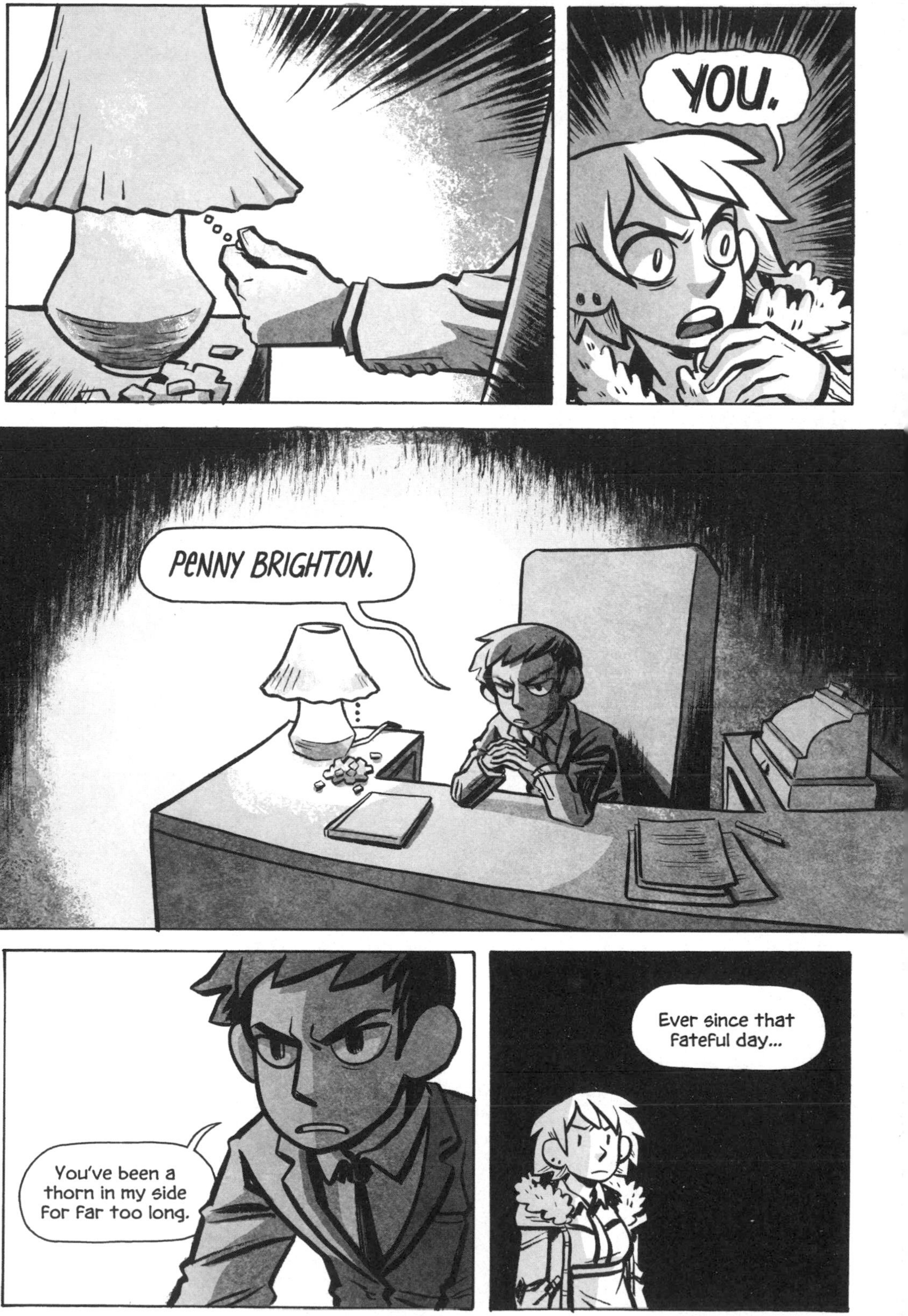
YOU.
PENNY BRIGHTON.
You've been a thorn in my side for far too long.
Ever since that fateful day...

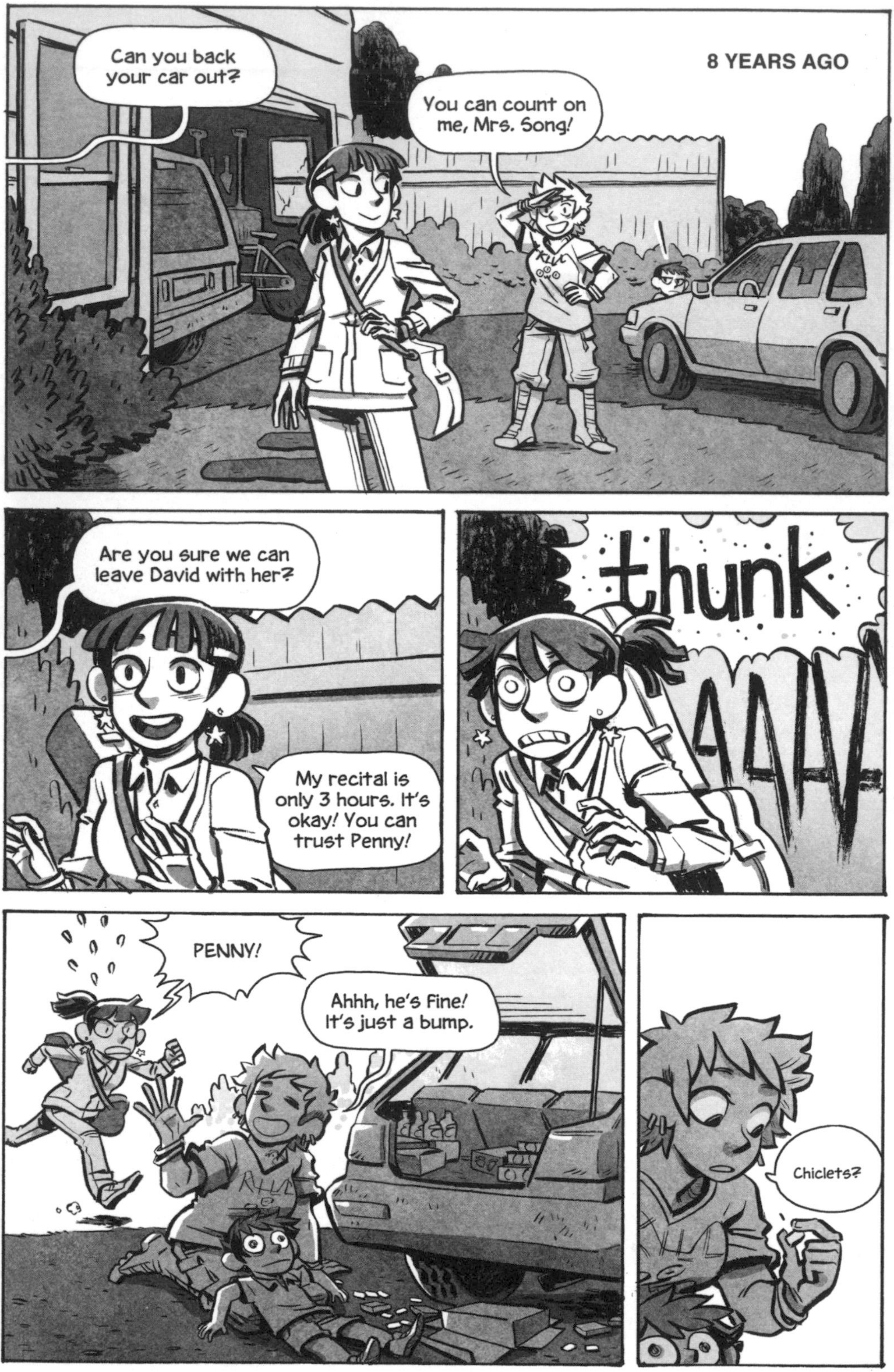
Can you back your car out?
8 YEARS AGO
You can count on me, Mrs. Song!
Are you sure we can leave David with her?
My recital is only 3 hours. It's okay! You can trust Penny!
thunk
PENNY!
Ahhh, he's fine! It's just a bump.
Chiclets?

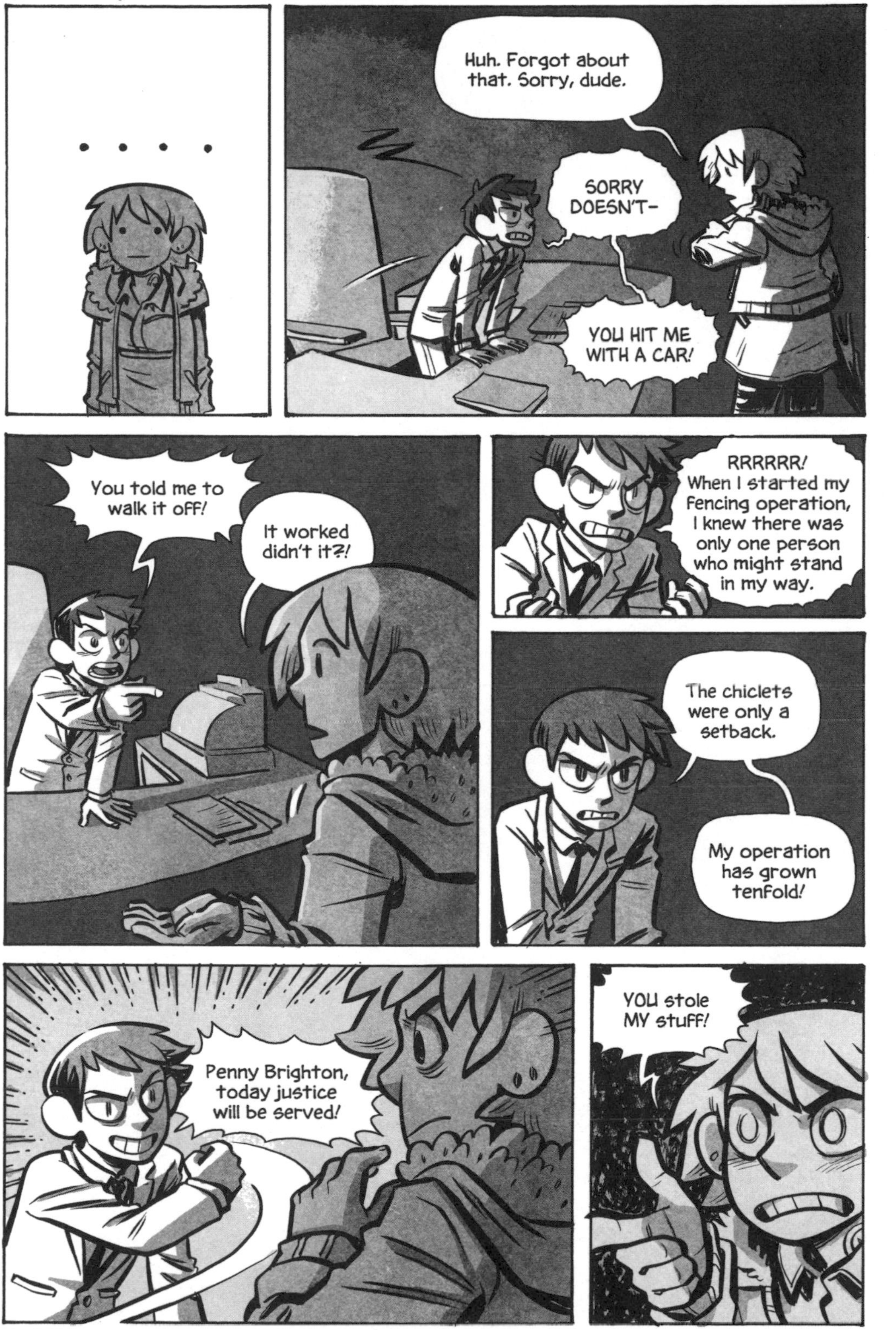
. . . .
Huh. Forgot about that. Sorry, dude.
SORRY DOESN'T-
YOU HIT ME WITH A CAR!
You told me to walk it off!
It worked didn't it?!
RRRRRR! When I started my fencing operation, I knew there was only one person who might stand in my way.
The chiclets were only a setback.
My operation has grown tenfold!
Penny Brighton, today justice will be served!
YOU stole MY stuff!

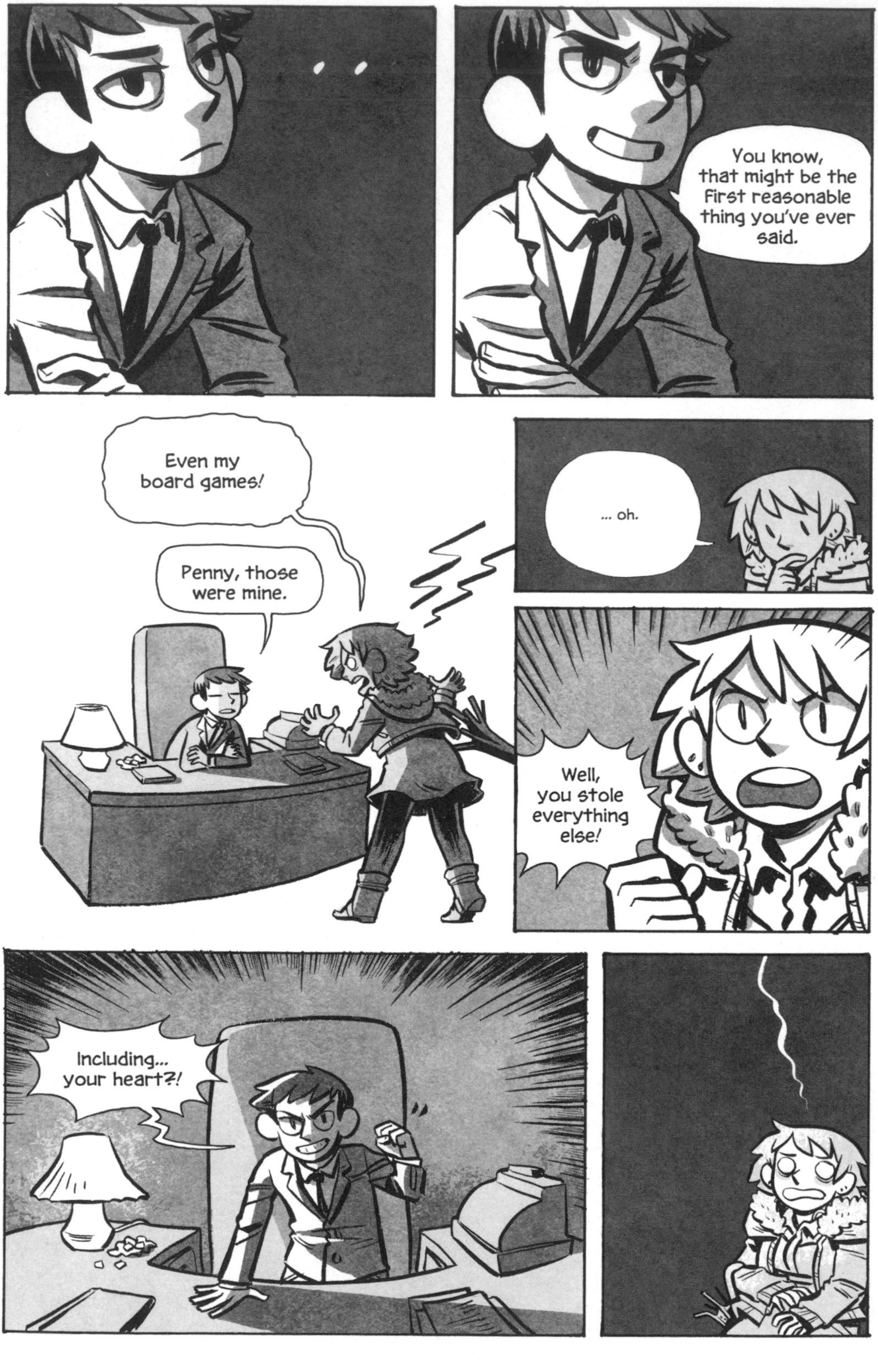
. .
You know, that might be the first reasonable thing you've ever said.
Even my board games!
Penny, those were mine.
... oh.
Well, you stole everything else!
Including... your heart?!

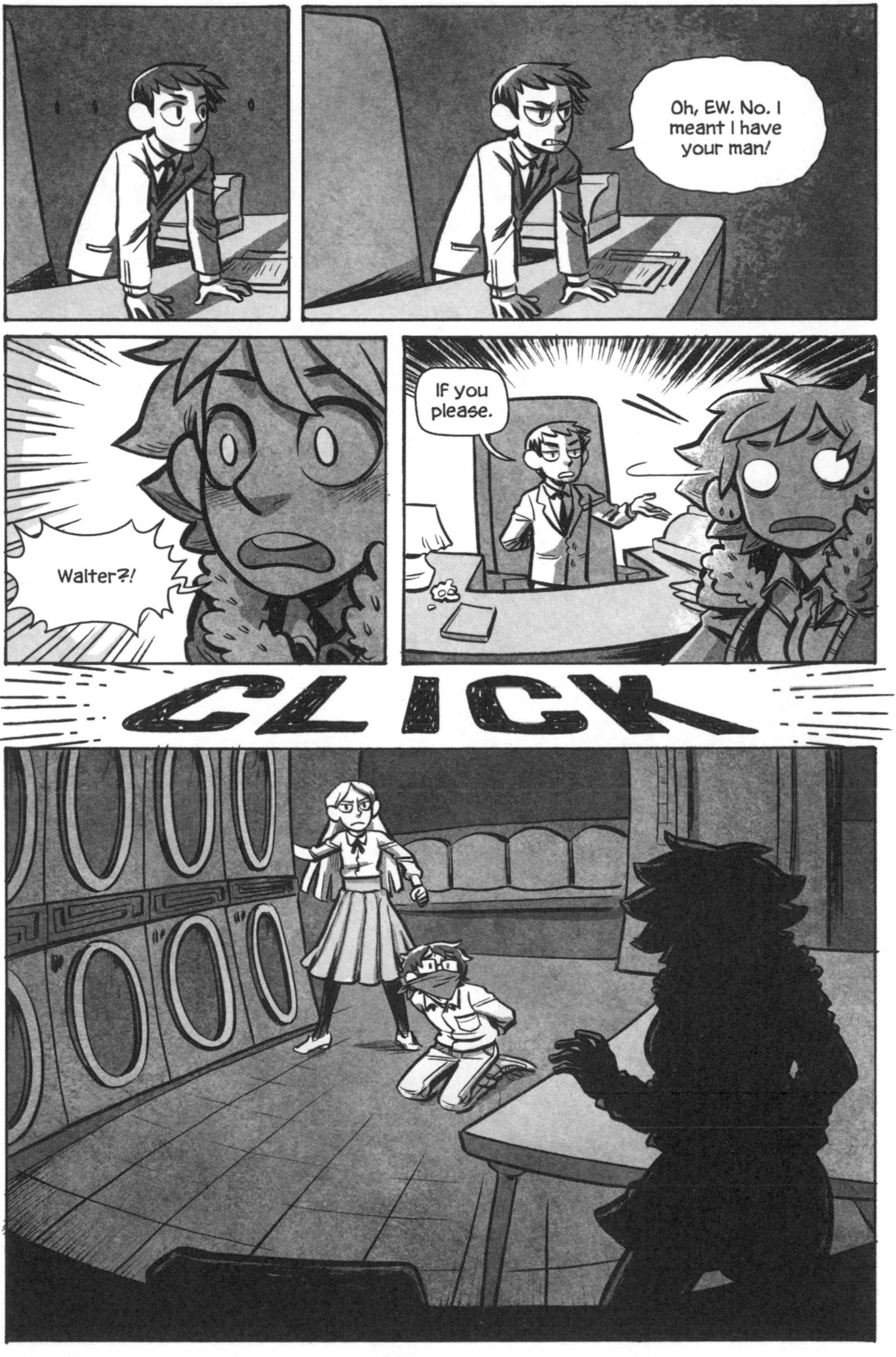

Oh, EW. No. I meant I have your man!
Walter?!
If you please.
CLICK

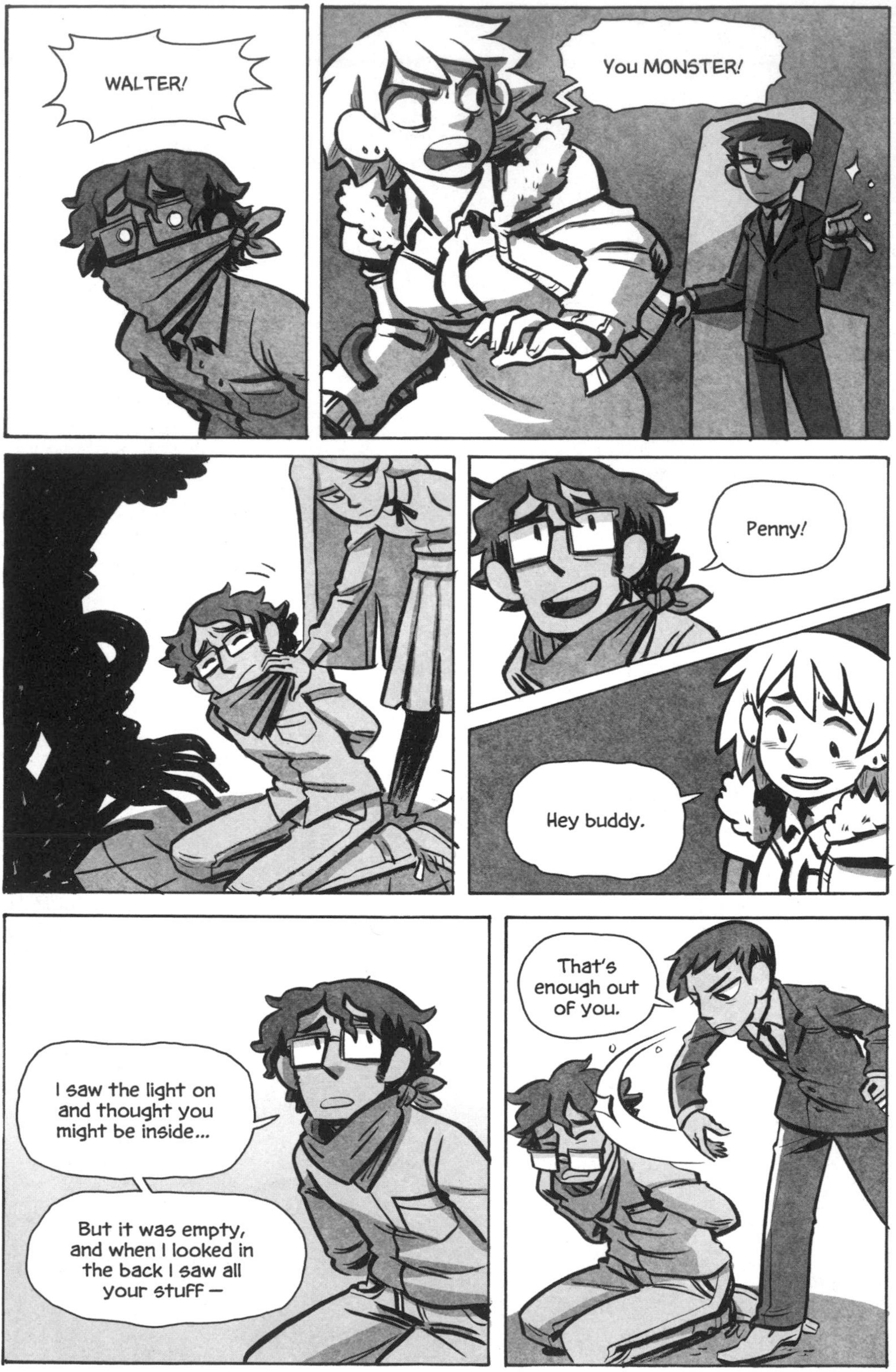
WALTER!
You MONSTER!
Penny!
Hey buddy.
I saw the light on and thought you might be inside...
But it was empty, and when I looked in the back I saw all your stuff —
That's enough out of you.

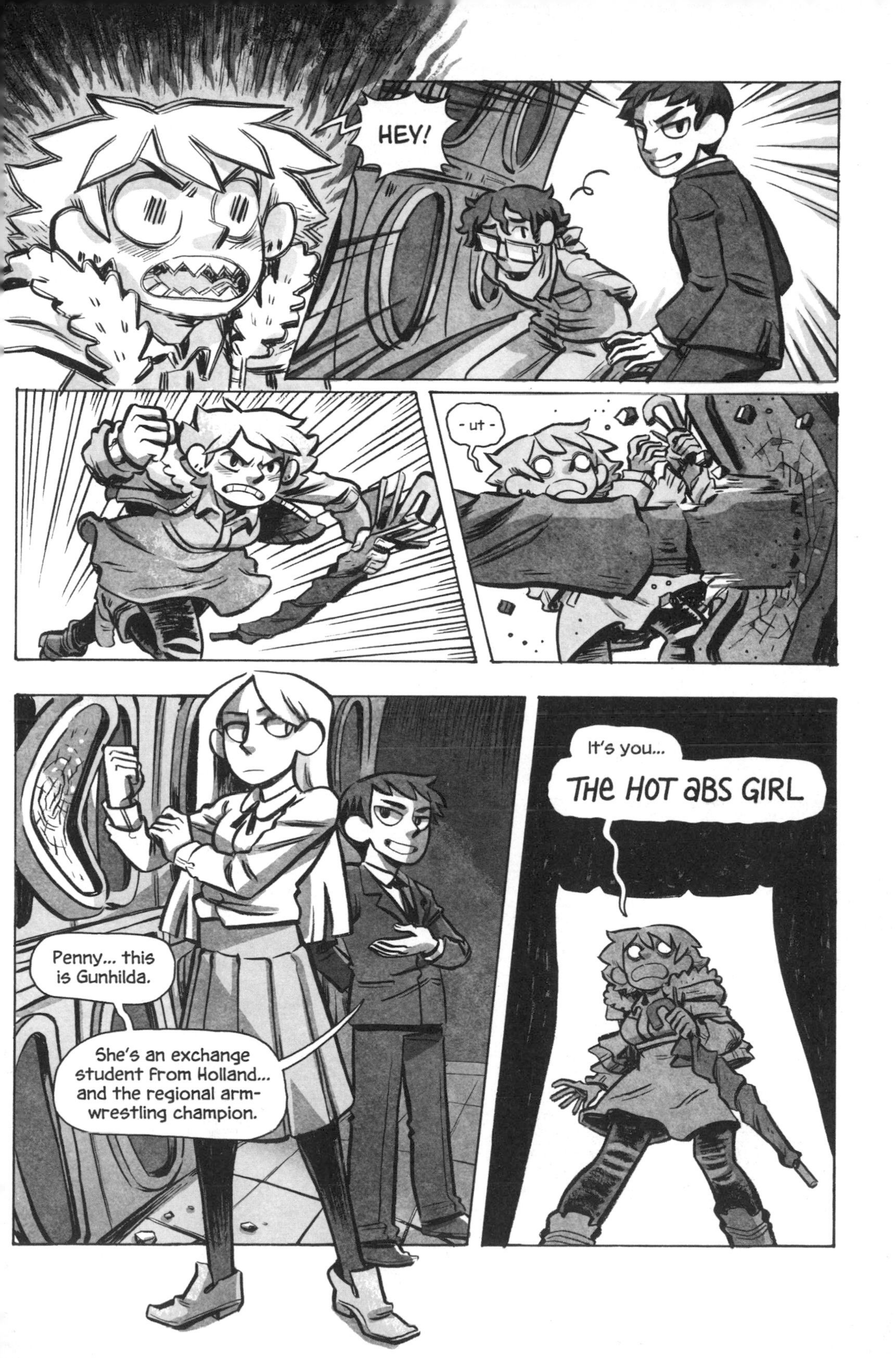
HEY!
- ut -
Penny... this is Gunhilda.
She's an exchange student from Holland... and the regional arm-wrestling champion.
It's you...
THE HOT aBS GIRL

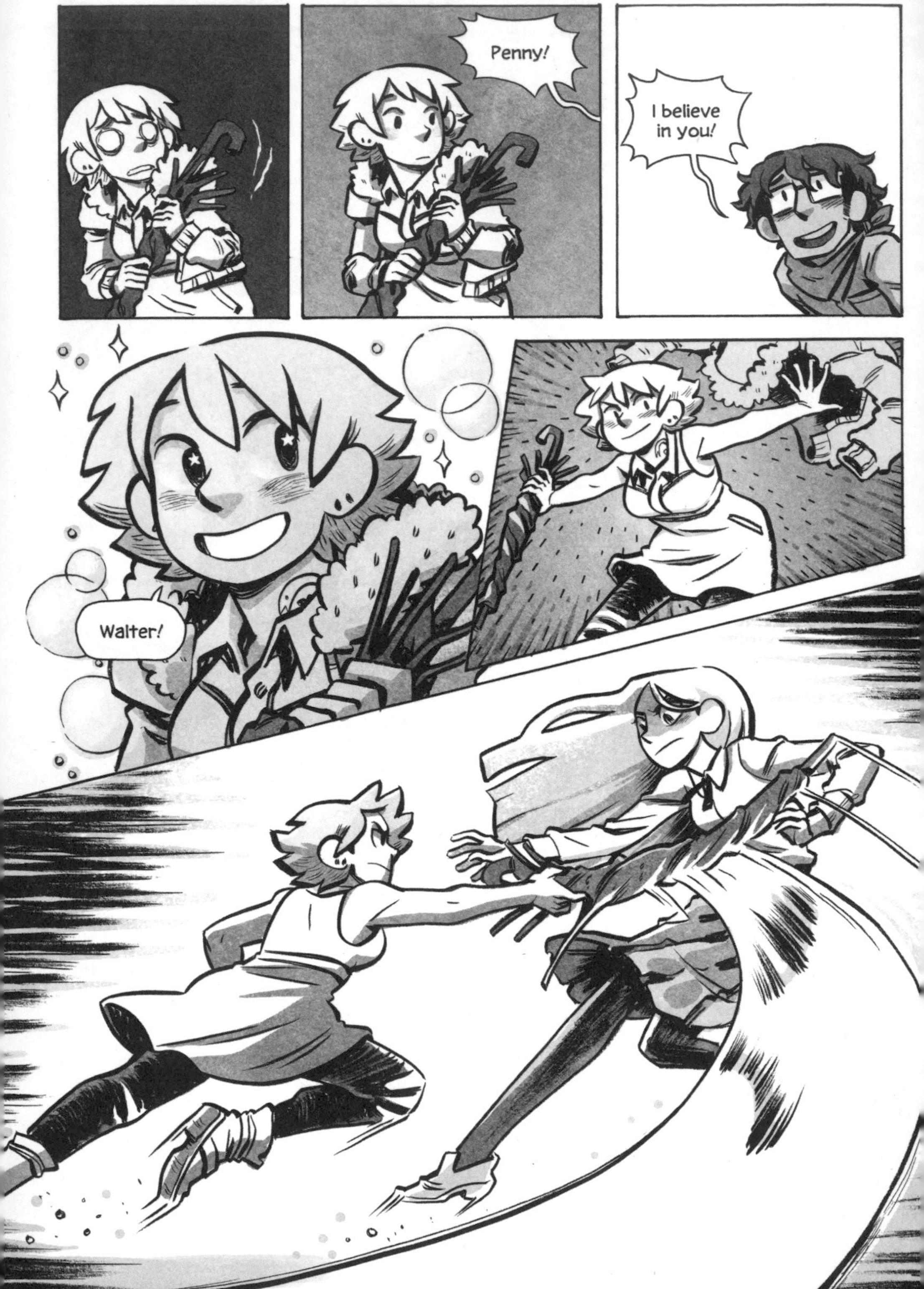
Penny!
I believe in you!
Walter!

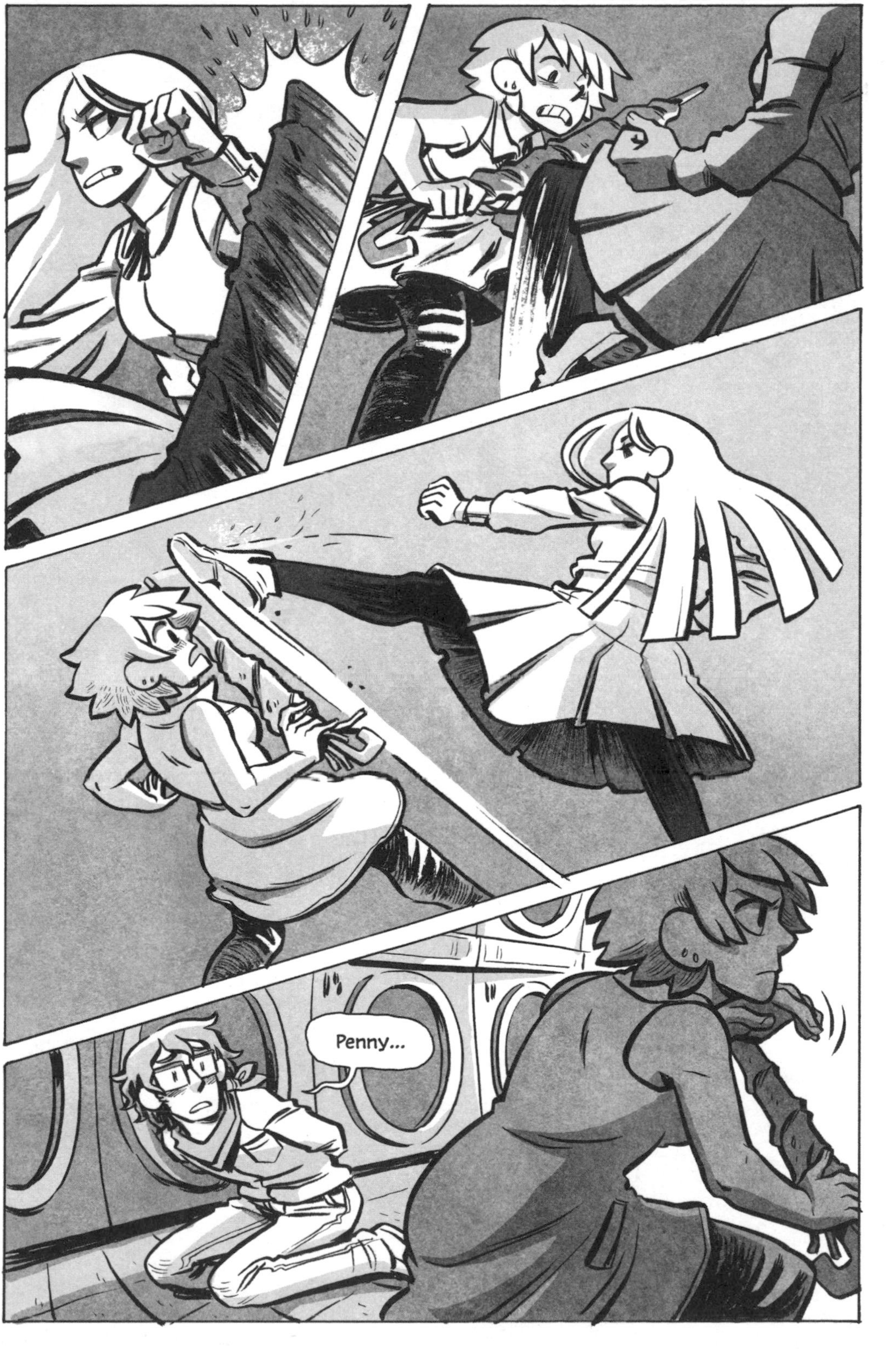
Penny...

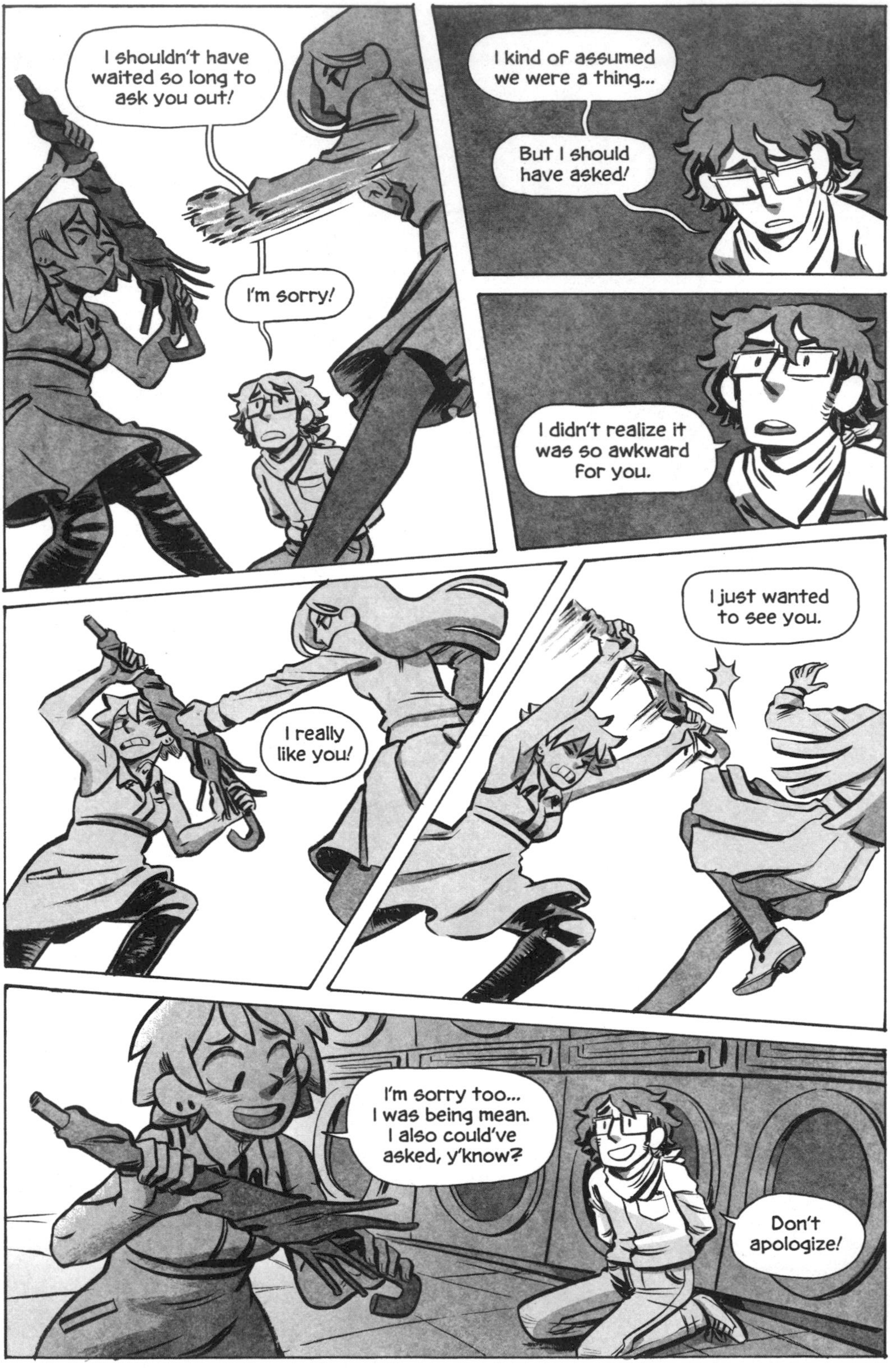
I shouldn't have waited so long to ask you out!
I'm sorry!
I kind of assumed we were a thing...
But I should have asked!
I didn't realize it was so awkward for you.
I really like you!
I just wanted to see you.
I'm sorry too... I was being mean. I also could've asked, y'know?
Don't apologize!

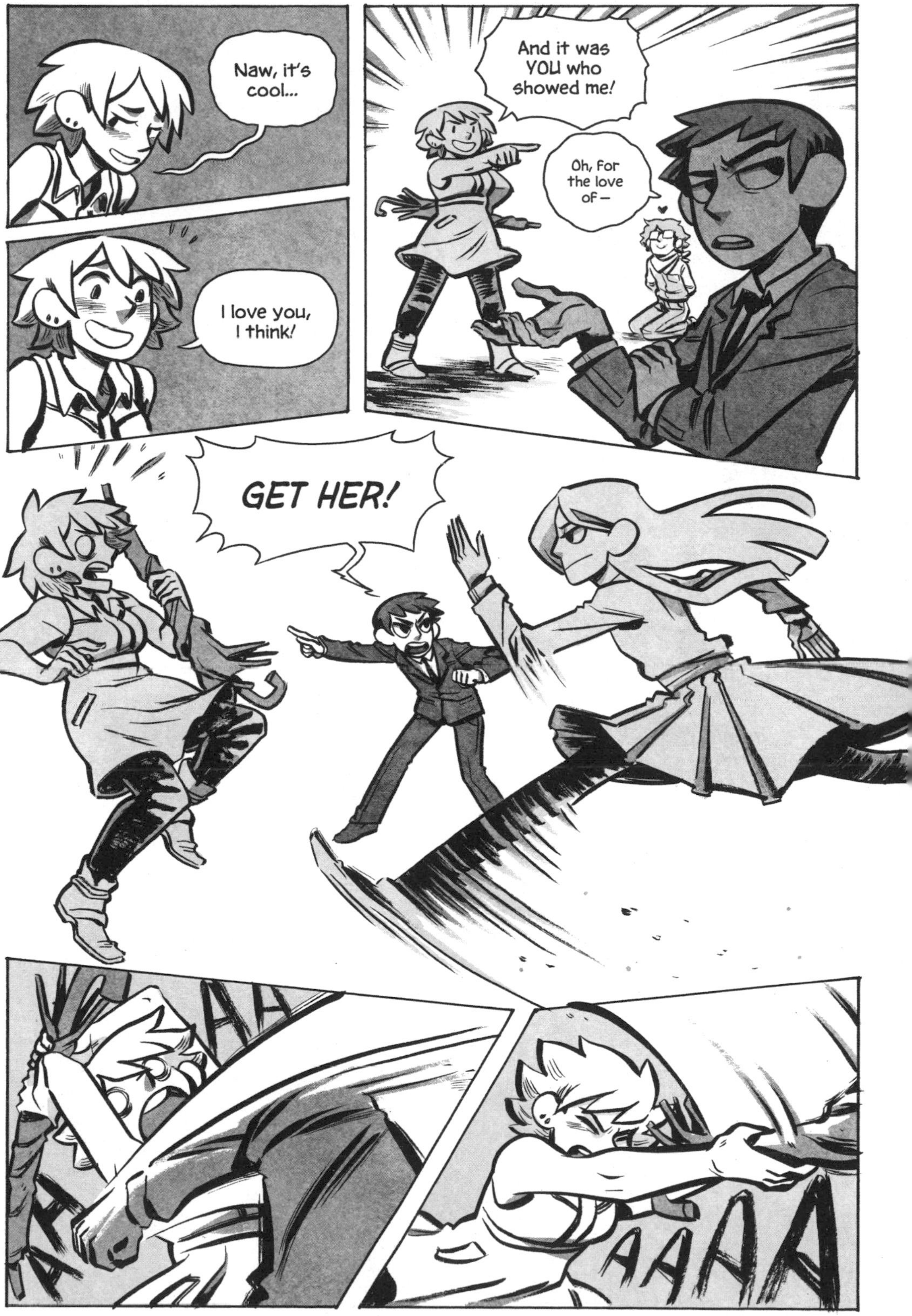
Naw, it's cool...
I love you, I think!
And it was YOU who showed me!
Oh, for the love of—
GET HER!
AAAA

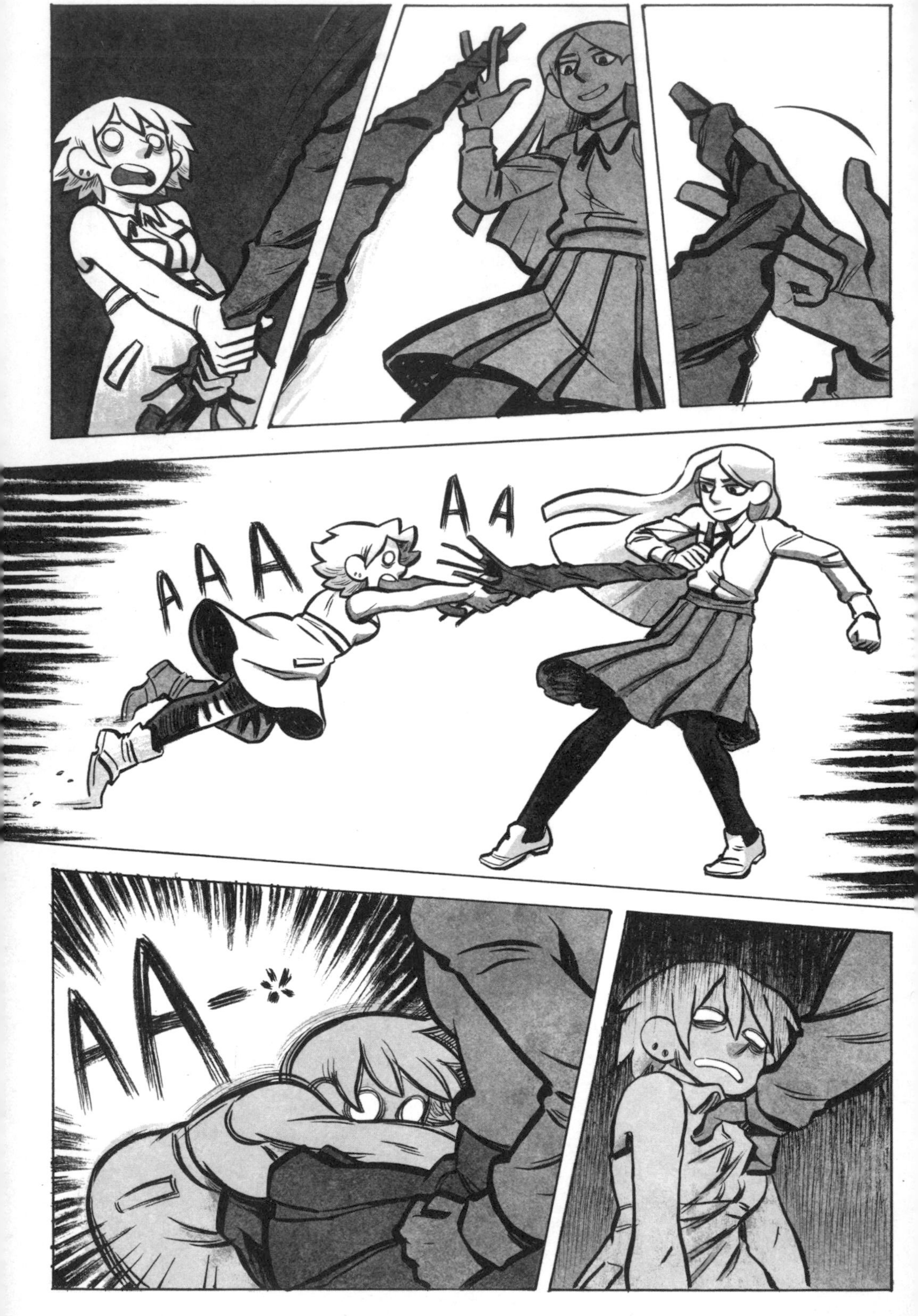
AAAAA
AA-

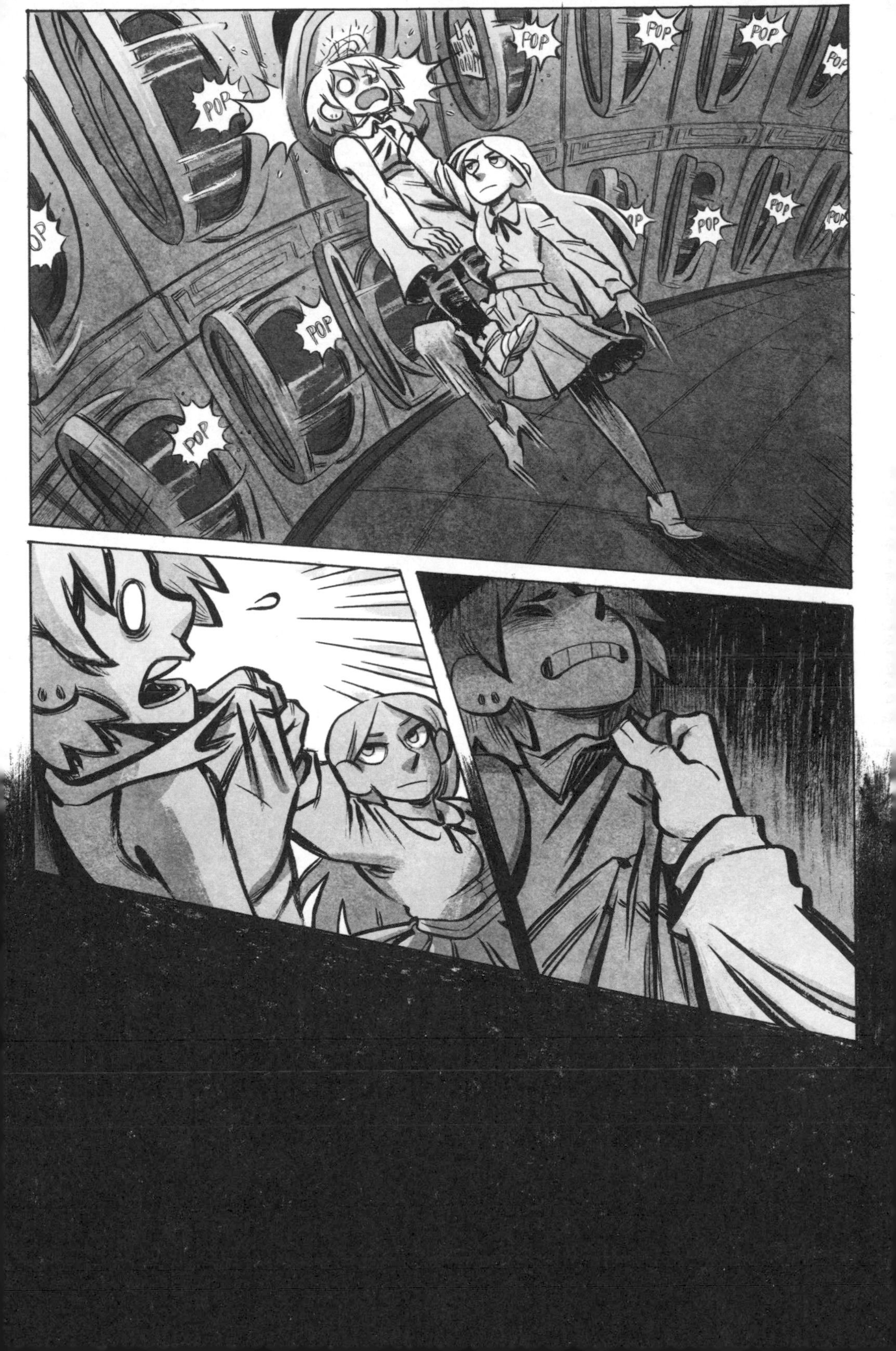
POP
POP
POP
POP
POP
POP
POP
POP
POP
POP

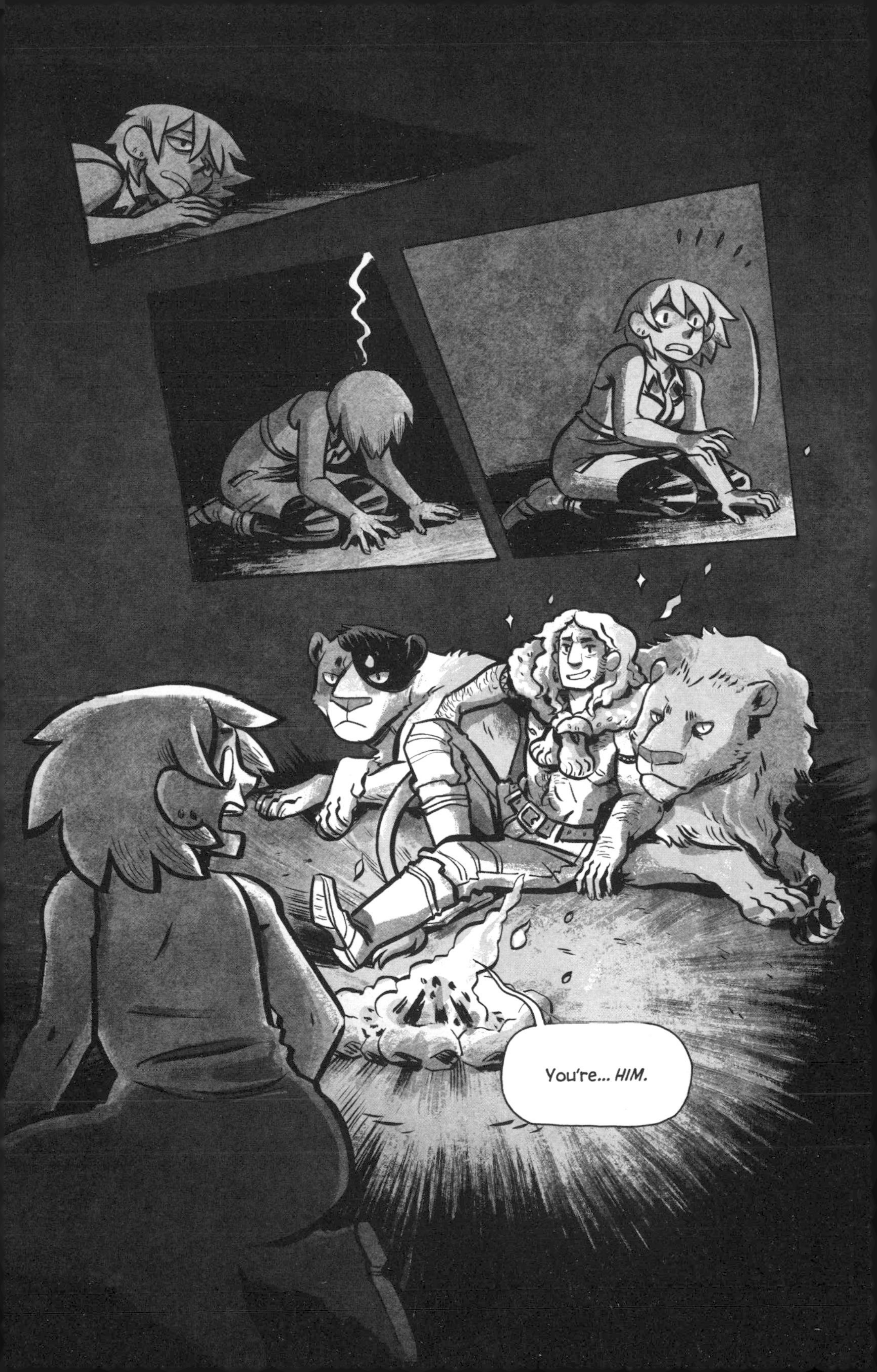
You're... HIM.

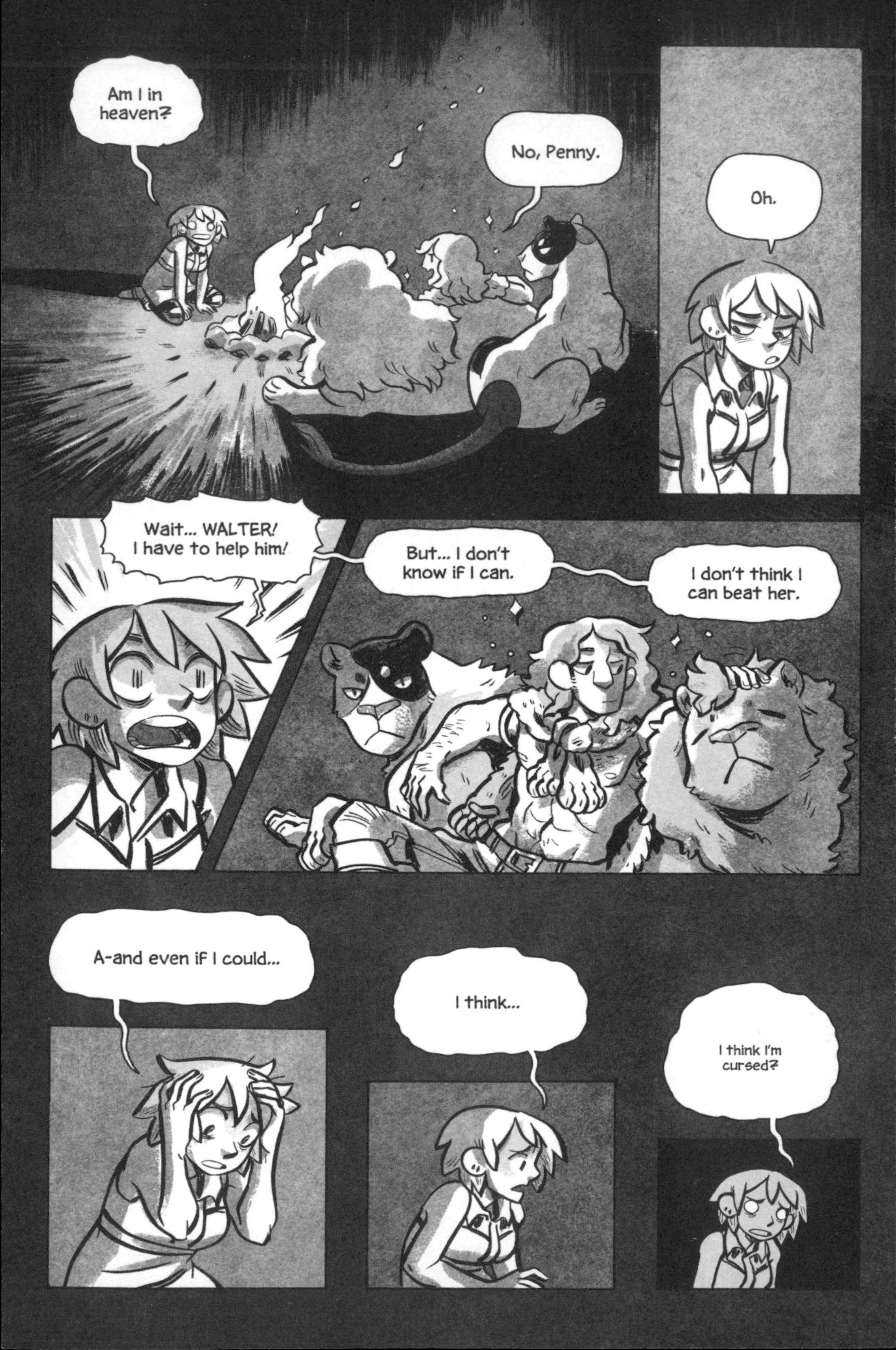

Am I in heaven?
No, Penny.
Oh.
Wait... WALTER! I have to help him!
But... I don't know if I can.
I don't think I can beat her.
A-and even if I could...
I think...
I think I'm cursed?

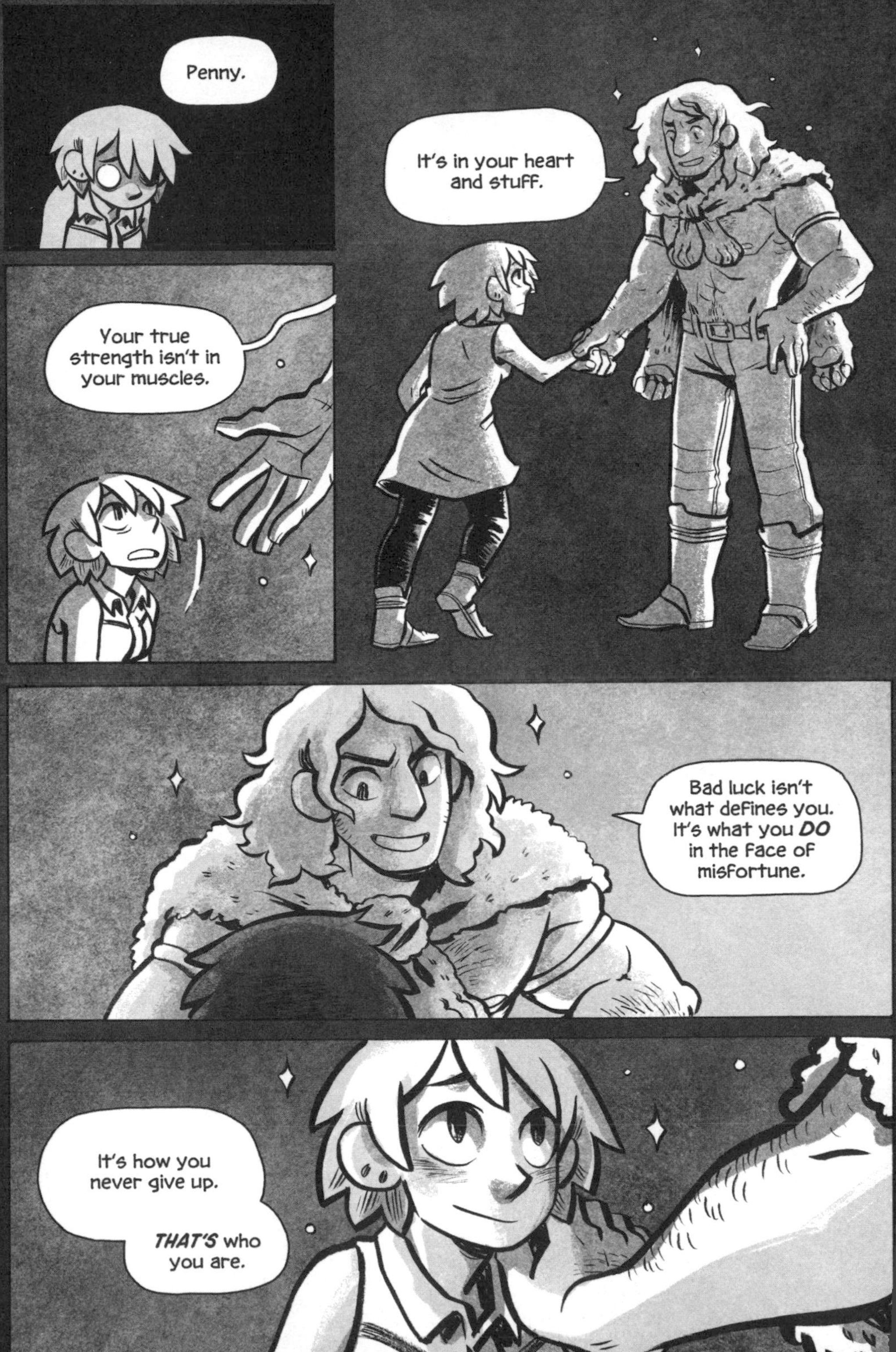
Penny.
It's in your heart and stuff.
Your true strength isn't in your muscles.
Bad luck isn't what defines you. It's what you *DO* in the face of misfortune.
It's how you never give up.
THAT'S who you are.

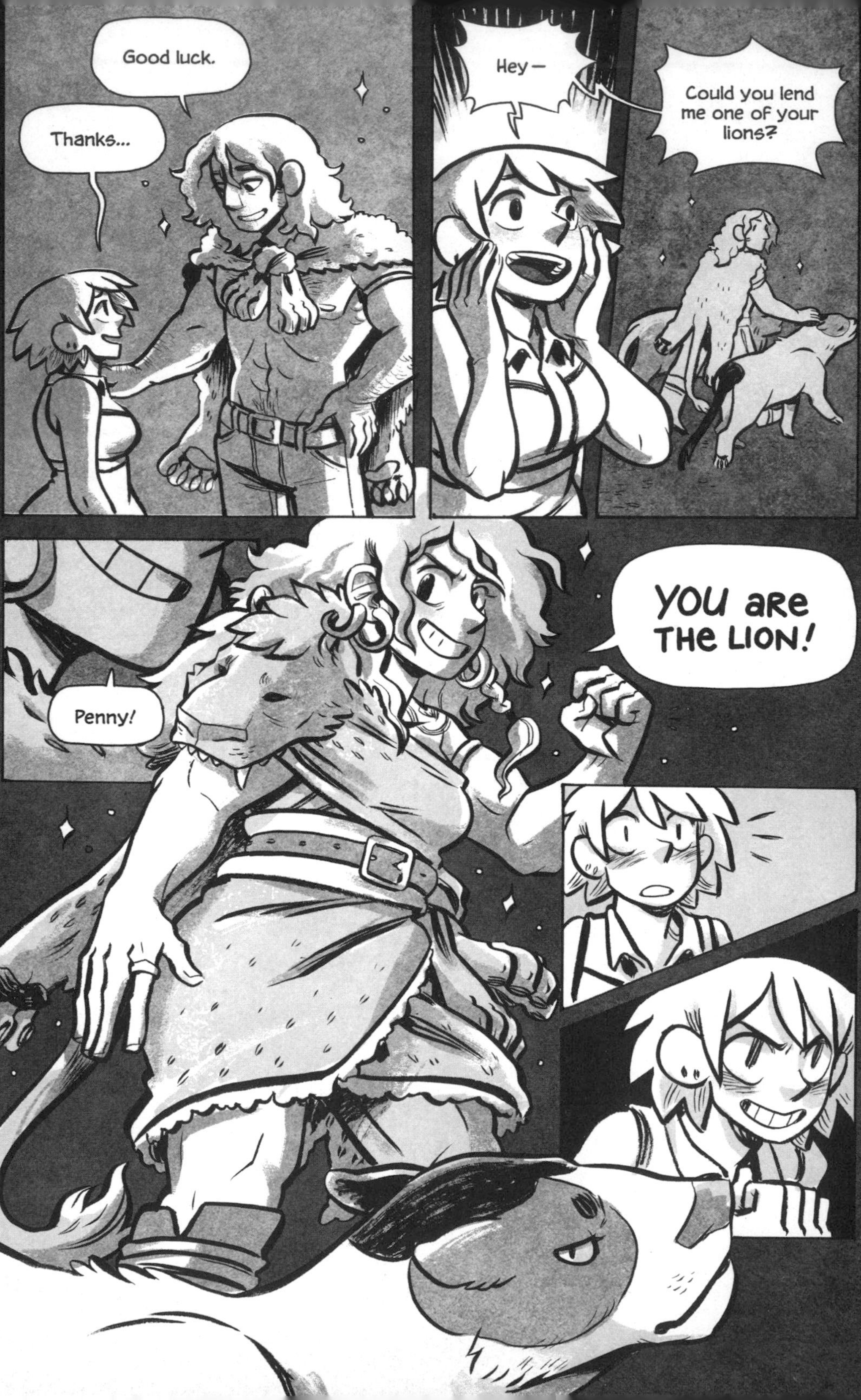
Good luck.
Thanks...
Hey—
Could you lend me one of your lions?
Penny!
YOU are THE LION!

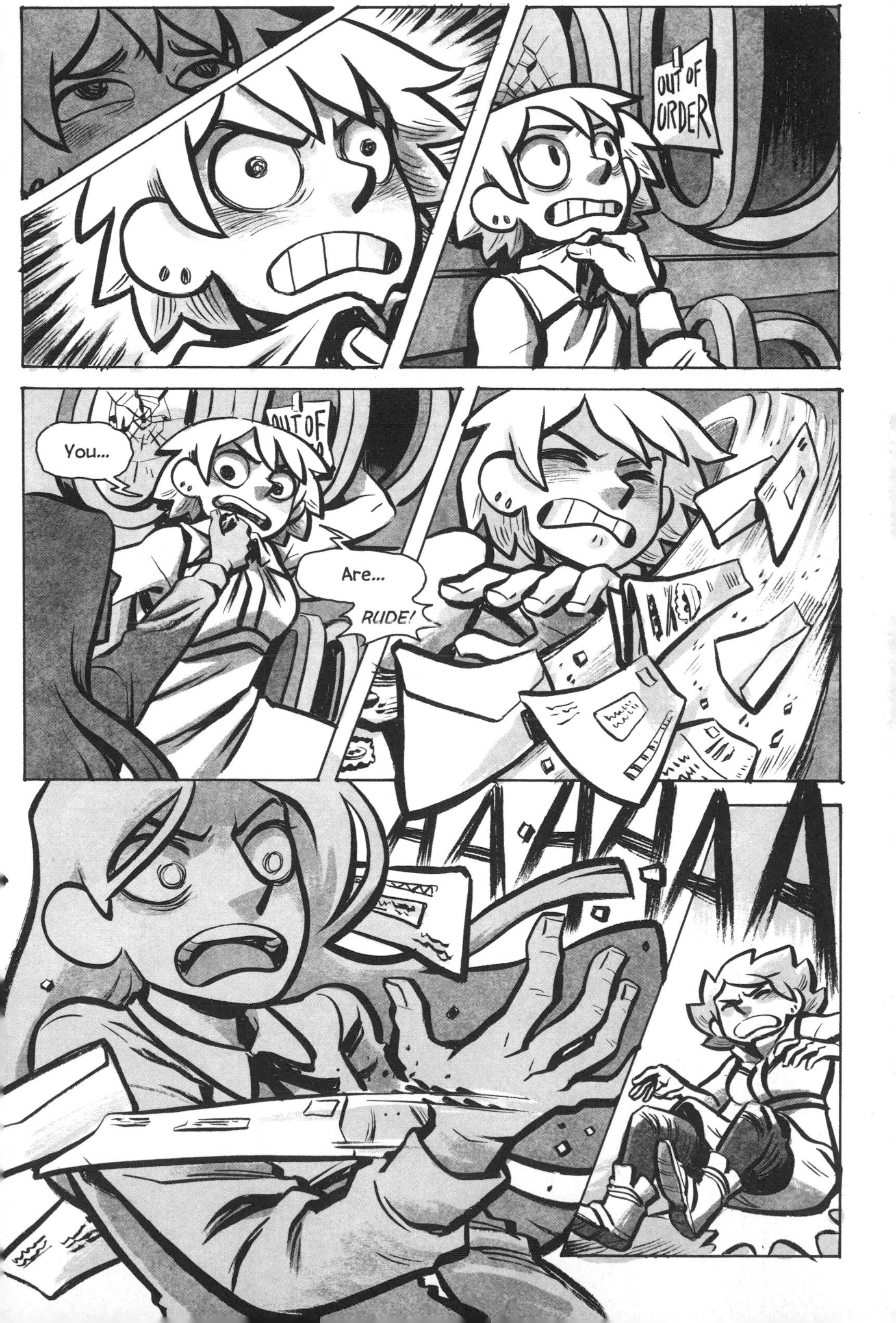
OUT OF ORDER
You...
Are...
RUDE!

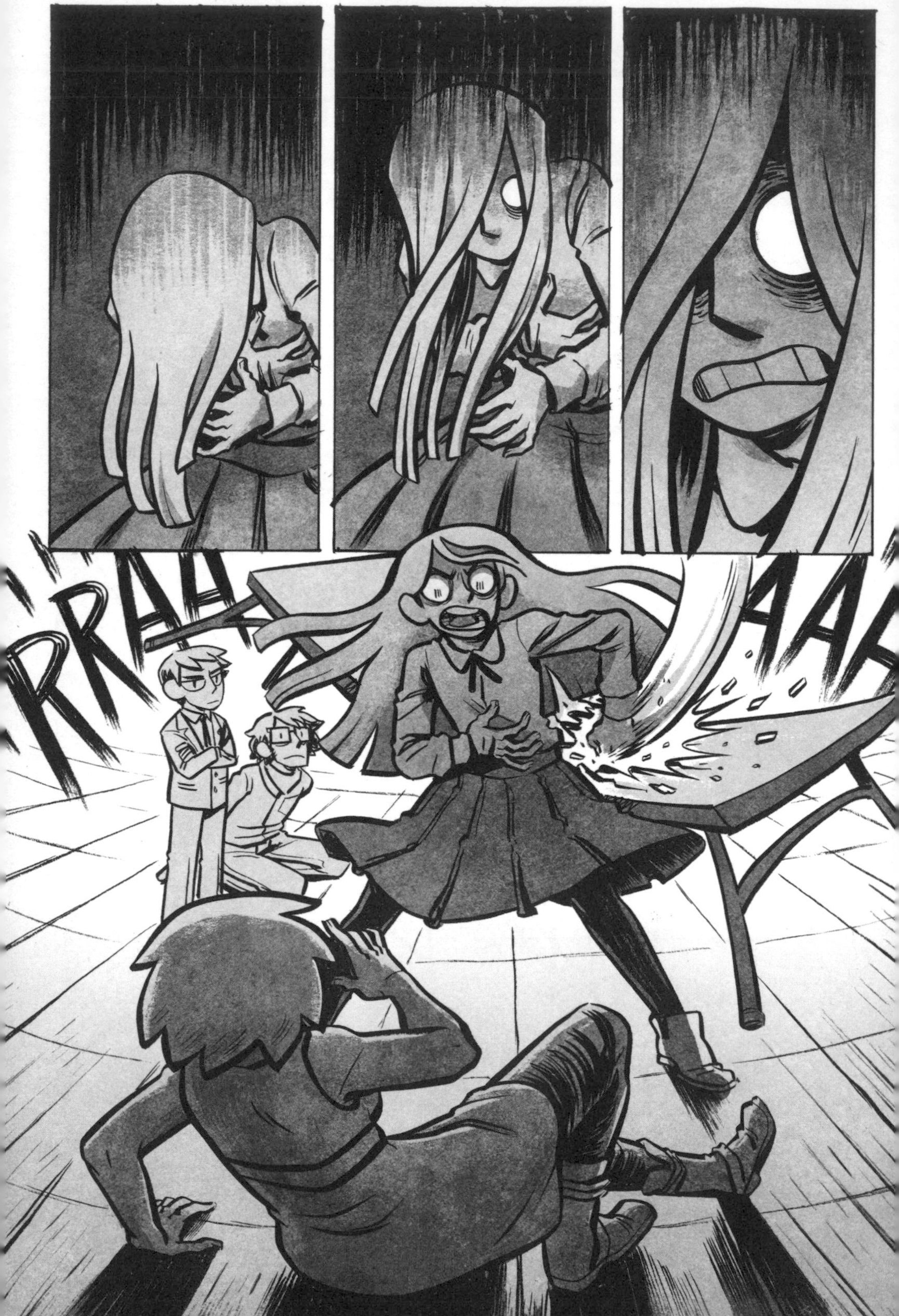
RRAAH AAAR

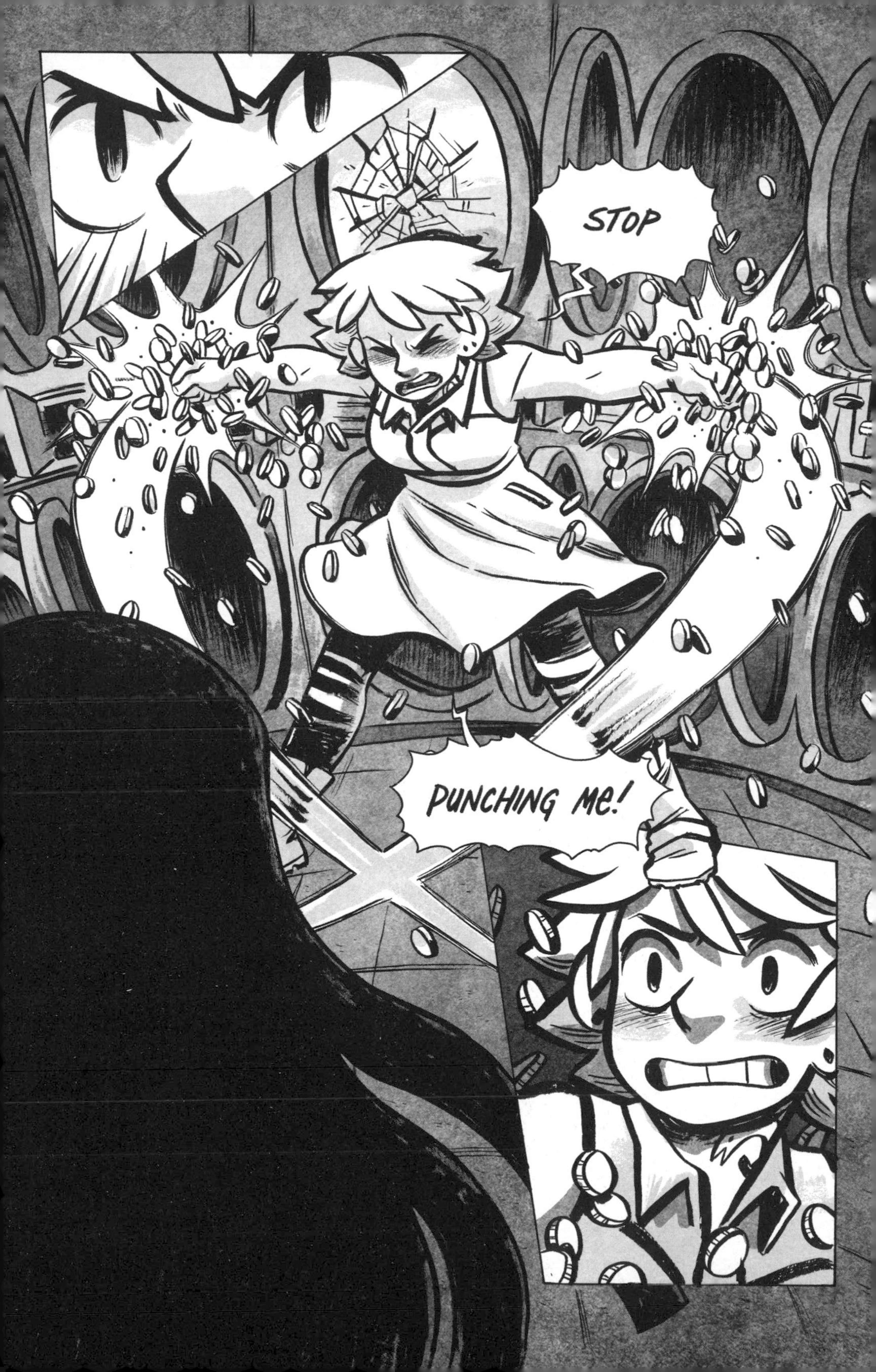
STOP
PUNCHING ME!

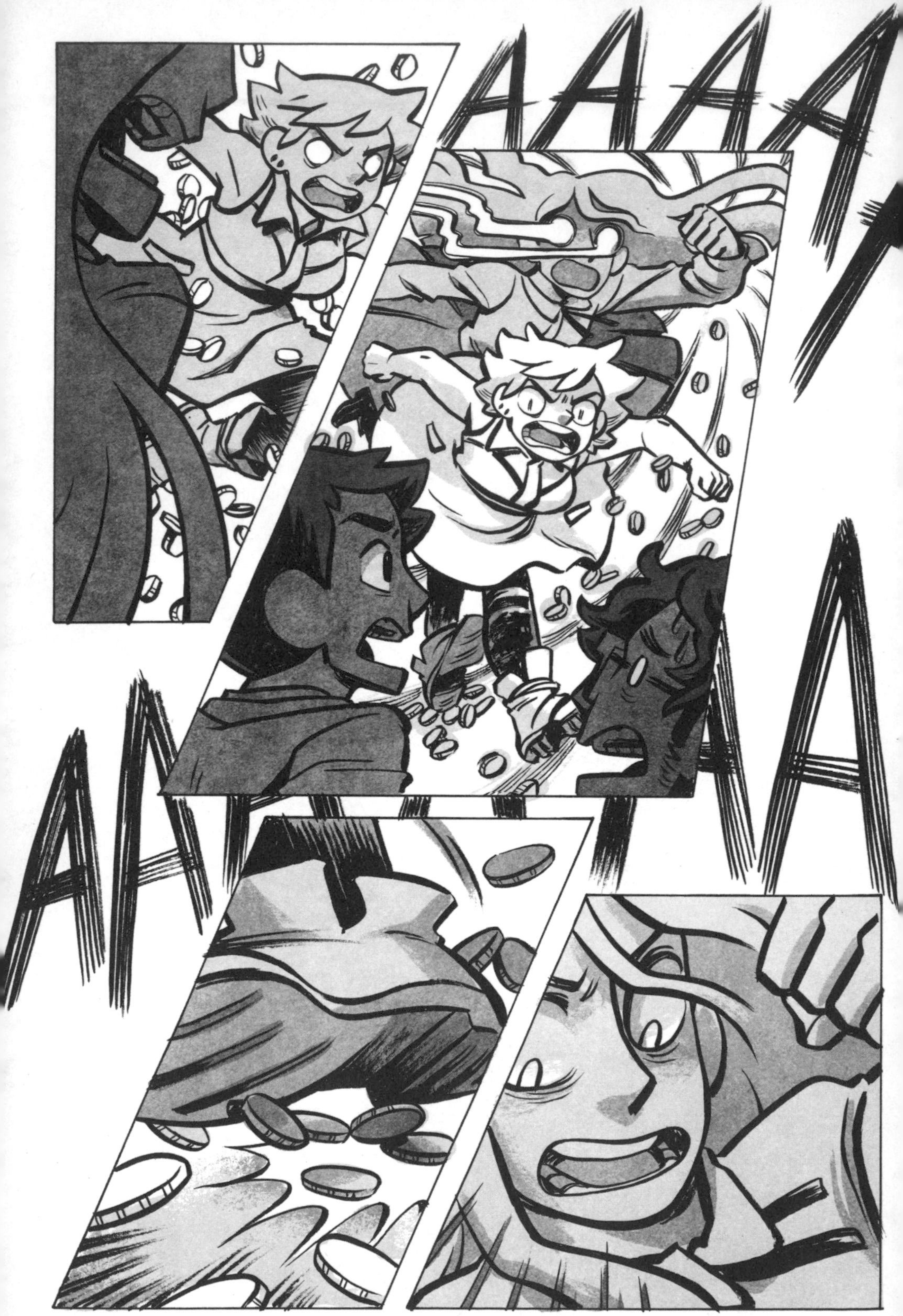
AAAAAAAAAA

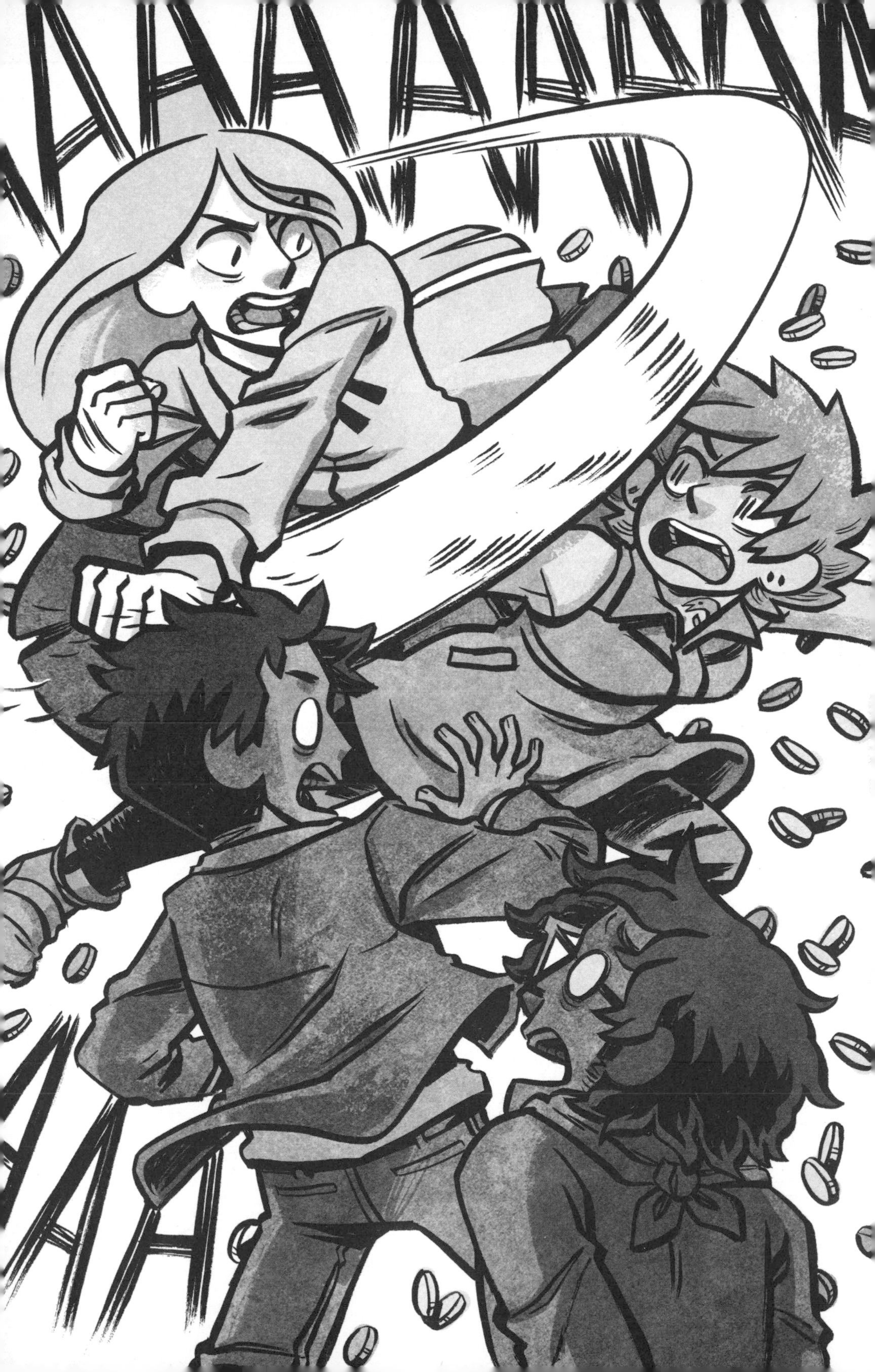

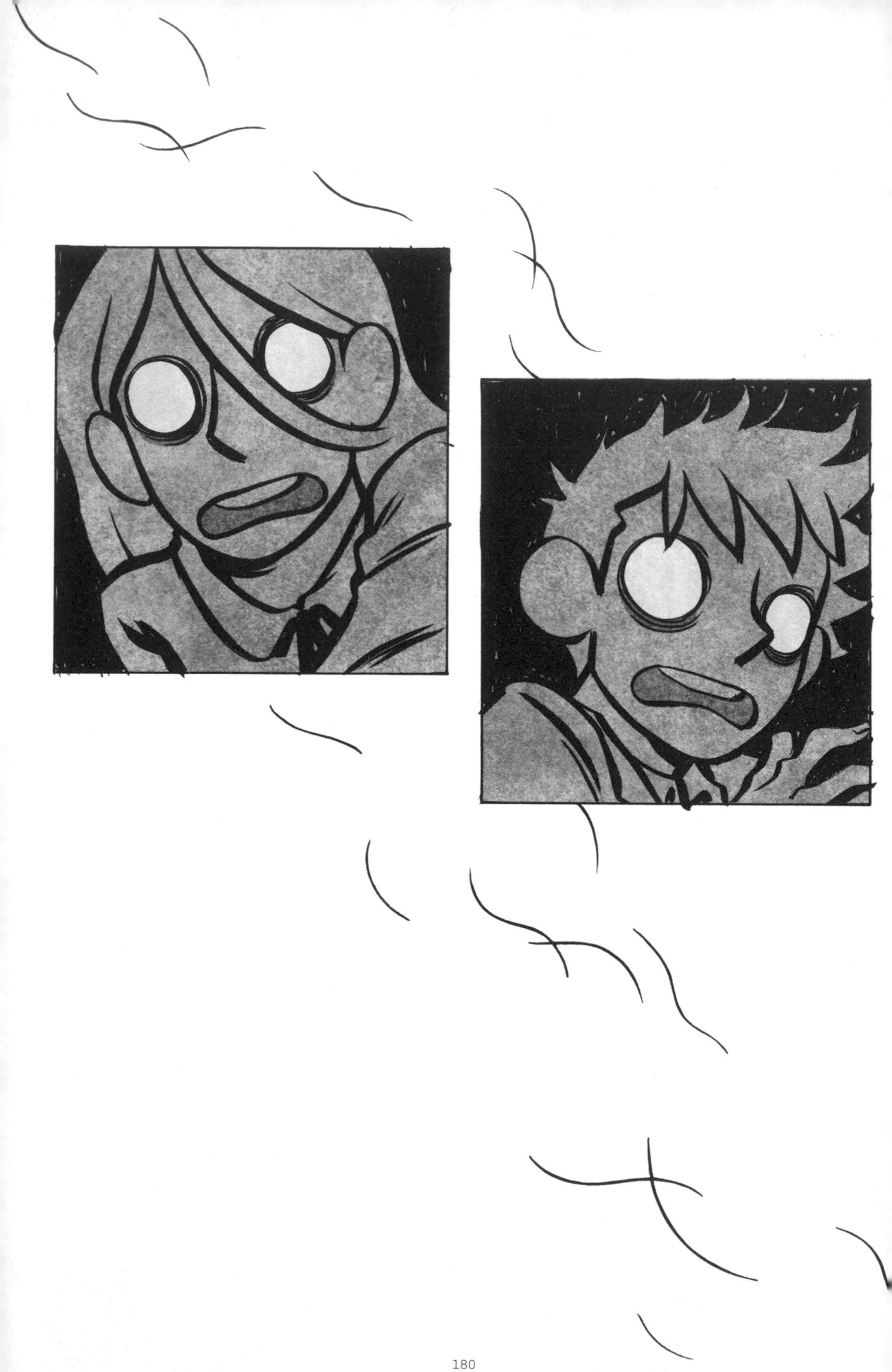

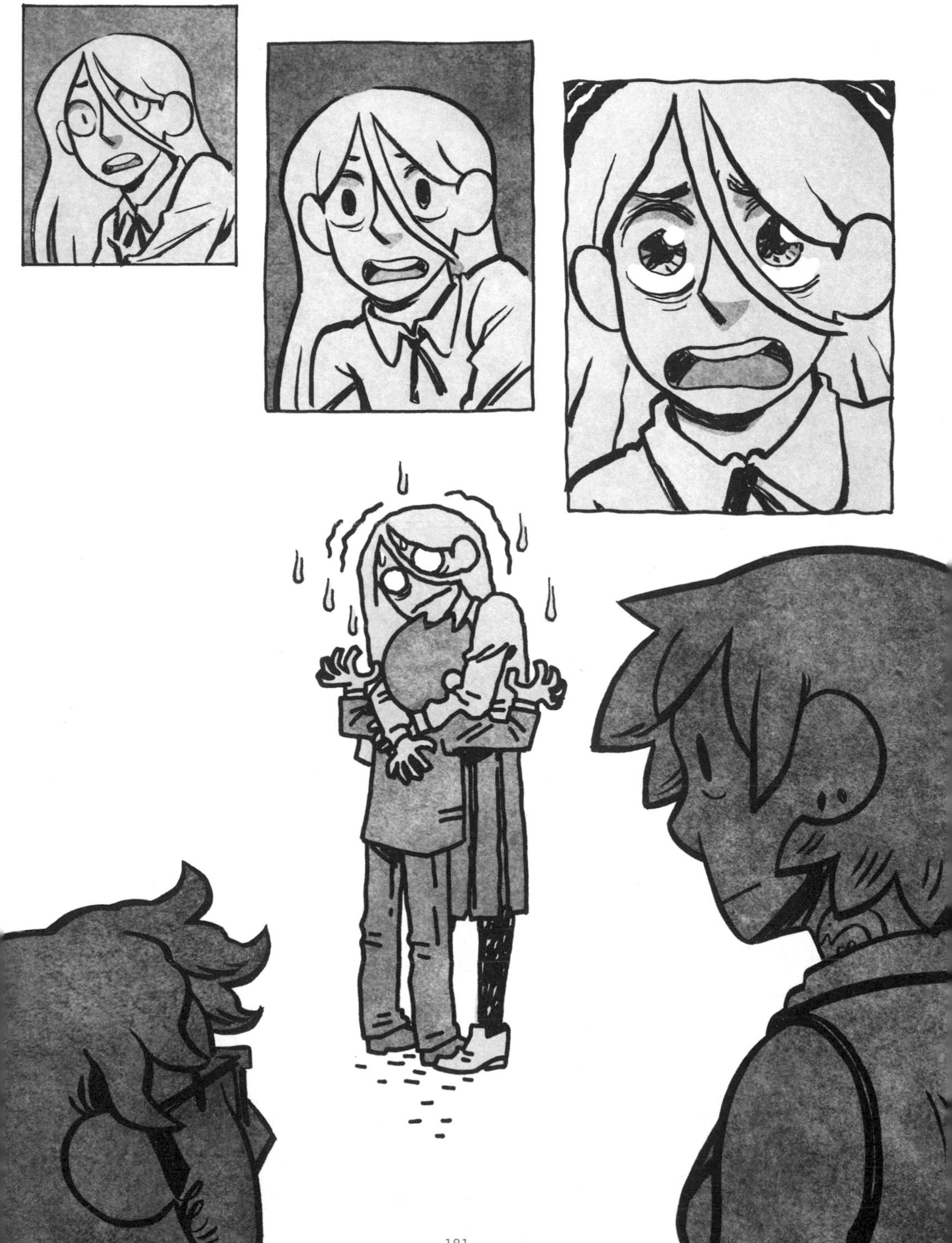

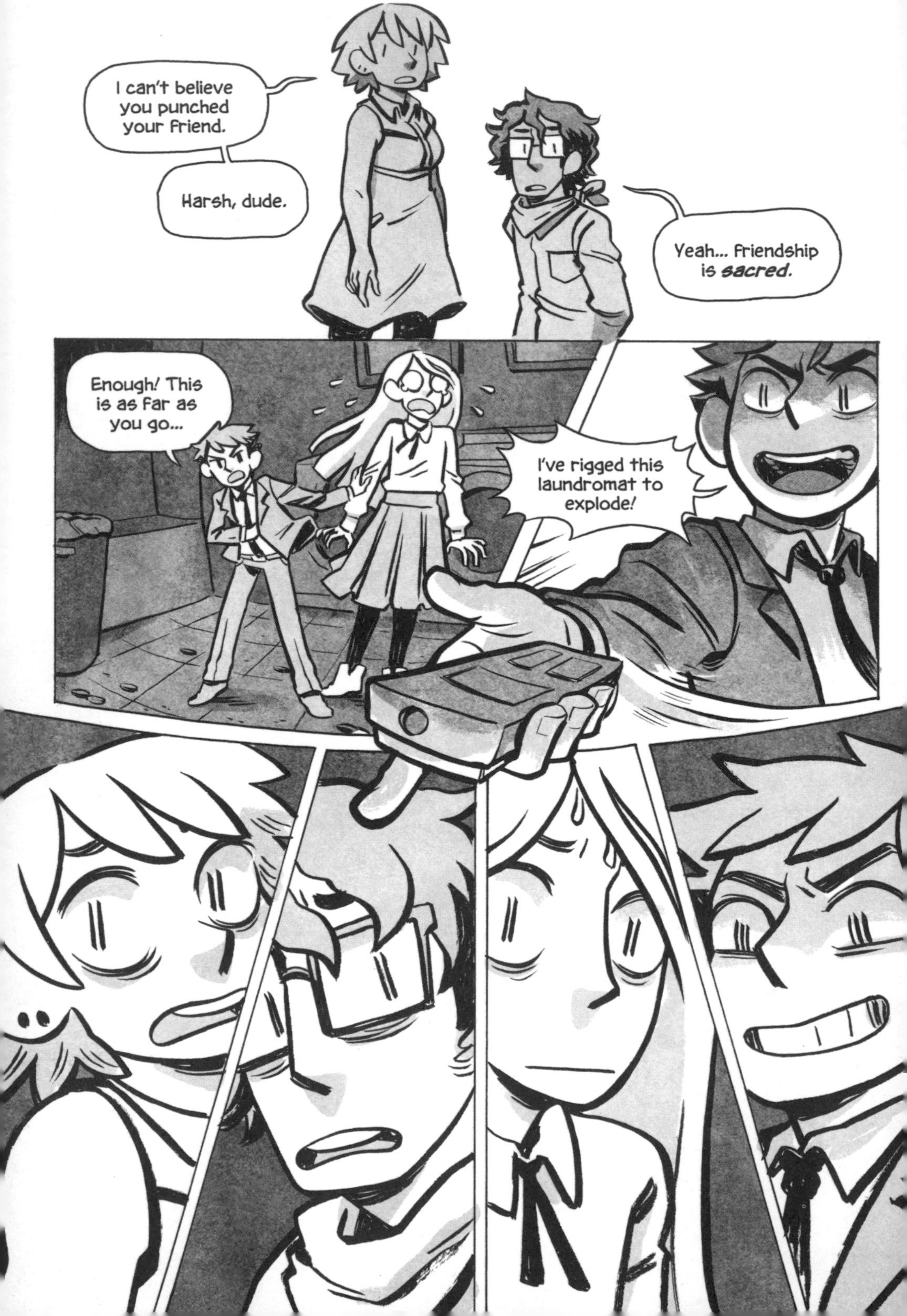
I can't believe you punched your friend.
Harsh, dude.
Yeah... friendship is *sacred.*
Enough! This is as far as you go...
I've rigged this laundromat to explode!

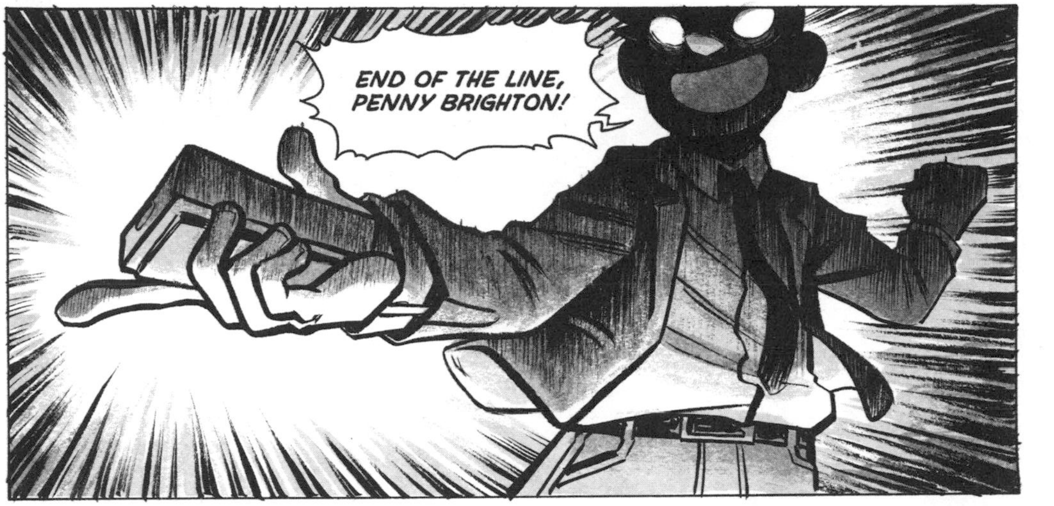
END OF THE LINE, PENNY BRIGHTON!

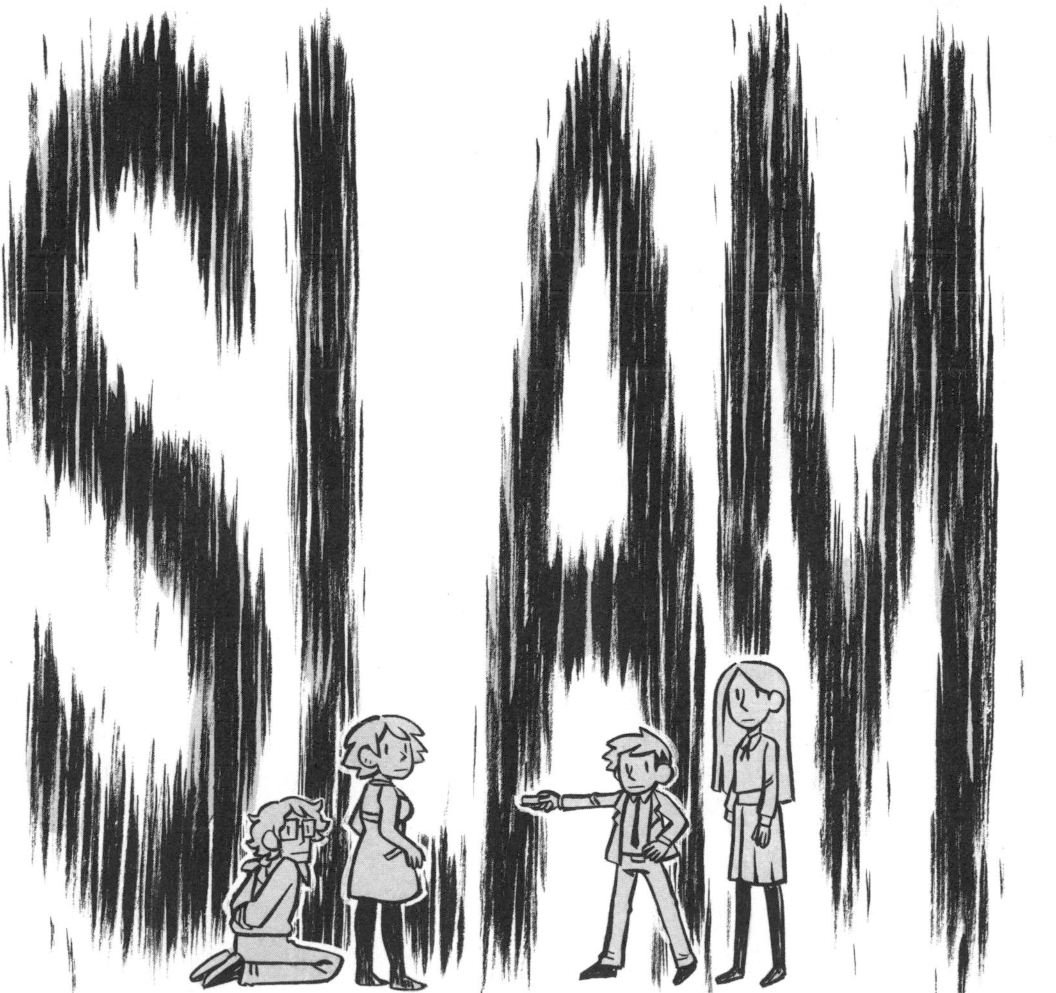
SLAM

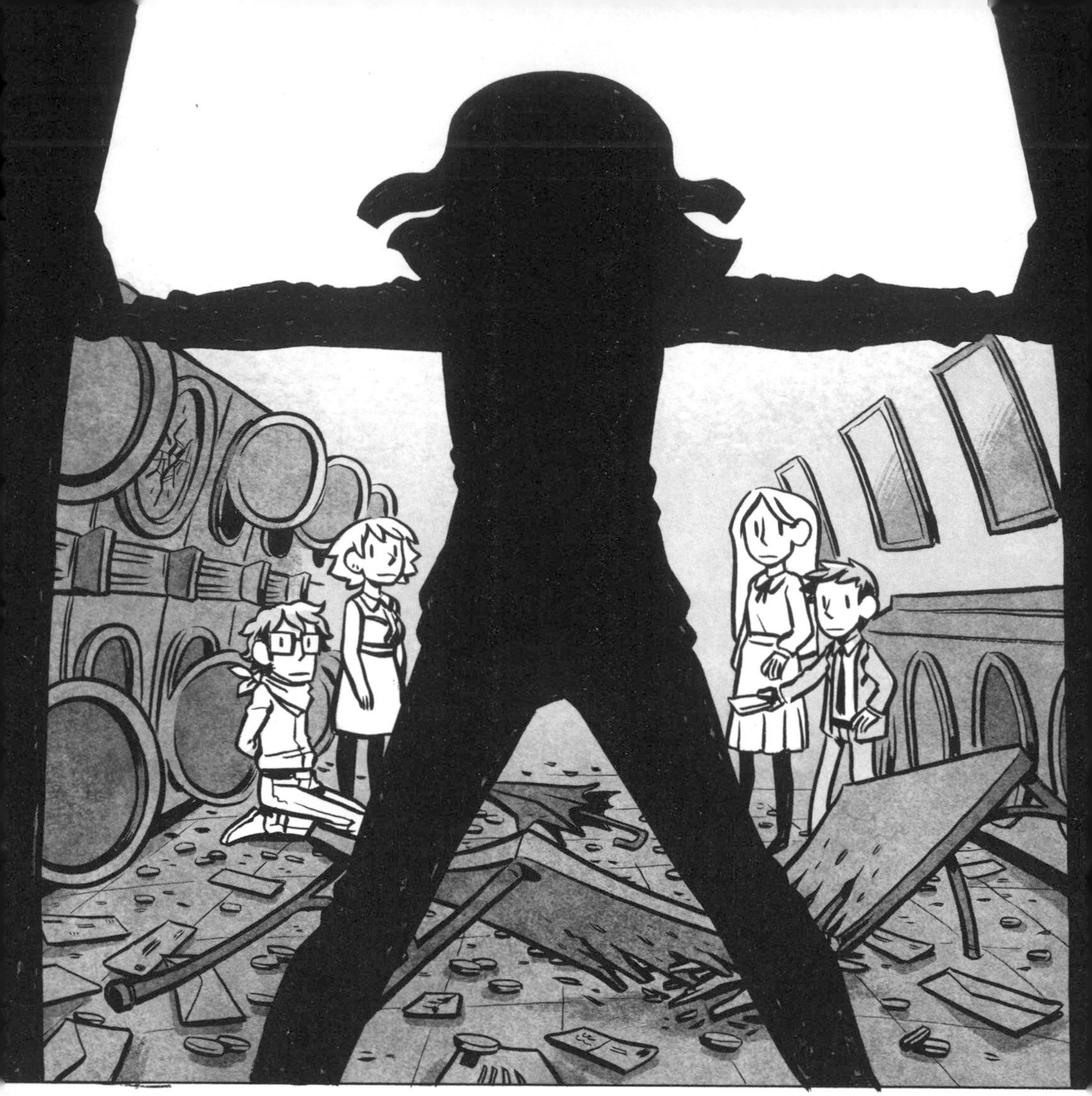

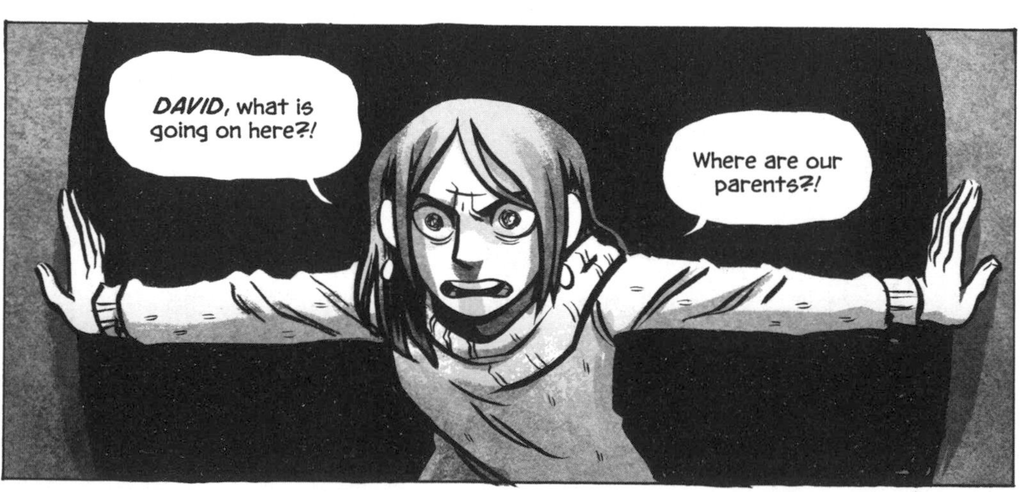
DAVID, what is going on here?!
Where are our parents?!

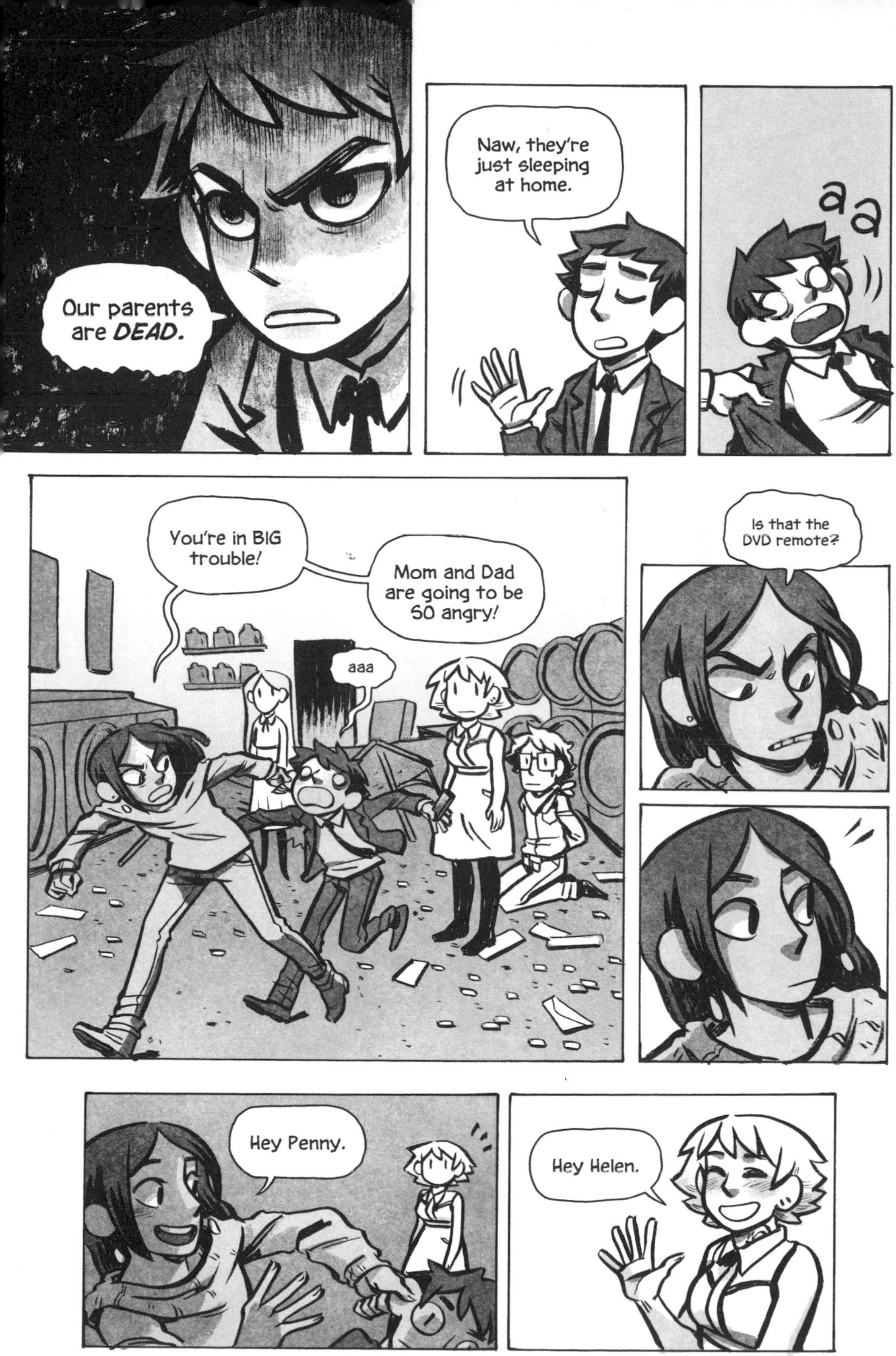
Our parents are DEAD.
Naw, they're just sleeping at home.
aa
You're in BIG trouble!
Mom and Dad are going to be SO angry!
aaa
Is that the DVD remote?
Hey Penny.
Hey Helen.

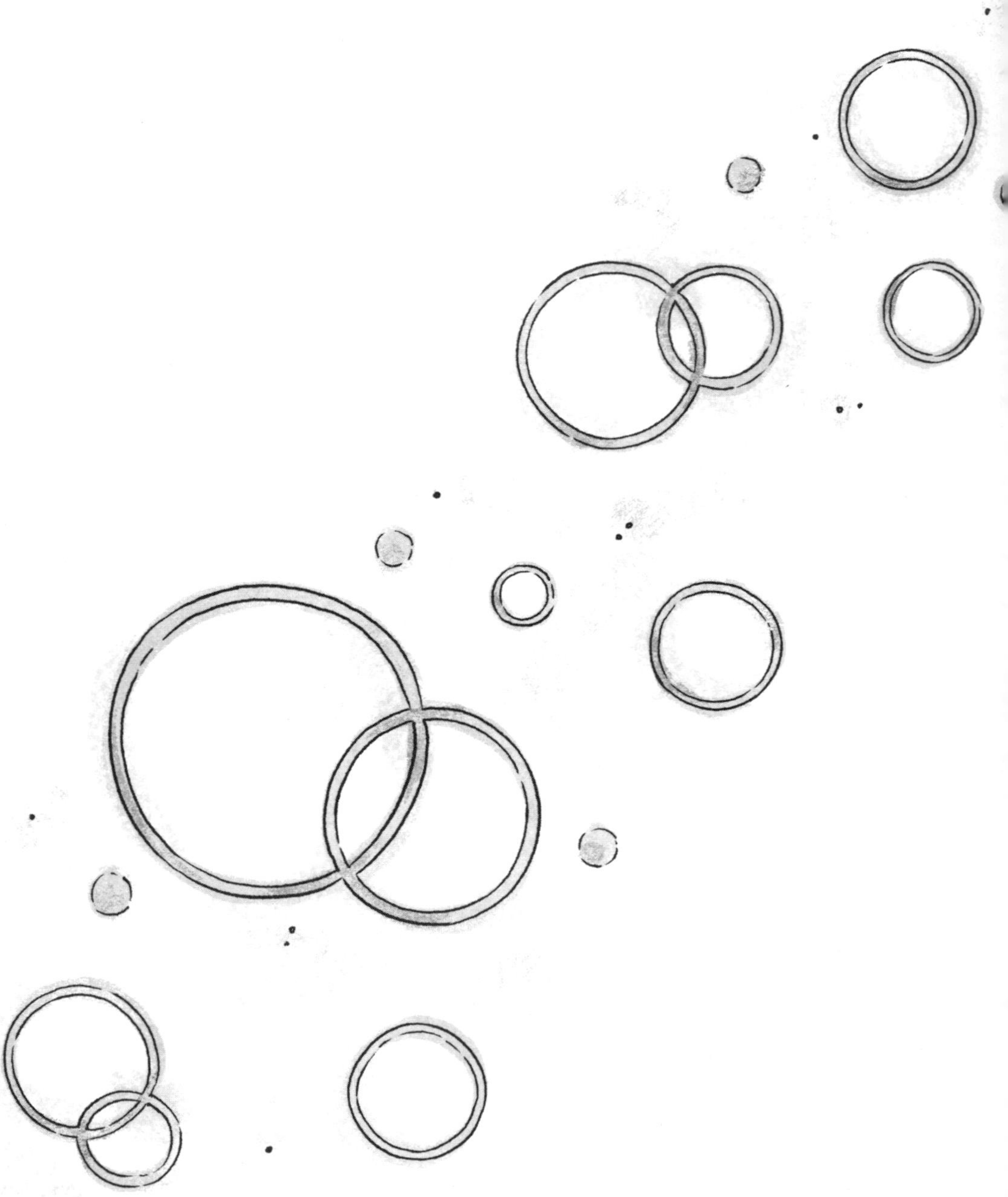

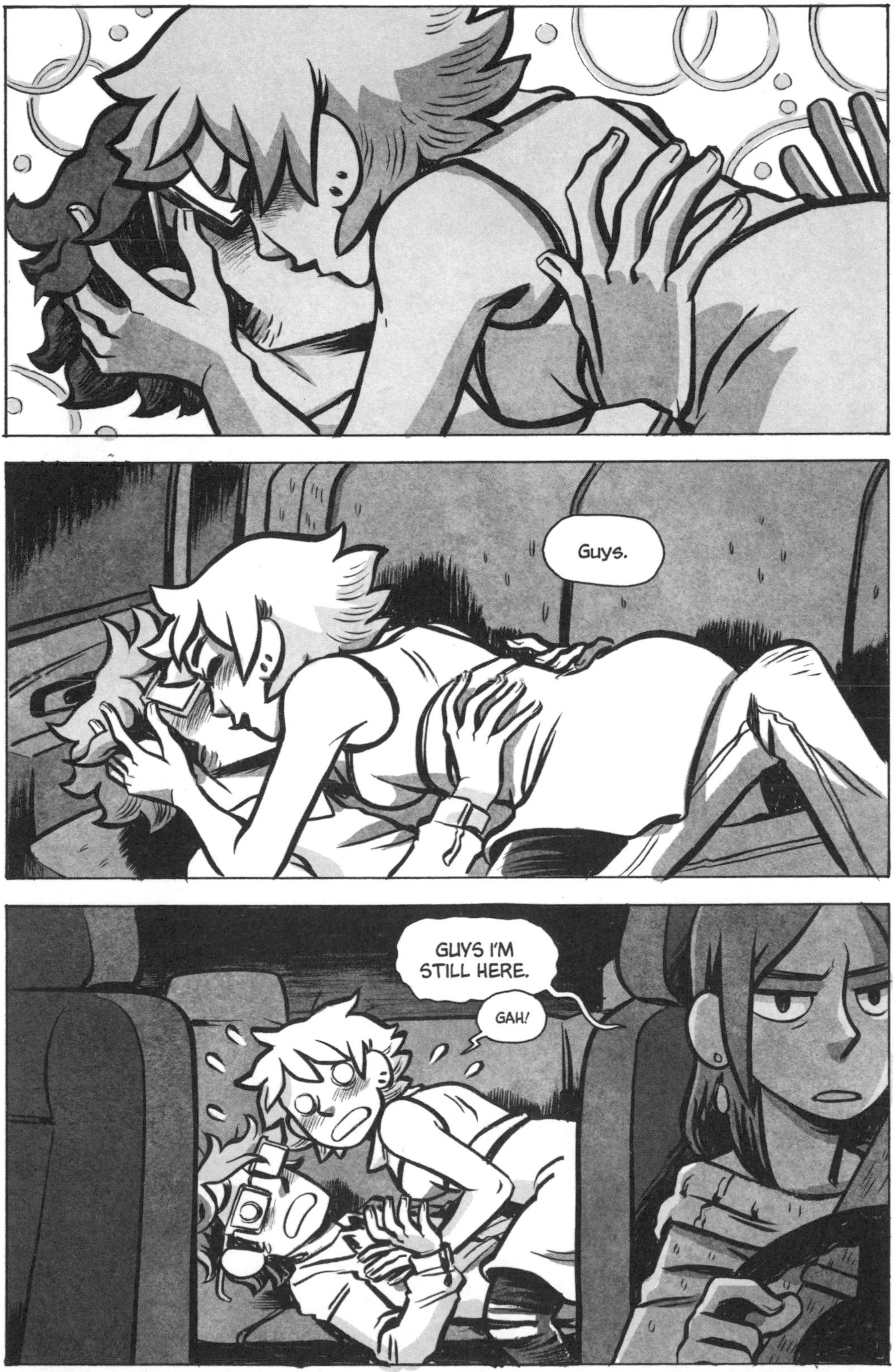
Guys.
GUYS I'M STILL HERE.
GAH!

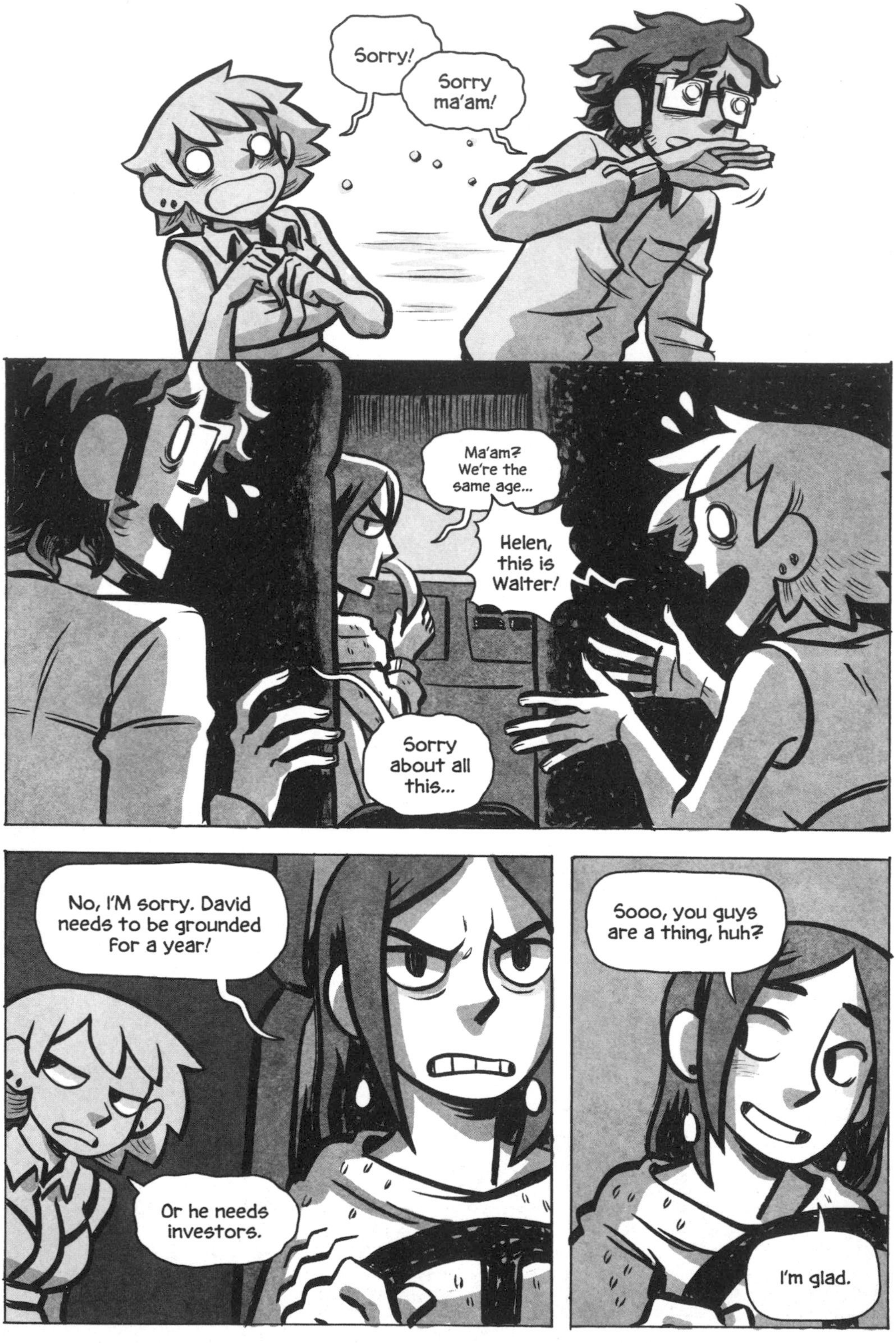
Sorry!
Sorry ma'am!
Ma'am? We're the same age...
Helen, this is Walter!
Sorry about all this...
No, I'M sorry. David needs to be grounded for a year!
Or he needs investors.
Sooo, you guys are a thing, huh?
I'm glad.

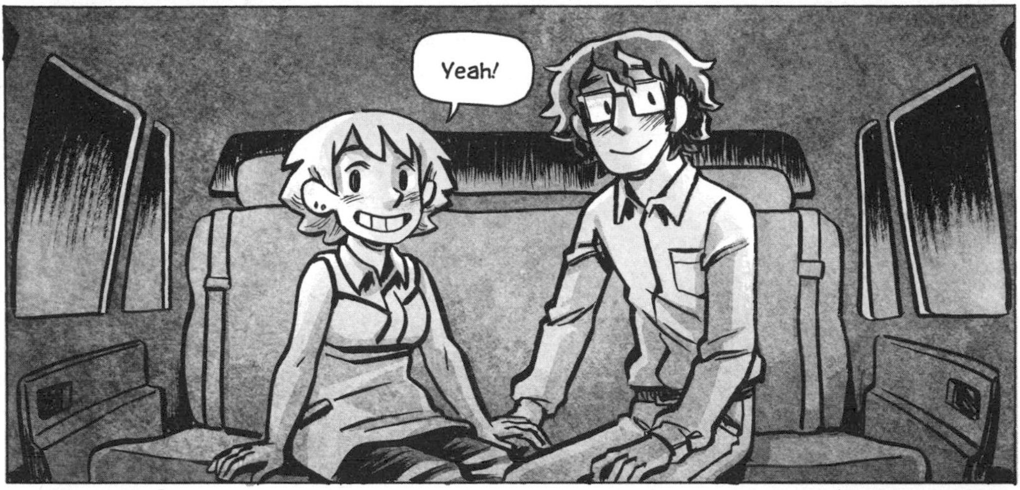
Yeah!

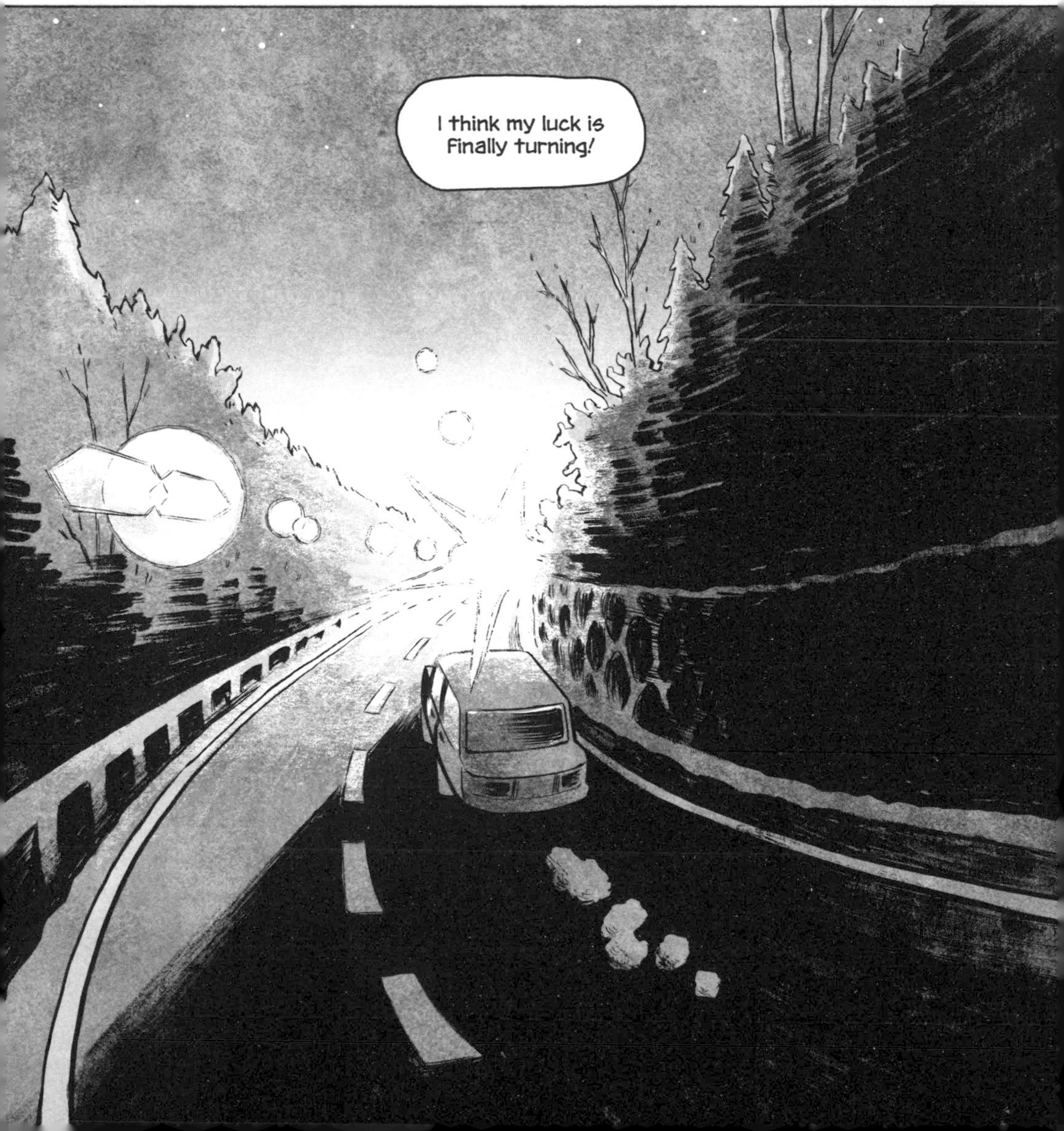
I think my luck is
finally turning!

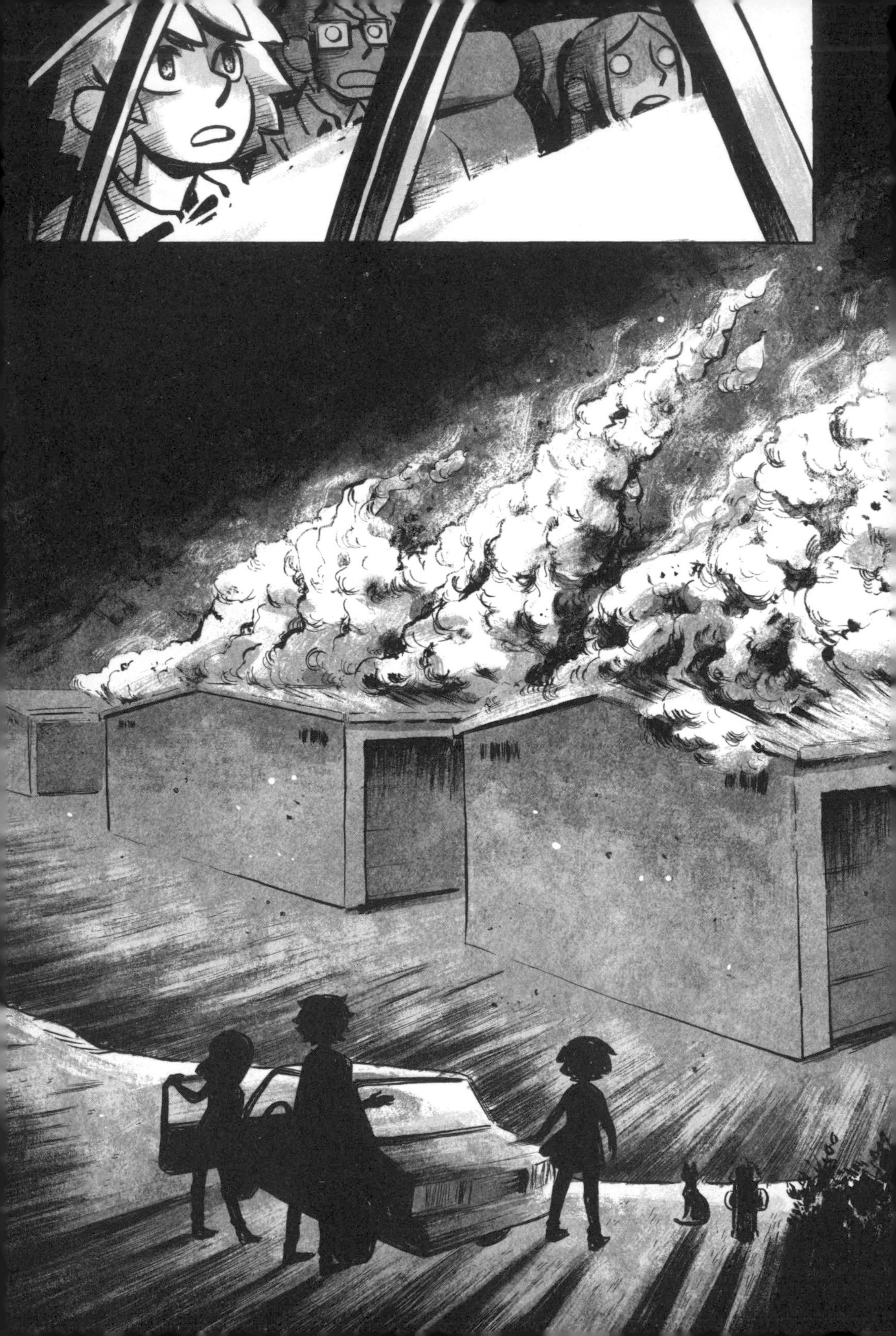

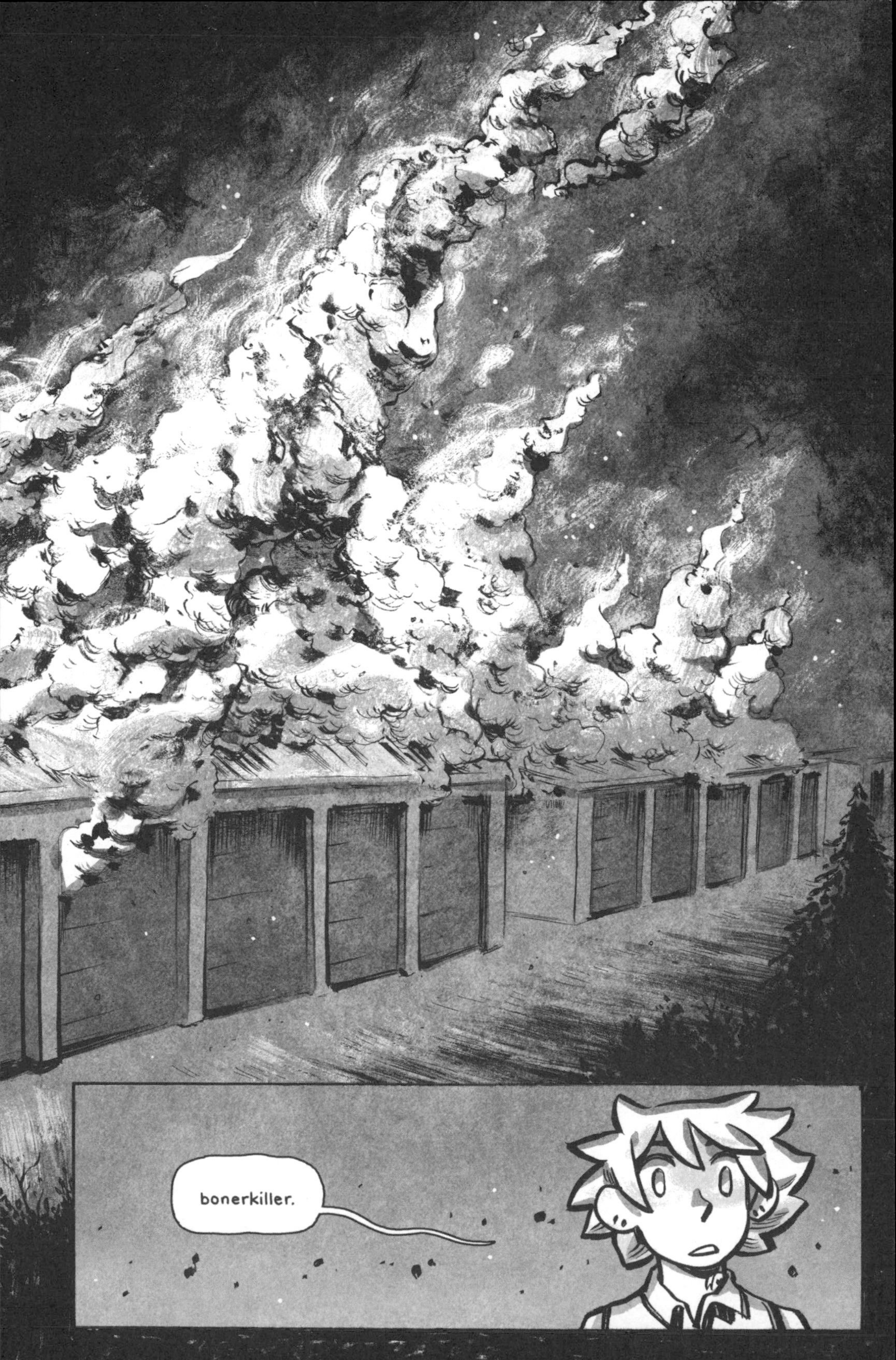
bonerkiller.

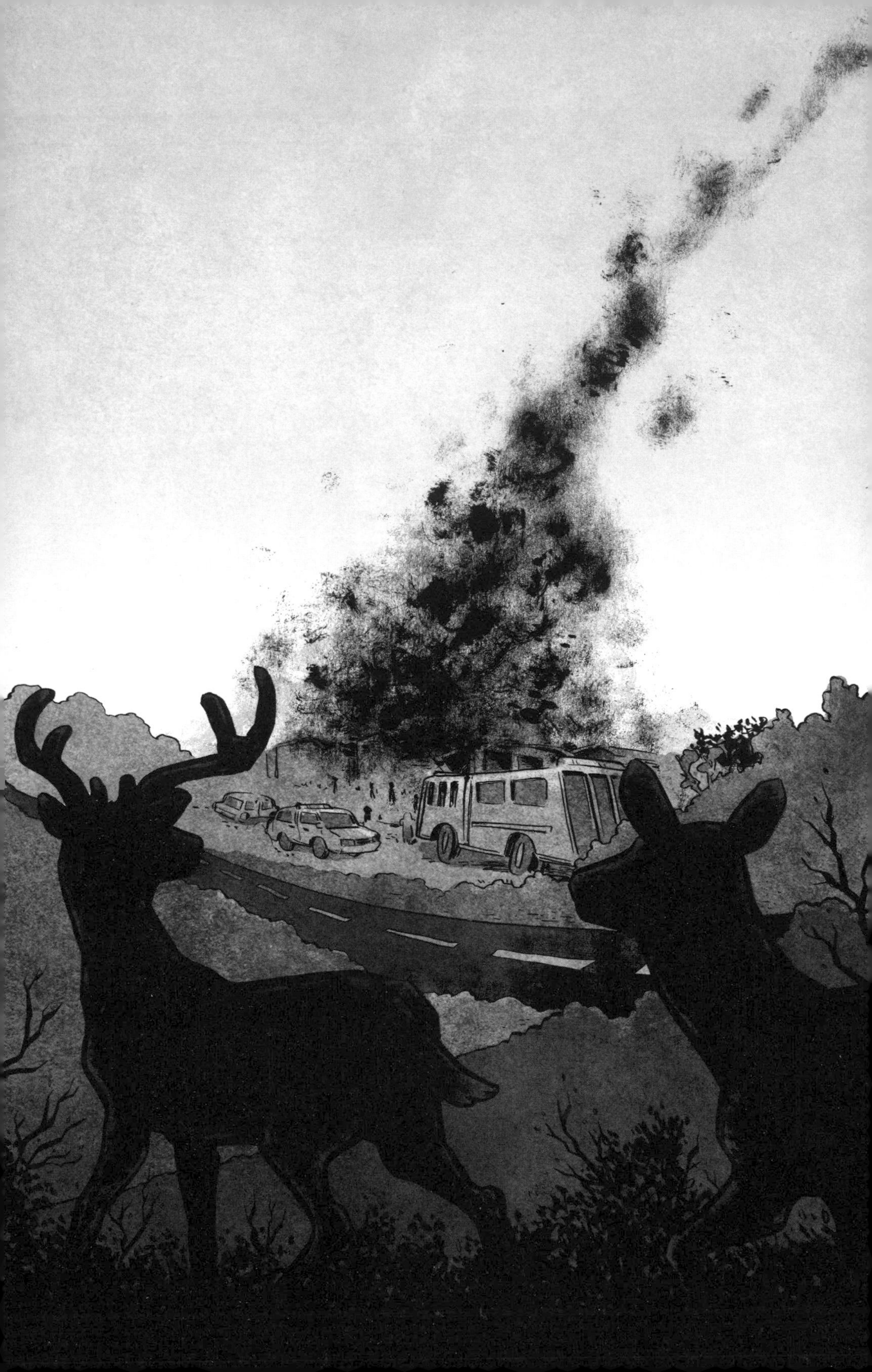

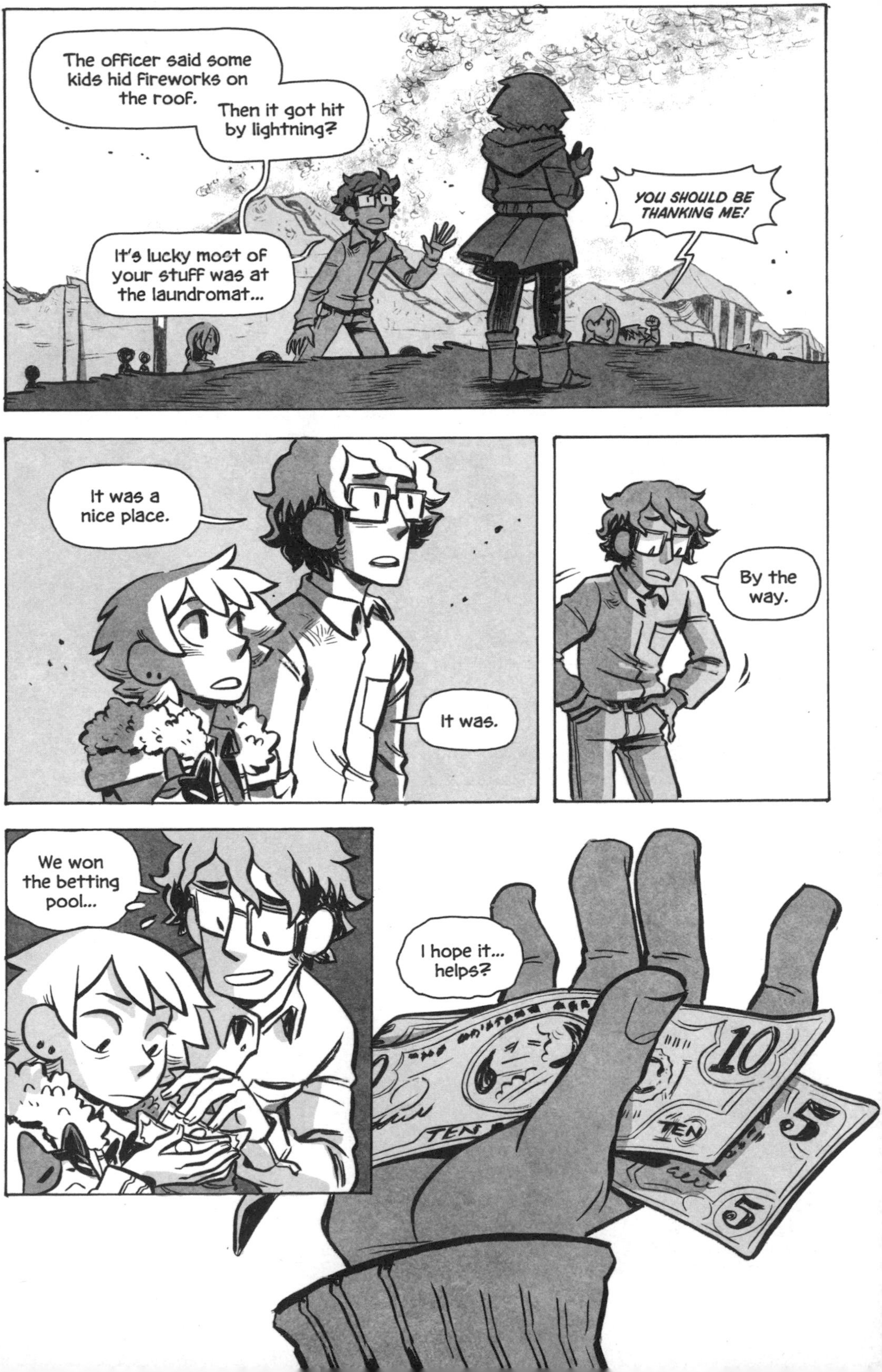
The officer said some kids hid fireworks on the roof.
Then it got hit by lightning?
It's lucky most of your stuff was at the laundromat...
YOU SHOULD BE THANKING ME!
It was a nice place.
It was.
By the way.
We won the betting pool...
I hope it... helps?
10
TEN
5

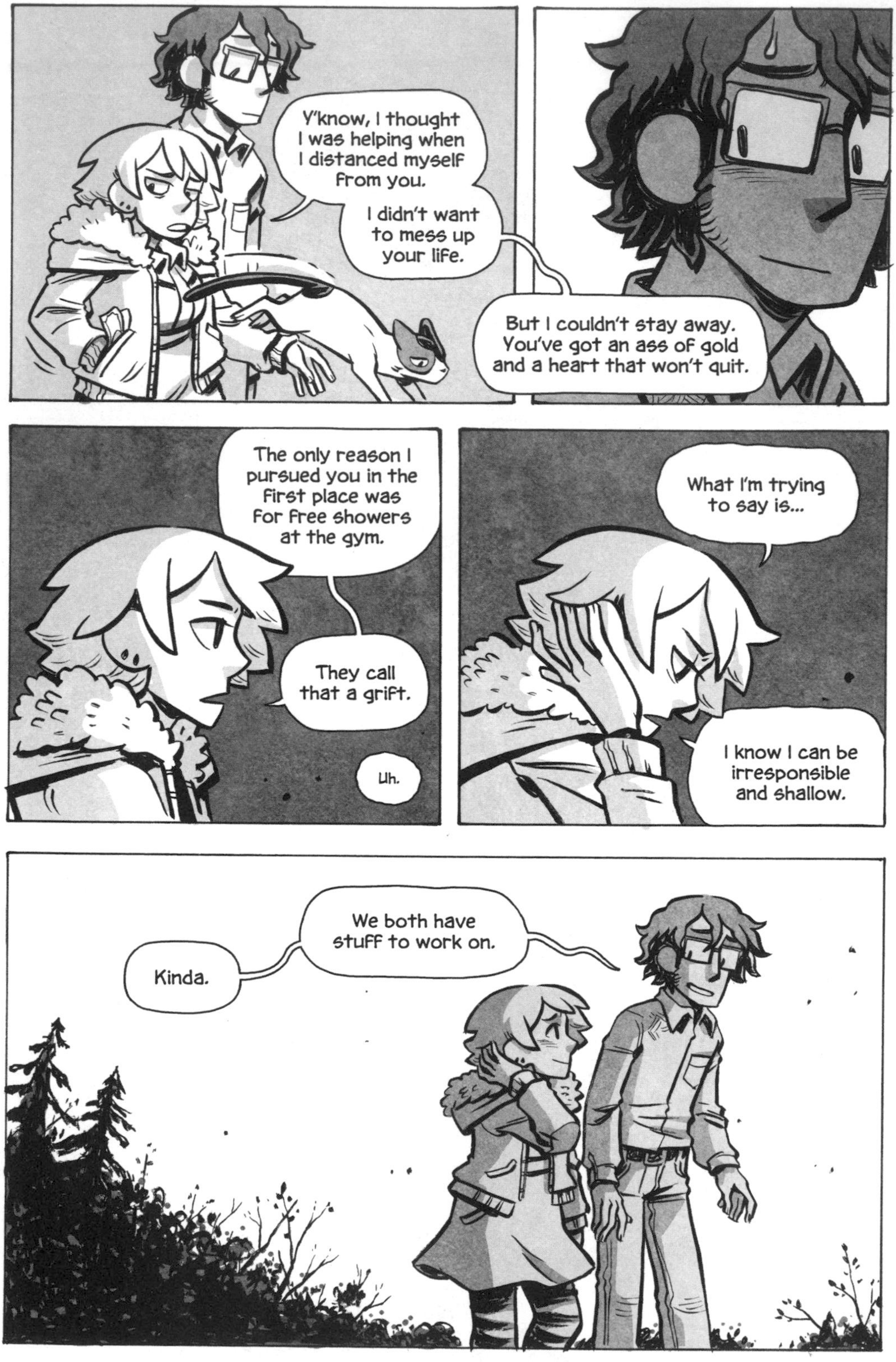
Y'know, I thought I was helping when I distanced myself from you.
I didn't want to mess up your life.
But I couldn't stay away. You've got an ass of gold and a heart that won't quit.
The only reason I pursued you in the first place was for free showers at the gym.
They call that a grift.
Uh.
What I'm trying to say is...
I know I can be irresponsible and shallow.
We both have stuff to work on.
Kinda.

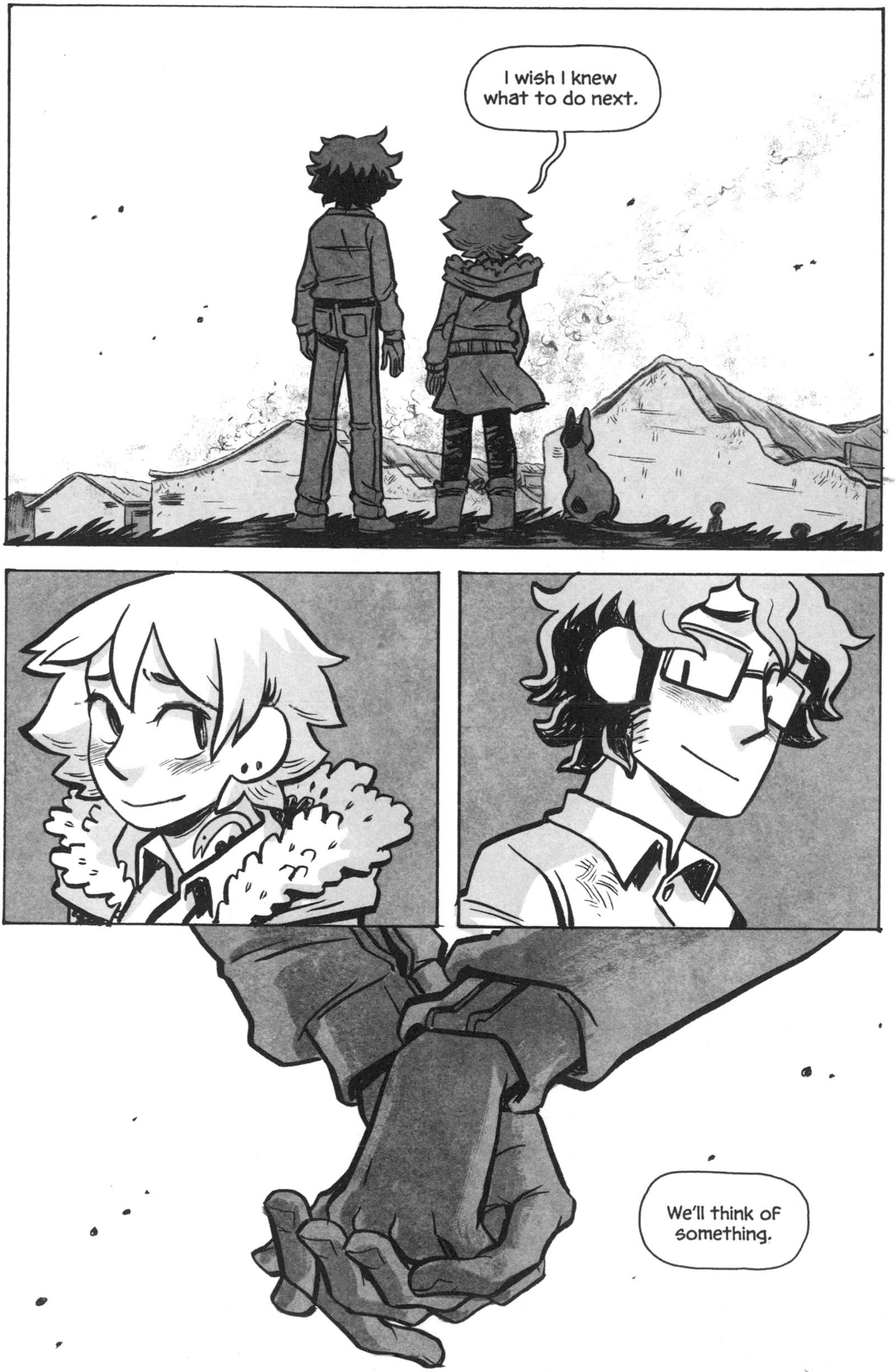
I wish I knew what to do next.
We'll think of something.

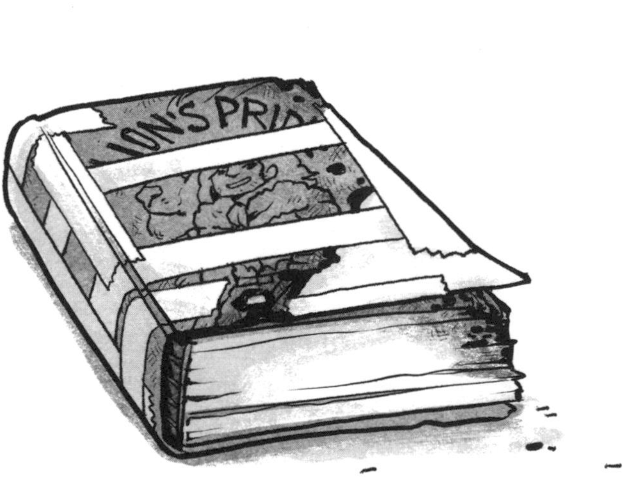
ION'S PRID

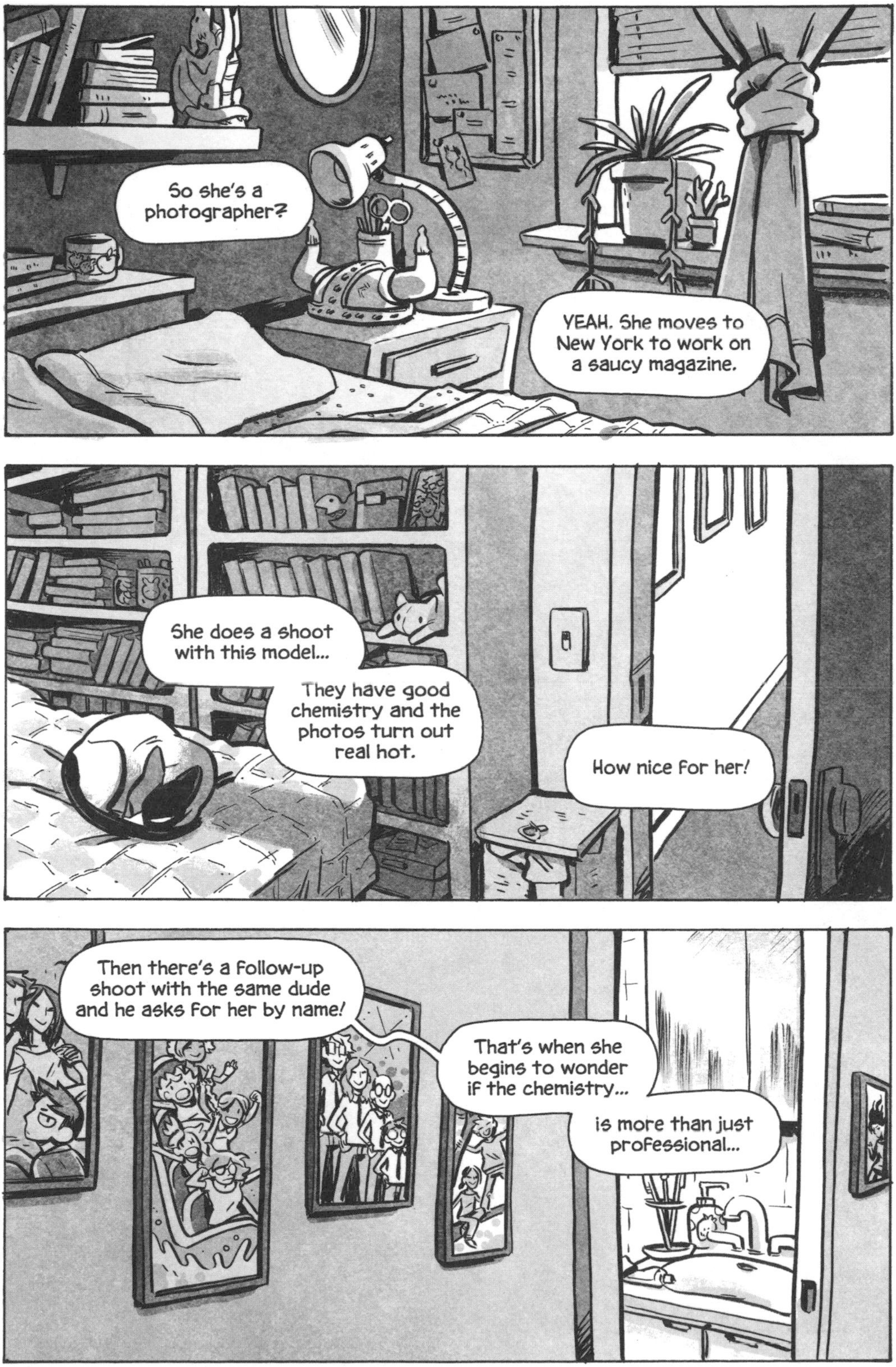
So she's a photographer?
YEAH. She moves to New York to work on a saucy magazine.
She does a shoot with this model...
They have good chemistry and the photos turn out real hot.
How nice for her!
Then there's a follow-up shoot with the same dude and he asks for her by name!
That's when she begins to wonder if the chemistry...
is more than just professional...

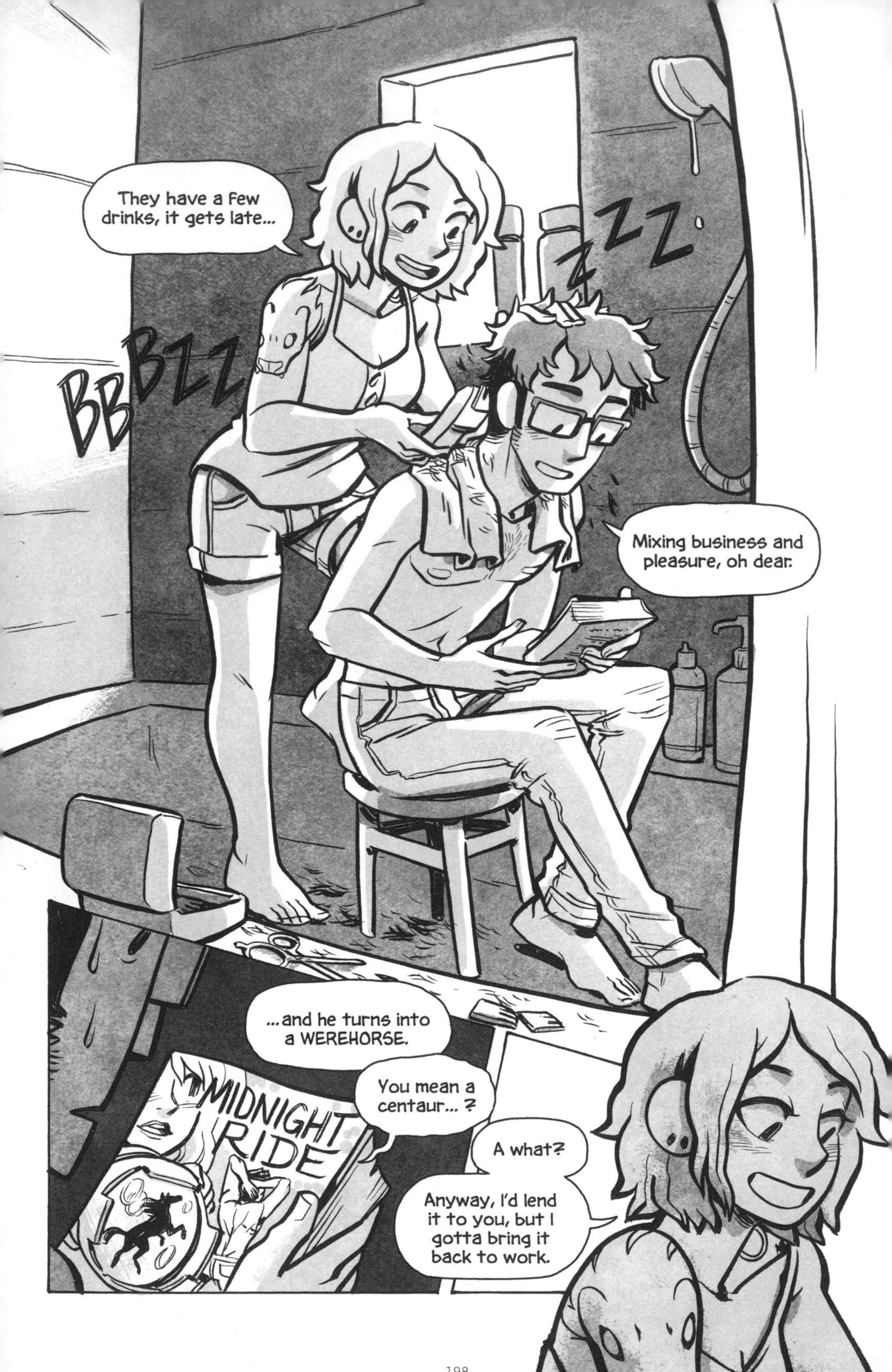
They have a few drinks, it gets late...
BBBZZZ
ZZZ
Mixing business and pleasure, oh dear.
...and he turns into a WEREHORSE.
You mean a centaur... ?
A what?
Anyway, I'd lend it to you, but I gotta bring it back to work.
MIDNIGHT RIDE

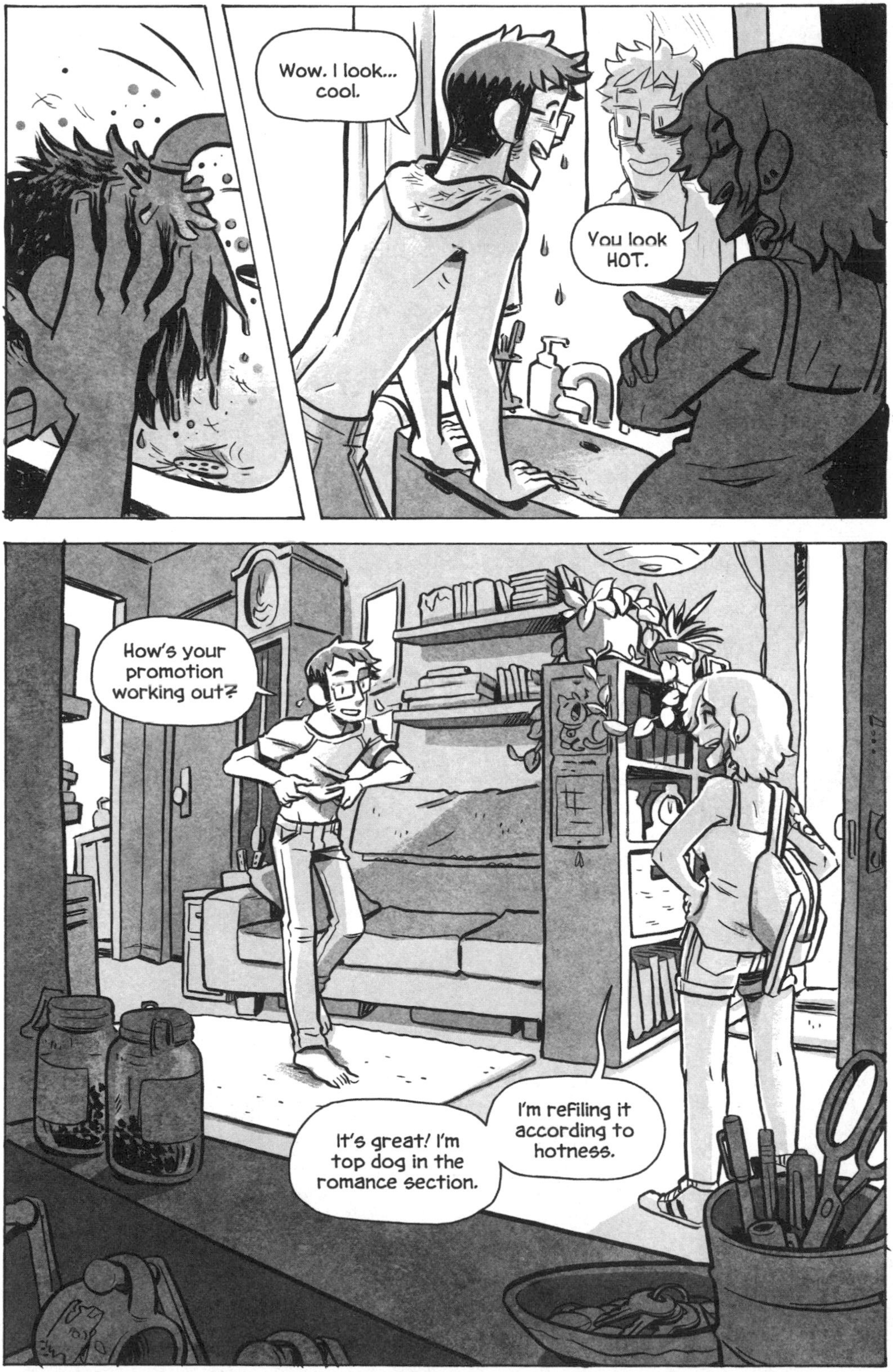
Wow. I look... cool.
You look HOT.
How's your promotion working out?
It's great! I'm top dog in the romance section.
I'm refiling it according to hotness.

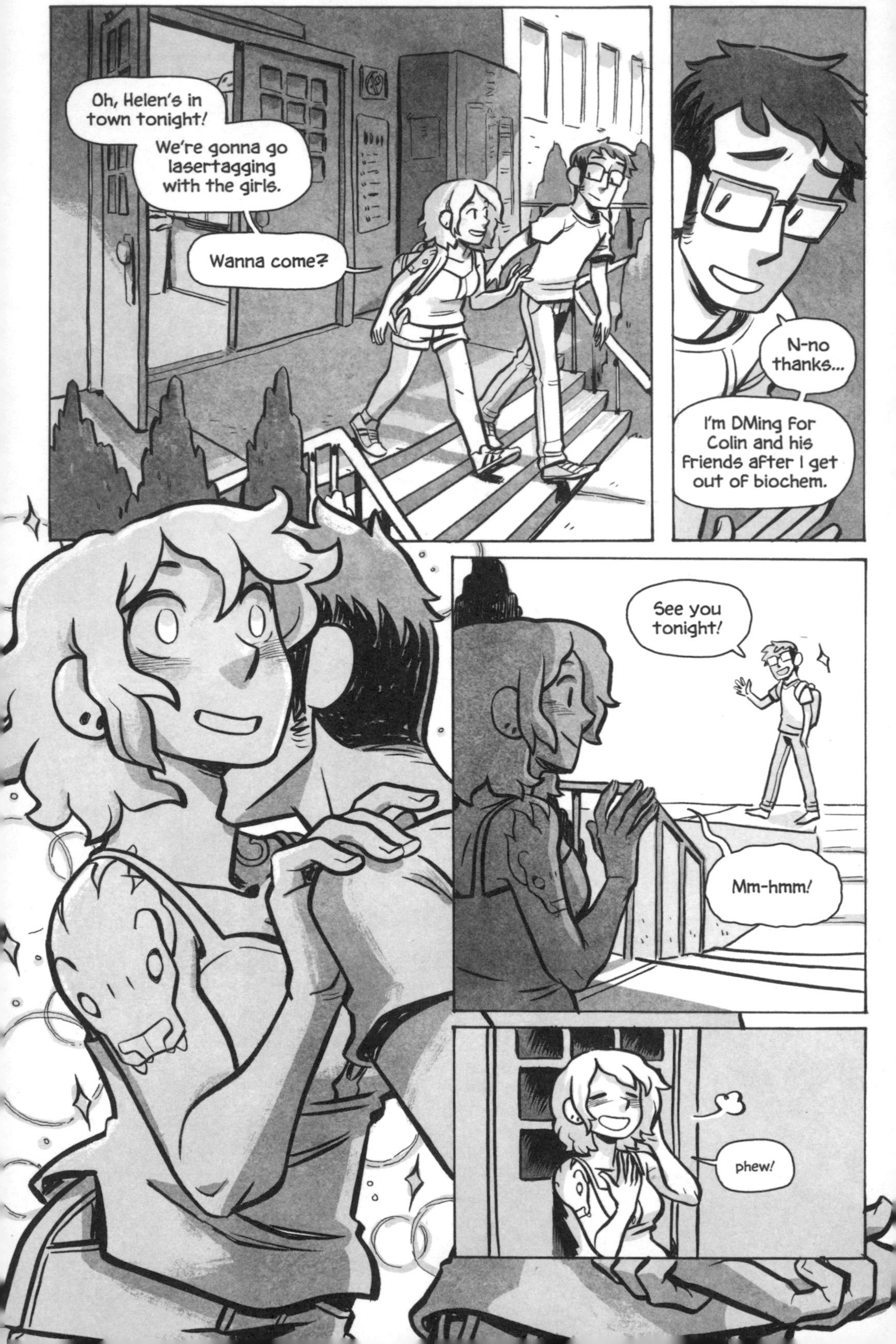
Oh, Helen's in town tonight!
We're gonna go lasertagging with the girls.
Wanna come?
N-no thanks...
I'm DMing for Colin and his friends after I get out of biochem.
See you tonight!
Mm-hmm!
phew!

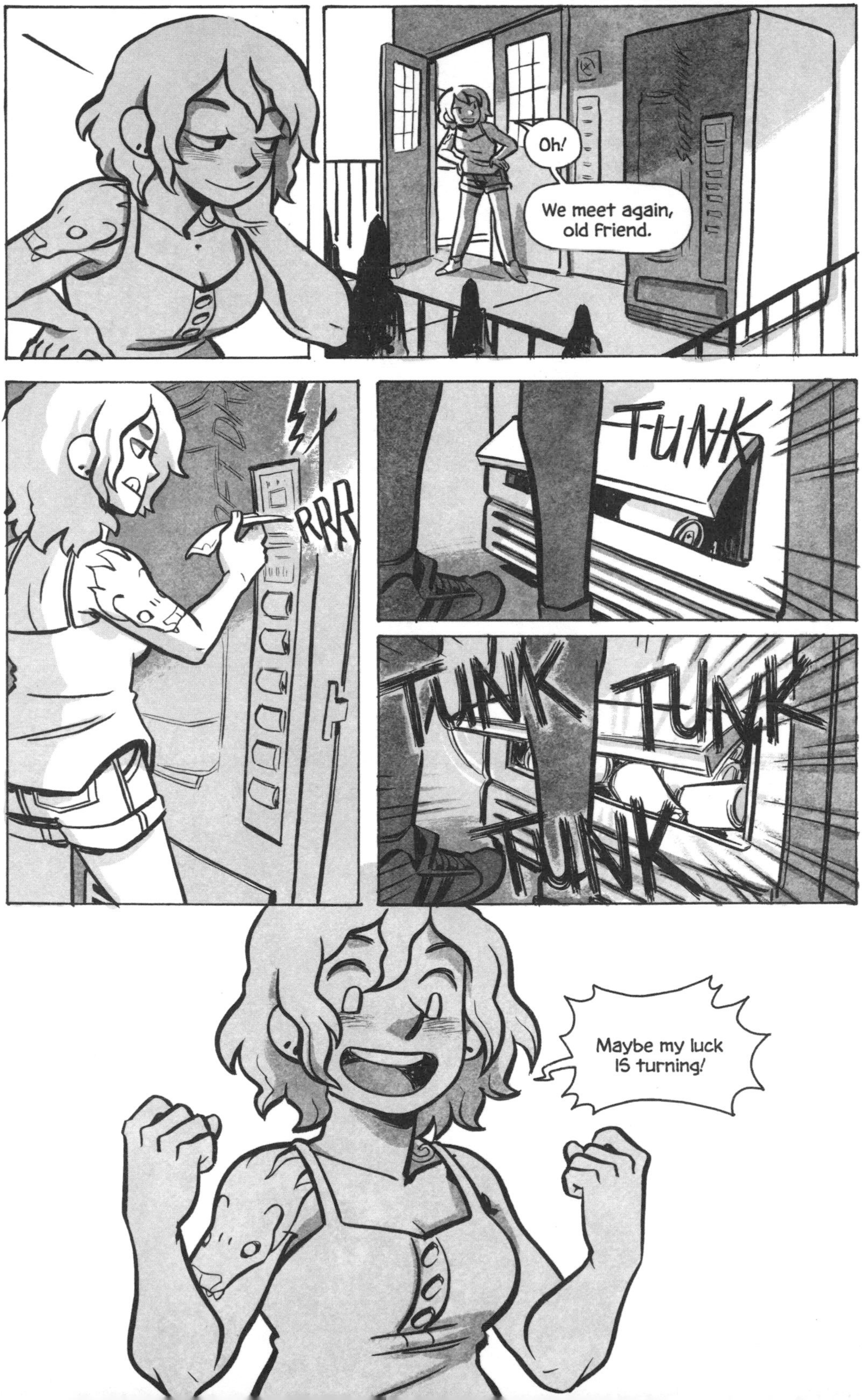
Oh!
We meet again, old friend.
RRR
TUNK
TUNK
TUNK
TUNK
Maybe my luck IS turning!

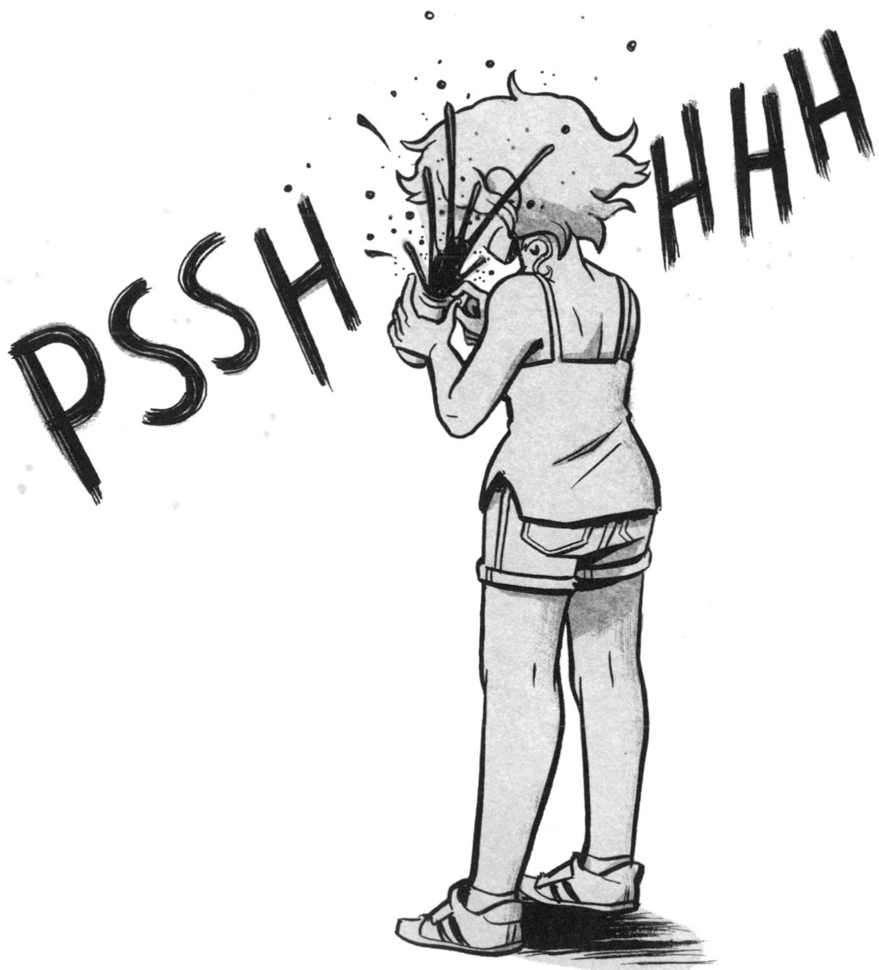
PSSHHHH

PEOPLE PENNY OWES MONEY/FAVORS TO

113420 • "Knight" Mike • @no381 & @renegal • 0tacoon • A Freaking Dork • A Miura • A Ro • Aaron Batman • Aaron Golas • Aaron Mitchko • Aaronn Adam Davies • Adam Hoks • Adam Kennedy • Adam Reibelt • Adam Stardust • Adam T • Adam Wyatt Goldstein • Adanska • Adrian Martinez • Agrue • Aimee Ainsley Y • Akemi Kuroe • Akiyo Nishimiya • Alan Resendiz • Alanna Woodbeck • Albert Vidal • Alec • Alenka Figa • Alex "Pizza King" Robinson • Alex Androski Alex Greenbaum & David Arenivar • Alex Heglin • Alex Horner • Alex Martin • Alex Pelayre • Alex Yi • Alexander "Galactus" Schroeder • Alexander Withey Alexandra • Alexandra Graudins • Alexandra Tortosa • Alexis Hadden • Ali Grotkowski • Alice • Alice Leigh W. • Alicia Mundinger • Alicia! • Alisa Chen Alison Wilgus • All Daves • Allan Butschler • Allen "DoctorBear" Homes • Allison Strejlau • Ally Hoyland • Amanda 'Pandacakes' Z • Amanda Santos Amber E Staab • Amelia O'Leary Amirul Khalid • Ana C. Castro • Andrea Calogero • Andrew "Codemaster" Kane • Andrew Baillie • Andrew Dal Cin • Andrew Duff Andrew Heintz III • Andrew Hornberg • Andrew Luczak • Andrew M Osberg • Andrew Simmons • Andrew Tyrell • Andrew Yen • Andrew Zienowicz Andy Benoit • Andy Hartshorn Andy Scheffler • Angela "Inky Phalangies" Boyle • Angela Zhang • Anh-Tu Nguyen • Anna Seitz • Anne E & Foley • Anne Williams Anonymous • Anouk Waning Ant • Anthony Joseph Gonzalez • Anthony McDonald • Apollo Lemmon • Aranea Push • Ardid • Arras Wiedorn • Ash Brown Ashley & her cats. • Ashley H. • Askari Kokkonen • Audra Furuichi and Scott Yoshinaga • Austin Murphy • Autumn Williams • Bagel • Baggetta • Bailey Bailey & Orange Kitten • Bailey C Britton • Banjoni Miller • Barbara Maria White • Becca Hillburn • Becky Punch • Bekka Lyn • Bel Tomov • Ben Elgin Ben Glazebrook • Ben Johnston • Ben Kirzhner • Ben Russell • Ben Turner • Benedict Alvin "ben-ben" Coo • Benny Peake • Betsy Albertsdaughter • Bettina Big Erik • Bill Icenrose • Billosopher • Blair Mueller • Bob C. Chesser (not the cool Bob) • Bobbie Sotelo!! • Bobby Burton • Bolkonsky • Boum • Brad Hunziker Brandon Hanvey • Brandon Puckett • Brandon "SBK" Mitchell • Brendan Harder • Brendan Marcy • Brendan Nicholas • Brenny Bear • Brenson Humphreys Brent Sieling • Bret Wilson • Bri Rudd • brian allred • Brian Dorfman • Brian Dwornik • Brian Felix • Brian Krulik • Brian Stone • Brian Townsend Brian Zielinski • Briareos Hecatonchires • Brie (like the cheese) • Brittany Cook • Brittany Schieron • Brittany Whittington • Brooks Sligh • Bruna N. Bryan "KoiVene" Quinto • bryan viau • Bryce Westgaard • Buzz • C. Ellis • C. Ellis • C. Ybay • C.N. Rowen • Caichee • Caitlin Benoit • Caitlin Stern • Caity Hall Cammie • Camu • Candace Ming • Cap'n Redbeard • Cara Adams • Cara Ferraro • Cara Judd • Carl Rigney • Carlos Shine • Carly Ho • Carmichael Micaalus Casey Gren • Cat and Cait • Catherine Cullen • CatherineHG • Cecilia and Naia Williams • Ceylan McGinty • Chalupa Batman • chance harris • Char Diotte Charibdys • Charity Pilcher • Charles Atencio • Charley V • Charlotte Sophie Ferguson • Charmaine Ong • Chelan Sweeney • Chelsea M Holt • Chessie Monks Chewie • Chibi Sara • Chloe "Too Sugoi to Die" Sewell • Chloe and Hanna Johnson • Chris "Shay" Rydberg • Chris Buecheler • Chris Burgess • Chris Chiu Chris Drackett • Chris Neveu • Chris Roberts • Chris Stuurman • Christen • Christina Foster • Christine and Scott Anderson • Christine Lee Duirs Chrys Anastasi • Chuck Gala • Ciaran Statham • Cindy Nakano • CJ Lew • Claire Murray • Clara So • Clare "muscles" Robinson • Clarence the cat Claudia & Caroline • Claudia Berger • Clayton Grey @ Laboratory • Clinton Hallahan, Esq. • CobaltBlue • Comrad Pirinja (Cameron H.) • Coni Yovaniniz Connie Wen • Conor .H.Carton • Coral • Cos Ryan • CrossXhunteR • Crystal Jayme • Cuddles the cat • cyborgify • Cynthia "Cynamille" Mund • D. Kent Kerr Dame Argust • Damien Trahan • Dan A • Dan Brown • Dan Catchpole • Dan Garatea • Dan Mitchell • Dan Schneiderman • Dana • Dana Rae • Dana Schlichting Dana Schwehr • DanChin • Daniel "BurnHavoc" Pawliw • Daniel Cushman • Daniel Dietsche • Daniel Earl • Daniel Sauve-Rogan • Dannel Jurado Danni Covarrubias • Danny Nicolas • Darryl Aoki • Dave C • Dave W • David • David 'Shonen' Law • David & Sinda Eggerman • David A. • David Cramlet David Fronk • David Kerr (Walter's DnD buddy) • David Lambe • David Lars Chamberlain • David M. • David Moraski • David Perzel, II • David Sims David van Rijn • David Walter • Davis D Morgan • Dawnya "Lins" Lynn • DCRurouken • deagol • Debbie Conway • Dechanique • Dennis M • Dennis Muldoon Dennys Antunish • Derek Huie • Desmond Ho • Devin Lee Gay • Devin Tuck • Devonition • Diana Mallery • Diana Sierra-González • Dieter Laskowski • Dilly Divi • Donnie Love • Dr Schratwieser • Dr. Kopong T. Limson • Dr. Stephen Berkowitz • dreamingsamurai • Drew Benedetti • Druin Roberts • Duckless Jon Dustin Doyle Grey • Dylan Evans Chinn • Ed Stahl • Edgar Guzman • Edward • Edwin Galeana • Edwin S. • EG Eisbar • Eilis Karr • Elaine Nguyen •Elena Ahn Elias "Banjo Man" Turner • Elisa Sguanci • Elise W (Sparrow) • Elizabeth Davidson • Elizabeth Williamson • Ella Quinn Lagerquist • Ellie Bee • elorg • Elvis Em Huff • Em9 • Embreane James • Emi • Emilee LB • Emilie Gray • Emily • Emily & Sioban • Emily Bowman • Emily Compton • Emily L. • Emily McMinn Emily Ott • Emma Levine • Emmis Touron • Eresu • Eric Fox • Eric Freeman • Eric Hartman • Eric Meadows • Eric Spitler • Eric Wei • Erica Zaback • Erik Erik Holland • Erik the Great • Erin Brown • Erin The Pâtissier • erinidge • Esiver • Esther Teng • Eva Cherney • Eva Jeanne Bieser • Eve B. • Ewan O'Sullivan Fabien CLAUDE • FAbster101 • Familia Torres • Finch • Fionna • Fletcher Rory Hamish Schmid • Frank Dominguez • G. Garrett • G. R. Brown Gabriel Schlesinger • Gaelen McFadden; That Poor Bananal • Gamma • Gareth Bracchi • Garrett Pauls • Gary Tyrrell • Gashley Au • Gene Endiape Genué Revuelta • George P. Burdell • Georgeo Brooks • Gibbs • Ginger Apolo • Glenn Lazo and Fer Frick • Glenn McAllister • glitterboots styles...... • Glo Mercado Gordon Ramsay • Gov • Grace Evers • Gracie Kath • Graciela Villegas • Grant E. McGee • Great General Kelbesque • Greg Mettler •Guilded Age Gunnlaugur Thor Einarsson • Hadsvich • Handsome Dan • Hanna Paquette • Hannah Howden-Roberts • Hannah Lee Stockdale • Hannah Rutqvist • Hannako L Hannele Kormano • Hat Ducks • Hazel Noguchi • Healy Rodman • Heather Lanza • Heather Matsune • Hegesippe Éspace • Heijmans Family • Helst Henrik Lindhe • Herman Clogmaster • Hillary Lovinggood • hiro4 • Holly Blankenship • Hubert Skorupski • Hugo Pour-Hashemi • Humanavatar • Ian ian " raggy ' moore • Ian Beck-Cross • Ian McAllister • Ian Mutchler • Ilana R. Niemi • impartialcredit • Ingo Lembcke • ioachim • Isabel • Isabelle Melancon Iter • ITW • J.A Pickford • J Brown • J Wagner • J. Driscoll • J.K. Hilbert • J.P. Meshew • Jace-Leia Newhook • Jack Attack • Jack McNab • Jackie Scott Jackie Sojico • Jacob Bean • Jacob Hansen • Jacob Mcloughlin • Jake Kesinger • JAMAR NICHOLAS • James • James "Ven'Tatsu" Morgan • James E. McAuliffe James Flaagan • James Olson • Jamie Fong • Jamie Rich • Jana Hoffmann • Janelle Krzykowski • Jano Rohleder • Jared "Marhalut" MacAdam Jared Sadewater • Jared Schilling • Jared Walske • Jasmine P. • Jason "Cheese" Smith • Jason Miles • Jason R. • Jay Crow Comics • Jay Jacques Jay Lofstead • Jean-Philippe Guérard • Jeanne • Jeff Abshire • Jeff Hess • Jeff Muse • Jeffrey Gene Liu • Jen Guignard • Jen Murphy • Jen Pope • Jenn Gall Jenna El-Amin • Jenna Zamie • Jenni • Jennifer N. Smith • Jennifer Staton • JennyHeee • Jeremy Mosuela Higley • Jeric Pereda • Jess "the Bookwyrm" Tuttle Jess Fink • Jess Graham • Jess Steffan • Jesse Morgan • Jesse Riggs • Jessica "Muscles" Eith • Jessica Bell • Jessica Corzantes-McGinty • Jessica Garvey Jessica Gonzalez-Wu • Jessica Harvie • Jessica Lynn • Jessie "Tine" Wilson JessiKristen • Ji "Inyuji" Eom • Jibs Monteef • Jill Jamieson Jim Arthurs and Crystal McDowell • Jimmy O'Dwyer • Jinx & Ami • JLRoot • Joaquín Cogollos Jocelyn Oudesluys • Joe Field • Joe Salazar • Joe Shea Joel Rosario • Joel Watson • Joeri 'SabreWing" Roels • Joey Science • Johanne Westen Noer • John "Jing" Nguyen • John Gallagher • John MacLeod John Michael Pesina • John Morel • John Sanders • John Shoe • Jojo • JoJo Seames • Jon • Jon & Leah Hayward-Crichton Jon Chaisson & Amanda Taylor-Chaisson • Jon Hex • Jon Vanneste • Jonas Pagé • Jonathan "Teddy" Marinaro • Jonathan D. Handler • Jonathan David Page Jonathan Schmidt • Jonathon Imperiosi • Jordan Klinefelter • Jordan Sekiya • Jordan Witt • JOSE!? • Josh • Josh • Josh "Elephante" Romano • Josh Campbell Josh Closs • Josh kimbap • Joshua 'Scud' Miller • Joshua Brock • Joshua Flanagan • Joshua Hall • Joshua Munro • Joshua Van Arsdale • Joshua W. Daniels Joy Kim • juan atherton • Juan Chanco • Juan de Dios Torreblanca Rojas • Juho S • Julia Burmistrova • Julia Van Steenberg • Julie • Julie Fiveash Justin Barber • Justin Bartl • justmega • K. T. Baker • k.c. gonzales • Kacy Smith • Kaeti Vandorn • kahai • Kai & Annika • Kail Yuan • Kait Feldmann Kaitlin Powell • Kaitlin Wilson • Kaitlyn Mugg • Kalle Stenberg • Kamryn Nordsiek • Karalyn • Karen Rohan • Karin D. • Karl Zahn • Kasey Golden

BASICALLY FOREVER

Kasey Van Hise • Kat Gems • Kat Lombard-Cook • Katie Holliday • Katie Kruger • Katie McDermott • Katie P. • Katie Rusch • kation • Katrina T. Pinvidic
Katten Korven • Kattryna C. Maxxwel • Katy and Rian • Katy Dalziel • Katy Day • Katy Kimsey • Kay "Fists o' Fury" Rossy • Kaycie D. • Kaye Bristol • Kayla Church
Kayla Heptonstall • Kayla Robinson • Kayla Witherow • Kearra • Keiji Miashin • Kel & Jor • Kellie Rios • Kelly Delahanty • Kelly Unrequited
Kelly Ying Sin Au-Yeung • Kelsey Liggett • Kenna Bathea • Kevin "Kyven" Mayo • Kevin (Disco?) • Kevin Levron • Kevin Lewis • Kevin Nolan • Kevin O'Neill
Kevin Pointer • Kevin Siegl • Kevin Virnig • Kevin Wong • Kia Mantey • Kii Bandaru • Kim Hoang • Kimberley Cole • Kiraly • Kit • Kitsu Maharu • Kitsunami
Kitty Ang • Kitty Wills • KittyKrunchXDLMAO • klio • Kona Cannon • Korey • Kou Chen • Kristen Levine • Kristen Toohill • Kristin H • Kristopher Grenier
KT Jayne • KT Smith • Kyle Elizabeth Huck • Kyle Harrison • Kyle Rose • Kyle W • L Hart • LadyKnightmare • Larke Stone and Zack Turnipseed • Lasso Hynninen
Laura Ault • Laura Light • Laurel Martinell • Lauren MacDonald • Lauren Williams-Hackman • Laurent Louf • Lawrence E. Minor II • Le Dang • Lea C.
Leah Webber • Leandro Nascimento • Lee Cherolis • Len "Smash Bro" Ahgeak • Lena Olson • Lexxy • Lidia Morris • Lila Papiernik • Lilette • Liliana S.
Lilly Crespo • Lily H. • Linda Edwards • Linda Shearer • Lindsay J. Resor • Lindsay Small-Butera • Lisa Brooks • Lisa Thomson • Lissa Pattillo • Liz Novaski
Liz Ritter • Liz Stewart • Lizbeth Hevia • Lizzy Dawson • locallunatic • Logan Arias • Logan Pettit • Logan Spoto • Logan Woods • Lorilyn • Lostdux
Louis Mastorakos • Louis T. Austin IV • Luc de Chancenotte • Luchacomico • Luchie • Lucky Nothin • Lucy Flawless • Luiz Mendez • Lukas • Luke J. Sabljak
Luke Maes • Luke Primous • Lulu Tang (lubibul) • Lydia Au • M Walk • M. Cash • M. Croll • M. Imamura • M&M Skiba • Mac Bentley • madclarinet • Maggie
Magnus C. M. • mancameron • Mandy & Scott Klein • Maqqy96 • Marc Mendes • Marcus "Arood" Olovsson • Marcus Zita • Mard • Margaret Lionsbeard
Marie Encarnacion • Marine Corporal D.B. Huckabone • Marissa Itkowsky • Marita Jackson • Mark "Moose" LaGuardia • Mark Fazzari • Mark Navarrete
Mark Skews • Mark Tollefson • Mark Wlodarski • Markus Magnitz • Martha Sullivan • Martijn "Tailed" Witlox • Martin & Mack • Mary E. Paduano • Mathias
Mathieu Marchand • Matt Brown • Matt Cassar • Matt Chin • Matt Cummings • Matt D Loux • Matt Gosper • Matt Haas • Matt Harrold • Matt K • Matt Keeley
Matt Kim • Matt Nelson • Matt Schmidt • Matt Warren • Matt Williams • Matthew "Nox" Abram Poff • Matthew Clement • Matthew Dietz & Jennifer Koudelka
Matthew LaRose • Matthew Mowczko • Matthew Reynolds • Matthew Shepard • Max Monast • Max Stein • Maxwell Motley • Maya Schmidt • Meagan Joyce
Meaghan Hartie • meeshay • Megan Boing • Megan Brennan • Megan Byrd • Megan Jinxy J • Megatron • Melanie Castle • Melissa Andrade • Melody Dawn
Meowe Cattemanne • Merili • Michael Armor • Michael Beguiristain • Michael Bingham • Michael Cooper • Michael Coppolino • Michael Ederer
Michael Escalante • Michael Heath • Michael Kaplan • Michael Krzak • Michael Martinez • Michael McKay • Michael Noback • Michael Rappe • Michael Taylor
Michael Tervoort • Michael Yamamoto • Michaël Archibald I. Montferrat Guérette • Michelle Johnson • Michelle Y. Morris • Michiel De Mey • Mickey Spencer
Mike Darlow • Mike Kauffman • Mike Rengel • Mikey Ward • Mikkel Thomas • Mint J. • Mira Danoake • Miriam Ayles • Mirko • Mistress CrankyBadger • MJ
MJ Fisher • Moohi • Moe Murone • Molly Hayden • Molly Watson • Monika Kalan • Monique Pihl • Monte Kowalsky • Moogle • Morvan DEGUELT • Mouse
Mr Bear • Mr. John A. Herph • Ms. Robin Dobashi • Nat & Finn • Nate Seymour • Nathan Kissel • Nathaniel Roberts • Nathanielle • Natisha Lavender-Duncan
Neeeeeeeev • Neil Cowan • Neil Graham • Nell • Nelson Zelaya • Neo • Niall Dalby • Nic Herzig • Nicholas Lowther • Nicholas Rivera • Nicholas Serratore
Nick Czarnecki • Nick Fagerlund • Nick Goodway • Nick Lee • Nick May • Nick Rajsky • Nick Taylor • Nicky Ward • Nicole Chartrand • Nicole LaChance • Niki
Niki La Teer • Niki Pell • Nikki De Backer • Noah Swartz • NoahThaBoah • noako • Nodoko • Noelle Eve • Nora Broderick • Nulani t'Acraya • Nut Case • Odeko
Olivia Decherd • Olivia Li • Olivia Rohan • Omar Hernandez • Ondine • onihat • Oscar "Ask" Wiberg • Otaku News • Owen F • Paddy Sheridan • Paige Jones
Paige Luther • Patricia Sanvictores • Patrick George • Patrick James Moylan • Patrick Mohlmann • Patrick Rennie • Patrick Grankvist • Patty Hyland • Paul <3
Paul Cosgrove • Paul M. H. • Paul Segal • Pencilears • Perry Maybrown • Pete Norton • Peter B • Peter Hafer • Peter J Pottorff • Peter James Maggs
Peter Kempson • Peter Sturdee • Philip Beverley • Philippe Johnson • Pierre from the merguez party • Pierre Lebeaupin • Pippin O'Leary • PK • PoiPoi
Prince Kit • PRIYA D:< • Puff Johnson • Punky Quiroz • Rachel • Rachel Dukes • Rachel Oaks • Rachel Schmitz • Rachel Tougas • Rae • Rahat Ahmed
Randall Spohn • Randy Laue? • Ray C Bennett • Ray Powell • Raynard Solomon • RB Miller • Reem • Regina Legaspi • Rei Chavez • Rewynd • Rhel ná DecVandé
Rianne Goodman • Ricardo Garcia Paredes • Richard B-L • Richard Maytidu III • Richard Suh • Riley O'Brien • Rin Ling • Riparian • RJ Guevara
Rob Van de Motter • Robert A. Carreras • Robert and Drea • Robert Decker • Robert Lee • Robert Mawdsley • Robert O'Neal • Robert Riley-Mercado
Robert Shimizu • Robert Sikorski • Robert Stallings • Roberta & Diego • Robin Moore @ytrahne • Rochelle Mantanona • Rodrigo Ortiz Vinholo • Roni Simunovic
Roonil Wazlib • Rory Morris • Rosalia • Ross Alexander • Rowgee • Roy Higashi • Rumbleroar Pond • Ryan Belden • Ryan CG Taylor • Ryan Mattson
Ryan Scott Green • Ryan Stevenson • Ryan Watson • Ryan Woerner • Salazar Goldman • Saleh Yassin • Sam Emo • Sam Grusky-Milin • Sam Schechter
Sam Watterson • Samantha F. • Samantha Netzley • Sam Fearing • Sami • San Carpenter • Sandi Gammon • Santi & Melissa • Santi Orozco • Sara
Sara Brueckman • Sara O'Neill • Sara Rude (Project Shiro Studios) • Sarah • Sarah Boyle • Sarah Elsewhere • Sarah Graley • Sarah Huang • Sarah K. Müller
Sarah Olson • Sarah Robertson & Kyle Shuttlesworth • Sarah Schanze • Sarah Ulloa • Sashah Li • Sayaka Wright • Scoopy • Scott • Scott Hastings Mitchell
Scott Jacobson •Scott Kaneshiro • Scott Morey • Scott Rubin • Scott Vandehey • scuffy • Sean Carner • Sean Holden • Sebastian Winslow • Selene • Sen
Seung Lee • Shaela "Starcat" Morin • Shamus and Lesley • Shane W Berry • Shannon Perry • Shawn Fassbender • Shawn Miller • Shay • Shelby Miksch • Shell
Sherry, Scott's mum • Shield Bonnichsen • Sho Ikeda • Shoona Browning • Shuri • SiG • Silent Sam • Simon Cotts • Siobhan Covill • Siobhan Mooney
SmoothGardener • Sofia Pinheiro • Sophie Burkland • Sophie Shanahan-Kluth • Sophie T. • Soren Moskjaer Lauridsen • Sparrow • Spenser C. Anderson
Spoinker • Squid & Lynx • Stasia Archibald • Stefan Feltmann • Stefanie Battalene • Stephanie "Shiba Master" Dill • Stephanie A. Williamson •Stephanie Bao
Stephanie Spiker • Stephanie Trimboli • Stephen Murdoch • Steve Flack • Steven "Shaggy" Shanahan • Steven "StevRayBro" Brown • Steven Cunningham
Stevie Coelho • Storm Luna • Stuart Telfer • Stumpy Pete • Summer Tangerine • Susan & Slava • Susanna Wolff • T C Hotaling • Tait Peterson • Talulah Leroux
tampon • Tanya "Cow Hat Ninja" Burr • Tavis Maiden • Taylor Cook • Taylor R. Martin • Taylor von Kugelgen • TeaDino • Ted Faliszek • Ted Hahn
Teddy Rodriguez's Mom • Teejeh • Toongkoh • Terry Chu • Tessa Evans • Tessa Manor • That Darn Ted • That IT guy...Brian...? • That Lady with the Purple Hair
That Lanky Bastard • That one girl at the bus stop • The Catalans • The Courier • the Makeout Hobo • The Miss Cat Lady LYR
The Phenomenal Philosophical Pharaonic Photogenic Pheonyx • Theo K • TheTabbehCat • Thomas Gagnon • Thomas Goembel • Thomas Polok • ThunderSpade
Tias • Tiffany Pascal • Timmi Gee • Timothy Christopher Isidore Bumpus • Timothy S. Broadwell • Tiso Spencer • Todd Ponder • Tom Briechle • Tom Cleary
Tom Stefan • Tom Whiteley • Tom Worthington • Tomio Ueda • Tony B • Tony Cosens • Tony Spencer • Tony Tran • Tracy Hirano • Tracy Ma • Tracy-Anne Moore
Travis Parker • Trev • Trillian S. • Tristan Lennon • Trixie • Tunnelman • Tylar Bright • Tyler Mann • Tyler McDowell • Ulrich Weidenhammer-Courtemanche
Valentine Fadie • Valerie Burk • Valerie D. • Valerio Varriale • Vanessa Gillings • Vanessa Pastore • Vanessa Satone • Vanessa Stefaniuk • Vegard Stenhjem
Hagen • Vehryn • Ver • Veronica Agarwal • Victor M.J. Ryden • Victor Mahnic • Víctor Pasanau • Victoria Sun • Virus Visal • Vivian Chan • Wagner
Wally Hastings • Whatshisface • Will Harrison • William "Bilbo" Davis, the Ringbearer • William Ford • William Milhans! • Willow • wolkilula • Wyn
Xavier "An Apple A Day" Alexander • Xib Vaine • Ymmy • Yoggleberry Soth • Yomi • Yomis McGroanis • Yu Shin Chuang • Yuki Okamura-Wong • Yurie Murayama
Yvonne Chung • Z. M. Tseng • Zach and Jamie • Zach Smith • Zach Zimmerman • zach! • Zachary Miller • Zache • Zack Penzien • Zegbert • Zen Sayer • Zoe
Zoe L • Zoe Mendez • Zoë Steel • Zoutroi • Zuluf Yakingun • Zuzu Swiatek

THANKS

Archer, Mike and Joe, for providing the basis for the three rude kids. You taught me how to chill.

James Lucas Jones, for your patience as we finished this book. We're grateful.

George Rohac, for your help in making this book a reality.

Katie, for always cheering us on.

ABOUT THE AUTHORS

YUKO OTA & **ANANTH HIRSH** live in Brooklyn, NY.

Yuko is a cartoonist.

Ananth is a writer.

They've worked with Oni Press, BOOM!, Dark Horse, Lerner Publishing, Red5, and more.

Ananth has a previous book with Oni Press, titled **BUZZ!** You can see more of Ananth Hirsh's work with Tessa Stone at **isthiswhatyouwanted.com**.

Ananth and Yuko's self-published books include **CUTTINGS**, a collection of fiction comics & related materials, and three collections of slice-of-life autobio titled **JOHNNY WANDER VOL 1, 2 & 3**.

They post comics at **johnnywander.com**.

EVERYTHING IS GREAT.

portraits by Kris Mukai

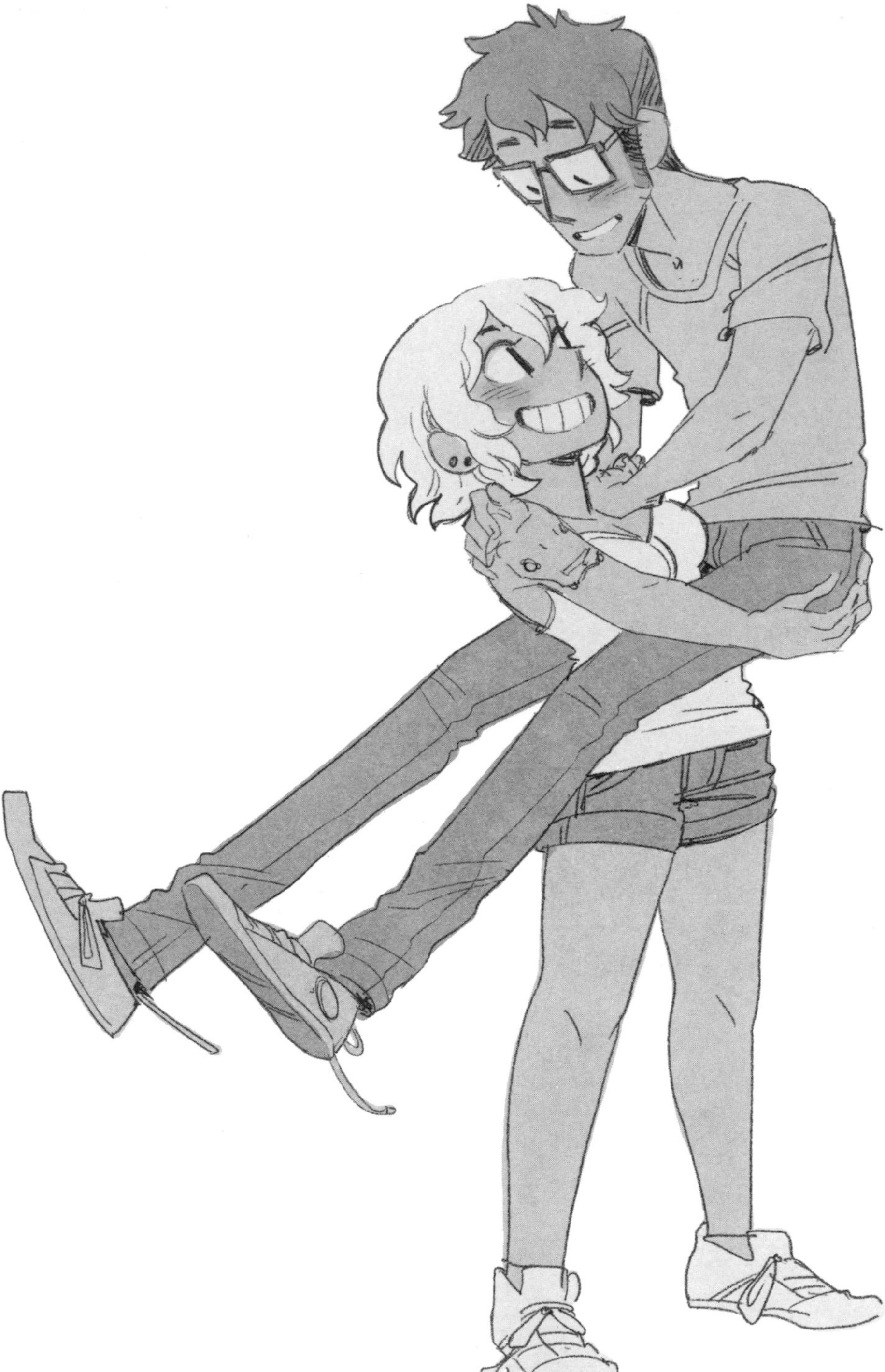